"*Poor Mary,*" he murmured. "*So much to learn.*"

He stood over her and raised her to her feet. She looked up into his eyes and then closed her own as his mouth came relentlessly down on hers.

The world swayed and spun. The floor seemed to disappear from beneath her feet, and a heavy, drugged sweetness took possession of her body as his mouth moved against her own, parting her lips and exploring her mouth.

Still keeping his mouth against hers, he swept her up in his arms and carried her down the corridor. . . .

—from QUADRILLE

By Marion Chesney
Published by Fawcett Books:

THE
LOVE MATCH

♡

QUADRILLE

Marion Chesney

FAWCETT CREST • NEW YORK

A Fawcett Crest Book
Published by The Ballantine Publishing Group
The Love Match copyright © 1989 by Marion Chesney
Quadrille copyright © 1981 by Marion Chesney

All rights reserved under International and Pan-American Copyright Conventions. Published in the United States by The Ballantine Publishing Group, a division of Random House, Inc., New York, and distributed in Canada by Random House of Canada Limited, Toronto. *The Love Match* was originally published by Ballantine Books in 1989. *Quadrille* was originally published by Ballantine Books in 1981.

http://www.randomhouse.com

Library of Congress Catalog Card Number: 98-92409

ISBN 0-449-00210-1

Manufactured in the United States of America

First Edition: August 1998

10 9 8 7 6 5 4 3 2 1

Contents

The Love Match

Chapter One

THE LARGE HOUSE in Hanover Square had a lost and abandoned look, as if no one lived there anymore. And yet servants could be seen going about their duties, and very occasionally a beautiful young lady would emerge and take the air accompanied by her maid.

The rooms seemed haunted by the voices of the bluestockings Mrs. Waverley had invited to her soirees. But Mrs. Waverley, that champion of rights for women, had betrayed her sex. She had married a colonel, now Baron Meldon, and had fled London. Society gossiped furiously after the announcement of the marriage and then forgot about her. They also forgot about her three adopted daughters, Fanny, Frederica, and Felicity. Fanny had married the Earl of Tredair; Frederica, Lord Harry Danger; and surely that third one had married as well.

But the third one, Felicity, was all alone. Mrs. Waverley had gone, leaving her the house and a treasure in jewelry, enough to keep Felicity in comfort until the end of her days. But Felicity was an independent lady. She had sold her first novel and was already hard at work on another. The servants were all women, Mrs. Waverley having never employed menservants, and the housekeeper, Mrs. Ricketts, was always at hand to accompany Felicity should she care to go out. Felicity had recovered from the blow of Mrs. Waverley's desertion of her, from the feeling of aching loss at being abandoned by her "sisters." But she had quarreled with Fanny and had tried to break up Frederica's marriage—sure Lord Harry did not mean to marry her—so they could hardly be expected to want to see her again.

In fact, she would have considered herself content had it not been for that ongoing nagging curiosity about her birth. Mrs. Waverley had adopted the three girls from an orphanage. Both

3

Fanny and Frederica and their then suitors had tried to find out why Mrs. Waverley had chosen them, why they had initially been kept at an orphanage that demanded high fees from the relatives of the orphaned, yet in their case there did not seem to be any relatives, and why Mrs. Waverley turned faint every time she saw the Prince Regent: Each time the girls had come up against a blank wall.

Of the three girls, Felicity had been the one who had most rigidly followed Mrs. Waverley's training. Women were little better than slaves, and marriage was a way of selling themselves into bondage. But now that Felicity was independently wealthy and had a profession, she found her nights plagued by romantic dreams. The Season was beginning again. The air was full of excitement as if throbbing with all the hopes and dreams of the young misses arriving by the carriageload to look for husbands.

She was not vain, but her looking glass told her she was beautiful. She had masses of chestnut hair, an elegant figure, a sweet face, and large hazel eyes. Fanny was still abroad, Frederica was also on the Continent, and there were occasionally reports in the papers of their happiness and beauty. Although Felicity did not yet know it, her determination to remain a spinster was already crumbling.

Yet still she often toyed with the idea of taking up the reforming process where the treacherous Mrs. Waverley had left off—at finding women who needed to be trained to educational independence. But women, thought Felicity bitterly, were all fickle. A man had only to smile on them and they forgot all their principles.

Mr. Harvey, the bookseller who was publishing Felicity's book, had cleverly spread gossip about it through society before publication. It was called *The Love Match* by a Lady of Quality. The heroine was a rake who broke men's hearts and left them weeping. Mr. Harvey was sure of its success.

So good was his promotion that by the end of the first day of publication every copy had sold out.

Felicity was sitting in her drawing room one day, admiring the handsome volume for the hundredth time, when Lady Artemis Verity was announced.

She put down the book and rose reluctantly to greet this unwelcome caller. Lady Artemis lived on the other side of

Hanover Square and had recently returned from Italy. She was a dashing widow who had been engaged to a Mr. Fordyce but had broken the engagement and run away from him. Her fine eyes were snapping with curiosity as she came into the room.

"I could not believe my ears, dear Miss Waverley," she cried, "when I learned Mrs. Waverley had become married." Lady Artemis giggled. "So much for all her theorizing and prosing on about the independence of women. And Frederica! Now Lady Harry Danger, I believe. Tra la. You bluestockings seem to know how to snatch the best husbands from the marriage mart. So how do you go on? Never say you are living here alone."

"No," lied Felicity, although she did not know quite why she lied. "My aunt is chaperoning me. A Miss Callow."

"Indeed! I should like to make her acquaintance."

"She is very old and frail and is lying down at the moment."

"You must bring her to tea." Her eye fell on Felicity's book. "I see you have been reading *The Love Match*. A sad sham."

"How so?" demanded Felicity angrily.

"Oh, everyone is tut-tutting over it and saying what a monstrous rake the authoress must be herself, but, my dear, I could swear it was all the imaginings of a virgin."

"I found it highly convincing," said Felicity stiffly.

"Well, you *would*, would you not?" Lady Artemis laughed. "But to any woman of the world . . . la, the ravings of an innocent. Men do not fall in love with such a philanderer. If she is still in prime condition, they get their lawyers to offer her a sum for her favors. If she is past it, then a shilling and a glass of rum is the usual fee."

"It is selling very well," pointed out Felicity.

"A novelty. But society will soon become wise to her, and her next book will be left on the shelves. I have not seen you about. Are you determined to keep to Mrs. Waverley's teachings and stay hidden from the world of men?"

"I have been busy of late," said Felicity. "But we shall no doubt meet soon."

"I look forward to meeting your aunt. Miss Callow, is it not?"

"Yes."

"Strange. I did not think you had any relatives . . . er . . . that you knew of."

"Well, I have," snapped Felicity.

She was still smoldering when Lady Artemis left. She picked up her book and scanned the pages. A blush mounted to her cheeks. Was it so naive? Was Lady Artemis being malicious? But, then, Lady Artemis could not know that she, Felicity, had written that book. Felicity bit her lip. Perhaps it was naive. How could she enlarge her experience? She could not attend balls and parties unchaperoned. She rang the bell.

Mrs. Ricketts, a tall, powerful woman, came in and stood with her hands folded.

"I have been thinking, Mrs. Ricketts," said Felicity, "that it is time I made my debut."

"You cannot do that on your own, miss," said Mrs. Ricketts. "Perhaps you had best advertise for some genteel lady to chaperon you."

"I don't want a stranger in my house interfering with my ways and my independence," said Felicity. "Why do not we dress you up finely, Mrs. Ricketts, and you can come with me?"

The housekeeper recoiled in horror. "I couldn't do it, miss, and that's a fact, me with my plain speech and plain ways. Me sit with them dowagers? Your social standing would be in ruins. Besides, you don't get no invitations, and you won't get none neither, not without some older lady to nurse the ground."

"Drat!" Felicity chewed her fingernails. "Never mind, Mrs. Ricketts, I shall hit on something."

To her surprise, she had another caller that day, the famous actress Caroline James. Caroline had entered the Waverley household the year before in the guise of Lord Harry Danger's sister, Lord Harry having employed her to befriend Frederica and so further his suit. Caroline had, furthermore, been engaged to be married to Colonel James Bridie, now Baron Meldon, he who had run off with Mrs. Waverley. The famous actress was a handsome woman and had conceived an admiration for the strong-willed Felicity.

"I put off coming to see you," said Caroline, "for actresses are not at all respectable, but a rumor reached me that you had been left alone, and I was anxious to reassure myself the world went well with you."

"Yes," said Felicity. "I am truly independent now. Mrs. Waverley left me this house and all the jewelry."

"Then you are indeed fortunate," said Caroline. The Waverley jewels were famous.

Felicity looked uneasily at her book, then said impulsively, "I wish to confide in you, Miss James. Have you read *The Love Match?*"

"Not yet," said Caroline, "but all London is talking about it."

"I wrote it," said Felicity, coloring slightly.

"How clever of you!" exclaimed Caroline.

"I felt until today it was indeed clever of me," said Felicity. "But a certain Lady Artemis called on me. She is a widow and very *mondaine*. She does not know I wrote it, of course, but she sneered and said it was obviously written by a virgin, that it was naive. The heroine in my book is a rake, or rakess, if there is such a thing. I wish to enlarge my horizons and go about in society. I told Lady Artemis I was chaperoned by an aunt, a Miss Callow, but Miss Callow does not exist."

"Then you must advertise for someone to take you about," said Caroline, unconsciously echoing Mrs. Ricketts.

"I don't want that," said Felicity fiercely. "I do not want to be under anyone's thumb again. Could *you*, my dear Miss James, not pretend to be Miss Callow?"

Caroline shook her head. "I have too many performances, too many rehearsals."

Felicity fell silent, and Caroline's blue eyes watched her sympathetically.

"Could you not," said Felicity, raising her eyes, "make me up to look like an elderly lady?"

"I could. But someone so young as yourself would not stand close scrutiny. What is your plan?"

"Oh, Miss James, if you could make me up to look like a dowager, I could entertain the ladies of the *ton* to prepare my own debut."

Caroline looked amused. "But when you are invited to a ball or party, you will be expected to arrive with this Miss Callow. You cannot split yourself in half."

"I shall worry about that when the time comes," said Felicity. "Please say you will do this for me."

Caroline hesitated, looking at the glowing, pleading face turned to her own. "You could come with me to the theater," she said, "and we could try something."

Felicity clapped her hands with delight. "Now!" she said. "Let's go now!"

The Marquess of Darkwater was strolling across Hanover Square when he saw Miss Felicity Waverley emerge with Miss Caroline James.

"What is that minx up to now?" he mused, watching as both ladies climbed into a carriage and drove off.

For the marquess not only knew who Felicity was but that she was the authoress of *The Love Match*. He had been present at the bookseller's when Felicity had first presented her manuscript and, unknown to her, had followed her home to find out who she was.

The marquess looked like one of the villains in Felicity's book. He was tall and tanned, with a broad-shouldered athlete's body. He had thick raven-black hair and piercing gray eyes. All Felicity's villains were handsome. The hero was plain-featured to show the readers that beauty of soul was more attractive to the rakish heroine in the long run than mere good looks. The marquess had returned from the West Indies the year before, where he owned sugar plantations. He was in his thirties and had been married to a delicate lady who had only survived the climate of the West Indies a few months before falling sick and dying. He had had some vague hope of finding a new wife in London, someone strong and brave enough to travel back with him to the plantations. But so far he had not met anyone to excite his interest . . . except, perhaps, Felicity Waverley, whom he considered highly unmarriageable in view of her spicy book. Unlike Lady Artemis, the marquess thought Felicity had a great deal of experience that no young lady should have in order to write such a shocking book, not knowing that the more purple passages of Felicity's prose had been culled from Greek and Roman classics.

He had hoped to meet Felicity at some society function, but it appeared Miss Waverley did not go out.

He went on his way but had only gone a few yards when he was hailed by one of his friends, Lord Freddy Knox. "Are you coming to our ball?"

"Of course." The marquess smiled. Lord Freddy had recently become married at the great age of nineteen to an heiress one year younger. The ball was to be the couple's first social engagement since their marriage. "Good," said Lord Freddy. "I do hope it will be a success. Cassandra can barely sleep a wink with nerves." Cassandra was his new wife, whose looks did not live up to her name, as she was small and plump and fair and vague, forever losing things and forgetting things. "Any fair charmer we can ask for you?" demanded Lord Freddy.

"No," began the marquess, and then his eye fell on the Waverley house. "Well, there might be."

"Only name her," cried Lord Freddy.

"Miss Felicity Waverley. She lives over there."

"I thought they were all married."

"No, I believe Miss Felicity is still unwed."

"There was a story going about," said Lord Freddy awkwardly, "that the three girls were foundlings and bastards adopted by Mrs. Waverley."

"And yet such lack of parentage did not stop either Tredair or Danger from marrying," pointed out the marquess.

"True. If you want her, you shall have her. But this Miss Felicity might think it odd to receive a card at this late date. The ball's on Friday, and this is Monday."

"Try," said the marquess.

"Oh, very well, although I don't think my Cassandra will like it."

Felicity sat in Caroline's dressing room. "I will need to try to effect this transformation myself," said Caroline, "for no one else must be in on the secret. Now, let me see. I think a rather nasty birthmark might answer."

"Why?" demanded Felicity. "I want to be a sweet white-haired old lady who will be doted on by the dowagers."

"Because if you have a disfiguring mark on your face, then people will not look too closely. Before I even begin on your appearance, you must learn to move and walk like an old lady."

The day wore on as Felicity went through "rehearsal" after "rehearsal" until she began to feel very weak and old indeed. Caroline then drew out wigs and makeup and white wax and got to work.

"You must always sit in a bad light," she said at last. "I have finished. You can look now."

She held up a branch of candles, and Felicity looked in the mirror.

A white-haired old lady stared back. A purple birthmark disfigured her left cheek, and white wax wrinkles crisscrossed her brow. The huge wig shadowed her face. "Never be seen without gloves," said Caroline, "or your hands will give you away. Do not sit too near the fire, or your wrinkles will melt. Now you will need to have all that taken off and then learn to put everything on yourself. It is a good thing Monday is the one night I do not have a performance."

"Surely you don't perform on Sunday."

"I rehearse. But don't tell anyone or they will close down the theater!"

At long last, Caroline pronounced herself satisfied. Then she said, "Before you embark on this mad scheme, I trust you are only going into society to *observe*. You may feel Mrs. Waverley betrayed you, but her principles were sound. It is a good thing for a woman to have her independence. It was you yourself who convinced me I should not marry."

"And you are happy?"

"Yes, I am very happy. My success is secure; I am thrifty; I shall have enough money to keep me comfortably in my old age."

Felicity looked again in the mirror. "This birthmark is quite repulsive," she said.

"It will serve its purpose," said Caroline. "Wear some of those famous Waverley jewels. All will look at those rather than at your face."

"I hate those jewels," said Felicity fiercely. "Mrs. Waverley enjoyed forcing us to wear them to excite the envy of the *ton*. I used to feel like some pasha's favorite. Fanny and Frederica must have hated them as well, for they left theirs behind. But if you think it will serve the purpose, I shall wear something dazzling."

Felicity returned home late, feeling weary. Mrs. Ricketts handed her a letter she said had been delivered that evening by hand. When she opened it, Felicity found a heavily embossed invitation card and a letter from Lady Freddy Knox. In it, Lady Freddy apologized for the lateness of the invitation, saying it had been dropped down the back of her desk by mistake.

"My first ball this Season," said Felicity with satisfaction. "I shall pen an acceptance."

"You cannot go, miss," pointed out Mrs. Ricketts. "You don't have a chaperon."

"I have now," said Felicity cheerfully, and told the appalled housekeeper of her plan.

In vain did Mrs. Ricketts argue and protest. Felicity was determined to go. She would accept for herself and her "aunt"; she would arrive alone and, on reaching the ballroom, say that her aunt was right behind her. She would make her entrance with a crowd of other people.

Mrs. Ricketts at last threw up her hands in despair. She resigned herself to the inevitable. Felicity would be found out, and there would be a minor scandal. Her hopes of a debut would be dashed, but at least the household could return to peace and quiet.

Felicity was glad of the invitation, for it meant she could put off playing the part of Mrs. Callow in society for another week.

But she had a longing to try out her masquerade on someone first, just to see if it worked. Then she thought of Lady Artemis Verity and sent a servant across the square the next day with a card in which Miss Callow requested the pleasure of Lady Artemis's company.

At one point, she thought she would not be ready in time. The whole putting on of makeup, wig, and wrinkles took much longer than she had remembered. She instructed the grumbling housekeeper to half pull the curtains in the drawing room closed and to tell the other servants they would receive instant dismissal if they so much as breathed a word of what was going on.

Lady Artemis arrived at four o'clock in the afternoon, her fine eyes sparkling with curiosity. She was ushered into the shadowy drawing room.

"Pray forgive me for not rising to greet you, Lady Artemis," said a frail voice from a wing chair by the fireplace.

Lady Artemis walked forward and made her curtsy. She looked at the little old lady sitting in the chair and then averted her eyes quickly from that ugly birthmark and looked at the glittering diamond brooch pinned on her gown instead.

"Where is your niece, Miss Callow?" she asked, looking around.

11

"She has contracted a chill," said Felicity, "and is lying down. She sends her compliments and begs to be excused."

"Poor thing," said Lady Artemis. "It is hard to believe such a strong character as Miss Felicity should succumb to anything. Are you but lately come to town, ma'am?"

"Yes, my lady."

"A great surprise. Mrs. Waverley led society to believe her girls had no relatives whatsoever."

"Maria Waverley is a sad and devious woman," croaked Felicity. "She lied to suit what ends I do not know. The girls are in fact sisters of the name of Bride."

"Indeed? Which county?"

"The Somerset Brides."

"Never heard of them."

"My lady, your manner distresses me. But, ah, then, the younger generation is mannerless to a fault," said Felicity gleefully.

"Oh, I am sorry, Miss Callow. What you must think of me! But to more cheerful topics. Does your presence in London mean that Miss Felicity will be able to make her debut like a regular debutante? Poor Fanny and Frederica had to be courted on the sly."

"Yes, I plan to take her everywhere," said Felicity, "my health permitting, of course."

Mrs. Ricketts brought in the tea things and stood about nervously until Felicity ordered her from the room.

"Tell me, Lady Artemis," asked Felicity, "why it was that your engagement to Mr. Fordyce came to naught?"

"You are well informed," said Lady Artemis with a little laugh. "I found I had made a mistake."

"In what way?"

"I simply felt we should not suit."

Her curiosity almost made Felicity forget her role of old lady. "Was his annual income not large enough?"

Lady Artemis put her teacup down in the saucer with an angry little click. "Miss Callow! I am a very rich woman. I do not need to marry a man for his money."

"I am sorry," said Felicity. "But, you see, love does not appear to enter into a society marriage."

"Be assured," said Lady Artemis dryly, "that it most cer-

12

tainly entered into the marriages of both Miss Fanny and Miss Frederica Waverley."

"If I could only be sure of that," said Felicity half to herself.

She leaned forward and picked up her own book with one gloved hand. "You told my niece that this was the work of a virgin, that the authoress had obviously no experience of the opposite sex."

"Yes, that is my opinion."

"You having, on the other hand, a great deal of experience?" said Felicity, enjoying all the license of being an old lady to the hilt.

Lady Artemis thought of her sexual antics with the ever-inventive Mr. Fordyce and blushed and then rallied. This old lady could not know of such goings-on.

"I am a widow," she said.

"Oh, yes, of course, that must help," mused Felicity. "But how do you suppose this writer could gain experience without . . . er . . . losing her virginity?"

Lady Artemis's eyes perceptibly sharpened, and Felicity raised her fan to her face. Ladies of the *ton* did not talk about virginity, especially elderly ladies of the *ton*.

"I suppose she must be content to observe, but that is hardly a substitute for firsthand experience," said Lady Artemis. "Tell me, Miss Callow, do you share Mrs. Waverley's views? Or rather, as we must now assume, the views Mrs. Waverley pretended to have?"

"I believe all ladies should be as highly educated as men," said Felicity, "and I believe more professional jobs should be open to them. Do you plan to marry again, Lady Artemis? You must forgive the curiosity of an old woman."

"Perhaps . . . if I find someone to please me. I am fortunate in being able to pick and choose."

"For Felicity's sake," pursued Felicity, "I must find out the marriageable, the eligible, men. Who is the top prize?"

"The Marquess of Darkwater," said Lady Artemis promptly. "But there is a drawback there."

"Which is . . . ?"

"He is a widower, handsome and rich, but any bride of his would have to travel back to those wretched plantations in the West Indies with him. The climate killed his first wife. She wrote to a friend of mine when she first arrived, complaining about the heat and flies and the dreadful provincialism of the other plantation owners. Do you know some of them adopt American manners and the ladies do not sit down to dinner with the men? She was vastly shocked that Darkwater did not keep slaves but freed all the Africans and paid them wages."

"Oh, excellent man!" cried Felicity.

"You do hold radical views, do you not? But of course there are many who are convinced that were they to wed Darkwater then they might persuade him to stay in England and send out an overseer."

Felicity looked at her speculatively. "And are you one of the hopeful, Lady Artemis?"

"La! I have not even met the man . . . yet. But he is a great friend of young Lord Freddy Knox, and so we are all sure of seeing him at the ball to be held by the Knoxes."

"Felicity has been invited."

"Indeed! Then it is fortunate for us other ladies that she holds such strong views on the rights for women. Nothing disaffects a man more."

Felicity stiffened. "And yet, Lady Artemis, Felicity led me to believe you shared her views."

"For a time, for a time. But, la, one wishes the gentlemen to adore one, after all."

"Like the Earl of Tredair, say? But, alas, he *did* marry Fanny without being the least bit put off by her principles."

"My dear Miss Callow, Fanny Waverley was very beautiful, as I recall."

"As is my Felicity," said Felicity, thinking that being one's own aunt had great advantages. For example one could sit and praise oneself all one liked.

Lady Artemis rose to leave. She heartily wished she had not mentioned Darkwater's name. What if that minx Felicity should steal him away? Somehow she must contrive to see him before that ball and poison his mind against Felicity.

"Again I must beg you to forgive me for not rising," said Felicity.

"Are you sure you are strong enough, ma'am, to face the rigors of a Season?" asked Lady Artemis, looking down at the huddled figure in the chair.

"I shall manage very well," said Felicity. "It is my wish to see Felicity married."

"I thought Miss Felicity was against the idea of marriage."

So she is, thought Felicity, but I am not telling *you* that, or it would be all about London. Aloud, she said, "She is not against marriage, only against marriages of convenience, which, as she is very rich, she does not need to make."

Lady Artemis discovered that the marquess had rented a house in Green Street. The next day, she made her way there, followed by her long-suffering maid, and walked up and down until she saw him appear, or rather she saw a richly dressed man appear and assumed it must be the marquess. As she came abreast of him, she stumbled and let out a scream. He raised his hat. "Have you hurt yourself, ma'am?" he asked politely.

"A little twist, that is all," said Lady Artemis. She smiled up at him. "May I present myself. I am Lady Artemis Verity and you, I believe, are the Marquess of Darkwater."

"At your service, my lady."

"Oh, if you could just give me your arm to the end of the street," said Lady Artemis, taking him literally. "My poor ankle hurts a little."

He offered his arm, and she leaned on it. "I believe you attend the Knoxes' ball, my lord?"

"Yes. Will you be there?"

"Of course I shall." She dimpled up at him. "May I hope for a dance?"

The gray eyes looking down at her turned a trifle frosty and he said "Certainly," but she realized dismally she had appeared too bold.

"I shall not keep you to it," she said. "I was only funning. There are many pretty young ladies looking forward to the pleasure of your company."

"I am sure none prettier than yourself," he said gallantly.

"Oh, but London is evidently to have a new belle. Miss Felicity Waverley is emerging from seclusion."

"Ah, yes, I have heard of her."

"Quite farouche," said Lady Artemis with a little laugh. "She holds strong views on the rights of women, yet she plans to marry some complaisant man and bend him to her ways."

"Then I wish her every success."

"Miss Waverley will no doubt be very successful. She pretends to appear helpless and feminine, but she is made of iron."

"I gather you do not like Miss Felicity Waverley."

"I?" Lady Artemis opened her eyes to their widest. "I admire her immensely. So strong, so ruthless, so cynical."

"We are now at the end of the street," he pointed out.

"So we are," she said gaily. "À *bientôt*, my lord."

She stood and watched him walk away. Such shoulders! Such legs! Really, the prospect of living in the West Indies seemed more attractive by the minute.

Chapter Two

FELICITY WAS CARRIED along on a wave of elation right up until half an hour before she was due to leave for the ball. Then the full enormity of what she was about to do struck her. Surely she would never get away with it!

She longed for the company of either Frederica or Fanny. Why had she quarreled with Fanny? Why had she been so stupid as to try to ruin Frederica's chances of marriage? Mrs. Rickett's doom-laden face was no help.

Nervously Felicity checked her appearance in the looking glass again. She was wearing a gown of fine white India muslin with an overdress of gold gauze fastened with pearl and gold clasps. A rope of fine pearls glowed against the whiteness of her neck, and she wore a little pearl tiara in her curled and pomaded hair. Her face was surely a trifle too pale. She reached for the rouge pot and then decided against it.

Oh, if only there were a real Miss Callow! For a brief moment, Felicity toyed with the idea of sending a servant to say she was unable to attend. But Lady Artemis's criticism of her book still rankled. She had to find out more about the real world. She, Felicity, did not even know what it felt like to be kissed by a man. Perhaps in the interests of literature she ought to begin by encouraging some man to kiss her. But how did you get a man to kiss you and then reject him? The critics had said her book was amusing and shocking. If she told some man she had only encouraged his advances to further her experience so she might get to work properly on her next novel, she would create more of a scandal in society than Fanny or Frederica had ever done.

Mrs. Ricketts entered to say the hired carriage was at the door. Mrs. Waverley had employed only women servants and had hired a carriage from the livery stables as she needed it, that way avoiding having men in her employ. Felicity allowed Mrs. Ricketts to put a swansdown-lined mantle about her shoulders. She picked up her reticule and fan.

The evening had begun.

As the carriage lurched forward through the crowded streets, Felicity wished she had ordered a sedan chair instead, although it was becoming increasingly hard to find one. The benefits of a chair were that you stepped into it in your own hall and were borne straight into the house you were visiting, and as the chairmen ran along the pavements, there was no danger of being stuck for hours in a press of carriages.

She was anxious to make her entrance and get it over with. The Knoxes' house was only a few streets away, but it was a social disgrace to arrive on foot. Her carriage lined up behind the other carriages in the street where the Knoxes lived.

At last it was her turn to alight. She hesitated a little on the pavement and looked up at the house. It consisted of four stories, but it was smaller than her own, not being double-fronted. It was not overwhelmingly imposing, and there were no liveried footmen lining the steps. She saw a large party about to go in and fell in behind them, following the ladies to a room at the side of the hall where they were to leave their wraps.

Felicity felt quite old. Another Season, another batch of fresh, hopeful faces up from the country. She left her cloak with a maid and then walked back out into the hall and up the narrow staircase. The ball was in progress on the first floor. Three rooms had been joined together by dint of removing the connecting double doors for the evening and taking out most of the furniture. Felicity presented her card to a footman and made her curtsy to Lord and Lady Freddy Knox. Lord Freddy was a genial-looking young man, and his small, plump wife seemed too nervous to wonder where this Miss Callow who was supposed to be escorting Felicity had got to.

Felicity passed through to the ballroom and began to edge around the floor to where she could see a free seat against the wall.

She sat down and looked about her. A few couples were dancing energetically in the small space provided. More people were arriving by the minute, and it looked as if there would soon be no room left for dancing.

And then she saw Lady Artemis. She was standing by the

door talking to a tall, handsome man. As Felicity watched, he turned and looked full at her. She studied him curiously, wondering whether to cast him in the role of villain or hero.

Definitely villain, she decided. Here was no plain yet honest hero but rather a tall, commanding man in exquisite tailoring and with a haughty, arrogant air. His eyes were as cold as the North Sea. His face was lightly tanned. He said something to Lady Artemis, still keeping his eyes on Felicity. Lady Artemis made a little moue, shrugged, and then began to lead him forward.

They came up to where Felicity was sitting, and she rose at their approach. "Miss Felicity," cried Lady Artemis. "Where is your aunt, Miss Callow?"

"Somewhere in the press," lied Felicity. "She recognized an old friend."

"May I present the Marquess of Darkwater. Lord Darkwater, Miss Felicity Waverley."

Felicity curtsied and the marquess bowed. "Would you care for some refreshment, Miss Waverley?" he asked.

"That would be very welcome," said Lady Artemis, quick to include herself in the invitation.

And then Felicity saw Mr. Fordyce, Lady Artemis's ex-fiancé. He was standing in the doorway. He was a small man with neat features and a trim figure. Lady Artemis's pansy brown eyes widened in alarm. "I am sure I see Lady Dunster signaling to me," she said, and quickly wove her way between the groups of onlookers and dancers to make her escape.

"Would you like me to present myself to Miss Callow first?" Felicity realized the marquess was asking.

"No, there is no need to bother her," said Felicity. "She is a very old lady and does not like to be troubled when there is no need."

"Meaning that you have decided for yourself I am safe and respectable?"

"Meaning that, yes, I should like some refreshment and, no, I do not think it necessary to trouble my aunt."

"Very well. Follow me and I will try to beat a path for us."

The rooms were now crammed. Dancing couples were colliding with spectators. The sound of voices beat upon the air, and the rooms were suffocatingly hot. A morning room on the half landing between the ground and first floors had been set aside for refreshments. There was nowhere to sit down. Waiters who were supposed to be circulating among the guests with glasses of wine, negus, champagne, and lemonade stood helpless, trapped in the press, their trays of drinks held high above their heads. The marquess, benefiting from his height, lifted two glasses from a tray and said to Felicity, "Out again, I think. There must be somewhere we can find space."

He led the way downstairs and paused on the bottom step. "I suggest we be unconventional and sit on the stairs, Miss Felicity. Or would you rather stand?"

"No, I am quite happy to sit down," said Felicity. She sat on a corner of the stair, and he sat close beside her to leave room for the guests who were ascending and descending. "I do not know what is in these glasses," he said, handing her one, "but it looks like canary." He took a small sip. "Yes, it is, and not bad at all."

"It is not at all like a ball," ventured Felicity. "I spent all day wondering whether I would remember the steps of the waltz, but I fear I am not even going to be allowed to dance."

"It is a sad crush, and the newspapers will hail it tomorrow as a success. Freddy was so afraid no one would come, he invited far too many people." He looked down at Felicity, noticing the pureness of her skin and the delicate rise and fall of her excellent bosom. It seemed amazing that such a pure and virginal-looking girl could ever have penned the words of *The Love Match*.

"I am led to believe you are a supporter of the rights of women," he said.

"Yes, in a muddled kind of way," said Felicity candidly. "I am not much of a campaigner. Also, I have come to believe women only listen to such views when there is no hope of them being married. But the minute some gentleman appears on the horizon, they revert to simpering misses."

"How very harsh. Most of them are not really simpering, you know. They are young and shy."

"But it is a sad life when the sole aim of a gently born girl is to trap a husband."

"Then why is the stern Miss Felicity Waverley appearing at such a frivolous event?"

"I weary of my own company."

"You have Miss Callow."

"Yes, but she is so very old, you see, that she cannot attend many functions or entertain much, so I am mostly on my own. Also, I like observing people."

"Ah, yes. Taking notes. You do not write by any chance?"

"Not I," lied Felicity. "I enjoy reading. I thought that new novel *The Love Match* was very fine."

"Well enough in its way," he said, looking amused, "but I should be frightened to meet the authoress. I would fear she would eat me alive."

"I am sure she is a charming lady," said Felicity. She took a sip of her wine and studied his mouth with interest. It was firm and well-shaped. She wondered what it would be like to be kissed by that mouth.

"My teeth are all my own," he said in a mocking voice.

"I beg your pardon, my lord?"

"You were staring at my mouth."

"Not I," said Felicity. "I was thinking of something else."

"May I ask what you were thinking about?"

"Lord Darkwater!"

The marquess looked up. Lady Artemis, slightly flushed and out of breath, smiled down at him. "You promised me a dance, my lord."

"Did I? I really do not think there is any room left to dance, Lady Artemis."

"Oh, but there is. You will excuse us, will you not, Miss Waverley?"

Felicity rose as well. "Of course," she said. She watched them mount the stairs together and wondered what to do. Then she found Mr. Fordyce had joined her.

"Have you seen Lady Artemis?" he asked.

"Lady Artemis has just left with the Marquess of Darkwater. I believe they are going to try to dance."

"What a good idea," said Mr. Fordyce. "Will you do me the honor, Miss Waverley?"

"Thank you," said Felicity.

They walked together up the stairs and then began to edge through tightly packed groups of people who were drinking or shouting to make themselves heard above the din.

"I do not think we should trouble to try to dance," said Felicity. "This is more like a rout than a ball."

"No, no," said Mr. Fordyce eagerly, for he had just spotted

Lady Artemis circling in the arms of the Marquess of Dark-water. He pulled her through a space in the crowd and onto the floor. Crammed in one corner a small orchestra was bravely playing away, occasionally hitting wrong notes when dancers collided with one of the players.

There were only three couples dancing. Felicity and Mr. Fordyce made up the fourth. When they came abreast of Lady Artemis and the marquess, Mr. Fordyce suddenly called, "All change partners." Lady Artemis and the marquess stopped dancing and looked at him in surprise. He quickly abandoned Felicity and seized Lady Artemis about the waist and forced her to move off with him. The marquess put his arm about Felicity. "It seems you are left with me," he said.

Couples dancing the waltz were supposed to dance twelve inches apart from one another, but the dancing space was so small Felicity found herself being crushed against the marquess. She tried to make the most of the experience. After all that was what she had come for—experience. So here she was, pressed tightly against a man. It was all very embarrassing. She felt hot and breathless. And then she very definitely felt a hand stroke her bottom. She jerked back, her face flaming. "How dare you, sir!" she hissed.

"How dare I what?" asked the marquess crossly.

"You fondled my posterior."

He looked startled and then smiled. "Use your wits, Miss Waverley. I was holding one hand in mine and have the other firmly at your waist. Any one of the gentlemen behind you must have seen this crush as a delightful opportunity. Now, apologize."

She looked at him, her lips trembling, for she had been badly shocked.

"Think, Miss Waverley," he chided. "I do not have three hands."

"Oh, you are right," said Felicity. "I am sorry. But what a scandalous thing to do."

He put his arm round her waist again. There was a scream from nearby them, followed by the sound of a slap. "It seems as if the bold fellow has got his comeuppance," murmured the marquess. He piloted her smoothly round the small space, noticing the party was beginning to get out of hand. People were drinking a great deal and becoming excited and bold with the proximity of so many bodies and the heat of the rooms.

Lord Freddy passed close to them, and the marquess said, "If you do not let some fresh air in here soon, Freddy, your ball will become a romp."

"Good idea," said Lord Freddy. He walked toward the windows, and with the help of two footmen, raised both windows. A gale blew into the room; the candle flames streamed sideways and went out.

The ballroom was plunged into darkness. There was a little silence and then giggles and scuffles and screams.

The marquess put both arms around Felicity and held her tight. "Stay still," he said. "Better I than some stranger."

He could smell perfume from her hair, and he could feel her breasts pressed against his chest.

Felicity stayed very still, motionless, in his arms.

I believe she is frightened of me, thought the marquess. It's hard to think she wrote that book, but I was there when she delivered the manuscript. Could she possibly have been delivering it for someone else?

Lady Artemis, a little way away, was struggling in Mr. Fordyce's crushing grip. "Leave me alone," she wailed.

"That is not what you used to cry when you lay naked in my arms," he said fiercely. He forced his mouth against her own, ignoring her mumbled protests. Lady Artemis's mind was screaming that she would never more be trapped into performing Mr. Fordyce's degrading lustful exercises, yet her wanton body betrayed her and her lips grew soft against his own.

"You may release me now," said Felicity crossly. "The candles are being lit."

He let her go a little, but kept one hand at her waist. Those normally cold eyes of his were lit with a mocking, teasing look. "This ball is going to become very wild," he said. "Do you not think we should find your aunt and leave?"

Felicity looked about her, at the flushed faces and glittering eyes, and shook her head. It was too good an opportunity to observe society at its worst. She knew from gossip that this occasionally happened. Bound as they all were by the strict laws of conventions, by the many social taboos, occasionally the *ton* would rebel and kick up their heels. Glasses were being snatched off trays as soon as they appeared, and toasts were being drunk. Lady Artemis, Felicity noticed, was no longer dancing stiffly in Mr. Fordyce's arms but was sinuously swaying. Both their faces were hot and flushed, and their lips looked swollen.

"I cannot stay with you all evening, even at such an affair as this," said the marquess. "It would occasion comment. Come. Let us find Miss Callow."

"I will look for her myself," said Felicity, and pulling free, she disappeared into the crowd. Lord Freddy hailed the marquess again. "What am I to do?" he said. "They will take the house apart."

"Serve only lemonade," said the marquess. "That will soon cool their fever."

Lord Freddy nodded and soon could be heard calling to the footmen.

Felicity was meanwhile deciding to make her escape. The press of people was too much and the noise of so many voices deafening.

And then a young man smiled down at her and said, "May I help you, ma'am? You seem in need of protection."

Felicity looked up into his face, and then smiled back. Here was the hero of her book. He had a square, plain face, a snub of a nose, clear blue eyes, and thick unruly fair hair. His figure was stocky, and his cravat was limp.

"Thank you," said Felicity. "I was on the point of leaving."

"Then follow me and I will take you downstairs," he said. "Allow me to introduce myself. My name is Bernard Anderson."

"And I am Felicity Waverley," said Felicity. "Do you really think you can get me out of here? There appears to be a solid wall of people between us and the stairs."

"Follow me," he said. He lunged at the crowd with such energy that people squeezed to either side to let him past, and Felicity quickly followed. She took a deep breath of relief once they had reached the comparative peace of the stairs.

"May I fetch your mother or your chaperon?" he asked.

"You are very kind," said Felicity. "But my aunt, Miss Callow, is an eccentric old lady, and I fear she has already left without me."

"But you have a carriage?"

"Yes, thank you, Mr. Anderson."

"Then I shall escort you to it."

As they stood on the step waiting for the carriage to be brought round, Felicity found herself very much at ease in Mr. Anderson's company. He prattled on about what a sad crush it was and how Lord Freddy had commanded the waiters and footmen to serve nothing but lemonade, but had forgotten to tell his wife, who had promptly countermanded the orders.

When Felicity's carriage arrived, he begged leave to call on her and Miss Callow the following day. Felicity thought quickly. She would need to receive him as Miss Callow, but as Miss Callow she could sing her own praises. So she thanked him prettily and said she looked forward to seeing him.

Mr. Anderson made his way back up the stairs, but before he reached the top he found himself confronted by his mother.

"What were you doing with Felicity Waverley?" demanded his mother. Mrs. Anderson was a big, imposing woman with big, imposing breasts that were thrust up by her corset so much that her heavy bulldog chin appeared to be resting on them.

"I was escorting her to her carriage, Mother," said Bernard mildly. "I promised to call on her tomorrow."

"You will do no such thing," said Mrs. Anderson. "Those Waverley girls are foundlings and bastards. And there is no dowry there. For it is rumored Mrs. Waverley ran off and left that one penniless."

Bernard's face fell. "She is awfully pretty," he mumbled.

"But portionless," said his mother. "Come. We are going home. You know you must find an heiress, Bernard, yet you waste your time squiring the most unsuitable female at the ball!"

In her guise of Miss Callow, Felicity sat in her darkened drawing room the next day and waited for callers. Mr. Anderson would come and she would see if she, as her own aunt, could get him to offer to take her "niece" on a drive.

But the first person to arrive was the Marquess of Darkwater. Felicity shrank back in her winged armchair and asked to be excused for not getting up.

"I came to pay my respects to Miss Felicity," said the marquess, sitting down opposite.

"I am afraid my niece is lying down," said Felicity.

"A pity. Last night was a sad romp, was it not?"

"Quite disgraceful," said Felicity sternly. "I would not have believed the *ton* capable of such shocking behavior. Felicity told me there were many loose screws present."

The marquess blinked and then said, "I trust she spoke favorably of me."

"She did not mention you at all," said Felicity maliciously. "But she did meet a most charming young man. A Mr. Anderson."

"Oh, yes?" said the marquess. "I do not know him."

"Well, you wouldn't. He is not *fast*."

"What a low opinion you have of me and on such short acquaintance. Besides, it is ladies who are fast, not men."

"Lady Artemis Verity," announced Mrs. Ricketts.

Lady Artemis sailed into the room, both hands outstretched in welcome. Felicity felt every bit like the grumpy old lady she was supposed to be. Lady Artemis was wearing a dashing bonnet and a high-waisted morning gown with long tight sleeves ending in pointed lace cuffs. Her face was glowing, and her lips were delicately rouged.

"My niece is resting," said Felicity before Lady Artemis could speak.

"What is happening to these young girls, Lord Darkwater?" said Lady Artemis. "No stamina."

"That is true," said Felicity. "One obviously toughens up with age."

Lady Artemis ignored her. Her eyes were fixed on the marquess. She began to talk about the ball, about the crush, and about how disgracefully everyone had behaved. The marquess replied pleasantly that at least the Knoxes had had their first success. Any affair where so many women fainted, so many coachmen fought outside for places, and so many gentlemen were carried out drunk was always deemed a success.

While he talked, Lady Artemis studied his handsome face. Here was a man who would make her an ideal husband. Not Mr. Fordyce, who had managed to get into her bed after the ball and had left her feeling peculiarly degraded. She had had several affairs since her husband died. Now she craved respectability. She had tried her best to be discreet, but she knew there were many whispers about her.

She urged the marquess to talk about the West Indies and listened to him eagerly, interrupting every now and then to say she longed to travel, to see such countries. Felicity sat hunched up in her chair behind her wrinkles, feeling forgotten.

At last the marquess rose to take his leave, and Lady Artemis rose as well. "We shall all need to be on our best behavior now, Miss Callow," said Lady Artemis. "After that ball, you know. Society has shocked itself and will become very prim and proper for a while."

"I shall tell Felicity of your call," said Felicity.

After they had left, she sat and brooded. She was just about to rise and go up to her room, when to her surprise, Mrs. Ricketts entered to say that a Mrs. Anderson had called. "I did not usher her up, miss, for she looks bad-tempered."

"I shall see her," decided Felicity. "Draw the curtains a little more, Ricketts."

Mrs. Anderson had come to see Felicity for herself. She was alarmed because her son had turned peevish on the subject instead of being his usual malleable self. Mrs. Anderson was a fairly rich woman in comfortable circumstances, but she was greedy and, being a doting mother, had an inflated idea of her son's attractions. Bernard should marry an heiress—on that she had her mind set.

She was startled to be told by the housekeeper that Miss Felicity was lying down but that her aunt, Miss Callow, would receive her. Now Bernard had mentioned the existence of this aunt, but Mrs. Anderson had not believed such a creature existed. No one had noticed any chaperon with Felicity at the ball.

When she entered, she curtsied to the old lady in the chair. But at first Mrs. Anderson's covetous eyes did not even notice that disfiguring birthmark. They had fastened on the old lady's jewels. Felicity was wearing fine kid gloves with rings worn over the gloves and heavy bracelets encrusted with jewels at her wrists. Six strands of the finest diamonds blazed at her neck. An oil lamp had been cleverly placed so that although Felicity's face was in shadow, the jewels caught fire and blazed with a wicked light.

Mrs. Anderson gulped and sat down. "Is Miss Felicity present?" she asked.

"No, Mrs. Anderson," said Felicity, taking an instant dislike to Bernard's mother. "She is lying down. My niece is a delicate flower, Mrs. Anderson, and was vastly shocked at the behavior of the guests last night."

"As was my son," said Mrs. Anderson. "He was fortunate enough to be of assistance to your niece."

"So Felicity told me," said Felicity. "He was all that was kind and helpful."

"Society does gossip so," said Mrs. Anderson with a false little laugh. "I was led to believe poor Miss Felicity had been abandoned and was unchaperoned."

"I am surprised you should listen to malicious gossip," said Felicity sternly. "Felicity is very well protected by me. She is plagued by fortune hunters . . . of course."

"Of course," said Mrs. Anderson weakly, looking at those glittering jewels.

"Apart from her own wealth," said Felicity, "which is considerable, she will, of course, inherit my fortune on my death."

Mrs. Anderson felt more wretched by the minute. Why had she not let Bernard call? She must make her escape and send him round immediately.

"Why did your son not come with you?" asked Felicity. She still thought kindly of Bernard but put his mother down as an avaricious, vulgar creature.

"He sent me . . . because he is very shy, don't you know . . . to get me to beg you to give him permission to take Miss Felicity on a little drive in the park. But she is not feeling at all the thing, so . . ."

"I am sure if he calls at five o'clock, my niece will be glad to take the air with him," said Felicity.

Mrs. Anderson beamed. "I shall go and tell the poor boy immediately. To be frank with you, Miss Callow, I have never before seen him quite so taken with any lady."

Felicity bowed her head in assent.

Mrs. Anderson rose in a flurry of silk, anxious to take her leave.

As soon as she had gone, Felicity cast a worried look at the clock. Four o'clock! She must work hard or she would never manage to transform herself back into Miss Felicity Waverley in time.

At five o'clock, Mrs. Ricketts was posted in the hall with instructions to tell Mr. Anderson that Miss Callow was lying down, and then summon Felicity.

Felicity had been wondering whether Bernard was worth all the trouble. Surely such a mother must have passed on her greedy traits to her son. But when she saw him standing in the hall, looking shy and awkward yet so very happy to see her, she was glad he had come.

They had a sedate drive in the park, Felicity carefully confining her conversation to observations on the people she saw and the inclemency of the English weather. Because of Bernard, Felicity began to contemplate the idea of marriage for the first time. Here was no man to bully her or enslave her, but a pleasant fellow who would allow her to run her own household. It would be a relief not to feel alone in the world. Of course, his mother was a problem, but Felicity felt sure she could easily put that lady in her place. It was the thought of the irregularity of her position, her lack of parents, her lack of support, that made Felicity feel quite weak. For the first time, she realized why even women of independent means finally crumbled and preferred to be married rather than to face the rest of their lives alone. At one point, the Marquess of Darkwater's face seemed to float in front of her eyes, his gaze searching and mocking.

But the marquess was a powerful and dominating personality. He would not allow her any freedom. Nor would such an aristocrat wish to ally his name to a girl with the background of a foundling hospital and orphanage. "And yet," said a treacherous voice in her head, "both Fanny and Frederica managed to find men who did not care about their birth."

Bernard was seeing Felicity Waverley as no one had seen her before, shy and grateful for each little attention and compliment.

Lady Artemis was driving round the square when Felicity arrived home. She saw Bernard Anderson tenderly helping Felicity to alight and saw the warmth and admiration in the young man's face.

She felt a stab of pure jealousy. Those Waverley girls always managed to get men to fall in love with them. She would find out the name of that young man and see if she could draw his attention to herself. She had flirted with Darkwater, but he had remained cold and uninterested. She was only twenty-seven, but she felt much older. She had always been secure in the power of her beauty. It became important to her to prove she could take at least one man away from Felicity.

* * *

The Marquess of Darkwater was sitting in his club, wondering about Felicity Waverley. He could not get her out of his mind. She was an odd contradiction. Had she really written that book? Or had that ugly and sinister aunt of hers written it for her?

His mind turned to the aunt. Unlike Lady Artemis and Mrs. Anderson, he had not been put off by the birthmark or dazzled by the jewels. She was remarkably like Felicity and with the same young, hazel eyes. Felicity had remarkable eyes, he mused, golden brown with green flecks. There was a nagging little suspicion about that aunt somewhere in his mind. He remembered the room, how it had been darkened and how the light had been carefully placed so as not to shine on Miss Callow's face. Like a theater scene.

He decided to call unexpectedly on the following day to find out who would receive him . . . Felicity or Miss Callow.

Chapter Three

FELICITY AWOKE THE next day with a feeling of anticipation. She lay in bed, enjoying that rare sensation and wondering dreamily what was causing it. Then she remembered Bernard Anderson. She was looking forward to seeing him again.

She did not have any romantic thoughts about him. Rather, she looked on him as a newfound friend. She need not dress up as Miss Callow and call on the parents of eligibles. Bernard would court her and, yes, she would very likely marry him and settle down to a contented life. She would invite Frederica and Fanny to the wedding and hope they had forgiven her. Perhaps they had not been in love either, but had merely wearied of the unnatural life they had been leading under Mrs. Waverley's protection. Should she ask Mrs. Waverley? Felicity's face hardened. Mrs. Waverley had not really cared for any of them. She had bought herself a family out of an orphanage, and the minute a husband had appeared on the scene, she had forgotten all about them. But, Felicity mused, she had left the house and all the jewels. Yes, it would only be fair to ask Mrs. Waverley.

She rose and dressed, ate a light breakfast, and sat down to work on the first chapter of her new novel. She had decided to use the same heroine, but her female rake had been left in the last book on the point of reform, and on the point of marrying her plain but honest hero. Clorinda, as the heroine was called, must now jilt the hero and continue her amorous adventures. Felicity needed a new villain. The Marquess of Darkwater's face rose before her mind. She began to write busily.

The day wore on, and when she looked up, it was three in the afternoon. With an exclamation, she dropped her pen and began to change into one of her finest morning gowns. Bernard would surely call. But no sooner had she dressed than

Mrs. Ricketts knocked at the door to say the Marquess of Darkwater was waiting in the hall.

Felicity bit her lip. She did not want to see him, but, on the other hand, he was now her villain and she should study him closely.

She opened the door and told Mrs. Ricketts to show the marquess up to the drawing room. She was to say that Miss Callow was out on calls.

"You can't see him alone, miss," said Mrs. Ricketts severely.

"Oh, yes, I can," retorted Felicity. "Leave the door of the drawing room open, and be on hand in case I want you."

Felicity ran to the mirror and checked her appearance. Her gown of palmetto green satin with long sleeves and a Vandyke ruff looked rich and stately. Her hair was dressed high on her head with little tendrils being allowed to escape and fall round her cheeks.

The marquess rose at her entrance and bowed and said he was sorry not to have the pleasure of seeing Miss Callow.

"Why?" asked Felicity curiously.

He raised his thin black eyebrows. "I find her a most interesting lady," he said. His eyes were mocking, and Felicity wondered whether he had penetrated her disguise on his previous visit.

"I have just come from Harvey, the bookseller," he went on. "You said you had read that novel *The Love Match*. Harvey hopes to have a new book from the authoress shortly."

Felicity feigned a yawn of boredom. "I have little time to read these days, my lord."

"But he told me a most interesting thing. It appears that perhaps our bold authoress gained her knowledge from Greek and Roman classics rather than from life, if you take my meaning."

"No, I don't," said Felicity rudely.

"It appears that instead of being the work of an experienced lady of the *ton*, it may instead be the work of a highly imaginative and well-educated innocent."

"Unlike you," said Felicity, "I do not have the necessary experience to judge the book."

"You surprise me." He held up his hand as Felicity glared at him. "I mean," he went on smoothly, "that Mrs. Waverley had the reputation of being a great educator. 'Tis said you and the other two ladies were better educated than many men."

"Perhaps," said Felicity.

There came the sound of a carriage stopping outside. Felicity rose and hurried to the window. But it was not Bernard Anderson, only a young man who had stopped his carriage to talk to a passerby.

She returned to her seat, looking downcast. The Marquess of Darkwater realized with a little shock that Miss Felicity Waverley was most definitely not enjoying his company. In fact, she was clearly waiting and hoping for the arrival of someone else. It was a new experience for him. His title, his looks, and his fortune had always insured that women looked on him with glowing admiration and hung on his every word.

"Perhaps you would care to accompany me on a drive tomorrow?" he found himself saying.

"No, that will not be possible," replied Felicity firmly. "I have other engagements, oh, not only for tomorrow but for weeks to come."

The snub was obvious. He rose to take his leave. "I am sure," he said, "Miss Callow would welcome a visit from me. Present my compliments and tell her I will call on her."

"I do not think that is a good idea," said Felicity.

"Why, I pray?"

"I regret to inform you, my lord, that Miss Callow took you in dislike. You must forgive her. She is old and set in her ways and not likely to change her mind."

He was suddenly very angry. Yet did not he himself firmly dismiss people he considered tiresome?

But he found his anger was so great he could barely take a civil leave of her.

At that moment, Bernard was sitting in the Green Saloon of his mother's house in Cavendish Square, and feeling miserable and awkward. He had been all set to go and call on Felicity with his mother's blessing but Lady Artemis Verity had come to call. Being a widow, Lady Artemis enjoyed the freedom of being able to call on Mrs. Anderson on her own. A young miss would have had to be taken along by her mother or chaperon.

Mrs. Anderson was flattered by the visit. She was even more

excited when she noticed the melting glances Lady Artemis was throwing in the direction of Bernard. Mrs. Anderson knew Lady Artemis was rich. Even better than that, she had a title and was well-established in the *ton*, unlike Felicity Waverley who was of doubtful birth and social standing to say the least.

And when Lady Artemis, with another flirtatious glance at Bernard, said she would be delighted if both mother and son would grace her box at the opera that evening, Mrs. Anderson was already mentally preparing her son for his wedding.

Bernard was terrified of Lady Artemis. She was undoubtedly very pretty in the accepted mode. She had rich brown hair with glossy ringlets falling on either side of her face. Her complexion was fashionably pale, her pansy brown eyes large and sparkling, and her features piquant and delicately formed. But Bernard was twenty and Lady Artemis was twenty-seven, and she appeared to him a terrifyingly older and sophisticated woman. He longed for the fresh and undemanding company of Felicity Waverley.

As soon as she had taken her leave, Bernard rose to his feet. "Where are you going?" demanded his mother.

"Thought I would call on Miss Waverley," mumbled Bernard.

"Nonsense, my son. Lady Artemis is a catch, and did you mark how she looked at you? Forget Felicity Waverley. No breeding there and no title either."

"But, Mother . . ."

"Do as you are told, Bernard!"

So, as usual, Bernard did what his mother told him.

After a week of isolation, Felicity would have welcomed a visit even from the uncomfortable Marquess of Darkwater. The London Season was well underway, yet she sat in the great house, ignored and alone.

She summoned up her courage, put on the disguise of Miss Callow, and went to call on one of Mrs. Waverley's acquaintances, Lady Dexter, a lady who had claimed to share Mrs. Waverley's radical views.

It took a great deal of courage to emerge into the daylight as Miss Callow, but Felicity felt it was the only way she could get invitations for herself and to find out what had happened to Bernard Anderson.

She was just about to go out when Mrs. Ricketts came to say that Mr. Fordyce had called.

"Tell him Felicity is resting and put him in the drawing room," said Felicity, "but tell him I am about to go on a call and can only spare him a few moments."

Mr. Fordyce got to his feet as the bent old lady came into the drawing room. "Forgive me for disturbing you, Miss Callow," he said. "I was anxious to speak to Miss Waverley."

Felicity walked forward leaning heavily on a stick and settled herself in the wing chair. "What do you wish to speak to my niece about?" she asked.

"I knew Miss Felicity when I lived in the house next door and was engaged to Lady Artemis Verity," said Mr. Fordyce. "I wondered, perhaps, if Miss Felicity saw much of Lady Artemis these days."

"As little as possible," said Felicity.

"But they were great friends at one time!" exclaimed Mr. Fordyce.

"I believe at one time it amused Lady Artemis to pretend to share my niece's views on the rights of women," said Felicity, "but that was only a pretense."

"You must not think ill of Lady Artemis," said Mr. Fordyce. "She is a creature of nature."

Felicity blinked. "Like a wasp?"

"No, Miss Callow, like a pretty fluttering bird."

"Dear me, Mr. Fordyce. I would like to be of help to you, but your fluttering bird is not to be found here."

"I do not understand what she is about," said Mr. Fordyce wretchedly. "Why she must needs seek out the company of that youth, Bernard Anderson, I do not know."

"We do know Mr. Anderson slightly," said Felicity. She experienced a sinking feeling in her stomach. "Is Lady Artemis enamored of him?"

"She cannot be, ma'am!" cried Mr. Fordyce. "What has a youth of his years to offer her?"

"Youth and kindness and a good heart," said Felicity wistfully.

"I beg you, Miss Callow, if your niece has any inkling of how Lady Artemis feels toward me, I would be most grateful if she would let me know."

Felicity bowed her head. "Be assured, Mr. Fordyce, my

niece is not intimate with Lady Artemis. Now I beg you to excuse me. I have calls to make."

So that was that, thought Felicity, as she climbed into her carriage. Faithless Bernard! Or was it that his greedy mother saw better game? For one moment, she contemplated canceling the call and returning to the house. Her book was barely started.

But the day was gray and cheerless and threatening rain, and the large house looked dark and gloomy. She climbed into the carriage and told the coachman to take her to Lady Dexter's.

"You have left the preparations for Felicity's Season a little late, Miss Callow," said Lady Dexter after her odd visitor had been given tea. Really, this Miss Callow was extraordinary, covered as she was with blazing jewels. It was hard to look at her face, for one's eye kept being distracted by all those flashing rings and bracelets and brooches. Lady Dexter remembered the attempts to thieve the Waverley jewels and marveled at the old lady's courage in being seen abroad with such a king's ransom on her. "I will see what I can do, Miss Callow," she went on. "Your visit is a great surprise, for Mrs. Waverley put it about that her girls were orphans and had not any relatives."

"Maria Waverley told a great deal of lies," said Felicity. "I do not like to see my Felicity suffer because of them."

"Oh, I agree. Now, I am giving a musicale tomorrow night, Miss Callow. Not knowing of your existence, I did not send you a card, but I should be delighted if you and your niece would attend. Many eligibles will be coming. Who is new on the market? There is Darkwater. Then there is Mr. Johnson. There is the divine Colonel Macdonald, but lately come to town to set all our hearts aflutter."

"We should be pleased to come," said Felicity, although wondering how she was to manage to arrive as Felicity and explain the absence of her aunt.

"Splendid. Now do not run away, Miss Callow, for I am expecting several ladies for tea, some of whom might prove useful to you."

Felicity passed inspection by the ladies of the *ton* very creditably. The jewels were passport enough. Society had very strict social laws to keep upstarts at bay. Breeding was all. Vulgar money could not buy entrée. Or so they claimed. But the older and more aristocratic the family, the more ruthless the determination to hold onto power and land. That was the reason so many weeping girls were led to the altars of London to marry old and diseased men. Girls might weep, but they, like their parents, knew what they owed their ancient names. Love could be found outside marriage. There was only one commandment there to obey—Thou Shalt Not Be Found Out. And so the bartering went on: my ancient name for your dowry. The ladies Felicity met that afternoon bowed down before her display of jewels and pronounced her a fascinating character.

The thieves who had originally tried to steal the Waverley jewels had been transported, the highwayman who had in turn tried to get them had been shot, and the underworld of London still buzzed with occasional rumors, but no one dared try where others had so disastrously failed.

But there was a new breed of villain on the London scene: the confidence trickster. The wicked lord in the novels Felicity and other ladies read who seduced and betrayed and left some innocent weeping in the snow with a baby in her arms existed in real life, but he was not an aristocrat but a clever and ruthless man masquerading as one. Society prided itself so much on the great wall of strict taboos and shibboleths it had built around itself to keep the unfashionables at bay, that smug and secure, it was often betrayed by its own greed. So as Felicity was able to masquerade as an old lady by dint of attracting all eyes to her fabulous jewelry, so Colonel Macdonald was able to gain entrée to the best houses because of his handsome face, charm of manner, and reputation of having gained a fortune from an Indian prince while commanding a sepoy regiment.

It was fashionable for military men to forget about wars and campaigns in civilian life. The bravest of soldiers often appeared as a dandy only interested in the cut of his coat or the folds of his cravat. Of course, they discussed serious matters together in their clubs, but Colonel Macdonald made sure he performed only in the company of the ladies, where such serious subjects were forbidden.

He had been born Angus Mackay, son of a Scottish weaver. He had served as a private in a Highland regiment in India and had deserted as soon as he saw that his regiment was to be posted to the Peninsular Wars. Before he deserted, he stole several items of regimental plate, which he sold in Glasgow. He had studied the manners and bearing of his senior officers. In Glasgow, he had become Mr. Guy Flint, a Virginian tea merchant, and there had courted and married the daughter of a wealthy Scottish merchant. He had managed to spend her dowry very quickly on luxurious living and had taken himself off to fresh pastures right after his young bride had presented him with a son. He moved to the lake district the poets had made fashionable and had begun to court the daughter of a local landowner. Again, his suit was successful. He married her, but, again, her dowry, although generous, was not enough to keep him in the luxuries to which he had rapidly become accustomed. He deserted her and moved south. He was after bigger game. He took on the name and character of Colonel James Macdonald, Member of Parliament for Linlithgow-shire. One would think that the very claim of being an M.P. would have exposed him, but Linlithgowshire was believed to be in Scotland, and Scotland was a world away, and society was used to Members of Parliament who represented odd and barbaric constituencies and who never put in an appearance at the House of Commons, and so he was socially accepted.

He was a fine-looking man with silver-blond hair, a Greek god profile, blue eyes, and a slight Irish accent, which fell most seductively on listening ears. He made a great joke of his accent, saying he belonged to the Irish branch of the Earl of Hopetoun's family and, sure, wasn't it a plague to have a good Scottish name and be cursed with an Irish brogue?

When he was not masquerading as Colonel Macdonald, he liked to escape to low taverns and thieves' kitchens, where he could be himself, and it was in one of these low dives that he first heard about the Waverley jewels. He was used to thieves' stories being either downright lies or wild exaggeration, and so he all but dismissed the story of the jewels from his mind.

That was until he met Lady Dexter in the street on the day of her musicale and heard about Miss Callow.

"I was never more surprised," said Lady Dexter, "for all the talk was that the girls were taken by Maria Waverley from an orphanage and had no relatives at all. In fact, she told me so herself. Then this Miss Callow came to call. There is one

Waverley girl left unmarried, Felicity, and this Miss Callow, who is the girl's aunt, wishes to bring her out. I had met Felicity Waverley, a glorious creature, so I told Miss Callow to bring her to my musicale this evening. But, I tell you, Colonel Macdonald, I was quite blinded by Miss Callow's jewels—if they are *her* jewels, for the Waverley jewels are famous, you know. Such fine stones! She must be quite a strong old lady, since the weight of all those gems must have been considerable."

"I look forward to making her acquaintance," said Colonel Macdonald.

"Don't let young Miss Waverley steal your heart away," teased Lady Dexter, "or we shall all be most terribly jealous."

He kissed her hand. "Now, who could tear me from your side?" he said in his soft, lazy brogue. "You know I adore you."

"Go on with you," laughed Lady Dexter, but secretly she was delighted. She was nearly fifty, and Colonel Macdonald made her feel like a young girl.

The colonel sauntered on his way, his mind racing. This could be it. If he could charm this Waverley girl into marriage and get those jewels, he could flee the country and set himself up for life.

Felicity decided she could not stand the strain of arriving on her own and then lying about her "aunt's" supposed indisposition, so she decided to gamble and see if she could make her explanations before she arrived. She accordingly sent a pathetic little note to Lady Dexter, saying her aunt was ill and had begged her to go on her own but she feared to do so as it was a very shocking thing to do. A note from Lady Dexter was delivered back by one of her footmen. Miss Waverley must come alone. Her maid could escort her to the door, and Lady Dexter herself would introduce her to the company.

Colonel Macdonald's first feeling on beholding Felicity Waverley was one of dismay. He was used to hearing wealthy girls described as "beautiful," meaning the girl's fortune lent her an allure. But Felicity Waverley *was* beautiful. When he first saw her, she was standing with Lady Dexter, being introduced to some people at the doorway of the music room. She was wearing a slip of a gown of white satin covered with an overdress of white French net decorated with a tiny blue spot.

39

She had white silk roses in her hair, the center of each rose being formed of seed pearls and tiny sapphires. But she wore no other gems. Her white throat was bare and her gloved arms free of bracelets. He found himself daunted by her beauty and wishing she had worn some of the famous Waverley jewels to give him courage to woo her.

For the first time, his usual confidence deserted him. His previous victims had both been on the plain side. He squared his shoulders as if going into one of the battles he had so neatly avoided by deserting and bowed low before Lady Dexter. "Introduce me to this enchantress, I command you!" he cried.

Lady Dexter looked amused and Miss Felicity Waverley decidedly annoyed. Lady Dexter performed the introductions and then, being hailed by a party of new arrivals, left Felicity with Colonel Macdonald.

"Your beauty leaves me dumbfounded," said the gallant colonel. He heard his voice sounding in his own ears and realized with some irritation that his carefully cultivated Irish brogue was slipping into a decidedly Scottish burr.

"On the contrary, you appear to have plenty to say, sir," said Felicity, fanning herself and looking over his shoulder. Bernard Anderson, his mother, and Lady Artemis were just entering the room. Lady Artemis said something to Bernard, who blushed. Felicity looked up at the colonel with new eyes. He was handsome and personable. Bernard must not see that she cared about his neglect one bit.

"You do not appreciate my compliments, I can see," the colonel was saying.

"It is rather hard to know how to receive them," said Felicity with a smile. "I can either simper, hit you playfully with my fan, or walk away."

"Then I had better try to be sensible," he said. "Oh, that my poor Irish tongue could find the magic to charm you."

"Is that your way of trying to be sensible?" asked Felicity, beginning to be amused.

"Sure, it's the best I can do," he said with a grin. "Will you be after letting me fetch you a glass of something?"

"Delighted, sir. Ratafia will do."

He bowed and left to find a glass of ratafia for her. His place was taken by the Marquess of Darkwater. "Where is Miss Callow?" he asked. "Not still indisposed."

"Alas, yes, my lord."

"You and your aunt are like those cunning little figures on a curiosity clock. You know, the clock chimes and little figures appear, one for rain and the other for sunshine, but never the two together."

"We are both unfortunate in that we have suffered from bad health, but I am glad our misfortune provides you with amusement."

"Your ill health does not amuse me, only the strange way it seems impossible to see the two of you together at the one time."

Felicity affected a yawn and stared around the room as if seeking distraction. Bernard caught her eye and gave her a look like a whipped dog. His mother saw that look and stepped in front of him to block his view of Felicity.

"A word of warning in your ear, Miss Waverley," Felicity heard the marquess say. "Colonel Macdonald claims to be a Member of Parliament for Linlithgowshire, but there is no such place. I fear he is an impostor."

"How interesting," said Felicity languidly. "Thank you for telling me, my lord. It adds a certain luster to his charm and looks, and adds spice to this dull evening. Ah, Colonel Macdonald. We were just talking about you."

"Evening, Darkwater," said the colonel cheerfully. The marquess ignored him completely, gave Felicity a stiff bow, and strode away.

"His spleen must be mortal bad," declared the colonel.

"You are a Member of Parliament, I believe," said Felicity.

"For my sins. Linlithgowshire—in Scotland."

"I have heard of the town of Linlithgow in Lothian, but not of Linlithgowshire."

"Oh, 'tis a small county," said the colonel airily. "The musicale is about to begin. May I have the honor of escorting you?"

Felicity's glance flicked over the guests, from the marquess's cold eyes to Bernard's sheepish ones, to Lady Artemis's mocking ones, and then she gave the colonel a radiant smile. "With pleasure," she said, placing her hand on his arm.

The musicale was unfortunately composed of amateur performers. Usually hostesses tried to secure the latest diva, but Lady Dexter considered such a practice a waste of money when there were so many ladies in society eager to perform for no fee whatsoever. Although she herself was a flirtatious and *mondaine* lady, she had a weakness for the company of middle-aged bluestockings, not the genuine ones, but the affected ones who considered that the way to compete with the masculine intellect was to roar out ballads in as deep a voice as possible.

Felicity felt the colonel pressing something into her hand. She looked down. Two little pieces of candle wax lay there. "Earplugs," whispered the colonel. Felicity gratefully popped the pieces of wax into her ears and endured the rest of the concert in an uncomfortable state of unease. It was not the muffled roar of the singers' voices nor yet the presence of the handsome colonel that was causing Felicity discomfort but an acute awareness that the Marquess of Darkwater was sitting behind her. She could sense his physical presence, and that presence seemed to be upsetting her body. She realized with a little shock that she was physically afraid of him, yet could not make sense of her feelings.

She could only be glad when the last red-faced lady had roared off into silence. She deftly removed the earplugs. "Thank goodness that is over," said the colonel cheerfully. "Supper, I think, and let's hope the supper is good enough to make up for the ordeal we have just endured."

The supper proved to be as good as he had hoped. He had a hard time enjoying the food, however, for Felicity kept asking him searching questions about the abolition of slavery and the Corn Laws, two subjects he knew little about and cared less.

He privately thought slavery was a great idea and the law that declared any black man setting foot anywhere in Britain was automatically a free citizen absolutely ridiculous. But it was fortunate he kept such views to himself. Felicity was now sure he was an impostor and adventurer and was amused by him, but she would never have forgiven him had she known he held such callous and unnatural views. Felicity regarded herself as an impostor, and that made her feel drawn to the colonel. She then asked him about his home in Ireland. The colonel, glad to be free from political questions, waxed eloquent over his family home. The fact that he had never been to Ireland and had never had a home since he had left the weaver's cottage he had been born in did not faze him. He described the old square building set among the gentle green hills of County Down and the fine stables he had and the splendid fishing on one of his own private lakes. He went on to describe the splendid alfresco meals he had had on the grounds of his estate when his cousin the Earl of Hopetoun and his family had come to stay. He conjured up mythical cousins and aunts and soon had Felicity in tears of laughter over their fictitious eccentricities. There was Aunt Jane who rode to hounds just like a man and swore like a trooper. There was gentle Aunt Phyllis who knitted garters for the peasantry, blind to the fact that the poor souls had no stockings to hold up. And there was roistering Uncle John, the terror of the neighborhood when he was in his cups. He told story after story, and Felicity listened to him, wide-eyed, delighted with his handsome face, soft voice, and his hilarious stories about the members of his family. By the end of supper, she was beginning to believe there might even be a place called Linlithgowshire.

The colonel had found out she had come unescorted and quickly secured permission from Lady Dexter to escort Miss Waverley home by riding alongside her carriage.

He promised to take her driving on the following day. Felicity smiled as she undressed for bed that night. Bernard was forgotten. She did not care if the colonel was an impostor. He was kind and funny and he made her laugh. And then, all at once, the smile died on her lips. She could feel the presence of the Marquess of Darkwater so strongly that she looked wildly about the room. With a little shiver, she climbed into bed, feeling haunted.

At that very same moment, the Marquess of Darkwater finished a letter to the Earl of Hopetoun telling that peer there was a certain Colonel Macdonald in London who was not only claiming to be M.P. for Linlithgowshire but to be a cousin of the earl. He sanded the letter and decided to send his servant off with it in the morning to catch the royal mail to Edinburgh. The new fast coaches only took thirty-four-and-a-half hours to reach the capital of Scotland. He had paid for a return reply. With any luck, he should hear from Hopetoun before another week was out. Damn Felicity Waverley. He should leave her to her fate. But somehow, he just could not get that girl out of his mind. . . .

Felicity decided to spend the earlier part of the following afternoon as Miss Callow and then change back to herself to go driving with the colonel.

Her first caller, to her surprise, was Bernard Anderson. When he learned Felicity was "out," he looked ready to flee rather than spend any time with Miss Callow, but Felicity in her role as her own aunt pressed him to stay for tea.

"You look very disturbed, young man," she croaked. "What is amiss?"

"I had hoped to see Miss Felicity," said Bernard wretchedly. "You see . . ."

He broke off and got to his feet in blushing confusion as the famous actress Caroline James was announced. Caroline's blue eyes twinkled as she surveyed Felicity in the guise of Miss Callow.

"I am delighted to see you," said Felicity. "Felicity is out at the moment. She will be devastated to have missed you. May I present Mr. Bernard Anderson to you? Mr. Anderson, Miss Caroline James."

"I say," said Bernard, thanking his stars his mother was not present. "I have seen you many times on the stage, Miss James. Such divine acting! Your Lady Macbeth quite frightened me."

"Thank you," said Caroline. "I mean, I should have hated to have played a Lady Macbeth people actually liked. Do you attend the playhouse often, Mr. Anderson?"

"When I can," said Bernard eagerly. He meant when he could escape from his matchmaking mama.

"I am sorry not to see Felicity," said Caroline. "It may surprise you to learn, Mr. Anderson, that Miss Waverley was the one who gave me the courage to go back on the stage instead of entering into a marriage that would, I am now convinced, have made me miserable. Of course, this all may seem strange to a young bachelor like yourself. Men do not know what it is like to be constrained to marry someone out of fear of insecurity or because a pushing parent demands the sacrifice."

"Oh, yes, they do," said Bernard in a hollow voice, and Caroline looked at him curiously.

Tea was brought in by Mrs. Ricketts. Felicity sank back into the shadow of her wing chair and watched with amusement as Bernard began to relax and talk easily in Caroline's company. Caroline was looking particularly fine in a blue velvet carriage dress with a wide-brimmed black velvet hat on her head. Felicity found she was glad she had not had to meet Bernard as herself. It had been a stupid idea even to think of marrying him. He was too puppyish, too naive, and too much under the thumb of his mother. The colonel on the other hand was tall and mature and very amusing. One would never be bored. She roused herself with a glance at the clock and realized she would need to get rid of her guests, for it would take her a full hour to take off her disguise.

Bernard and Caroline left together. "I do not have my carriage, ma'am," said Bernard eagerly, "but I would be honored to escort you."

"Very well," said Caroline, and Bernard waved down a passing hack.

When they reached Caroline's address in Covent Garden, Bernard helped her down, paid the hack, and stood on the pavement with a sort of extinguished look on his face that went straight to Caroline's heart.

"Something is troubling you," she said gently. "I do not have to be at the theater for two hours yet. Come upstairs and we can sit and chat."

Her flat was a modest apartment above a bakery. It was all exotic and exciting to Bernard—the cozy parlor with a screen in the corner plastered with playbills, various theatrical costumes and plays lying about, the cheerful fire, the noises of the street coming up from outside and the general feeling of freedom.

He drank wine and looked dreamily at the fire while Caroline went into her bedroom and changed into a loose-flowing gown and then came back and sat on the other side of the fire and said, "Now tell me all about it."

And Bernard did. All about his mother, all about how he was being forced into marriage with Lady Artemis—"and she frightens me," he said. "She is such a *knowing* sort of lady."

"Did you hope to court Felicity?" asked Caroline.

"I don't know now," said Bernard. "I thought it would be jolly to have a friend my own age, but Mama . . . Well, there you are. She holds the purse strings."

"What would you do if . . . I mean, say you were free to work for your living; what would you do?"

Bernard ran his hands through his thick fair hair and stared at her wildly. "What would I do? Oh, ma'am, I would be a carpenter."

"A worthy trade. You would need to serve an apprentice-ship."

"But I have," exclaimed Bernard. "When my father was alive, we lived in Mealchin in Berkshire. There was a carpenter in the village and he taught me all his skills. My father—he died two years ago—was amused by my enthusiasm, but my mother was furious. She could not do anything to stop me when father was alive, but when he died, well, it transpired she had set her heart on me marrying an heiress and so we moved to town. I am a simple sort of chap, really, and would have made an excellent tradesman. Life is very unfair. There is probably some poor carpenter somewhere who dreams of how wonderful life would be if he could only be a gentle-man of leisure and go to all the *ton* parties."

"No doubt. I am afraid you must excuse me now, Mr. Anderson. I am due at the playhouse."

Bernard thought of his mother's disapproving face; he thought of Lady Artemis, who made him feel so awkward and clumsy and gauche. He clasped his hands together and stared at Caroline James. "Oh, how I would love to watch you from the wings," he said. "To be a part of the theater. To be behind the scenes."

"That can most certainly be arranged," said Caroline. "But your mother will be waiting for you."

"Let her wait," said Bernard. "Please . . ."

"How old are you?"

"Twenty."

"A great age," said Caroline with a mocking smile.

"I am a *man*," declared Bernard, standing up and striking his breast in the best Haymarket manner.

"And I am turned thirty," said Caroline, "an old lady compared to your youth. Oh, very well. You may come with me. But do not get in anyone's way!"

The play in which Caroline was appearing was called *The Beau's Delight or Miss Polly's Fancy*, a lightweight piece of nonsense that was drawing large crowds. At several points in her performance, she remembered Bernard and glanced toward the wings, both right and left, but of her young cavalier, there was no sign. It was the last night of the play, and the theater was crowded to the gods. When it was over, she sat in her dressing room removing her makeup. The manager of the playhouse entered. "I want to talk to you about that young fellow you brought along," he said.

"I'm sorry," said Caroline quickly. "He is in love with the theater. I thought it would do no harm. I assume he made a nuisance of himself and you sent him packing."

"On the contrary," said the manager, Mr. Josiah Biggs, drawing up a chair and sitting down by the small coal fire, "he has made himself very useful. That is what I want to talk to you about. He repaired some scenery for me in a trice. So deft and busy with his fingers! I fell into conversation with him. We began to talk about transformation scenes, and he got some paper and a pencil and drew out plans for a stupendous waterfall operated by a clockwork device, not like that tin thing at Vauxhall, but using real water."

"You would flood the stage and drown the harlequin," said Caroline.

"Not the way your Mr. Anderson has planned it. Is he really a gentleman?"

"I am afraid so, and one with a mother who would tear you limb from limb."

"I could be the talk of the nation with such a device as that waterfall," said the manager dreamily. "You gave up marriage to a baron to stay on the stage. Why should not this Mr. Anderson amuse himself by working with us for a little?"

"Colonel Bridie was not a baron when I knew him," said Caroline, "although I would have given him up just the same. But this is different. I was an actress in my youth and *returned* to the theater. It would not answer."

"I have given him the offer of a job."

"He cannot take it. He goes in fear of his mother."

But Bernard, who joined the party in the Green Room that night, appeared to have forgotten his mother's very existence. His eyes were shining, there was sawdust on his coat, and he was talking happily to various members of the cast. When Caroline took her leave, she found Bernard at her elbow.

47

"I am going to escort you home," said Bernard firmly. He appeared to have grown in stature in one evening.

When Caroline reached the baker's shop under her flat, she turned to Bernard and held out her hand. "Good night, Mr. Anderson," she said firmly.

Bernard held tightly onto her hand. "I was offered a job this evening," he said proudly.

"So I heard," said Caroline, trying to tug her hand free.

"Might I not come up with you and talk about it for a little?"

Caroline's face hardened. "Certainly not!"

"Oh, just for a little, please, Miss James. This has been the most wonderful evening of my life."

Caroline relaxed. Mr. Anderson really just wanted to talk.

"Just for a little," she said, "and then you really must be on your way."

Mrs. Anderson paced up and down the hall of her town house all night long, listening to the hoarse call of the watch, waiting for her son to come home. She had had to attend a rout on her own. Lady Artemis Verity had been there, and because of Bernard's absence, Lady Artemis had spent most of her time talking to that ex-fiancé of hers, Mr. Fordyce. Pale dawn light began to creep into the hall. Mrs. Anderson began to feel seriously alarmed. Bernard must have been attacked by footpads.

And then at six o'clock she heard his key in the lock. Bernard came in quietly. "Morning, Mother," he said coolly, and made for the stairs.

Mrs. Anderson's massive bosom swelled. "Have you nothing to say to me?" she cried, head back, eyes flashing fire.

"No, Mother," said Bernard quietly. "Nothing at all."

Speechless with amazement, she watched him mount the stairs to his room.

Chapter Four

WHILE BERNARD ANDERSON fell into a dreamless sleep, Felicity awoke. She drew back the bed hangings and looked at the little French gilt clock on the mantelpiece. She turned over on her side and tried to go back to sleep, but her mind was racing.

Fragments of conversation with Colonel Macdonald floated through her head. "I have never been married. I never before found anyone I was willing to share my life with . . . until now."

It was as good as a proposal of marriage. She had spent last evening in a mood of happy elation. But what now of all her previous strictures and beliefs about that prison called marriage? She had always considered marriage a sort of genteel serfdom. But life with the colonel would never be dull. He was so happy and carefree. He had admitted with an endearingly rueful smile that he had little money. Felicity had confessed that although she did not have a bank balance, she did have the Waverley jewels and was about to start selling a few in order to pay the servants and to cover the daily expenses of running the house. Colonel Macdonald had promptly said if she would trust him with them, he could get her a very good price, so Felicity had agreed to hand a few items to him that very afternoon.

The Marquess of Darkwater's handsome, saturnine face rose in her mind's eye again, and his caution rang in her ears. Had she been too trusting? Everyone knew about the Marquess of Darkwater, his unlucky marriage and his background. No one seemed to know much about the colonel apart from what he told them. Lady Dexter had sung the colonel's praises, but when Felicity had pointed out the colonel was a very odd sort of politician in that he seemed to fight shy of political subjects, Lady Dexter had laughed and said he never bored the ladies with tedious discussions. Felicity was lonely. She realized that was the root of her problem.

Felicity frowned. She should really write to either Frederica or Fanny, begging their forgiveness and so put an end to loneliness. But she was an independent lady, a published author. She should not be so weak-kneed.

But as the time for the colonel's call approached, Felicity, sorting out a few jewels, became more and more worried about Colonel Macdonald. It certainly would not hurt to lose such a few trinkets when she had so many, yet, because she was a woman and alone, pride made her want to be sure she was not being gulled.

As a young miss, she could hardly interrogate the colonel. But in the guise of her aunt, Miss Callow, she could ask as many searching questions as she wanted.

With great care, she donned her disguise and then went down to the drawing room and waited for the colonel to arrive. On a small table beside her, she placed two fine rings, one ruby and one sapphire, and a collar of diamonds. Mrs. Ricketts was ordered to draw the curtains but to light only one candle and to place it on the table next to the jewels. Felicity wanted to keep the colonel's attention on the flashing jewels and not on herself.

The colonel was ushered in. At first he looked taken aback to find "Miss Callow" and not Felicity, but then his eye fell on the jewels and he found he could not look away.

He was sorely in need of money. Triumphant and sure of Felicity, he had gambled heavily the night before and had lost a large sum of money to a Mr. Herd, a wealthy landowner. But the colonel had already lost money on a previous occasion to this same Mr. Herd, and Mr. Herd coldly said he expected to be paid promptly. The colonel had promised to meet him after he had seen Felicity. He would use the money for the jewels to pay Mr. Herd, tell Felicity the jeweler would pay a sum the following week, and then in the intervening week, do his damnedest to get her to promise to marry him.

"My appointment was with Miss Felicity," he said to the little old lady in the high wing chair.

"I know," said Felicity, "and I know why you are come."

The colonel wrenched his eyes away from the jewels and

50

looked at her directly and then quickly averted his gaze. Gad! What an ugly birthmark. Had Felicity changed her mind?

"Sit down," commanded Miss Callow. "I believe you have offered to sell a few items of jewelry for us."

Colonel Macdonald heaved a sigh of relief. The game was still on.

"Yes, ma'am," he said. "I would do anything to be of service to Miss Felicity." He was about to boldly add he had also come to ask leave to pay his respects, but then no doubt Miss Callow would proceed to ask him all about his income and prospects. Better persuade Felicity herself.

Felicity shrank back further into the shadows in order to study him better. She could see he was nervous and uneasy, but it did not seem the uneasiness of the lover.

She leaned slightly forward. "Felicity tells me you are a Member of Parliament."

"Yes, ma'am."

"There is a bill at present being read in the House that interests me. It is—"

"Ah, sure," he interrupted quickly, "you must not be bothering your poor head with such things, ma'am. You see, I can get a good deal for those jewels if I get them to the man quickly." He half rose.

"Please remain seated," said Felicity. She felt a wave of sadness engulf her. The colonel was not interested in turning his charm on what he thought was an ugly old woman, and his eyes, which were fastened on the jewels, held a naked look of avarice. Thank goodness I have discovered what he is really like in time, thought Felicity. Aloud she said, "I do not see any need for haste, Mr. Macdonald. Nor do I now wish the Waverley jewels to go to some anonymous jeweler. I shall take them myself to Rundell & Bridge. So much safer to deal with a known and reputable firm."

The colonel felt a sharp stab of fear somewhere in the pit of his stomach. He had put it about society that he was in easy circumstances. If he did not pay his gambling debts, then he would need to flee London. He had become accustomed to luxuries. His credit with his tailor, his club, his grocers, and his wine merchants had run out. He did not want to start off again penniless in some provincial city. He looked at the jewels again. He could raise enough on those to take him to Paris, and

54

there he could emerge with a new identity and play the field. It was a pity about Felicity, for it would have been grand to have had the pleasure of such a beauty in his bed.

Still, he tried. "Come now, ma'am," he cajoled. "Let me be speaking with Miss Felicity herself, and she will vouch for my good character."

"Miss Felicity is guided by me in all matters," said Felicity. "I wish to retire." She reached out a hand for the bell.

"Don't touch that, or it will be the worse for ye!"

Felicity looked up in amazement. Colonel Macdonald had got to his feet and was drawing a wicked-looking knife from his pocket.

And then downstairs came a knocking at the street door. "Stay still," hissed the colonel, holding the point of the knife at her throat. "Not a word."

From downstairs came the Marquess of Darkwater's voice and Mrs. Ricketts's answering one saying that Miss Felicity was out and that Miss Callow was entertaining someone and perhaps would not like to be disturbed but she would go and find out.

The colonel backed away until he was standing behind the door. "If you value your life, you old baggage," he hissed, "you will tell her to send Darkwater away."

Felicity stared at him in baffled fury. But if she did not obey, then he might stab Mrs. Ricketts as well.

"Do not come in," said Felicity as Mrs. Ricketts appeared in the doorway. "Tell the marquess I am not free."

"Yes, mum," said Mrs. Ricketts. She turned and went away.

"Good," whispered the colonel. "We will sit and wait until the coast is clear, and then we will go to your bedchamber, old lady, and we will find the rest of the jewels."

"You will hang, you greedy scoundrel," said Felicity.

Colonel Macdonald shrugged. "May as well be hanged for a sheep as a lamb."

Downstairs, Mrs. Ricketts held open the street door for the marquess. "Miss Callow does not wish to be disturbed," she said in a loud voice. But as the marquess made to leave, she caught his arm and whispered urgently, "Please go up, sir. Something is wrong. I know it." She slammed the door loudly so that anyone listening would think the marquess had left.

The marquess looked at her in surprise and then ran lightly up the stairs.

He stopped short at the tableau that met his eyes. Miss Callow was shrinking back in her chair while the colonel held a long sharp knife in front of her.

The colonel saw him. "Come one step nearer, and I will kill her," he said.

Unnoticed by him, Felicity had been slowly drawing up her knees. As the marquess hesitated, Felicity kicked out with all her might, the serviceable half boots she considered correct dress for an old lady striking the colonel full in the stomach. As he doubled up, the marquess moved like lightning and struck him full on the chin with a massive blow of his fist. The colonel was driven backward by the blow. He crashed into a chair opposite, then crumpled up and lay half across it, dead to the world.

"Oh, bravo!" cried Felicity, leaping to her feet, "A flush hit, sir. Bravo!"

The marquess took off his gloves, took out his handkerchief, and wound it around his bleeding knuckles. Then he looked at Miss Callow, and a flash of amusement lit up his eyes. Her white wig had slipped to one side revealing the glossy chestnut hair of Felicity Waverley.

"I mean," quavered Felicity, remembering her role all too late, "we are monstrous pleased to be rescued."

The servants came running in, Mrs. Ricketts carrying a length of cord with which she proceeded to tie up the colonel.

"Drag him out to the landing and shut the door," ordered the marquess, "and give me a few minutes in private with Miss Callow."

"Yes, my lord," said Mrs. Ricketts. "Mary, Beth, Joan, seize a hold of this fellow."

They removed the colonel by pulling his unconscious body to the floor and then sliding it across the rugs and out onto the landing. Mrs. Ricketts turned in the doorway. She tried to signal to Felicity that her wig was askew, but Felicity was looking at the marquess. But the marquess saw Mrs. Ricketts and jerked his head. She gave a resigned sort of curtsy and withdrew, closing the door behind her.

"The jig is up, Miss Felicity," said the marquess.

"Yes, I am so glad that villain has been unmasked," said

Felicity. She sat down in the wing chair. One of the wings caught at her wig and it and the cap she was wearing fell off and landed on the floor.

The marquess began to laugh. "I mean *you* have been unmasked, Miss Felicity. What a fright you have made of yourself!"

Tears started to Felicity's eyes. "So you know," she said weakly.

The amusement left his face. "Come, Miss Felicity. Go abovestairs and change back to your normal and beautiful appearance while I deal with the authorities."

Felicity nodded dumbly, too upset to protest. But she scooped up the jewels before she left the room. She was so rattled by the colonel's attack on her, she was worried the marquess might prove to be a thief as well.

The marquess went out after her, stepped over the colonel's unconscious body, and told Mrs. Ricketts, who was waiting in the hall, that he would return shortly with the constable and a magistrate.

Upstairs, Felicity wearily removed her disguise. She felt terribly lost and tired. All around her in the west end of London were young misses with mothers and fathers to turn to in an emergency. Her thoughts turned again to the mother she had never known, and she longed to give up completely, to lie facedown on the bed and cry her eyes out.

Colonel Macdonald recovered consciousness. He cautiously felt with his fingers at his bound wrists. Feverishly he began to work at the knots. The rope was thick, and Mrs. Ricketts had not made a very good job of tying him up. Soon he had his wrists free and then his ankles. For one mad moment, he thought of trying to get at least some of those jewels. But Darkwater might be somewhere about, and if he were not, he would surely be returning with the forces of law and order. Groggily the colonel got to his feet. He slid down the banisters. Mrs. Ricketts had left her post in the hall to go down to the kitchens. He quietly opened the door and walked down the stairs and then he began to run as hard as he could, down toward the river, down to where that sordid network of alleys, wharves, and slums would swallow him up.

The marquess was furious when he returned to find the colonel had escaped. But he sat with Felicity while the magistrate, the beadle, and the constable asked questions. When they had finally taken their leave, he said quietly to Felicity, "I did not tell the authorities of your ridiculous masquerade. Now tell me why you found it necessary to pretend to be your own aunt. Were you trying to chaperon *yourself* at the Season?"

Felicity nodded dumbly.

The marquess looked at her bent head. "Have you no one to care of you, my child?"

"No, my lord. Except, of course, Mrs. Ricketts."

"A housekeeper, however worthy, is not enough to protect you from charlatans. Colonel Macdonald pretended he was going to sell some jewels for you. Why? Are you so destitute?"

"No, my lord. I own this house and all the Waverley jewels. I have no money in the bank and wanted to sell a few items."

He glanced about him. The money she had received for her book would certainly only last a short time in Regency London. He had an impulse to tell her he knew she was the author of *The Love Match*, but decided against it.

"Then I suggest," he said, "that you allow me to escort you to a reputable jeweler, where you may sell the items yourself. Tell me what you know of your family. The other two Waverley girls, Fanny and Frederica, are now titled ladies. Can you not write to them and ask them for protection?"

Felicity hung her head. "I cannot. I quarreled with them. I do not know if they have forgiven me."

He rang the bell and ordered tea to be brought in; Quite like the master of the house, thought Mrs. Ricketts with dawning hope.

He waited in silence while tea was served and while the obviously upset Felicity had time to compose herself.

"Begin at the beginning," he said, "and tell me how you came to be in this odd situation."

Felicity spread her hands in a gesture of resignation. Then she began to speak.

"We were taken from an orphanage, that is, I and Fanny and Frederica, by Mrs. Waverley and brought up in an odd way. We were allowed little social life; we were constantly warned against the evils of men and marriage. Mrs. Waverley is a very good teacher, and she educated us herself. Then Fanny ran away to get married, and later Frederica. But Mrs. Waverley herself deserted me to get married to Colonel Bridie, now

Baron Meldon. She left me this house, as I told you, and all those wretched jewels. There is a considerable amount of fine jewelry. Mrs. Waverley would make us dress very drably when we went out but liked to attire us as richly as barbaric princesses when she entertained at home. I felt Fanny had betrayed me, and then I tried to prevent Frederica's marriage, for I really truly believed Lord Harry Danger did not mean to marry her. Both the Earl of Tredair, who married Fanny, and Lord Harry made attempts to find out the mystery of our parentage but were both unsuccessful. Since Mrs. Waverley had almost convinced us we were all foundlings and bastards, we might have let the matter rest. But it did seem as if someone or some people were determined to stop us from finding out anything." She gave an embarrassed laugh. "We even began to think we might be royal bastards, for every time Mrs. Waverley saw the Prince Regent, she turned white and he looked monstrous upset. Then the orphanage itself only housed girls who were being kept there by wealthy relatives. They told us we were charity cases, but I found that hard to believe as no one on the ruling body of that orphanage showed any signs of charity whatsoever.

"I decided never to marry. I agreed with Mrs. Waverley's views, even though she had betrayed them, because women are the lesser sex and marriage is a form of slavery. But I began to think there might possibly be exceptions to the rule," said Felicity wistfully. "I hear reports that both Fanny and Frederica are very happy. I was . . . I am . . . lonely. I thought, don't you see, that being of independent means I could perhaps find a companion, an equal. Yes, I suspected Colonel Macdonald was an impostor, but he seemed so gay, so charming, and I am by way of being an impostor myself. Baron Meldon, who married Mrs. Waverley, was at one time engaged to the actress Caroline James. She called here, and I hit on the plan of being made up to look like an elderly lady. That way I could chaperon myself. Now you have discovered my trick; there is nothing left for me but to settle down to a solitary existence."

"But what is stopping you from writing to Lady Tredair or Lady Harry?" asked the marquess.

Felicity sighed. "We were brought up to be rivals. Pride,

combined with fear they might still be angry with me—That is what is stopping me."

She fell silent. He sat opposite her, very much at his ease, the candlelight shining on his handsome face. He studied her for some moments, noticing the purity of her skin and the gleaming cascade of her chestnut hair.

"I sometimes hate Mrs. Waverley," said Felicity suddenly.

"And yet," he said, "she saved you from the orphanage and left you independent. She educated you well and made you all so independent-minded that at least Fanny and Frederica found two gentlemen who were prepared to treat them as equals, or so I believe."

"Perhaps," said Felicity slowly. "But I think I hate her because I feel in my bones she knows the identity of our parents. Before she met the baron, she was very possessive and did everything to bind us close to her, almost as if she had bought herself a ready-made family to protect her from the world."

There was another long silence, and he shifted restlessly, and she wondered whether he was becoming bored, and that thought gave her a sharp pain. Soon he would rise to take his leave, his curiosity satisfied, and she would never see him again.

"It is a fascinating mystery," he said. "Have courage, Miss Felicity. Surely you and I would be better employed finding out where you come from than spending our evenings in hot rooms talking to a lot of charlatans and bores."

"I do not see how we can succeed where Tredair and Danger failed," said Felicity.

"They were both men deeply in love, and having secured their hearts' desire, they lost interest," said the marquess. "But we, Miss Felicity, are heart-free and intelligent. Before we set about our investigations, we must find a chaperon for you. No, do not look so surprised. I know what you are thinking. I shall not tell anyone of your masquerade. As far as society is concerned, Miss Callow has retired to the country. Now, I have a fourth cousin, resident in London, a poor relation. I had planned to do something about her plight, for she is companion to an old harridan and having quite a miserable time of it. Allow me to fetch her here. We may have to travel, and you cannot drive off with me on your own."

From being in the depths of misery, Felicity began to feel quite light-headed with excitement. She clasped her hands together and looked at him beseechingly. "It would be wonderful if we could solve the mystery."

He raised an admonitory finger. "Be warned, Miss Felicity, that the outcome may not be what you hope."

"Anything is better than not knowing," said Felicity. "Where do we start?"

"I think," he said, "we will start with Mrs. Waverley herself."

The marquess's fourth cousin, Miss Agnes Joust, was a thoroughly silly woman, and was suffering as much as any woman without any strength of character can when she finds herself in a nasty predicament. Miss Joust had survived three months as companion to a Mrs. Deves-Pereneux. Mrs. Deves-Pereneux was a gross, overfed bully. Miss Joust was thin and faded and fortyish. The only thing that lightened her days was the knowledge that her handsome relative, the Marquess of Darkwater, was in London. She had not seen him for many years until he had called on her a bare month ago. Miss Joust had fallen violently in love with him on the spot. She wrote him little notes about the happenings of her days. Occasionally he would reply, and she kept his letters in a sandalwood box on her toilet table, reading and rereading them. One of her favorite dreams was that he would arrive in person again, but this time he would sweep her off, away from the horrible Mrs. Deves-Pereneux.

Miss Joust had no faith to console her. Every Sunday for the past three months she had prayed for deliverance from her mistress, and every Monday came along to show that God had not paid any attention. Therefore, it followed that God did not exist, and Miss Joust became determined to punish Him by telling Him so. Mrs. Deves-Pereneux liked to walk home from church. It was half a mile, and the going was slow and painful for both women—for Mrs. Deves-Pereneux because she was fat and for Miss Joust because her mistress leaned too heavily on her arm and grumbled and wheezed.

They were just reaching the bleak red brick house in Bloomsbury where Mrs. Deves-Pereneux lived when Miss Joust saw a smart curricle approaching and her heart began to hammer hard as she recognized the driver.

"Why, 'tis Lord Darkwater," she cried.

"What's he want?" grumbled Mrs. Deves-Pereneux. "Got no right to come calling on servants without a by-your-leave, and so I shall tell him."

Tears started to Miss Joust's weak eyes. Mrs. Deves-Pereneux, a frightful old snob, had no intention of being rude to a lord, but it did her heart good to torment Miss Joust.

But the old lady was quite put out when the marquess said he wished to see Miss Joust in private. "Servants," said Mrs. Deves-Pereneux nastily, "have to give notice when they are expecting callers."

"I was under the understanding that Miss Joust was your companion," said the marquess icily as he followed them into the gloom of the downstairs parlor.

"Well, well, *paid* companion," said the old lady, but in a mollified tone, for she had noticed Miss Joust's nose had turned red, a sure sign of acute distress. "I shall retire for a few moments, my lord, and then you may have the honor of taking tea with me."

"That will not be possible," he said coldly. "My time is short."

Miss Joust groaned inwardly. A few moments bliss in his company would mean days of cruelty as Mrs. Deves-Pereneux exacted her revenge. An hour, say, would have made such treatment bearable.

As soon as her mistress had lumbered out, Miss Joust began on a long, prepared speech, well-rehearsed for just such an occasion. But he interrupted her and said, "I had hoped to do things pleasantly, but that old fright never does anything pleasant. I have found a congenial post for you, Miss Joust. Go and get your trunk packed. We will leave immediately."

Miss Joust clasped her hands to her bosom. The marquess's well-tailored coat of Bath superfine and leather breeches and top boots faded to be replaced by a suit of shining armor. Somewhere in her ears she could hear a celestial choir and the snort of his milk-white steed outside the door.

"Are you all right, Miss Joust?" asked the marquess anxiously, for her eyes were now closed and she was breathing rapidly.

Miss Joust opened her eyes. "I will do as you command, my lord," she said firmly, "and escape this dungeon!"

With head thrown back, she strode out of the room.

The marquess experienced a qualm of doubt and then reassured himself with the thought that half the spinster companions and chaperons in London were decidedly weird.

Then there came sounds of the very devil of a row, coming from upstairs. He could hear the deep bass of Mrs. Deves-Pereneux's voice punctuated with the shrill protests of Miss Joust.

The afternoon dragged on, the noise upstairs went on and on, the clocks ticked, and the fire died in the hearth. The marquess was just about to rouse himself and go upstairs to find out what was going on when the door opened and a much-flushed and exhilarated Miss Joust stood there, carrying a trunk, while the bulk of her mistress loomed behind her.

Mrs. Deves-Pereneux's curses and complaints followed them from the house. The marquess could not be bothered telling her what he thought of her and so pretended to have been struck deaf.

"You will be relieved never to see her again," he remarked as he drove through the streets of Bloomsbury.

"Oh, my lord, you have saved me from the jaws of hell," exclaimed Miss Joust, and then in a more practical tone, "Where are we going?"

"There is a young lady in need of a companion."

"Young? How young?"

"Nineteen or twenty, I should guess."

"Oh."

"I had better tell you the whole story."

As the marquess talked, Miss Joust began to feel more at ease. This Felicity had had a weird upbringing. And a bluestocking! Bluestockings were notoriously ugly. Nothing more tedious for a man than the company of a young bluestocking. Mature men like the marquess must find the feminine company of a *mondaine* older woman like herself infinitely preferable. For Miss Joust lived in a fantasy world. When she looked in her glass, she did not see a long-nosed spinster with drab brown hair and thin lips, but a calm, medieval beauty with an air of mystery. She was still convinced the vicar of the church in which she had prayed so uselessly to God was in love with her and had not declared his passion because of the fearsome Mrs. Deves-Pereneux. The fact that the marquess might have arrived because of some divine intervention did not occur to

60

Miss Joust. She had shown Him she could manage very well on her own, thank you, and so she did not believe in Him.

Felicity and Miss Joust sized each other up like two stray cats. Felicity decided quickly that Miss Joust would do. She appeared to be a silly, nervous woman, but not a bully. Miss Joust was taken aback initially by Felicity's beauty, but she quickly recovered. It was just like the gallant marquess to offer to help Miss Waverley, but he would soon discover she came from very low origins indeed. One had only to look at her! No lady was ever so obviously beautiful. One had only to look at Emma Hamilton. Low origins meant Miss Waverley would remain unmarriageable. Miss Joust had not yet learned the happy fate of the other two Waverley girls.

There was, moreover, nothing of the lover in the marquess's demeanor. Miss Joust, her main worry laid to rest, was able to appreciate her comfortable surroundings, the finely appointed bedchamber allotted to her, and the excellence of the cuisine. Her head was full of dreams. They were to set out for Meldon in two days' time to confront Mrs. Waverley. Miss Joust could see it now: Mrs. Waverley would produce papers proving Felicity's father had been a low felon. The marquess would fall very silent and then he would seek her out. "You cannot stay in such a household," he would say. Miss Joust, wearing her best lilac sarcenet with her hair loose, would exclaim, "Alas, what is to become of me?" He would then gaze at her with a smoldering look and reply, "Fear not. I have found you another position." "Where?" demanded Miss Joust. "What as?" "As my wife," he cried, seizing her in his arms. And that was such a lovely dream that Miss Joust smiled dreamily all through dinner and paid little attention to Felicity, who wondered whether to be cross or amused.

Miss Joust decided to pay attention to her surroundings by the time the pudding was brought in. That way, she could save a little of the splendid dream for bedtime. "How do you pass your days in London, Miss Waverley?" she asked.

"Really, Miss Joust, I have just been telling you how I pass my days. Are you usually so inattentive?"

"Oh, no, Miss Waverley. I am just so glad to be away from that dreadful woman. So fatiguing. She quite addled my poor wits. Do tell me again."

"Firstly, you may call me Felicity, and I shall call you Agnes. I do not have much in the way of a social life. I read a great deal. Do you read much, Agnes?"

"Yes, though I have not had the leisure to indulge my tastes of late. Mrs. Deves-Pereneux would have me read to her quite shocking and unsuitable books, you know. *The Love Match* was the last book. Quite dreadful. As if any woman of society would be so loose in her morals."

"I thought it was an excellent book," said Felicity crossly. "Why should people read books about rakes and philanderers with complacency yet shudder at the idea of a woman doing the same thing?"

"Ah, you are young, Felicity. Ladies have a natural modesty that curbs their actions. We all know we are put on this earth to be the support of some gentleman, as the ivy wraps itself around the strong oak."

"Well put," said Felicity acidly. "Ivy is a parasite and will soon destroy the strong oak with its clinging dependency."

"La! How fierce you are. Simon told me you were a bluestocking."

"Simon?"

"The Marquess of Darkwater."

"Forgive my ignorance, Agnes. I am not on such terms of familiarity with his lordship as to call him by his Christian name, or even to know of it."

"It is different in my case," said Agnes Joust, her nose turning pink. Her nose turned red when angry and pink when she was lying. "Us being related, you know."

"With relatives as rich as Darkwater in your family, I am surprised you have to earn your living," commented Felicity.

"Well, one does not want to be a burden and . . ." Agnes was about to add that she was just one of many indigent relatives but thought better of it. "Would you like me to read to you, Felicity?"

"No, thank you. I am perfectly capable of reading to myself."

"Perhaps you would like me to demonstrate an interesting new stitch?"

"Do not be so worried about earning your keep," said Felicity with quick sympathy. "Your main job will be to chaperon me on our travels. In the meantime, you may rest as much as you like."

Agnes felt a sudden rush of gratitude for Felicity. Such a pity she wasn't a lady.

Felicity was glad to retire to the privacy of her room as soon as possible. She looked wearily at the few pages of manuscript on her desk. Would she ever write another book?

Chapter Five

THE NEXT DAY, Felicity checked over the inventory of the Waverley jewels, the huge box that now held them open on her bedroom floor. She was wondering where she could put them for safekeeping. She had removed the items she meant to sell that day. As she was kneeling on the floor, bending over the box, there came a faint scratching on the door and Agnes walked in. She stopped short at the sight of the jewels, blazing like a pirate's treasure.

"I do not like to be disturbed before noon," said Felicity shortly.

"Oh, what wondrous gems!" cried Agnes. She walked slowly forward, her eyes shining. "Oh, how I would love to be able to wear jewels like that!"

"I am wondering where to put them for safekeeping," said Felicity, half-irritated, half-amused by her companion's raptures. "You may choose something to wear today, if it would please you."

Agnes fell to her knees beside Felicity and began to lift piece after piece out of the box, holding the jewels up to the light. "Do not take all day," snapped Felicity. "Select something and be off with you."

Agnes seized an emerald necklace and bracelet from one of the many trays and darted from the room.

"It is not at all the thing, you know," said Felicity later when Agnes joined her in the drawing room, "to wear such gaudy baubles with a morning gown."

"Oh, I know," breathed Agnes, "but just for this little while. I feel like a queen."

"Mr. Bernard Anderson has called," said the housekeeper from the door of the drawing room.

Felicity hesitated and then said, "Send him up, Ricketts."

Bernard entered at a half run. He fell to his knees in front of the startled Felicity and cried, "Oh, I am in love, and I am so very happy!"

Agnes let out a squawk and darted from the room and shut the door. She went halfway down the stairs, her hand to her breast, her heart beating hard. How wonderful. That very personable young man was obviously proposing to Felicity, and Felicity would accept him, and she, Agnes Joust, would be maid of honor, and the marquess would squeeze her hand tenderly and whisper in her ear, "This wedding has given me the idea of marriage, Miss Joust . . . or may I call you . . . beloved?"

Inside, Bernard was pouring out a tirade of gratitude that Felicity had introduced him to the most wonderful woman in the world, Caroline James.

"I am glad you are happy, Mr. Anderson," said Felicity. "But please do rise and take a seat and tell me calmly what has happened. Are you engaged?"

"I have not dared ask her," said Bernard. "I have taken a job in the theater, you know."

"No, of course I do not know. And what has Mrs. Anderson to say to that?"

"She is furious, but there is nothing she can do," said Bernard simply. "Do you think there is hope for me with Miss James?"

"Mr. Anderson, I really do not know. I have not seen Miss James since that day you met her. I am afraid you will need to ask her yourself."

"I stayed the whole night with her," said Bernard. He saw Felicity's raised eyebrows and blushed. "I mean, I stayed all night and talked and talked. It was so wonderful."

Outside on the staircase, the Marquess of Darkwater was finding to his irritation that his way was being barred by Agnes.

"Hush!" she said. "They must not be disturbed."

"What on earth are you babbling on about, you widgeon?" snapped the marquess. Agnes blushed painfully. His words and tone were like a bucket of cold water being thrown over her. The fantasy marquess of her dreams had a much better script.

"A Mr. Anderson is proposing marriage to Felicity."

"And did Miss Waverley order you from the room?"

"N-no, but you see . . ."

"He may prove to be another charlatan. You should not have left her."

He mounted the stairs and opened the drawing room door. Bernard was now seated respectably in a chair with Felicity in a chair opposite. Felicity rose and curtsied and made the introductions.

The marquess looked from Bernard's glowing face to Felicity's amused one and said sharply, "Well? Am I to congratulate you?"

"Why?" asked Felicity bluntly.

"I gather from Miss Joust you have just received a proposal of marriage."

Agnes let out a faint bleating sound.

"If Miss Joust had stayed in the room," said Felicity, "she would have learned that Mr. Anderson is indeed on the point of proposing to someone . . . but not to me."

The marquess found he was feeling relieved but put it down to the fact that he was looking forward to the unraveling of the mystery about Felicity and did not want anyone else on the scene.

"I will bid you good day, Miss Waverley," said Bernard. "I pray you will come to my wedding."

"Gladly," said Felicity. "Good luck!"

After he had left, the marquess asked curiously, "What was all that about?"

"Mr. Anderson is enamored of the actress Caroline James. He hopes to marry her."

"A boy like that!"

"Miss James is very beautiful."

"Granted. But there is a great difference in their ages."

"Quite. Miss James is, I should guess, about your age, and Bernard, near to mine. Women marry older men every day. I do not see what is so wrong in that."

"Women do not wear so well."

"Only because they are worn out with childbirth," said Felicity sharply.

"My dear Felicity!" cried Agnes. "You must not say such things."

The marquess turned and looked at his relative and then his

eyes sharpened. "I gather those are not your jewels, Miss Joust."

"No, dear Felicity was kind enough to lend them to me."

He turned back to Felicity. "As for the Waverley jewels, do not trouble to sell any of them at the moment. I will pay all expenses, and we can settle our accounts later. I suggest we take them to my bank for safekeeping, and that includes those you have on, Miss Joust."

Agnes's hand fluttered protectively to the necklace at her neck. "Oh, but surely dear Felicity will need some for the journey."

"I am grateful to you, my lord," said Felicity. "Those jewels have brought me nothing but trouble. But please do render me an exact account of all expenses when this adventure is over."

"I have my carriage. I think we should take them to the bank now. If you do not mind, I shall send an item of news to the *Morning Post* to say the jewels are lodged in the bank. You do not want your servants to be imperiled."

Felicity called Mrs. Ricketts and two of the maids to help her carry the jewels downstairs. Her mind was working busily. She did not know what she thought of the marquess now, only that it was a relief to have some of her worries taken off her hands.

Agnes came with them to the bank and watched sulkily as all the jewels including the emerald necklace and bracelet were locked away in the vaults and Felicity tucked the receipt from the bank in her reticule. But soon a dream arose to console her. Felicity had been proved to be of low birth. The marquess came to rescue Agnes from her post as he had rescued her from Mrs. Deves-Pereneux. As they drove away from Hanover Square, he handed her a flat morocco leather box, and when she opened it, there were the emeralds. "I bought them for you, my beloved," said the dream marquess. "Poor Miss Waverley was only too glad to get the money for them. Of course, she cannot live in London anymore now that the scandal of her birth is out. But *we* can, my darling, as man and wife."

This was such a good dream, Agnes spent the rest of the day adding to it and embroidering it.

Felicity was already beginning to find this companion tiresome. She retired to her room early to prepare for the journey on the morrow. The marquess had proved not to be a villain. His only interest in her was as a provider of a mystery to amuse him. He had pointed out they were both heart-free. Felicity had often dreamed of having the company of some man as a friend. Now it seemed she had it. So why did she feel so low?

After some thought, she put it down to her dread at meeting Mrs. Waverley again. She could never think of her as Baroness Meldon.

It was a blustery sunny morning when they set out for Meldon. The marquess's traveling carriage was comfortable and well-sprung. Felicity was tired after a night during which she had had little sleep and soon dozed off.

Agnes gazed hungrily at the marquess. She was sure he was longing for an opportunity to say something intimate to her. He was shy, of course. That was it. Since his wife's death, it was rumored he had shunned the company of the ladies. Perhaps he needed a little encouragement.

She smiled at him fondly and said, "It is a fine day, is it not, Simon?"

The marquess looked at her coldly, and she blushed under his gaze. All at once, her use of his first name seemed like the impertinence it undoubtedly was. He took out a book and began to read.

Agnes could not bear the silence. After a little while, she gave a genteel cough and said tentatively, "What are you reading, my lord?"

"*The Use of Phosphates in Increasing the Yield of Wheat,*" he said without raising his eyes.

"How interesting!" cried Agnes. "I dote on phosphates."

He raised his eyes. "So you know about phosphates?"

"Yes, my lord. They are those pretty blue flowers, are they not?"

"Phosphates are salts that enrich the earth, like fertilizer," he said. He lifted his book higher this time, as if to barricade himself from further questions.

"Silly me," said Agnes with a tinkling laugh.

She did not feel at all stupid. A woman's role in life was to make a man feel superior on all occasions.

Felicity awoke and yawned and stretched. She blinked and

looked around. Agnes put a playful finger to her lips. "Shhh," she admonished. "Our gallant companion is deep in literature."

"What are you reading?" Felicity asked curiously.

With an edge of irritation in his voice, the marquess told her.

"Oh," said Felicity in surprise. "Is that Hulm on phosphates, or Jardine?"

He looked at her in amazement. "Jardine, Miss Felicity. Never say you have read it."

"Yes, indeed. Mrs. Waverley considered a knowledge of the latest innovations in agriculture an essential part of my education."

"You poor thing!" exclaimed Agnes.

"On the contrary, I found it fascinating. Is this to improve your plantations, my lord?"

"No, I own a small estate in Surrey that is not in good heart."

The pair plunged into a long discussion on crops, phosphates, and drainage.

Agnes was just wondering whether it was possible to go into a decline through sheer boredom when a dream came to save her. The marquess was standing in the middle of a plowed field, hatless, shirt open at the neck, in leather breeches and thick shoes. She herself was wearing a simple peasant dress—lilac muslin, perhaps?—with one of those leather bodices. "This land is all ours, my sweeting," said the marquess, gathering her to his side with one hand and pointing across the field with the other. A warm wind blew Agnes's hair across her cheek, and he tenderly brushed it aside. She frowned in irritation. With his third hand? This dream needed more work. She resolutely closed her eyes. In no time at all, she was fast asleep.

The former Mrs. Waverley, now Baroness Meldon, and her husband were dozing in front of the fire in the parlor after a hearty meal. The sound of carriage wheels crunching on the drive outside made both sit up.

"Callers," said the baroness bitterly. In London, it was easy. If one did not want to be disturbed, then one's servant simply said one was not at home, but in the country, everyone for miles around seemed to know exactly when one was at home or out. "I hope it is not the vicar," she added. "A most stupid and encroaching fellow."

A footman came in carrying a card on a silver tray, which he presented to the baroness. The servants had quickly learned which one of the pair held the purse strings and managed the household.

The baroness fumbled for her quizzing glass and held it up scrutinizing the card. "The Marquess of Darkwater," she read. "Don't know the man. What does he want, do you think?"

"Perhaps a friend of the Prince Regent," said the baron importantly, brushing grains of snuff from his coat and straightening his wig.

"Show his lordship in," said the baroness, getting to her feet.

The baron had turned away from the door and was arranging his crumpled cravat in the glass when he heard his wife's exclamation of dismay. He swung around. His eyes went straight past the marquess to where Felicity Waverley stood, and he turned a slightly muddy color.

Felicity had told the marquess she did not think their visit would be welcomed, but he had not expected them to be greeted with such shock and dismay.

The baroness wanted to forget all about the three girls she had adopted from the orphanage. The baron alone knew he had received his title from the Prince Regent on the understanding that he married Mrs. Waverley and took her away from London. Why the Prince Regent should go to these lengths, the baron did not know, nor did he care. He had a title and a rich wife. Now, as he looked at Felicity, he dreaded that the prince would somehow learn of her visit and be displeased.

"Felicity," said the baroness faintly. "Why are you come?"

"May we sit down?" asked Felicity impatiently. "We have journeyed from London to see you."

"It is too small and stuffy here," said the baroness with a distracted look about her. "We will repair to the Green Saloon."

The small party followed her across the hall and into a large, chilly, and very grand room. The baron had bought the house and estates with his wife's money. He loved his new home and he loved his title. Could the Prince Regent remove a title through displeasure?

The marquess sat down and looked at Baroness Meldon curiously. She was a massive stately woman like a figurehead on a ship. She looked at him, and she looked at Agnes, but she would not look at Felicity.

"We are come," said Felicity, "because I feel it is important to trace my parents."

"But that is impossible," said Mrs. Waverley. "And pointless. I gave you the jewels and the house. Why should you wreck your life by trying to find out about parents who were probably not even married?"

"Why should you believe that?" put in the marquess.

"They were charity cases at the orphanage," said the baroness angrily. "I gave them a home. I took them to my bosom. Did they thank me? Did they give me love? No!" She struck her breast. Agnes looked at her with approval. The baroness was behaving just as a lady ought.

"We are all grateful to you," said Felicity. "You know that. We might have loved you had you not kept us like prisoners in the house in Hanover Square. We might have loved you had you not tried to set us against one another."

"Viper!" cried the baroness.

"In truth, Felicity, I must say you are too hard," said Agnes.

"Do not interfere in matters that are not your concern," retorted Felicity. "You must have some idea, ma'am. Why was it when Tredair tried to find out from the orphanage, they sent a messenger to warn you of his visit?"

"Because they considered it none of his concern."

Felicity leaned forward. "Then tell me, ma'am, why it is you turn faint when you see the Prince Regent and why his majesty looks most uncomfortable. Are we royal bastards?"

The baron exploded into wrath. "Take yourselves off!" he shouted. "Begone from my house and leave my wife in peace." He rang the bell and told the footman who answered it, "These persons are leaving. Have them escorted off the estate and make sure they are not allowed to return."

The marquess was about to expostulate when he saw two letters lying open on a desk by the door. Felicity had got to her feet and was now raging at the baroness. He moved quietly to the door, straining his eyes to read the letters.

"You *unnatural* woman," Felicity was saying. "There is no need for this rudeness. And what of your famous principles? What of all your lectures on the evils of marriage?"

"Saints preserve us," screamed the baroness. "Am I to be molested in my own house, you strumpet? You came from the

71

gutter, and you will no doubt return to the gutter when this fine lord has tired of you."

"You have a mind like a kennel," raged Felicity. "What of your precious background?"

She found the marquess had taken her arm, and she tried to shake him off. "Come along, Miss Waverley," he said. "There is nothing for us here."

The fight suddenly seemed to go out of her, and he led her from the room.

When they had gone, the baroness said, "Ingratitude always makes me feel ill, my love. I am going to lie down."

"I'll be up soon," said the baron. "Do not fret. I will make sure those tiresome people are not allowed to trouble you again. I must write an urgent letter."

He sat for a long time at the writing desk. He did not particularly want to remind the Prince Regent of his existence, yet perhaps it might be better to tell him one of the Waverley girls was ferreting about. He bent his head and began to write.

The marquess found a comfortable inn to stay the night in the village of Meldon. He studied Felicity during supper. Agnes was prattling on, acting, as she fondly believed, the part of hostess and marchioness-to-be. Felicity, he thought, could do with a good cry. He wanted to tell her what he had found out but was reluctant to say anything in front of Agnes, who would cackle and exclaim. He regretted having chosen her to be a companion to Felicity, but, on the other hand, he was sorry for her, as he was sorry for all poor relations, neither fish nor fowl, treated with contempt by both servant and master. After they had finished the pudding and the covers had been removed, the marquess said, "Miss Joust, I am sure you are tired and this business is really not your affair. Please leave us."

Agnes bridled, and her long nose turned red. "I feel it my duty to point out it is not at all the thing to leave Felicity unchaperoned."

"We are in a public dining room, Miss Joust, not a private parlor. You force me to order you to leave us."

Agnes got reluctantly to her feet. She dropped her fan and made a great work of picking it up. She then spent a long time arranging her shawl about her shoulders. At last, she left.

She stood outside the dining room, fretting. What were they talking about?

What if they were talking about *her*?

Then a rosy dream began to curl about her brain. They *were* talking about her. She could see the marquess, leaning back in his chair, toying with his glass of wine. "Miss Waverley," he was saying, "I do hope all this is not too much for Miss Joust. My late wife was not strong, you know." In the dream Felicity answered something or other. "Yes," the dream marquess went on, "I worry about her. Will she be strong enough, for example, to endure the climate of the Indies?"

Agnes went out to stroll in the inn garden just in case he should care to come looking for her.

"I think I found something out," said the marquess. "Oh, cry, for heaven's sake. You will feel better."

"I don't want to cry," lied Felicity, although her eyes glistened with unshed tears.

"Then listen to this. While you were shouting at the baroness, I noticed two letters on the desk in the corner. One was a business letter from a firm of lawyers in Scarborough. I could not make out the rest. There was no time, but enough to know it was about money and business. The lawyers are Baxter, Baxter, and Friend, Whitestairs Walk, Scarborough. If Mrs. Waverley—I think of her as that, you know—if she has her business run from Scarborough, then that is probably where she came from. If we find out who exactly she is, where she was born, and who she married, we might have a clue as to your birth."

"Scarborough," said Felicity in a hollow voice.

"Yes, Scarborough. I suggest we return to London tomorrow and make preparations for the long journey."

"You are very good, my lord," said Felicity. "I do not know why you should go to so much trouble on my behalf."

"Because it amuses me," he said with a smile.

And Felicity decided at that point that she really must escape to her bedchamber and burst into tears.

The marquess had said it would take two weeks to put his affairs in order and to make preparations for the long journey to Scarborough in Yorkshire.

Felicity found time lying very heavy on her hands. Agnes

73

was beginning to irritate her immensely. She kept urging Felicity to take the Waverley jewels out of the bank—"just for a little, you know. So terrible to think of them lying in a dusty vault where no one can see them." Felicity protested wearily that the jewels should remain where they were until she returned from Scarborough. To escape from Agnes, she went to Covent Garden to see Caroline James. She was fortunate in finding the famous actress at home. Caroline welcomed her warmly and then listened in amazement as Felicity recounted her adventures at Meldon.

"So the third Waverley girl is to have a titled marriage," teased Caroline.

Felicity looked surprised. "What can you mean?"

"Why, this Lord Darkwater is going to a great deal of effort and expense on your behalf."

"Oh, as to the effort, he says he is bored and the mystery amuses him, and as to the expense, I have promised to reimburse him."

"Come now. There must be more to it than that."

Felicity frowned. "No. We have become friendly, that is all. I was mistaken in him. My first impression of him was wrong. He is a gentleman on all occasions and, believe me, there is nothing warmer in his attitude than that of friendship. But tell me about yourself? Mr. Anderson called on me to tell me he had taken a job at the theater."

"Yes, and a dreadful scene his mother made, too. I must confess, I thought the boy would soon tire, but he seems engrossed in his work and is very enthusiastic."

"About his work—or about you?"

Caroline turned pink. "It is calf love, nothing more. He will soon grow out of it."

"And if he doesn't?"

"We'll see. I am much too old for him."

"And yet the difference in your ages is almost the same as the difference in age between myself and Darkwater."

"But that is not the same. Darkwater is a man."

"What is that to do with it?"

"You must know you are being deliberately naive. This is a man's world, or had you forgot."

"No, I am not likely to forget, particularly as I am burdened with a silly woman Darkwater has chosen to be my companion. But if one is of strong mind and independent spirit, then the conventions, most of them made by men, do not matter."

"We'll see. How goes your writing?"

"Not at all. I appear to have run out of ideas."

"With all the adventure in your life! Perhaps, like Miss Austen, you should base your writing on people and places you know well."

"I do not find Miss Austen much of an inspiration," said Felicity gloomily. "Genius is never inspiring. I had better get back to Hanover Square before my companion drives my servants mad with her airs and graces."

"Who is she?"

"A Miss Agnes Joust. A poor relation of Lord Darkwater. He rescued her from a tyrant of a mistress, but she does not seem in the least grateful to be with me."

"Get rid of her!"

"I shall speak to Darkwater about her when we return from Scarborough."

The Marquess of Darkwater walked through the gilded splendor of Clarence House. It was almost two weeks since he had been in Meldon. He found a letter from the Earl of Hopetoun waiting for him in which that peer angrily denied any knowledge of Colonel Macdonald.

The marquess had made all the necessary preparations for the journey north and planned to leave as soon as possible. But before he could call at Hanover Square to tell Felicity he was finally ready, he had received a summons from the Prince Regent.

The Prince Regent was lying in a darkened saloon on a chaise longue, wrapped in a Chinese dressing gown with a turban made of cloth of gold on his head.

The marquess bowed and kissed the fat hand languidly extended in his direction.

"How may I be of service to you, Sire?" he asked.

"Hey, that's what we like in a man," said the prince. "Straight to the point with an offer of obedience and duty."

The marquess frowned. His offer had been a courtly gesture, not to be taken seriously.

The prince propped himself up on one elbow. "Sit down, man, and take your ease. We have good news for you."

"Which is?" asked the marquess, pulling up a chair beside the chaise longue and sitting down.

"We are leaving for Brighton tomorrow and wish you to accompany us."

"Sire, I am about to set out on a journey. I am flattered and pleased Your Majesty should wish my company, but I must refuse."

"You will obey your sovereign," said the prince wrathfully. "We command you to accompany us to Brighton."

"Why?"

"What d'ye mean, *why*? Is our wish not enough?"

"In this case, Sire, no, it is not. Your Majesty has many friends and admirers to accompany you to Brighton."

The prince looked more like a large cross baby than ever. He thought of the letter he had received from Meldon. He had decided to keep Darkwater with him in Brighton until such time as he considered the marquess had forgotten all about the Waverley girl. But perhaps he was worrying overmuch. Darkwater had an estate in Surrey. Perhaps he was bound there. Or, better still, back to the West Indies.

"Well, well, where are you bound that is so important?"

"Scarborough," said the marquess.

"You shall not go. It does not please us."

"May I ask why, Sire?"

"No, you may not," roared the prince. "Odd's fish, are we to account for our actions to every petty lord? Get out of our presence!"

The marquess rose and bowed and began to walk backward toward the door.

"Stay!" cried the prince. "When do you set out?"

"In two days' time, Sire."

The Prince Regent slumped down against the cushions and put a hand before his eyes. The marquess bowed his way out and shut the door behind him.

He drove straight to Hanover Square and told Felicity to make ready. They were leaving that very night.

Felicity exclaimed at the hastiness of the departure and demanded to know why. He replied he was bored and did not want to hang about London any longer. He did not want to scare her by telling her the real reason. He felt sure the prince would try to stop him. The secret to the royal distress lay in Scarborough and in the mysterious Mrs. Waverley's background.

Chapter Six

FELICITY WAS NEVER to forget that mad drive to the north of England. The marquess's traveling carriage pulled by six black horses moved at an amazing rate.

The marquess was driving his team himself. Agnes became so sick with the constant swaying motion that Felicity opened the trap in the roof and begged him to slow his pace because Agnes was ill. He called down heartlessly that if she looked like she was dying, he might consider stopping. Otherwise, he advised Miss Joust not to be sick in the carriage but to put her head out of the window.

"What did he say?" asked Agnes faintly.

"He is very concerned about you, but says that speed is of the uttermost importance," lied Felicity.

A faint color came back to Agnes's wan cheeks. "Dear Simon," she murmured. "So solicitous."

Felicity was beginning to feel quite sick herself and heaved a sigh of relief when they finally stopped at a posting house for the night.

The marquess opened the carriage door. Agnes collapsed into his arms and appeared to faint dead away.

"Was there ever such a woman?" he said crossly. "Here, John," he ordered one of the grooms, "carry Miss Joust into the inn."

Agnes felt herself being lifted in strong arms. She had been so busy pretending to be unconscious, she had not heard the marquess's order to his groom. She pretended to recover consciousness and wound her arms around John's neck and said, "Oh, that this moment could last forever."

She opened her eyes wide and gazed up into John's weather-beaten face.

"Put me down, sir," she cried, writhing like an eel. "Where is your master?"

"Right behind, miss," said John, tightening his hold. "My lord said I am to carry you into the inn and carry you I shall."

Furious, Agnes lay rigid like a plank, and like a plank, John propped her up against the wall of the hallway of the inn.

Agnes was furious. She had been nearly at death's door, and no one had cared. She would show them. She allowed Felicity to help her up the stairs to her room. One of the many things Agnes did not like about Felicity was that that self-sufficient young lady did not consider it necessary to employ the services of a maid. Agnes collapsed on the bed as Felicity efficiently ordered the chambermaids to unpack such items from their luggage as they would need for a night's stay at the inn.

Agnes was torn between pretending to be ill and staying in her room, or putting on her best lilac silk gown and dazzling the marquess. The lilac silk gown won the toss.

They had a private parlor. To Agnes's disappointment, the marquess was abstracted and said little. Felicity looked wan and tired, and he asked sharply, "Are you sure you are fit to travel tomorrow, Miss Felicity? I am afraid our headlong dash has been a little too much for you."

"And for poor me," said Agnes pathetically.

He ignored her and looked at Felicity.

"I shall be well enough after a night's rest," said Felicity. "What of you, Agnes?"

"I suppose so," said Agnes sulkily. Really, it was too bad of Simon. She was his flesh and blood and not some little parvenue of suspect birth like Felicity Waverley. What would he have done if she had been really ill? Agnes half closed her eyes. She could see in her mind's eye the darkened inn room and hear the hushed voices around the bed. "I fear you may have been the cause of her grave malady, my lord," the physician said. "Ah, no, never say that!" cried the marquess, falling to his knees beside the bed. Agnes stretched out a hand as pale as alabaster to lightly touch his dark locks. "I forgive you, Simon," she whispered.

This scene was so very affecting that tears began to roll down Agnes's cheeks.

"Poor Agnes," cried Felicity. "It has all been too much of a strain for you. Come and lie down, and I shall go to the kitchens myself and make you a posset."

Agnes's agile brain raced. All at once, she had a plan in her mind, a plan that would get her the marquess's sympathy and might get Felicity accused of trying to murder her. Like some ladies of this first part of the nineteenth century, Agnes took a small quantity of arsenic to add luster to her hair and to keep her skin clear. She had enough of the poison with her to insure she would be very sick but in no danger. She would put the arsenic in the posset Felicity brought her and then say she had been poisoned.

"Thank you my dear," she said faintly. "That would be most welcome."

Felicity took her up to her room, helped her undress, and put her to bed. She then went back to the parlor to say good night to the marquess.

He gave her a rueful smile. "I engaged Miss Joust to look after you. I am afraid she is not a suitable companion."

But Agnes's plight had touched Felicity's kind heart. "She means well," she said. "The journey was a hectic dash. Is such speed really necessary?"

"Yes."

"But why?"

"If Mrs. Waverley has something to hide, she may have written to Scarborough to alert her lawyers."

Felicity shook her head in bewilderment. "She has no reason to know we are bound for Scarborough."

"She may have guessed. It is better we reach there as fast as possible."

"Very well," said Felicity reluctantly. "I only hope Agnes manages to get a good night's sleep. At what hour do we depart in the morning?"

"Six o'clock."

Felicity groaned.

She made her way to the kitchens and ordered the cook to produce the necessary materials for a posset, made it up, and carried it in a cup on a tray to Agnes's room. Agnes was lying in bed with her eyes half closed. Felicity noticed with surprise that Agnes's hair was still piled on top of her head and that her lips were slightly rouged. She did not know Agnes had prepared for her famous deathbed scene.

80

"Dear Felicity," said Agnes. "Leave it beside me."

"Would you like me to stay with you until you fall asleep?" asked Felicity.

"No, Felicity, I shall do very well." Agnes waited until Felicity had gone and then climbed from her bed and found the paper twist of arsenic she carried in her reticule. She carefully measured some grains into the cup. She knew she was going to have an uncomfortable time of it, but was sure she had not put in enough to make her actually vomit.

But Agnes had misjudged the dose. Felicity's room was next door, and she was aroused in the night by Agnes's screams for help.

She ran next door. The room reeked of vomit, and Agnes was standing, clutching her throat. "Poison," she screamed. "Poison."

The noise alerted the marquess. He took one look at the situation and called for the inn servants. Soon a glass was pressed into Agnes's hand, and his stern voice was commanding her to drink it. She threw the contents down her throat as the marquess seized the chamber pot and stood at the ready. Agnes spluttered, and her eyes bulged. It had been hot water liberally laced with rock salt.

Agnes was dreadfully sick. But by the time the physician arrived, she was lying weak and pale in the bed, purged of all the poison, and able to start to accuse Felicity. "I think it was that posset," she said faintly. "See, you may examine it. There is a little in the cup."

The physician was a dour Scotsman who had been roused from his bed. "It certainly appears to be some sort of poisoning," he said, and Agnes closed her eyes in satisfaction. But his next words were not at all what she had expected. The doctor was examining the contents of the toilet table. He then picked up Agnes's reticule and said, "Mind if I look in here, my lord?" and then without waiting for permission, he drew open the strings of the reticule and tipped the contents out on the table.

He picked up the twist of paper, gently opened it, and carried it over to the oil lamp to examine the contents. "Arsenic," he said, his face grim. "These silly women, playing with death. They will do it."

"That is not mine," cried Agnes. "I do not know how it got there!"

And then came the marquess's voice, as cold as ice. "If you are suggesting Miss Felicity put some in that posset and put the rest in your reticule, Miss Joust, then I suggest you recover as quickly as possible and find your own way back to London."

The physician came to the bed holding the oil lamp and peered down at Agnes. "I thought so," he said. "Do you see those moles, my lord? Here, and here?" He pointed to a mole on Agnes's chin and then one on her forehead. "An arsenic-eater, quite definitely."

"Was a man ever plagued by such a dangerously silly woman?" said the marquess furiously. "Well, Miss Felicity? Shall we continue on our journey and leave her behind?"

Agnes burst into frightened tears. "I am sorry, Felicity. It was wicked and silly of me. Yes, I do occasionally take arsenic and was ashamed to confess to the practice." Tears poured down her cheeks.

"It is all right," said Felicity. "No one is going to send you away. My lord, we cannot travel tomorrow."

He looked furious, and then suddenly his face relaxed. "Very well," he murmured. "It might be interesting to see what happens. I may be worrying overmuch."

Agnes was genuinely weak and ill the next day. At one point, she managed to struggle from the bed and look out the window. Her window overlooked the inn garden, and the sight that met her eyes did little to cheer her. It was a fine, sunny, very English afternoon. A light wind was pushing great fleecy clouds across a blue sky. The sun shimmered on the winding river bordering the inn garden. Walking along the riverbank was the Marquess of Darkwater and Miss Felicity Waverley. Felicity was wearing a lilac muslin gown—*my* color, thought Agnes, gritting her teeth. It was high-waisted and had long tight sleeves ending in points at the wrist. It had a little gauze ruff at the neck and three deep flounces at the hem. Under the hem, little lilac kid shoes peeped in and out. On her head was one of the new transparent hats, a circle of stiffened gauze decorated with white flowers. The lilac gown, like the matching parasol she carried, was ornamented with a little white spot.

The marquess was in morning dress: blue coat, striped waistcoat, pantaloons, and Hessian boots. He was laughing at something Felicity was saying, and she was smiling up at him. Agnes got back into bed and rang the bell.

When a chambermaid came in, Agnes groaned pathetically and said, "Fetch Miss Waverley. I am nigh to death."

The minute the chambermaid had left, Agnes got up again and looked down from the window. Soon the chambermaid appeared below, the streamers of her cap flying. She stopped before the couple and began to talk. Felicity looked startled and made a move to leave, but the marquess placed a hand on her arm to restrain her and said something to the chambermaid. Agnes crawled back into bed and practiced a few groans. She waited and waited. At last the door opened, and, to her horror, neither Felicity nor the marquess appeared but the crusty Scottish doctor, who gave her a draft of something, told her to behave herself and stop wasting his time, and left. It was shortly after he had gone that Agnes realized he had given her a heavy sleeping draft, the doctor having put her down as a hysterical woman who needed sedation. So when Felicity did look in, Agnes was sleeping peacefully. She returned to the garden to tell the marquess the news, and found him in the company of two gentlemen. Felicity was versed enough in the ways of the world to recognize such men as gentlemen when she saw them, although the less initiated might have assumed that men attired in many-caped coats despite the warmth of the day and wearing belcher neckcloths belonged to the stables. Here then were two Corinthians with clothes and manners to match.

"Who's the filly, Darkwater?" asked one as Felicity approached them.

"That is Miss Waverley," said the marquess, "and if either of you refer to her as a filly again, I shall take great pleasure in ramming your teeth down your throat. Miss Felicity," he said, as she reached them, "allow me to present Sir George Comfrey and Mr. Peter Harris."

"Pleasure," said Mr. Harris laconically. He did not remove the straw he had been chewing from his mouth. He was a squat, brutal-looking man with blue jowls and broken teeth. Sir George Comfrey was tall and thin with a long nose and slanting pale green eyes. He looked like a fox.

He made an elaborate bow.

"What brings you here, Harris?" asked the marquess.

"Same as yourself," said Mr. Harris. "Traveling north. Stay with m'friend in Harrogate. When do you leave?"

"It depends on the health of Miss Waverley's companion. She was taken ill last night. Hopefully we might be able to leave tomorrow."

"You said you were bound for Scarborough? What takes you there, Darkwater?"

"I am going there on business of a private nature."

There was a little silence. Both men exchanged glances. Felicity wished they would leave. It had been so comfortable walking in the garden with the marquess and talking about all sorts of things. "Care to broach a few bottles in the tap?" asked Comfrey.

"No," said the marquess pleasantly. "I prefer the company of Miss Waverley."

The two men began to move reluctantly away.

"Are they friends of yours?" asked Felicity.

"No, mere acquaintances. The darker side of Prinny's entourage, I think."

Felicity looked shocked. "I do not think our Prince Regent would relish the company of such fellows. Forgive me for speaking plain, my lord, but I could not like them."

"Then we shall avoid them. There are always such characters on the fringes of the court. Sporting is all the rage, and quite a number of men wish to look and sound like a cross between their own coachmen and gallows birds."

Agnes joined them for dinner that evening. The deep sleep had refreshed her, and she wanly declared she felt quite her normal self. Felicity insisted they should stay one more day to make absolutely sure Agnes did not have a relapse. The marquess frowned impatiently but said nothing. He felt uneasy about the sudden appearance of two of Prinny's toadies.

He did not see what those two could do to stop their journey north, if such was their intention. He posted two of his grooms in the passageway outside their rooms with instructions to rouse him at the slightest sign of anyone approaching.

The marquess found it hard to get to sleep. He tried to remember his wife as she had been when he was courting her and to remember if he had felt the easy companionship in her company he had enjoyed with Felicity in the inn garden. But all he could remember was it had been a strict and correct courtship and he had not really been alone with her until their wedding night. He closed his eyes in pain as he remembered that night. How she had writhed away from him and called him a monstrous cruel and unfeeling brute. After that miserable night, she had complained of headaches and backaches and every kind of malaise. He was sure she was making every excuse she could think of not to sleep with him. Although he had tried to cherish her, to treat her with tenderness, she had infinitely preferred the company of her lady's maid. He had been most surprised when she had died, to find she really had been a frail creature, yet he had nothing with which to reproach himself. Before he met Felicity Waverley, he had never before envisaged a woman as being a friend and companion.

He was just about to slip off gently into sleep at last when a voice in his brain asked, What would *you* do if you wanted to stop three people journeying north?

"I would wreck their carriage," he answered crossly in his mind. All at once, he sat bolt upright. The carriage!

Felicity, too, was awake. She could not stop thinking about the marquess. She turned over and over in her mind everything they had said that day. She thought of the charm of his deep voice, of the humorous twist to his mouth, and of the way his normally cold gray eyes had lit up with laughter as he had looked down at her. But there was something about this journey and the frantic need for haste that he had not told her. And what of those two ugly men, Harris and Comfrey?

And then she heard a low voice in the passage outside. She ran to the door, unlocked it, and looked out. The marquess was talking to his groom. He looked up when he saw Felicity and said sharply, "Get back to bed."

"Where are you going?" she asked softly.

"Just as far as the stables to see that everything is all right."

She closed the door, but stood irresolute. The stables. All at once she did not like the idea of his going out in the blackness of the night with Harris and Comfrey possibly around.

Feeling silly, but determined to go ahead with it, she opened her trunk and took out a small pistol and primed it. Then she pulled a warm cloak with a hood over her nightgown and slipped her bare feet into a soft pair of kid shoes. She made her way swiftly out into the passage and down the stairs. The inn door was standing open. Outside, a high wind was blowing, and a small bright moon was racing through the clouds. The stables were at the back of the inn. She felt in her pocket for the cold reassuring smoothness of her pistol and hurried across the yard.

The marquess had checked the horses. All was well. He made his way through to the carriage house, moving as silently as a ghost. Just as silently, the groom crept behind him.

All appeared to be quiet and still, yet there was an atmosphere of danger in the air. The wind sighed around the building and pieces of straw drifted across the floor. The carriage gleamed softly in a shaft of pale moonlight coming in through a high barred window at the end. Feeling confident now that he had been imagining things, he strode forward. And then a sickening blow struck him from behind and, as he went down, he could hear a groan behind him from the groom, who had also been attacked.

He lay on the cobbles fighting to keep conscious while the whole world seemed to whirl about him.

"Right, Comfrey," said Harris. "Bring that ax over here. A few blows on the wheels of this carriage should be enough, and then we'll be on our way."

Slowly the marquess eased himself up onto one elbow and shook his head to clear it. Harris was standing by the gleaming panels of the coach, an ax in his hand. He raised it to bring it down on the wheels when a clear feminine voice called out, "Hold hard, or I shall blow your brains out!"

Harris dropped the ax and he and Comfrey swung around to face the doorway. Felicity Waverley stood there, a small pistol in her hand.

Comfrey began to laugh. "Pick up the ax, man," he said to Harris. "She ain't going to do anything with that toy."

Harris bent down to pick up the ax and a bullet whizzed through his hat. He stayed where he was in a half crouch as if frozen. The marquess struggled to his feet. Felicity was reloading her pistol. "Are you unhurt, my lord?" she called.

"Yes," he said, moving toward the two men.

"Do not get between me and the line of fire, my lord," said Felicity coolly.

The marquess nodded and unhitched a coil of rope from the wall. Stumbling slightly, for he still felt groggy, he tied up the two men. "It was only a joke, Darkwater," pleaded Comfrey. "See here, did it for a wager, don't you know?"

"You can explain matters to the justice of the peace," said the marquess. His groom groaned and shifted. He went and bent over him and then felt his pulse. The landlord of the inn came running in followed by some of his servants.

"These men tried to wreck my carriage after attacking me and my groom," said the marquess. "Call the constable and have them taken to the roundhouse for the night."

He waited until Harris and Comfrey had been bundled out and then went to Felicity. "Where did you learn to shoot like that?"

"Mrs. Waverley taught me," said Felicity.

"What an extraordinary woman," he said with a grin. "Finding out about her past is going to be a pleasure."

"Are you badly hurt?" she asked.

"My head is quite hard, but I must confess I feel pretty sick."

The landlord came back with more servants, and the groom was carried out. Instructions were given to rouse the Scottish doctor from his bed again to attend to the groom.

"And now," said the marquess, "back to bed, Miss Felicity. We will go to the authorities in the morning and find out what these two ruffians have to say for themselves."

"There is something wicked about this," said Felicity with a shiver. "Someone is very anxious to stop us from finding out about Mrs. Waverley."

She looked white and strained. He had a longing to take her in his arms, but prudence held him back. He was not sure of his feelings. And then at the back of his mind, he was always haunted by the coldness of his wife.

"They were probably doing it for a wager," he said, although he didn't believe it. "Come along, Miss Felicity."

They made their way out. The inn was ablaze with lights and the courtyard full of guests demanding to know what had happened.

Felicity was glad to escape to her room. She had a longing to tell him she had changed her mind, that she did not want to find out anything about Mrs. Waverley. Her dull existence in Hanover Square now seemed like paradise. What was she doing risking her life on the Great North Road when she had a comfortable home and the efficient Mrs. Ricketts to take care of everything?

Agnes was furious to learn she had slept through all the excitement. She eagerly asked Felicity to repeat over and over again what had happened. Agnes was bitterly jealous. Knowing how to prime and fire a pistol was a most unmaidenly talent, yet she wished she had been the one to save the marquess.

They were sitting in the private parlor having a late breakfast when the marquess came in, looking grim. "They've gone," he said, sitting down at the end of the table.

"Harris and Comfrey?" exclaimed Felicity. "How can that be? They were surely locked up in the roundhouse."

"They were visited during the night by the local justice of the peace, Mr. Haggerty. I roused Mr. Haggerty and demanded an explanation. He is a weak, shiftless man. He began to bluster that the two criminals were fine gentlemen who had only been playing a prank. I swore and said I had been struck nigh unconscious and my groom attacked as well, that they had been on the point of wrecking my carriage. He apologized but said he was sure a fine gentleman like myself would not wish to press charges. I said I most certainly did, and he said he would send men out to look for the pair." He fell silent, wondering again if the pair had used the magic of the Prince Regent's name to escape.

Agnes shivered. "They may come back and attack us!"

"I doubt it," said the marquess, but he added silently, But someone else may.

Agnes wanted to continue to play the ailing invalid, but the thought that if they waited any longer at the inn they might be attacked by Harris and Comfrey decided her against it.

The little party set out again at dawn the next day. Agnes could not help noticing that the marquess's attitude to Felicity had noticeably changed. Before he had always been courteous and polite. But now there was a warmth in his smile and admiration in his eyes when he looked at her.

Blowsy strumpet! thought Agnes furiously. She would come to a bad end like her sisters, or not her sisters, but those other two. Then Agnes realized for the first time that she did not know what had happened to the other two. Before her job with

Mrs. Deves-Pereneux, she had been taking care of an elderly lady in the country and so had not heard much town gossip. Agnes did not read the newspapers either, or she would have learned of the adventures of the famous Waverleys.

"Do you ever hear from the other two ladies?" she asked.

"Who?" Felicity was looking dreamily out the window.

"I mean the other two ladies who were adopted with you. I gather they do not reside with you anymore."

"Oh, Fanny and Frederica? They are married."

Of course they are, thought Agnes. Mrs. Waverley, who could buy all those fabulous jewels, had no doubt bought them lowly but honest husbands.

"And where are they now?" asked Agnes.

"Both are still on the Continent, I believe," said Felicity. "Fanny, Lady Tredair, is now in Paris, and Frederica, Lady Harry Danger, is in Rome. Goodness, how tired I am, but it is hard to get any rest with the sickening motion of this carriage."

"Mrs. Waverley, or rather, Baroness Meldon, no doubt worked hard to secure such good husbands," said Agnes, who had hardly been able to believe her ears at the sound of both titles.

"On the contrary, she worked very hard to stop either of them marrying. Both married without even a dowry."

For one brief anguished moment, a flash of common sense penetrated Agnes's mind, a mind normally cobwebbed by dreams and fantasies. Such was the power and attraction of the Waverley girls that neither birth nor lack of dowry had stopped two of them from marrying the best in the land. She, Agnes, should appreciate that she was well-treated as a companion and strive to hold this post for as long as possible.

But jealousy combined with fantasy soon took over again. The marquess's voice seemed to sound in her ears. He was confiding to Agnes his worries about Felicity. "As soon as I saw her waving that pistol about, Miss Joust," he was saying, "I knew she could not be of gentle birth. No lady even knows one end of a pistol from the other."

So Agnes's dreams grew stronger as the miles and days flew past and the air grew colder and fresher and was tinged with the salt of the sea.

At long last, the marquess's voice from the box shouted down, "Scarborough!"

Felicity tugged at the strap and let down the glass and leaned out. Cliffs and elegant buildings and a magnificent stretch of blue sea and an odd feeling of recognition and familiarity braced the Yorkshire air.

Somehow she knew the long journey to find the identity of her parents was nearly over.

Chapter Seven

THE SEASIDE OF the aristocracy had grown from the fashion for visiting spas. The move from inland spa to seaside had been gradual. It had begun at Scarborough, where a mineral spring by the seashore had first attracted visitors to the town. Some enthusiasts had bathed there in the seventeenth century when the government had even considered taxing bathers on the grounds that the seas belonged to the kings of England. At that time, a few aristocrats sporting naked in the sea had not been enough to make Scarborough fashionable. The impetus started in the middle of the eighteenth century when Dr. Richard Russell set about promoting the use of seawater to cure disease—taken internally. According to Russell, seawater in half-pint doses, mixed if necessary with port or milk, could cure scurvy, jaundice, gonorrhea, gout, and other ailments.

The fashion for seaside holidays having been established, the visitors set about creating the same atmosphere that prevailed at the inland spas. Assembly rooms were built, establishments for taking the waters and bathing in them were set up by doctors and professors of the new science, reading rooms were built at which card games and raffles were included among the amusements, and every social event was designed to provide a medium for getting to know other visitors.

The marquess was anxious to go to the lawyers as soon as possible before the news of their arrival was published in the social columns of the local papers. He obviously did not consider Scarborough a very safe place for them to reside in for very long, thought Felicity wistfully, as she stood on the balcony of her hotel room and looked out across the sea. It was such a jolly place, and the changing colors of the sea were fascinating.

And then a tall man came into view, walking along the

esplanade in front of the hotel. He was holding onto his hat. He sported a fine pair of black military sideburns. There was something about his manner, and the confident air of the man, that forcibly reminded Felicity of Colonel Macdonald. The man looked up and saw the slight figure on the balcony. He tugged his hat down over his eyes and went on his way, his pace a little faster than before.

Colonel Macdonald, now the Comte D'Angiers, his Irish brogue changed to a lisping French accent, hurried on his way. When he had gone some distance, he turned about and looked back at the hotel. The figure on the balcony had gone, but he had recognized Felicity Waverley. He thought of those jewels and his mouth watered like that of a hungry man thinking of a sumptuous banquet. He had done well at cards at the gaming tables of Scarborough and was feted and petted by the ladies and had as many social invitations as he could desire. But he wanted to secure enough money to end his shaky life of cheating and lying.

He slowly turned about and made his way back to the hotel. He reminded himself that with his hair dyed and his new Frenchified air, Felicity would hardly recognize him unless he got too close.

He hesitated outside the hotel, then squared his shoulders and strolled inside. The manager came forward to welcome him. The comte was a prime attraction with the ladies, and his presence in the hotel usually meant extra guests for tea and other refreshments.

"Any new guests, m'sieur?" drawled the comte.

"Yes," said the manager importantly. "The Marquess of Darkwater."

The comte frowned and half turned, about to escape. But perhaps his eyes had been deceiving him. "Did he come with a party, or alone?"

"His Lordship came with a most beautiful young lady, a Miss Waverley, and her companion, Miss Joust. Why, I believe that is His Lordship coming down the stairs."

The soi-disant comte moved behind the screen of a potted palm and looked through its fronds. It was indeed the marquess and Felicity. He watched as they exchanged a few pleasantries with the manager. Then they went outside and walked off along the esplanade.

He moved out from the shelter of the palm and approached the manager again. "I see no sign of the companion," he said.

"Probably in her room," said the manager. The comte thought quickly. Companions were poor sorts of creatures, easily gulled. "I seem to remember meeting a Miss Joust in London," he said. "Perhaps you could present my card and ask her if she would do me the honor of taking tea with me on the terrace?"

The manager bowed, took the card, and hurried off. The comte made his way to the terrace, which, in fact, was a long narrow room with French windows overlooking the sea. It was not the fashionable hour for tea, so there were few people about.

Agnes had been moping in her room when the comte's invitation was delivered to her. She had been feeling very low at being left behind by the marquess, but the marquess had begun to think the less Miss Joust knew of Felicity's affairs the better. He had put her down as an unstable, gossipy woman.

She did not stop to consider that she had never met any French comte in London. Excited and elated at the invitation, she dressed in her best lilac gown, ran to Felicity's room and borrowed a handsome cashmere shawl, and then made her way downstairs to the terrace.

That the comte must indeed know her appeared to be borne out by the fact that he rose and bowed as soon as she entered the room. But the comte, looking at the long-nosed dab of a creature, knew immediately this must be Miss Joust. Companions were always stamped with the mark of faded gentility.

As she came up to him, he seized her hand and kissed it, clicking his heels together.

"I am enchanted to meet you again," he said.

Agnes blushed and simpered. He held out a chair for her, then snapped his fingers. The comte ordered tea and cakes, then sat down next to Agnes.

"I have been trying to recall where we met, my lord," said Agnes.

"Sure . . ." he began, then remembered in time he was supposed to be French, not Irish. "*Ma foi,* Miss Joust," he said. "I have a terrible confession to make. We have not met."

"Indeed!"

"I saw you driving out with Miss Waverley, and I made it my business to know who you were."

93

This was like one of Agnes's very best fantasies. That she had only been companion to Felicity for a very short time and how truly amazing it was that the comte should have had a chance to see her in London and then miraculously appear so quickly in Scarborough did not enter her mind. She threw him a killing glance, and he looked suitably smitten, as though by Cupid's arrow.

He began to ask her what they were doing in Scarborough, and Agnes looked down her long nose and said it was all very mysterious and dear Simon would be furious with her if she told anyone.

"Simon?"

"The marquess is my cousin."

"If you are a cousin to a *marquis*," exclaimed the comte, "I am *bouleversé* that he should allow you to work as a companion to such an eccentric young lady."

"He did not want me to, of course," said Agnes. "But I prefer to earn my keep rather than be anyone's pensioner." Agnes was not surprised to hear Felicity described as eccentric. Young ladies who carried pistols and knew how to use them were eccentric in the extreme.

"Most commendable. But an onerous task, considering the dangers attached to it."

"Dangers?"

"I assume Miss Waverley has all her famous jewels with her. Attempts have been made before to steal them."

"No," said Agnes crossly, thinking of that dear emerald necklace. "She lodged them all in Simon's bank before we left."

The comte nearly rose to his feet and left there and then. But apart from his desire to get his hands on the jewels, he also wanted revenge on Felicity. He remembered her masquerade as Miss Callow and how her disguise had slipped when she had kicked him in the stomach. He had decided she had deliberately disguised herself and lured him to her home with a promise that he would be able to sell the jewels for her, only to unmask him.

Then he heard Agnes complain, "So silly to lock all the jewels away and not even take a few trinkets for the journey. Yet she leaves the bank receipt for the jewels lying about where anyone might pick it up."

The comte let out a slow breath. He was glad the waiter arrived at that moment with the tea things, for his excitement was so great, he felt it must show on his face.

He did not immediately return to the matter of the jewels. He encouraged Agnes to talk and quickly learned that she was in love with the marquess and was bitterly jealous of Felicity and that she coveted those jewels almost as much as he did himself.

He slid in little barbed remarks. It was a pity one so fair as Miss Joust should have to wait hand and foot on a lady of doubtful background. Then he flattered her. Did she know lilac was her color and she should never wear anything else? Did she know her eyes were like moonstones? And Agnes's eyes shone like pale oysters in a barrel of dough, and her yearnings for the marquess dimmed and faded to be replaced by yearnings for this handsome comte.

"It is a sad life being a companion," said Agnes, "and also dangerous."

"How so?"

"I shall tell you this in confidence. May I trust you?"

"Word of a D'Angiers," he said, putting his hand on his heart.

Agnes leaned forward and looked to the right and left. Then she said slowly, "On the journey north, Felicity tried to poison me."

Mad, quite mad, thought the comte. But he exclaimed in horror and begged for more details.

"Simon had been paying me . . . well, extra attention. He is, how shall I say, a little bit overwarm in his attentions to me. Felicity noticed. I was sick from the mad pace at which we were traveling, and she offered to make me a posset. She laced it with arsenic! Had not Simon heard my cries and given me an emetic, I should most certainly have died."

"But milord, the marquess, did he do nothing to have her brought to justice?"

"She! She made sheep's eyes at him, and then she bribed a savage Scottish doctor to say I was an arsenic-eater."

The comte correctly interpreted all this to mean that Agnes was an arsenic-eater, had tried to bring disgrace on Felicity, and had overdone things and been unmasked. He had a weak pang of sympathy for Felicity. What a fright this woman was!

But the afternoon wore on as he charmed and flattered, and when he finally begged Agnes not to reveal their meeting, Agnes readily agreed, although she would not for one moment admit to herself the real reason for complying with the request, which was fear this comte should fall in love with Felicity if he set eyes on her.

He got her to agree to slip out that evening after Felicity had gone to bed and to take a walk with him in the moonlight. Agnes felt it was the happiest moment of her life.

The marquess and Felicity sat facing Mr. Baxter, the senior partner of Baxter, Baxter, and Friend. He repeated that Baroness Meldon owned some property in Scarborough that she rented out and that her main business affairs were handled by a firm in the city of London. He did not know anything of the baroness's background and implied that if he did, he would not reveal it.

When the marquess and Felicity finally took their leave, Felicity asked, "Do you think he was warned of our arrival?"

The marquess shook his head. "He was behaving just like any ordinary provincial lawyer. But why should she buy property in Scarborough if she has no connection with the place? I wonder where it is."

"He would not even tell us that," pointed out Felicity.

"But somewhere in that musty office is a box, which, I feel sure, would tell us a lot more. Leave it to me."

"What are you going to do?"

"Break in after nightfall."

"That will not answer," said Felicity practically. "When he returns in the morning and finds the shattered door, we will be the first suspects."

"He will not find anything out of order," said the marquess. "I managed to get hold of a set of these before I left London." He drew a ring of skeleton keys from his pocket.

"Let me come with you," said Felicity eagerly.

"No, stay and get some rest."

He remained resolutely deaf to her protests. "And do not breathe a word of my plans to Miss Joust. She is a good-hearted lady but silly and gossipy."

Felicity had long ago come to the conclusion that Agnes was not good-hearted in the slightest, yet she felt a great pity for her. Felicity was firmly convinced all women had such a hard role to play in life, it was no wonder they turned out such poor creatures. She could not find it in her heart to blame Agnes for her silliness. She thought Agnes had poisoned herself not to try to get her, Felicity, accused of murder, but simply to draw attention to herself. Also Felicity had gradually realized that Agnes was in love with the marquess, and that awareness had made her treat her companion with more kindness than she deserved.

Felicity decided to spend the evening after dinner being pleasant to Agnes. But she had become so used to London hours, she had forgotten dinner would be served at four in the afternoon. Agnes, because she had stayed on the terrace with the comte, had missed dinner, too, but declared wanly she could not eat a thing and would go to bed early.

The marquess ordered a late supper for himself and Felicity, late for the hotel, but at the London hour of seven in the evening.

He was abstracted and talked little. Felicity began to worry that he was becoming bored with the whole affair.

When dinner was over, he asked her to lock the door of her room and to make sure Miss Joust kept her door locked as well.

Felicity went to Agnes's room. She knocked at the door but did not receive any reply. She tried the handle, but the door was locked. Assuming Agnes had gone to bed, Felicity sighed with relief. She would have the rest of the evening to herself.

But she did not want to stay confined in her room. It would be pleasant to go down to the terrace and drink coffee and listen to the sound of the sea. When she reached the terrace, she wondered at the propriety of what she was doing. She really should not be unchaperoned. But the tables in the terrace room were empty except for four old ladies drinking negus and eating sweet biscuits.

They all bowed as Felicity passed, and Felicity dropped them a low curtsy and sat at the table next to theirs.

She was soon to know they had all learned her name. Addressing her as Miss Waverley, they introduced themselves. The spokeswoman for the group was a Mrs. Crabtree. "Do you and Lord Darkwater plan to stay in Scarborough long?" she asked.

"Not very long," said Felicity.

97

"Not on holiday, then?" asked Mrs. Crabtree after much whispering.

"Yes, in a way," said Felicity, wishing she had sat at another table.

More whispering transpired and then Mrs. Crabtree asked, "You come from London?"

"Yes, ma'am."

"Ah, the dear Season. I wonder you can bear to leave it. Does the Prince Regent attend many functions?"

"Yes, Mrs. Crabtree. His Royal Highness enjoys parties as much as ever."

"How beautiful he was as a young man," sighed Mrs. Crabtree. And "Beautiful . . . beautiful . . ." murmured her friends in a sort of Greek chorus. "Our young Prince Florizel. We were all in love with him."

One thin lady leaned forward and muttered fiercely in Mrs. Crabtree's ear.

"Yes, but she don't want to know about a scandal like that," said Mrs. Crabtree. She smiled at Felicity. "Old gossip. One of our dashing young matrons set her cap at the prince all those years ago. Her poor husband. Such a to-do."

Felicity sat up straight, her eyes suddenly shining with excitement. "Was this matron's name Waverley, Mrs. Waverley?"

"No, no." Mrs. Crabtree shook her head, and the Whitby jet ornaments on her cap glittered in the lamplight. "It wasn't that. Now, what was it?" The ladies put their heads together and whispered and muttered, but not one of them could remember the name. "She wasn't from here," explained Mrs. Crabtree. "York, I believe."

The marquess sat at the desk in the lawyer's office going through a pile of receipts and books and papers. They were all connected with three buildings in Cliff Place East. The lawyers had records of having received money for the rentals and then of sending bank drafts to Mrs. Waverley at Hanover Square and then, more recently, to Baroness Meldon at Meldon. The marquess took a note of the address. The office contained no other clue. He could only hope there was some elderly resident in one of the properties who remembered Mrs. Waverley.

He put everything back in place, glad that the office, unlike most lawyers' offices, was so well-dusted. That meant he did not have to worry about leaving smears and fingerprints.

Having spent a long time finding the right key on the ring to open the office door, he was able to close it quickly and make his escape. Although it was early in the evening, the town streets were deserted. The residents went to bed early. Only the fashionable, elderly dowagers and visitors stayed up late in the hotels.

He was walking along the blackness of the esplanade when he nearly collided with an amorous couple who were locked in each other's arms. He muttered an apology, swerved, and went on his way.

"That was Darkwater!" cried Agnes. "Did he see us?"

"No," said the comte. "He did not, my darling."

"Oh, then, kiss me again," said Agnes.

"I cannot," said the comte, who had had more than enough of Agnes. "I fear I could not restrain my passions. Oh, that we could be wed!"

For once in her life, Agnes very nearly fainted—such was her emotion on hearing those beautiful words.

"But why can't we marry?" she asked, pressing close to him.

"I am a poor man. I lost all my fortune. My parents were guillotined, and I was brought to England as a young boy. I have my wits and talents and a certain skill with cards, but I could not ask any lady, especially one of gentle birth and sensibility such as yourself, to share my vagabond life."

"Take me!" said Agnes, throwing her head back. "We will wander the roads of England together, like gypsies, stealing an occasional crust of bread and living on berries."

He sighed. "It does seem an unfair life when such as Felicity Waverley has a fortune in jewels and thinks so little of them that she leaves them to molder unseen in some bank vault. No! Forget I ever spoke of marriage. It is impossible."

He waited hopefully in the darkness. How long would it take the silly bitch's mind to work it out?

"I could take that receipt for the jewels," said Agnes at last. "We could collect the jewels and flee the country."

He almost laughed with relief. But instead he said passionately, "I cannot expose you to such danger. Come, I will kiss you one last time."

Agnes, dizzy with passion and mad with hope, spent quite half an hour persuading him to let her do what he had been manipulating her into doing in the first place. Then she said in dismay, "But could we get to London in time? If Felicity finds the receipt missing immediately after I have taken it, she will write to the bank and send the letter by the royal mail coach, and nothing is faster than that."

"All you need to do," he soothed, "is to let me have the receipt for an afternoon. I will make a fair copy, which you will return instead of the original."

A sharp stab of fear shot through Agnes's brain. A cynical voice in her mind pointed out he appeared to have thought of everything. But his lips found hers again, and she gladly shut out that nasty voice.

The marquess stopped outside Felicity's room and then decided to wait until morning. It was too late to speak to her. But the sight of that amorous couple wrapped in each other's arms in the blackness of the night had roused and stirred his senses and brought old dreams and longings flooding back.

He raised his hand and knocked gently. He was about to turn away when the door was opened by Felicity. She was wearing a white nightgown trimmed at the throat and wrists with fine lace, and over it she wore a white silk wrapper lined and trimmed with swansdown. Her thick chestnut hair was brushed down on her shoulders. "Come in," she cried.

"I should not have come," he said awkwardly. "You had better leave the door open."

"It is too cold to sit in a draft," said Felicity, "and no one is about this time of night." He walked in, and she shut the door behind them.

"I was successful in finding out where the properties are, but nothing else," he said. "But perhaps there might be someone there who can tell us something about Mrs. Waverley."

Felicity knelt down on the hearth and picked up the tongs. "I had better make up the fire," she said. "It has turned chilly." He knelt down beside her and took the tongs away from her. "Let me do that," he said.

She smiled at him suddenly. He knelt there beside her and then gently put the tongs back on the hearth and turned to her. The candlelight was shining on her hair, and her eyes were large and dark. Her lashes were so long, he could see the shadow of them on her cheeks. He could smell the light flower perfume she wore. He put his hands lightly on her shoulders and bent his head toward her lips.

He felt her tremble slightly under his hands. He remembered his wife's disgust at any physical intimacy whatsoever. He could not bear any form of rejection from Felicity Waverley. That he realized with a stab of pain. He shook her shoulders lightly and said huskily, "Go to bed. It's late. We'll talk in the morning."

Felicity nodded dumbly but did not meet his gaze. He rose and left the room.

Felicity got shakily to her feet. She had been so sure he meant to kiss her. She had wanted him to kiss her. She clenched her hands into fists and glared bleakly about the room. How terrible to fall in love with the very man who might find out your birth was so disgraceful, he could not possibly marry you!

The marquess had hired a curricle to drive about the town. It also meant he could avoid taking Agnes along with them as he would have had to do if he and Felicity had been in a closed carriage.

It was perhaps unfortunate for the comte's plans that the marquess chose to be especially kind to Agnes at breakfast. He felt guilty about leaving her behind. She was, after all, related to him and had had a poor sort of life, filled with snubs and neglects. He smiled at her and asked solicitously after her health and apologized for the first time for the rigors of the journey. Agnes blossomed under all this attention and became convinced once more the marquess was enamored of her. She felt very powerful. Here she was, Agnes Joust, with two handsome men competing for her favors. The comte had asked her to meet him that night on the esplanade and to give him the receipt. He had said it would be safer to make the substitution overnight instead of leaving it to the insecurity of a bare afternoon.

When Agnes was finally told she was again being left behind, she accepted it with good grace. Of course, dear Simon was anxious to get this tiresome business about Felicity over and done with. She gave him a conspiratorial smile of sympathy.

She planned to take her knitting downstairs. She would need, of course, to keep her eyes on her work. With such dangerous charms as she had been proved to have, she must watch she did not ensnare any other poor gentleman.

She would go to meet the comte that evening just the same. Perhaps she might even let him kiss her in farewell. It would be a touching scene, but she would tell him gently that her heart belonged to Simon. Perhaps he might be so distraught he might dash himself on the rocks below the esplanade. Agnes gave a delighted shudder. She would try to hush it up, but it would get into the newspapers somehow, that Agnes Joust, fiancée of the Marquess of Darkwater, had driven an attractive French aristocrat to his doom. Women would stare at her jealously and accuse her of being a Delilah, but Simon would proudly take her arm as they walked out and, with flashing eyes, defy anyone to say anything against her. She might even allow Felicity to come on a visit after they were married, and gently, as a married woman, point out to the spinster Felicity the folly of a lady learning too much. "Brains should be left to the men," she would say. "You know I have always told you that, Felicity dear. Now, there is a nice young man coming to dinner tonight who would suit you very well. The curate. Not very handsome, but a lady in your position cannot look too high."

Felicity dressed in one of her best outfits to go driving with the marquess. She wore a morning gown of apple blossom sarcenet with a high ruff and a large mantle of pale blue mohair in the form of a cloak. On her head was a yellow straw hat with a brim *à la Pamela*, ornamented with a broad plain blue ribbon.

She felt shy in the marquess's company and longed for a return of their old easy companionship.

As they walked from the hotel together, she heard an elderly voice calling, "Miss Waverley! Miss Waverley!"

Felicity turned around as Mrs. Crabtree came hurrying up to her. Felicity introduced her to the marquess. "Such a little thing," said Mrs. Crabtree, "but I thought it might interest you. That lady we were talking about the other night, you know, the one whose name I could not remember."

"Yes," said Felicity. "What was it?"

"It came to me in the middle of the night. It was Bride. Yes, yes, her name was Mrs. Bride."

Chapter Eight

"You have had a shock," said the marquess as he climbed in beside Felicity and picked up the reins. "What was all that about?"

"Drive on," said Felicity quietly, "and I will tell you." He flicked the reins, and the horses tossed their manes and set out along the esplanade at a brisk trot. They had gone a little way when he slowed their pace and then said, "Now, what did she say that upset you so?"

"That was a Mrs. Crabtree," said Felicity. "I met her last night. She and her companions were talking about an old scandal. The Prince of Wales came here as a young man. One of the local matrons set her cap at him. I asked if the lady's name had been Mrs. Waverley, and Mrs. Crabtree said no. She has just told me she remembers the name. It was Bride. Mrs. Bride."

"And what is the significance of that?"

"That was the surname we had at the orphanage, Fanny, Frederica, and I. Bride. Oh, do you think . . . ?"

"I do not think it possible that the now Prince Regent stayed long enough to father three girls in Scarborough, however long ago, without the scandal being generally known. The occasional by-blow can be hushed up, but not three of them."

"So you think it might be a coincidence?"

"No, not exactly. It only adds to the mystery."

He turned into Cliff Place East, a cul-de-sac. The buildings were three stories high and made of red brick, in good order, and with the steps well-scrubbed.

The houses were divided up into apartments. They rang bells and knocked at doors, but no one appeared to have heard of Mrs. Waverley. The rent was collected by a man from the lawyer's office; that was all they knew.

"Is there anyone quite old living here?" asked the marquess. He was told there was an old lady called Mrs. Shaw who lived in the attic at number seventeen.

It seemed a long climb up to the attic, and Felicity wondered how an old lady managed to cope with so many stairs.

Mrs. Shaw answered the door herself. She was a dwarf of an old lady, with wisps of white hair escaping from under an enormous cap. Her face was crisscrossed with wrinkles, and she had ugly white hairs sprouting from her chin, but her faded gray eyes were sharp with intelligence. They introduced themselves and were ushered in, the marquess ducking his head to avoid bumping it on the low ceiling. The room was neat and clean, a clutter of odd bits of furniture, bric-a-brac, shawls and fans, and a linnet in a cage by the window.

The marquess explained they were trying to find out about a Mrs. Waverley, and Mrs. Shaw shook her head. "I can remember everyone I ever met, and I never knew a Mrs. Waverley," she said.

"But she owns this property," cried Felicity.

"Ah, but I never met or knew the owner of this property," said Mrs. Shaw. "Someone in London, I believe."

Felicity turned her head away to hide her disappointment. The marquess was just picking up his hat and gloves again to take his leave when Felicity suddenly said, "But did you ever know a Mrs. Bride?"

"Ah, her," said Mrs. Shaw with a cackle of laughter. "What a woman!"

"Tell me about her," said Felicity.

"She was a buxom, handsome lass who had just given birth to a baby girl. Her husband was a rich landowner. I think he owned coal mines in Durham, although they lived in York. They came here so Mrs. Bride could drink the waters and recuperate after the birth. The Prince of Wales, a wild young man at that time, came here, and well, they barely tried to hide their love for each other."

"Mrs. Bride and the prince?"

"Yes."

"And what happened?"

"Such a scandal it was," said Mrs. Shaw dreamily. "Such excitement. And then all at once it was over. The Brides disappeared from Scarborough, and the prince's fancy was taken by someone else, quite a plain woman."

"Do you know her name?"

"Let me see, it was a Lady Torry, a Scottish lady."

"Do you know exactly where in York the Brides lived?"

"I could not say. No one here ever saw either of them again."

"So we had better travel to York today," said the marquess as they climbed into the carriage again. "I am sure if we find out about the Brides, we will find out about Mrs. Waverley."

They were turning out of the cul-de-sac when Felicity thought she saw two people she recognized, but when she twisted about and looked back, there was no one there.

"That's odd," she said. "I thought I saw Comfrey and Harris. They were standing at the corner of the street. But I must be mistaken."

"Just in case you are not mistaken," he said grimly, "we had better set out for York right away."

Agnes was upset at the speed of their departure. She scribbled a hasty note to the comte to say she had gone to York and that Darkwater had sent a servant to reserve rooms for them at the Swan Inn. She felt for a moment she should tell him she could not see him again, but then the idea that a jealous suitor in hot pursuit might bring the marquess up to the mark occurred to her, so she sent him her love instead.

But she did wish she had told the comte to be careful in approaching her again, for the marquess's servants were all armed, pistols primed and ready, and Felicity was calmly sitting in the traveling carriage and priming her little pistol like a veteran.

"Why are you doing that?" cried Agnes. "It is a sunny day, and we shall reach York by nightfall. There is no fear of highwaymen."

"You never know" was all Felicity would say.

"Are you any nearer in solving the mystery?" asked Agnes curiously.

"Perhaps. I do not know."

"Poor Simon," sighed Agnes. "I am sure it is a burdensome task for him. I am sure he now wishes to wed and to return with his bride to the West Indies."

Felicity carefully placed the loaded pistol on the seat beside her and said in a colorless voice, "I did not know he was interested in any lady."

Agnes gave a sly little giggle. "I will not betray Simon's secret, but be assured, he is on the point of proposing marriage."

"Why did he not tell me?" asked Felicity. "I would have gone on with the investigation myself."

"Well, it is not likely he would confide something of such an intimate nature to you," said Agnes. "I, being of his own blood, am a different matter."

"And who *is* this lady?"

"I was told in confidence," said Agnes primly.

Felicity felt very low. She had thought he had been on the point of kissing her last night. She must have been mistaken. Of course he had no interest in her. He had been friendly and charming, but he had shown not one sign of wishing their relationship to be anything more serious, and he had had ample opportunity to do so, had he wished.

The carriage jolted across the moors, the sun shone down, and Felicity felt more miserable than she could ever remember feeling in the whole of her life.

Then as they were traveling through a tract of deserted moorland, the horses suddenly reared and plunged. The carriage slewed across the road, and there came a hoarse cry of "Stand and deliver!"

Agnes screamed and flung herself facedown on the floor. There came several sharp explosions. Felicity seized her pistol, let down the glass, and leaned out. The carriage dipped and swayed as the marquess and his coachman jumped down from the box. The grooms and outriders were standing around two men who were sitting on the ground, one nursing his leg and the other his arm.

Felicity opened the door and climbed down onto the road and went to join the marquess.

"Take off their masks," ordered the marquess. The groom, John, stooped down and ripped off the masks. From behind them, Agnes's hysterical screams sounded from the carriage.

"Harris and Comfrey," said Felicity.

"They are both lucky to be alive," said the marquess. "Go back to the carriage and keep that silly woman away while I question these men, Miss Felicity. Tell her they are highwaymen."

Felicity reluctantly returned to the carriage. Agnes was writhing on the floor, letting out piercing screams for help.

"Now, now, Agnes," said Felicity wearily. "It is all over. Two highwaymen held us up, but the marquess or his servants wounded them."

Outside on the road, the marquess leveled his pistol at Harris and Comfrey. "One of you had better talk," he said. "I can put your masks back on and shoot you dead and say I thought you were the highwaymen you pretended to be."

Harris cursed and clutched his wounded leg. "It was a joke," he said hoarsely. "Did it for a wager."

The marquess turned to John. "Shoot him in the other leg, John," he said. The groom raised his pistol and took aim.

"No," screamed Comfrey. "Leave Harris alone. I'll tell you. I don't know what it's about but a friend of Prinny's told us to stop you somehow and turn you back to London. He said there was a purse of gold in it for us. We didn't ask any questions."

"Then hear this," said the marquess. "You may make your own way to the nearest doctor and get your wounds attended to and then I suggest you return to London as fast as possible and tell the Prince Regent or whoever of his courtiers employed you that I shall be coming to see the prince on my return, and if he does not want a scandal to break about his ears, he had better leave me alone. Do you understand?" Both men nodded dumbly.

Agnes could hardly believe it as the coach began to roll forward again. She tried to catch a glimpse of the highwaymen, but by the time she put her head out of the window, the coach had turned a bend in the road and they were lost to view.

"What is Simon about?" she asked. "Why did he not keep a guard on them while he sent someone for the constable?"

"I do not know," said Felicity, more shaken by Agnes's news that the marquess meant to marry than by the attempted attack. "Please be quiet, Agnes, and stop asking questions. I have the headache."

Agnes sat back sulkily. She had screamed her best, yet the marquess had not even put his head in at the door to see how she was. She was glad she had not given the comte his quittance.

They arrived among the narrow lanes and twisted and jumbled buildings of York as night was falling. The old Tudor houses overhung the street, cutting off what little light of the day was left.

The Swan Inn was near the Minster, a bustling, prosperous place. They were all hungry, having not stopped to dine on the road, and were soon seated in a private parlor to enjoy a late supper. The landlord apologized for the paucity of the fare while his waiters set down a meal that would not have disgraced the finest table in England. There was a first course of macaroni soup and boiled mackerel, followed by entrées of scallops of fowl and lobster pudding. The second course consisted of boiled leg of lamb and spinach, roast sirloin of beef and horseradish sauce, and the third course of roast hare and salad, soufflé of rice, cheesecakes, strawberry jam tartlets, and orange jelly.

Agnes forgot her love life and ate her way steadily through the meal. Her downfall came with the strawberry tartlets. Neither the marquess nor Felicity wanted any, so Agnes ate the whole plateful, and by the time the covers were removed and the port passed round, she was feeling decidedly ill. She said weakly to the marquess that she wished to retire to her room for a few moments and made her escape. Instead, she went to the outside privy and was very sick indeed, after which she felt quite refreshed, Agnes being quite accustomed to gorging herself and then being ill. She then went to her room to bathe her face and put a little rouge on her cheeks. Simon should not be left alone with Felicity for too long. So wearisome for the poor man. Felicity would no doubt be talking about crops or drainage or some such boring thing.

Just before she left, she glanced out her window, which overlooked the inn yard, and saw the Comte D'Angiers strolling across the cobbles. She half raised her hand and then backed away. He would expect her to take that receipt for the jewels. And why bother? Why ruin her chances of being a marchioness?

A silence fell between the marquess and Felicity after Agnes had left the room. At last he said gently, "What is the matter? I know you have had a dreadful fright, but I am sure something else is troubling you."

"I feel guilty," said Felicity in a low voice.

"About what?"

"About you, my lord. You are chasing across the north of England on my affairs when you should be in London making preparations for your wedding."

"I? What or who put such a silly idea in your head?"

"Agnes . . . Miss Joust . . . said you were about to marry."

His lips tightened. "Miss Joust becomes sillier and more wearisome by the minute. I have no intention of marrying anyone at the moment."

"Oh." Felicity knew she should feel relieved, but she continued to feel low in spirits. That "no intention of marrying anyone" had done the damage.

She looked at him from under her lashes. He was leaning back in his chair, studying her face with a mixture of affection and amusement.

Felicity wished he would look at her in some different way, that he would show some sign of being attracted to her. Her head ached. She rose to her feet, and he rose as well. "Excuse me, my lord," she said. "I must lie down."

He stood aside to let her pass, and then his hand seemed to shoot out of its own volition to catch her by the arm. "Felicity," he said.

She looked up into his eyes. He was looking down at her warily, apprehensively.

How she found the courage to do it, how she instinctively knew she must do it, she never knew. But something made her put both her hands against his chest. He gently brushed a tendril of hair back from her face.

"Felicity," he said again. His lips met hers in a cool, firm kiss, almost a boyish kiss. Felicity's body leapt into flame, her lips softening against his. He gave a muffled exclamation and held her closely, burying his mouth in hers, delighted and amazed at her answering passion, moving his hands to caress her cheeks and then burying them in the thick tresses of her hair as his mouth explored hers and his lean hard body fused against the softness of her own. At the back of his brain, he felt he should say something, make some declaration of love, but he was frightened to break the spell. His whole world had narrowed down to this raftered inn room with the smells of wine and cooking, the smoky fire, the flower perfume she wore, the feel of her lips and skin, the ecstasy of that young body pulsing against his own.

Agnes softly opened the door and then stood, stricken.

They did not hear her. The marquess slowly gathered Felicity up in his arms and sat down, cradling her on his lap.

Agnes quietly closed the door again and leaned her back against it, her face flaming with mortification. She might have known it. Felicity Waverley was a slut! He would not marry her. He could not marry such as she. But while he was dallying with that tart, that wanton, that Felicity, he could not notice the pearl of womanhood that was Agnes Joust. She adjusted her shawl about her shoulders with shaking fingers and went downstairs and out into the courtyard of the inn and looked about. A black shadow moved in the blackness of the corner of the courtyard near the stables. She made her way toward it, calling softly, "My dear comte! Is it really you?"

The marquess freed his lips at last and said softly against Felicity's hair. "Do I frighten you?"

"No. Yes. Are you dallying with me because I am available?"

"You enchant me."

He tenderly kissed her throat. "Now I must leave you," he said.

Felicity shivered, suddenly cold. "Why? Where are you going?"

"To get a special license, my love."

Felicity Waverley's hazel eyes blazed with love and relief. "Oh, Simon," she cried, and flung herself against his chest with such force that the chair toppled backward and spilled them both onto the floor. He rolled over on top of her and then kissed her lovingly and longingly, straining her to him.

He said at last, "Do we need to go on with this business? Does it really matter who or what Mrs. Waverley was? Or this Mrs. Bride?"

Felicity sighed. "Yes, it does. I have a feeling we are very close to the solution."

"Then we will go ahead with it. But you must realize we will be married whether your parents turn out to be jailbirds or something equally horrible. I do not want you turning to me and renouncing me through some mistaken idea of honor."

"I'll never let you go," said Felicity.

"Then kiss me again."

"Kiss me again, darling Agnes," the comte was saying.

Agnes held back a little. Disappointment in the marquess was making her more inclined to be more suspicious than she would normally have been. "Before I kiss you," she said, "when are we to be married?"

"As soon as we collect the jewels, light of my life."

Agnes looked mutinous. "If you loved me, you would get a special license and marry me now. Perhaps it is only the jewels you want."

The comte thought quickly. He had been married twice before. What difference would a third make? And he could soon be shot of her once he had his hands on the Waverley jewels.

"I shall get a special license in the morning," he said. "Now kiss me."

"Meet me on the steps of the Minster tomorrow at ten in the morning with the special license," said Agnes, "and then I will give you the receipt."

Drugged and dizzy with kisses and caresses, Felicity stirred in the marquess's arms. "I do not think we should tell Agnes," she said softly. "She is a little in love with you, I think."

"I will put her on the London stage tomorrow!"

"But she has nowhere to go."

"One of my aunts in Devon will, I think, accept Agnes as a guest until I find somewhere to settle her. I shall send her to London with a generous amount of money so she may stay at one of the best hotels before journeying on to Devon. She must go as soon as possible because I am going to marry you as soon as it can be arranged."

"But does it not take two weeks to get a special license?"

"Not when so many of the clergy are in need of money. I shall marry you again in London. Will you come to the Indies with me?"

"Of course. I am very strong. You must not worry about me. It must have been a sad blow losing your wife. You never speak of her."

"The marriage did not last very long. I . . . it was not really a marriage."

"Why?"

They were now sitting in an armchair in front of the fire. He said against her hair, "I frightened her. Physically. She would not have me in her bed. I do not want to frighten you or disgust you, Felicity, for if you rejected me, I could not bear it."

Felicity took a deep breath. "Come now, Simon. Come to my bedchamber and let us lay your ghosts."

"After marriage, my brave girl. Kiss me again and then I shall go out in the streets of York to find a special license."

But it took the marquess at least half an hour to tear himself away from more kisses and embraces.

Agnes heard the marquess returning at two in the morning. Her room was next to Felicity's. She opened her door a crack to make sure it was he. A dim lamp in the corridor showed her it was indeed the marquess, and he was knocking softly at Felicity's door.

As Agnes watched, Felicity opened the door. She was wearing a filmy nightgown with priceless lace at the neck and wrists. She stretched up and wound her arms around the marquess's neck and then she drew him into the room and closed the door behind them.

Slut! thought Agnes furiously. She dived into bed and put the pillow over her ears in case any disgraceful sounds of lovemaking should penetrate from the next room.

"I not only have a special license," the marquess was saying, "but I think I have found out where we can go to solve the mystery. The clergyman who gave me the license was quite old. He hemmed and hawed at the speed of the matter, but he needs money badly in order to feed the poor of his parish, and I paid him well. We fell to talking. He had never heard of anyone called Waverley, but he did remember a Mr. Bride. He said the rector of St. Edmund the King by the south gate of the city had a wealthy landowner called Bride among his parishioners and there was some dreadful scandal years ago. We shall go to this rector in the morning. Now I am going to leave you alone before I misbehave myself."

He lifted her up and carried her to the bed and laid her gently down on it. He bent his head and kissed her tenderly. She pulled him down on top of her, and the bedsprings creaked, and next door Agnes bit the bolster in a fury and pulled the pillow more tightly about her ears.

At last, he disengaged himself. "We will be married the day after tomorrow," he said. "We can wait till then."

The marquess arose early the next morning and summoned Agnes to the private parlor. He looked tired but happy. Agnes thought he looked soiled.

"Your duties with us are finished, Miss Joust," said the marquess. "I have made arrangements for you to catch the royal mail coach at six this evening. I shall give you enough money to allow you to live at the best hotel in London for a week, and then I suggest you go to Aunt Tabitha's in Exbridge in Devon. She is kind, and you may stay there as her guest until I manage to make provision for you. I do not like to think of any relative of mine condemned to spend the rest of her days working as a companion. When I return to London, I shall see my lawyers and arrange for a settlement to be made on you. You will have a yearly pension and a sum of money as a dowry."

Agnes stared at him with her mouth open. It was a generous offer. More than generous, although her vanity stopped her from realizing the marquess was possibly the only man in England kind enough to consider her to be still of a marriageable age. But the better side of her nature was soon silenced by her jealousy. She longed for revenge on Felicity, and what better revenge was there than taking away the Waverley jewels?

But she could not refuse to go. She would try to get the comte to travel on the mail coach with her.

She waited eagerly, hoping the marquess and Felicity would set out early so she could meet the comte at the Minster at ten o'clock.

To her relief, they set out at nine. She hurried to Felicity's bedchamber and found to her annoyance that the door was locked. But as she was known to be Felicity's companion, she was able to persuade the landlord to unlock the door with the spare key.

She went straight to Felicity's traveling desk, hoping that, too, would not prove to be locked. But she raised the lid easily and looked inside. She ignored the other papers as she scrabbled about, looking for the receipt. At last, she found it. She was arranging the other papers back in place when her eye fell on a letter from a London bookseller. In it, the bookseller was congratulating Felicity on the good sales of her first novel, *The Love Match*, and said he was looking forward to receiving her next manuscript.

Agnes was flooded with a heady feeling of triumph. Before she got on that mail coach, the marquess, dear Simon, should know Felicity Waverley had written that dreadful, that shocking, book.

When she met the comte on the steps of York Minster under the shadow of the great twin towers, she was by far the happier and livelier of the two. The comte had had no intention of paying any large sum of money to get a special license at short notice. He had become an expert forger and so he had been up all night forging the license. He held it out, and Agnes blushed and smiled and handed him the receipt for the jewels. "But you must be quick," she urged. "Felicity has poisoned Simon's mind against me, and he is sending me off on the mail coach this evening at six. He says he will give me enough money to stay at a grand hotel in London before journeying to Aunt Tabitha in Devon."

The comte thought quickly. He was staying in modest lodgings, but he had very little money left.

"I will not have time to book a seat on the mail coach myself, Agnes, my precious. Could you please secure a place for me, and I will reimburse you?"

Agnes readily agreed. "Try to stop Miss Waverley or Darkwater from coming to see you off," he added. "I cannot conceal my love for you, and they might see it in my face. The bank receipt will be easily forged. I shall get it to you within the hour, and then we may look forward to our marriage."

Agnes sighed romantically and agreed.

Felicity and the marquess walked with the rector in the walled garden of his home while the old man rambled on and digressed and then suddenly began to talk about Mr. Bride. "He was a very strict man. He was a printer at one time, and he gradually bought up land. He was called a landowner, but he did not own broad acres belonging to one estate. He had pieces of land here and property there and then coal was discovered on one of his pieces of land in Durham and then on another. He became very rich indeed. He married a young lady some fifteen years his junior in this very church. She was the daughter of a curate and had practically nothing in the way of a dowry. She had three daughters, one after the other, and after the birth of the last, he took her to Scarborough to recuperate, leaving the new baby and the other two with a nurse.

"He returned from Scarborough and came to see me. He was a broken man. He said his wife had had an affair with some highborn gentleman and he would never forgive her or speak to her again and he had turned her out in the streets. I cried out in vain against his cruelty. I begged him to make some provision for her. He said he did not want to be reminded of her. The next thing I heard, he had sent the children away. What became of Mrs. Bride I shudder to think. People are very cruel.

"Then five years later he died. His will was published, and it was a great surprise. He left all his money to Mrs. Bride. Whether the lawyers found her or not, I do not know."

"But did Mrs. Bride not return to her father?" asked the marquess.

"She tried. But her mother was dead and her father in ailing health. He would have nothing to do with her."

"Have you ever heard of a Mrs. Waverley?" asked Felicity.

"Let me see. I remember a Miss Waverley who was a close friend of Mrs. Bride. She, too, was a curate's daughter and lived in a village outside York called Lower Demper."

"Let us go to this Miss Waverley now," urged Felicity after they had bade the rector good-bye.

"I think we should go tomorrow morning. I have made arrangements for us to be married at two tomorrow afternoon. Besides, we must say good-bye to Miss Joust. You may learn some sad news, Felicity. It is more than likely you are the daughters of poor Mrs. Bride who was turned out in the streets to die. But if that is the case and Mrs. Bride is indeed dead, then the Bride fortune belongs to you and your sisters."

"I would rather find Mrs. Bride alive," said Felicity.

They went immediately to Agnes's room on their return. She was sitting waiting demurely, her bonnet on her head and her corded trunk at her feet. In her hand she held a letter, which she handed to the marquess. "Read that," she said, then sat back with her hands folded and a smile of triumph on her face.

"That's my letter!" cried Felicity, her face flaming. "You have no right, no right at all, to read my correspondence."

The marquess handed the letter to Felicity and said coldly to Agnes, "Are you ready to leave?"

"But the letter!" cried Agnes, starting up. "She wrote that book."

"I knew Miss Felicity wrote that book long before I met her," said the marquess. "I thought she must be a very fast young lady. Then I discovered her racy knowledge came from a good grounding in the classics. I hope after we are married Felicity will continue to write."

Agnes's nose turned bright red. "Marry? You cannot marry her. She is a wanton."

"Miss Joust, if you persist in insulting my future wife," said the marquess evenly, "I must withdraw my generous offer."

There was nothing the now-frightened Agnes could do but beg Felicity's pardon. But her spite had had the effect of stopping either Felicity or the marquess from going to the mail coach to say good-bye to her. John, the groom, was sent instead.

Agnes climbed into the mail coach. The comte was already there. She sat down beside him. "We shall be married as soon as we reach London," she said.

"Alas," said the comte, "the special license I got in York will not serve in London. We must wait a few days until I find another."

"Give me the receipt for the jewels," said Agnes, a sharp fear gripping her.

"There is no need, my love. I have it safe."

"Give it to me," said Agnes evenly, "or I shall return to the inn and tell Darkwater what we have done."

He reluctantly handed over the receipt, which Agnes popped down the front of her dress and wedged in the top of her corset.

The couple waited tensely as the clocks of York began to chime six o'clock.

"Will he never move?" cried the comte.

"Always waits for the Minster clock," said a fat lady who had just climbed in.

Then there was a great boom from the Minster clock, the

first stroke of six. The coachman cracked his whip, and the mail coach began to move off.

Agnes tried to remind herself she had nothing to fear, she would soon be married to this handsome man. But no rosy fantasy came to soothe her, only increasing dread that he meant to cheat her.

Miss Waverley, it transpired, ran the village school. She sent word to them that she refused to be disturbed until school was over. The marquess smiled at Felicity and said they may as well pass the time by getting married as planned. To Felicity, it was all a dream, the dark church, the hired witnesses, the brief service.

"I don't really feel married," she said timidly as they left the church.

"It will grow on you," he remarked cheerfully.

"I still cannot get over that you knew all along I had written that book," said Felicity.

"I think I probably fell in love with you then," said the marquess, "when I saw you standing in that dark bookshop, clutching your manuscript. Now let us find out what this Miss Waverley has to say for herself."

Miss Waverley ushered them into her home, a small cottage beside the school. She was a tall, thin lady with a mannish figure and a stern face.

Felicity explained that she suspected Mrs. Bride might be her mother and wondered whether she was still alive.

Her heart beat hard as Miss Waverley replied, "She is still alive."

"Where may I find her?"

"I would like to write to her first and see whether she wants to see you," said Miss Waverley. "She does not reside near here. She lives in the south. If you give me your address in London, I will write to you there and let you know what she says."

"And is she indeed my mother?" asked Felicity desperately.

"If you tell me a little of your history, Miss . . . ?"

"Lady Darkwater," said the marquess. "We are newly wed."

Miss Waverley bowed from the waist. "My felicitations, Lady Darkwater."

"All I can remember is the orphanage," said Felicity. "The

Pevensey orphanage. Fanny has some memory of another place before that, but not anything very clear. A Mrs. Waverley came to the orphanage one day and adopted the three of us, Fanny, Frederica, and me. We lived with her in Hanover Square until she ran away to marry Baron Meldon. Tell me about Mrs. Bride. We came looking for Mrs. Waverley's past and found Mrs. Bride's."

"You know about the scandal?" asked Miss Waverley.

Felicity nodded.

"She came to me, quite distraught. By that time, my parents were dead and I was even then running the school. She had always been a heedless, flighty thing, and I told her a woman with an uneducated mind had no resources. And so I proceeded to educate her. She had an agile mind and soon outstripped my knowledge. And then after five years, I read that Bride had died. I contacted his lawyers despite Mrs. Bride's protests that he would have left her nothing. On the contrary, he had left her everything. I told her she now had her chance to build a school for young ladies and educate them as I had educated her. But the flighty part of her was still there. She said she was going to go to London to find her daughters. She settled a generous annuity on me, but I preferred to remain here and teach."

Felicity looked at Miss Waverley's stern face and then said slowly. "You do not need to write to my mother. I know who she is. She changed her name to Waverley, did she not? She went to the orphanage and adopted her own daughters. Oh, why did she not tell us who she was? Why did she treat us so unnaturally, keeping us mewed up, playing tricks on us, setting us against one another?"

"It is her story," said Miss Waverley harshly, "and you must ask her her reasons." She stood up to indicate the interview was at an end.

"I shall never forgive her. Never!" cried Felicity as they drove back to York.

"Then you will always wonder and wonder why she did it," pointed out the marquess. "The social column of the *Morning Post* today says both Lady Tredair and Lady Danger are back in London. There is an address for Fanny, Lady Tredair. Write to her and suggest the three of you to go to see Mrs. Waverley."

"Perhaps," said Felicity. "I should be relieved to find my parents were actually married and not criminals, but had they been, then they would have had an excuse for sending me to an orphanage."

As he drove into the inn yard, he said, "Do not look so downcast, my love. Remember we are married. Are you still worrying about Mrs. Waverley?"

"No, Simon. I was wondering if losing my virginity was going to be very painful."

"You have no doubt read extensively on the subject?" he said, half-exasperated, half-amused.

"Yes," said Felicity, hanging her head.

"Well, my love, there is no need to rush into things. I can wait." He helped her down from the carriage and tossed a coin to a hostler who had come running out.

He tucked her hand in his arm and led her toward the inn. "I would not frighten you or hurt you for the world," he said gently. "You have had an upsetting day."

Felicity frowned and worried all the way up to her room, remembering what he had said about his first wife.

At the door to her room, he kissed her gently on the forehead. "I shall see you at dinner," he said. "I must speak to the landlord. We are late again."

Felicity looked up at him, her eyes wide and dark. Then she turned and opened the door, then seized him by the hand and pulled him inside.

"What are you doing?" he asked, as she tore off her bonnet and pelisse and began to fumble with the tapes of her gown.

"I am getting into that bed with you," said Mrs. Waverley's daughter, "before I change my mind."

The York Minster clock boomed out the first stroke of midnight. Felicity lay with her head on her husband's naked chest. She awoke and rolled on top of him and luxuriously stretched against him, marveling how well their bodies fitted together.

He awoke, and his arms went tightly around her. "What are you doing, my wanton?" he asked.

"Still trying to complete my education," mumbled Felicity as his hands slid down to her bottom.

* * *

The next afternoon, Felicity sat at her writing desk and sleepily pulled a blank sheet of paper toward her. She began to write: "Dear Fanny." Then she frowned and tore up the paper, took a fresh sheet, and wrote: "My very dear sister."

At last she finished the letter and sanded it. She opened her desk to find a stick of sealing wax, when her eye fell on the bank receipt for the jewels. She picked it up and looked at it. Something was not quite right about it. The receipt, she remembered, had been in heavy black ink. But the ink now was a faded brown. The comte had not used the best ink for his forgery.

She stared at it. Agnes had been searching in this desk, which was how Agnes had found the bookseller's letter.

She picked it up and went through to her husband's room.

"Simon," she said, "do but look at this receipt. There is something odd about it. Do but mark the color of the ink. Then the bank manager, Mr. Lombard, had an odd curly flourish at the end of the *d*."

The marquess took out his quizzing glass and studied the document. He let out his breath in a long hiss. "A forgery. Damn that long-nosed grasping bitch."

"Can we let the bank know in time?"

He shook his head. "She went by mail coach, and nothing is faster than that. She will probably go straight to the bank as soon as she arrives."

"But they will surely not give her the jewels without a letter from me."

"Whoever forged this for her, if she did not do it herself, will no doubt forge a suitable letter for her."

"Then I am penniless . . . apart from the house in Hanover Square."

He put his arms around her. "After the riches you gave me last night, my sweeting, I do not care a damn about the Waverley jewels."

"Are you sure?"

"Come to bed and I will show you how very sure I am."

As he unfastened the tapes of her gown, Felicity said shyly, "Do people make love all day and night like us?"

Her gown fell to the floor followed by her petticoat. He put his hands over her naked breasts and sighed against her hair. "Who cares about what other people do. It is what we do to each other that matters. Damn Agnes Joust. The jewels will never bring her one fraction of the pleasure we enjoy."

Agnes Joust followed the bank manager down to the vaults, her heart beating hard. At Limmer's Hotel, the comte was waiting for her return. He had given her a forged letter supposed to come from Felicity. He had tenderly kissed her good-bye and promised to marry her on the following morning.

But Agnes did not believe him. The part of her mind that had manufactured all those fantasies to trick her and comfort her did not seem to be able to work anymore. She now knew his hair was dyed. She knew his French accent was false. She knew she was afraid of him. On her way to the bank, she had torn up his forged letter. She presented herself to Mr. Lombard, the manager, as Miss Waverley's companion and said Miss Waverley had instructed her to fetch a few items from the box. She looked a highly respectable lady, and she did have the receipt. The manager saw no reason to doubt her. Agnes felt sure if she only took some of the jewels and not all, Felicity would not trouble to report her to the authorities.

She had brought a large wash leather bag with her. Into it, she put the emerald necklace and bracelet. She would never sell *those*. Then a diamond parure, a sapphire brooch, a diamond tiara, twelve fine rings of various precious stones, and a collar of rubies.

She remained calm and ladylike until she was seated once more in the hired hack that had brought her, and then she burst into tears because nobody loved her and she was nothing more than a common thief.

She returned to the hotel where, unknown to the comte, she had packed her luggage early that morning and left it downstairs. She sweetly told the manager that she was leaving and that the Comte D'Angiers who was abovestairs would settle the bill. The hack was still waiting. She went straight to Rundell & Bridge, the famous jewelers, and, looking the very picture of respectability, sold the diamond parure for a very large sum of money indeed. Afterward she returned to the hack and continued on to the city, where she bought a seat on the mail coach for Dover. Napoleon no longer terrorized Europe, and she could travel freely. She endured the long miles of the journey in a frozen calm. She endured all the rigors of a rough crossing without complaint. She traveled in a foul stagecoach to Paris, barely noticing the discomfort. Once in Paris, she went to the best hotel, bespoke the best suite of rooms, telling the manager her lady's maid would be arriving shortly. Then she roused herself enough to go around the suite and turn all the pornographic pictures the French assumed the English visitors would adore to the wall. After that she lay on the silken cover of the bed and listened to the sounds of Paris.

And then all at once, that part of her mind that had seemed to be frozen for so long came back to life. Paris was full of handsome and dashing men. She would go downstairs to dine, and she would wear her lilac silk gown and the emeralds. *He* would approach her. "I am smitten with your beauty," he would say. He would be tall and blond and English. He would not be a mere marquess, but a duke. Agnes closed her eyes and smiled and followed the dream all the way back across the Channel to her triumphal wedding at Westminster Abbey, and was happy last.

The Comte D'Angiers trudged along the Dover road, his boots cracked and his fine clothes covered with chalky dust. He had been wandering ever since his escape from the hotel. He did not know what had gone wrong. He had been so sure of Agnes, so very sure. He was wondering who he was going to pretend to be next. He would wait until nightfall and then stagger up the drive of some country home and say he had been attacked by highwaymen and his luggage and carriage stolen. He looked to right and left as he walked along, searching for a suitable mansion. Perhaps he should pretend to be a comte still. The ladies were his mark, and the ladies all had a soft spot for French aristocrats.

Then he saw a pair of imposing gateposts. He stopped before he reached them. He did not want the lodgekeeper to see him. He climbed over the wall and slipped quietly into the green gloom of a small wood. He heard someone coming and lay down in a tangle of brush and brambles until he heard whoever it was go away. He would wait until dark, walk to the drive, then stagger up it and collapse artistically on the doorstep.

The owner of the mansion was a choleric squire with a passionate hatred for poachers. He stared wrathfully at his lodgekeeper. "What d'ye mean, Jem . . . there's a ruffian on the grounds?"

"I marked him approaching the lodge," said the lodge-keeper, "but he never come past. Shabby individual. Must have climbed over the wall."

"Get the gamekeepers out and tell them to shoot on sight this time. I'm wasting no more time in court."

Night fell and a full moon rode above, silvering the landscape.

The comte rose stiffly from his hiding place, his bright blue coat grass-stained. He made his way cautiously toward the drive. He could not risk going to the gates in case the lodge-keeper refused him admission. He would say he had staggered over the wall after he had been beaten up by the highwaymen. He hoped there was some pretty lady in the house whose heart would be melted by his plight.

And then there was a flash of fire, and something struck him with a blow like a hammer in the chest. He cried out in sheer amazement, and as he fell dying to the ground, his last thought was that somehow it was all Agnes Joust's fault.

Chapter Nine

THE THREE SISTERS sat in the drawing room of Baroness Meldon's home and awaited the arrival of their mother. The baron was visiting an old friend in a neighboring county, and his servants had not felt able to turn away three titled ladies from the gates.

The double doors to the drawing room were thrown open and Baroness Meldon, or Mrs. Waverley, as she would always be to her daughters, walked in.

Her eyes ranged coldly from Fanny's golden beauty to Frederica's gypsyish looks to the slim elegance of Felicity.

"Why are you come?" she demanded harshly. "I have no time for you."

"Why not, *mother dear*?" demanded Felicity.

The baroness held onto a chair back for support. "You know?" she whispered.

"Yes, we know," flashed Frederica. "But what we do not know is why you should rescue us from that orphanage where we were placed through no fault of yours, yet not let us know we were your children."

"But why must you know?" demanded the baroness passionately. "You never cared for me, any of you. You have all married well. What do you want of me?"

"We demand an explanation, and we will stay here until we get it," said Fanny in a cold, hard voice.

The baroness sat down and put her hands on her knees like a fisherwoman and glared at them. "Very well. I hope I have trained your brains sufficiently so you will understand and not be shocked.

"I had just given birth to you, Felicity. It had been a hard labor, and the doctor advised Mr. Bride to take me to Scarborough to take the waters. I had never been in love with your father. Does that surprise you? But my family had no money, and I was tired of being poor. I craved fine clothes and jewels and fun. My husband was a dour, withdrawn man, very religious. My life in York was dull and tedious.

"And then we went to Scarborough. Scarborough. What a magical place it seemed. All light and color and fine people and witty conversation. Then the Prince of Wales arrived with his entourage. I persuaded my husband to let me attend a ball that a certain Lady Torry was giving in the prince's honor. He saw me and asked me to dance—me, and nobody else. We fell madly in love. He was so beautiful then. We tried to be discreet, but word finally got to my husband. I told him I was going to live with the prince as his mistress. Then emissaries arrived from King George's court. I do not know what they said to the prince, but he refused to see me. My husband took me back to York. He said not a word on the journey, but when I got down from the carriage, he told the servants to keep me outside. He called me a harlot and told me to make my living on the streets. I went to my father, and he turned me away as well.

"I finally went to Miss Waverley, a schoolteacher. She told me I was suffering from neglecting my mind and education. She told me that men were beasts and fickle and only interested in women to satisfy their desires. I did not believe her.

"She lent me money, and I went back to Scarborough to see the prince. This time I did see him. He held me to him and kissed me and then he told me I must go away and never see him again. I asked him why. The pompous fool said I was causing a scandal and I owed it to England to leave him alone."

She fell silent, and the girls waited. Then she began to speak again.

"The contempt I felt for him soon cured me of my infatuation. All my hate was reserved for Mr. Bride. I learned through my spies that he had become slightly deranged and claimed you were probably not his daughters and so he had a nurse take you south and pay a foundling hospital to take you, and then he had you transferred to the orphanage. You were neither foundlings nor orphans, but then, money can take care of everything.

"When he died and left me all his money, it was like a

miracle. I planned to take you out of the orphanage, and when the time was right, I would tell you I was really your mother.

"But there was no natural bond between us, no affection. I cried out for your love, and you spurned me."

"That is not true," said Frederica hotly. "You would whisper wicked tales to one of us about the other so we were constantly quarreling, and when we found out what lies you were telling, we did not trust you. You could have had all our love had you told us the truth at the beginning."

"How could I tell you the truth?" demanded the baroness. "I did not want anyone to know Mrs. Waverley was the once-scandalous Mrs. Bride. I gave you love. . . ."

"You fed us on a diet of constant emotional blackmail," said Felicity. "With all your knowledge and education, you should know nothing disaffects anyone more than that."

The baroness shook her heavy head sadly. "So ungrateful. So unkind. I am lucky to be married to a fine man. I shall try hard to forgive you, but I confess I have no liking left for any of you."

"I suppose we should not have expected anything else," said Fanny to Felicity and Frederica. She turned to her mother. "Well, we thank you, Mother or Baroness or Mrs. Waverley. I am sure I speak for all when I say that despite the lack of love on both sides, there is a home with one of us should you ever need us. Had it not been for your education, we might not all have been lucky enough to marry men who wanted us for ourselves alone."

The three sisters rose to leave. "Do you still have the jewels?" the baroness asked Felicity.

"All but a few items that were stolen from me," said Felicity. "I know the name of the thief, but my husband does not want to pursue her because of the scandal it would cause. Why do you ask? Do you want them back?"

"Yes," said the baroness, fingering a heavy rope of pearls about her neck. "I have only a few trinkets left."

"Then you may have the lot," said Felicity. "I never want to see any of them again."

"Come, let us not quarrel," said the baroness, all smiles at last. "You will deliver the jewels as soon as you can, Felicity, my chuck? Now we will take tea."

"No, I thank you," said Fanny. "I feel we have spent too much time here already."

"As you will," said the baroness indifferently. "But the jewels. I must have the jewels. I was a fool to leave them behind."

"And what did you make of that?" demanded Felicity as they got back in their carriage.

"Strangely enough, she behaved exactly as I expected her to," said Frederica. She put her arms around both her sisters and hugged them fiercely. "We have found one another and that is all that matters."

The baron arrived home that evening and said to his wife, "The servants say three titled ladies called."

"Oh, them," said his wife. "They were collecting for some charity. Do you remember, my love, that I left all the jewelry to Felicity?"

"Yes, and a damn silly thing to do, or so I thought at the time."

"Well, the dear girl has written to me to say she is giving it all back to me. So sweet!"

"Don't wear it all at once," said the baron. "You used to look like a French ambassador's house during a victory celebration."

"Always funning," said his wife with a fond smile. "Such a wit."

"Yes, I know," said the baron complacently. "I always thought it was my wit that charmed the Prince Regent into giving me the title."

The baroness's eyes narrowed a fraction. She was sure she knew why the prince had given him that title as she knew why she was somehow never allowed to go to London. But then she looked around at the comfort of her house and thought of her precious jewels soon to be returned to her.

"I am sure you are quite right, dear," said the champion of women's rights. "But then, you always are."

The Marquess of Darkwater was finally ushered into the royal presence. He was not at all surprised to learn the prince had not yet gone to Brighton. He looked around the gathering of courtiers and said with a low bow, "What I have to say to you, Sire, should not be overheard."

The prince looked at him apprehensively, but he waved his fat hand, and the company filed out.

"Now, Darkwater," said the prince sulkily, "state your business."

"I am come," said the marquess, "to tell you I know all about that affair you had in Scarborough years ago with a Mrs. Bride, so there is no reason to set your bully boys on me again."

"We don't know what you are talking about."

"Yes, you do. Comfrey and Harris told me they had been set on me."

The prince seemed to crumple. "We have had enough of scandal," he said. "Our public hates us. We had to stop it."

"But if Your Royal Highness had simply told me the truth," said the marquess, "I would have held my tongue. You had me believing the Waverley girls were your children."

"Odd's fish, man!"

"And all it turns out to be is that a youthful fling of yours nearly ruined a woman's life. Why did you misbehave with a respectable Yorkshire matron? There are plenty of dashers at court to oblige you."

"You would not think it to see her now," said the prince mournfully, "but she was so fresh and innocent and beautiful. Word got to the king. We could not do anything other than give her her quittance. You will not speak of this, Darkwater?"

"Not I, Sire. I only want your assurance that I and my wife will be left in peace."

"Our word of honor."

"Then I shall take my leave."

"I loved her," said the prince, dropping the royal "we." "I loved her very much."

The marquess sighed. This poor fat prince would never love his wife because he fell hopelessly in love with quite unsuitable women—Mrs. Fitzherbert being his current passion, a passion that showed no signs of dying.

He bowed his way out backward and, wheeling about, strode through the gilded, overheated rooms until he reached the fresh air outside. He was walking along Pall Mall when he found himself being hailed by Mr. Fordyce.

"Darkwater," cried Mr. Fordyce. "We are surely both the happiest of men. I read of your marriage to Felicity Waverley, and tomorrow you may read of my re-engagement to Lady Artemis."

"I congratulate you, Fordyce. When is the wedding to be?"

"Almost immediately. My bride-to-be says she cannot wait." He kissed his fingertips. "Such fire! Such love! One day, she was all coldness and then the next, she was in my arms. Will you attend the wedding?"

"We should be delighted. We do not sail for the Indies for another month or two."

"Lady Artemis has gone to call on Lady Felicity. Ah, if only I could hear what my darling is saying now, how she is describing her love for me."

"So I had to promise to marry the fool," Lady Artemis was saying. "Faugh! Trapped like a rabbit."

Felicity blushed slightly. "But did you not consider, Lady Artemis, that . . . er . . . such a thing would happen?"

"Not I. I consulted some quack during my last marriage and the idiot told me I should never breed. Children! I detest children. With all your knowledge, do you not know any way to get rid of the brat?"

Felicity wished Lady Artemis would leave and take her troubles with her. "I do not suggest you answer any of the advertisements offering such a service," she said. "It is said the women only bleed to death or die of infection."

Lady Artemis stood up and walked to the window. "I suppose I shall have to go through with it and then farm the wretched baby out to some nurse. I declare! There is young Lord Western lately come to town. Such an Adonis! Such legs. He is talking to that frumpy Miss Nash. Fie, what a waste. I shall descend and see if I can make life difficult for her."

After Lady Artemis had left, Felicity crossed to the window and looked down into Hanover Square. The handsome Lord Western had been leaning against the side of a vis-a-vis talking to a young lady and her mother. Lady Artemis sailed up, parasol twirling. She stopped and spoke. Lord Western laughed. Soon Lady Artemis and Lord Western were walking off round the square in the direction of her house.

Felicity shook her head. Poor Mr. Fordyce. Did he deserve

such a wife? And then Mrs. Ricketts came in to say Caroline James had called.

Felicity's face lit up with pleasure, and she went to meet the actress with both hands outstretched in welcome.

"Tell me all your news," said Caroline, who then listened as Felicity recounted her adventures.

"You do not need to worry about a plot for a book." Caroline laughed. "You have had so many adventures. Why do you still live here? Darkwater has his own house, has he not?"

"We are staying here to make preparations for our journey to the West Indies," said Felicity. "We have to find jobs for the female servants, except the inestimable Mrs. Ricketts. Fanny and Frederica are quite jealous that I am to have her with me. She says she longs to see a country where the sun shines all day long. And what of you? And what of Mr. Anderson?"

"We are to be married," said Caroline. "His mother has left town in disgust. I fought against it. He is so young, you know, but . . . I am very happy with him. Do you think I am doing wrong?"

"Not at all," said Felicity. "I shall dance at your wedding."

Caroline took her leave, feeling elated and happy. No one in the theater seemed to consider her proposed marriage to Bernard odd, and Felicity seemed to think it was all right. She walked all the way to Covent Garden and mounted the stairs to her apartment. Bernard was lying on his stomach on the floor, drawing up sketches for yet another fantastic piece of stage machinery.

"You will make me jealous," laughed Caroline. "The manager says you attract more people than the actors."

"Where did you go?" he asked anxiously. "You were gone a long time."

She knelt on the floor beside him and smoothed the hair from his brow. "I went to see Felicity Waverley. She is now married to the Marquess of Darkwater. I told her we were to be married, and she was so delighted at the news, I felt happy and decided to walk home."

He kissed her tenderly. "You are always so sure someone will exclaim in horror at the idea. Now come and look at this design for a flying harlequin, and tell me it is the most wonderful thing you have ever seen."

* * *

The Marquess of Darkwater arrived home in time to change for dinner. "No Waverley sisters?" he teased. "I was sure I would find Fanny or Frederica here. It is a wonder their husbands see anything of them at all."

"It is marvelous to have a family," said Felicity. They were standing in his bedroom, which he never slept in but only used as a changing room. He stripped off his shirt. "Where is my valet, George? He is never around since we moved here."

"He is the only male servant in a household full of female servants," said Felicity. "He lives like a king with housemaids running errands for him and Mrs. Ricketts getting Cook to make treats for him. Shall I call him?"

"No, I'll dress myself. Kiss me first."

She put her hands on his naked chest and smiled up into his eyes. He caught his breath, then held her close and kissed her fiercely. "It's been so long," he whispered at last.

"I know," said Felicity. "Since dawn this morning."

His busy hands felt for the tapes of her gown, and his mouth came down on hers again.

Mary, the little housemaid, who had been posted at the top of the stairs, listened hard. She heard the master's dressing room door opening and closing. Then there were sounds of footsteps, and her lady's bedroom door opened and closed. Mary listened harder until she heard a key clicking in the lock.

She ran down the stairs and into the servants' hall. "Oh, mum," she cried. "They're at it again."

"Watch that tongue of yours," snapped Mrs. Ricketts. "Well, they won't be wanting any dinner, and it's a shame to waste it. Pass the lobster, Mr. George, and pour the iced champagne, but see that Mary only gets half a glass because she does giggle so...."

Quadrille

For Eileen and Tom Kerr
with love

Chapter One

"I DO NOT want to go to Clarissa's," said Lady Mary Challenge, standing beside the open window to try to catch a breath of cool air.

"You will do as you are told, madam," said her husband, Colonel, Lord Hubert Challenge, from his position in front of the looking glass.

Mary stifled a little sigh. So it had begun and so it would go on in this loveless marriage. He issued the commands, she must obey. She turned and surveyed her husband who was shrugging his muscular shoulders into his evening jacket. The room was lit by one branch of candles on the mantelpiece and his reflection looked almost satanic in their wavering light. It was a handsome if swarthy face with a strong chin and a firm mouth. He had a patrician nose and large, beautiful brown eyes, very well spaced and ornamented with long thick lashes which detracted not one whit from his overpowering air of masculinity. His thick black hair sprung in two wings from his high forehead and his tall figure moved with athletic grace as he turned to face her.

Mary turned away. She did not want to read the expression in his eyes, for she knew she looked dowdy. Her dress of heavy silk was overfussy, giving her immature figure an awkward air. She had a smooth madonna-like face with an almost translucent skin and two large gray eyes and a quantity of fine, light brown hair, but it was her shy cringing air which made her appear dowdy, rather than her unfashionable clothes.

"I told you before that Lady Clarissa is an old friend of mine," said Lord Hubert, turning away from her and searching through the card rack for the correct invitation.

"All Brussels knows of your friendship with Clarissa," thought Mary, but she did not have the courage to say it aloud.

Mary knew herself to be a wealthy heiress. She knew also that Lord Hubert had married her for her money in order to save his ancestral home. Mary had naively expected love to blossom in this arranged marriage. But no sooner was she his wife than, three weeks after they were married, his regiment was ordered to Brussels.

He hadn't wanted her to go with him but she had insisted with a pertinacity foreign to her shy nature and he had shrugged and agreed. She had fondly imagined a grim battlefront—for wasn't that ogre Napoleon back to ravage Europe?—where she would have her husband all to herself.

But never in her wildest dreams had she imagined the sophisticated, glittering scene that was Brussels, where every society beauty seemed to be gathered to dazzle and charm her susceptible husband. And Clarissa, Lady Thorbury, was the most beautiful of all. Already Mary had heard it rumored that Clarissa had been her husband's mistress before their marriage and before her subsequent engagement to Viscount Peregrine St. James.

"There are rumors that Napoleon's troops are at Quatre Bras," ventured Mary timidly to try to turn the conversation away from Lady Clarissa.

"Gossiping women," said Lord Hubert impatiently. "What do they know of military matters?"

Mary opened her mouth to point out that it was the elderly Colonel Chalmers who had given her the news but her husband had already marched to the door and was holding it open.

She bent her head and walked before him down the stone steps from their rented apartment and out into the warm June night. The streets were thronged with carriages, their lamps gleaming and flashing in the dark blue night. Ladies laughed and flirted their fans and the officers escorting them seemed as merry as ever. But the undertone everywhere was war. War stalked the cobbled streets and brooded in the darkness of the Park. The laughter had an edge and faces were lit with a hectic look.

Lady Mary was suddenly afraid for her husband. She wanted to talk to him about the forthcoming battle. At first it had seemed during the past carefree sunny days that Napoleon was merely some type of low criminal who would soon be fettered and chained by the might of the allied armies. But frightened rumors and scared whispers had grown in volume. Every time she had tried to convey her fears to her husband he had snapped back that she knew nothing of such things, and so she had to hug her fear to herself. She was too timid and retiring and countrified to make any friends among the dashing Brussels belles and so she had no one to confide in.

"Not that I ever had anyone to confide in," thought Mary bitterly. Her parents, two grim members of the untitled aristocracy, had passed her over to the care of a nurse and then a governess since that day she had surprised them by coming into the world when her mother was forty-eight and her father fifty.

When she reached her seventeenth birthday, they had seemed to notice her for the first time. "Why, Mary, you have become a woman," her mother, Mrs. Tyre, had said with a grim smile. The next week she was affianced, whether she liked it or not, to the impecunious Lord Challenge, the Tyres having decided it was time they had a title in the family.

Mary had fallen desperately in love with Lord Hubert with all the aching, tremulous passion of first love. But on their wedding night, he had brutally told her that he did not seduce virgins. It was an arranged marriage, nothing more. He would not interfere with her, provided she left him alone.

But still she had hoped. Until the day they had arrived in Brussels and Lady Clarissa had appeared as their first guest, looking at Lord Hubert with melting eyes. Every line of her body could be seen plainly through a transparent muslin gown, hinting at all sorts of untold intimacies.

Damn Clarissa! Mary's eyes filled with unshed tears. The carriage rolled to a halt and Mary braced herself for the ordeal.

At first she thought it was not going to be as bad as she had feared. Clarissa welcomed them, hanging onto the arm of her fiancé, Lord Peregrine. Lord Peregrine was a thickset, brutish man with a fat, blue chin and a great hooked nose. He had small twinkling eyes and his face was always creased up in a jolly laugh; but nothing could disguise the atmosphere of suppressed rage that he seemed to carry about with him. Mary did not like him one bit. But he was Clarissa's fiancé and therefore his presence surely meant that Clarissa would be too occupied to flirt with Lord Hubert.

Clarissa was a buxom redhead of about thirty years. Her dress of gold tissue was damped to cling to her body and Mary could not help hoping she caught a fatal chill. Clarissa had eyes which were strangely narrow and slightly tilted. They were of a pale green color and gave her appearance the lazy sensuality of a cat.

The company chattered of everything but war, and Mary wondered why they did not seem to feel its brooding presence creeping in from the streets.

Apart from Clarissa and Lord Peregrine, Mary and Lord Hubert, there were two other couples present.

There was a Major Frederick Godwin and his wife, Lucy. Major Godwin was a big, slow-speaking man, handsome in a florid way. He had thick, fair hair and a fine pair of military sideburns. His wife Lucy was small, pretty, vivacious and cruel. Her husband stared at her in dumb adoration while she pouted and flirted with all the men present. She had curly blonde hair confined over one ear with a blue silk ribbon and a ball gown of celestial blue muslin which enhanced the Dresden china perfection of her features.

The other couple struck Mary as being a very odd pair to find in high society. Their names were Mr. and Mrs. Witherspoon and they were hearty, jolly, middle-aged and very vulgar. They "my lorded" and "my ladied" all the titles to death, and when they weren't doing that they were claiming friendship with every notable in Brussels, from the Duke of Wellington to the Prince of Orange.

Mrs. Witherspoon patted her hideous turban complacently and turned her full attention on Lord Hubert. "Was you going to open up your town house in London?" she asked.

"If I come out of this affair alive," he said coldly.

"Such a fine house it is too," said Mrs. Witherspoon, laying a fat white hand on his jacket sleeve. "Such a pity it had to be kept closed all these years. St. James's Square, it is, I believe. It's a wonder you didn't sell it when you was so down in funds."

There was a startled silence, and then Lord Hubert looked down at the hand on his jacket as if some white slug were crawling up his arm.

"You seem to be well versed in my affairs, madam," he remarked, turning away.

"Oh, ain't I just," crowed Mrs. Witherspoon, peering round to see his averted face. "I know all about you, my lord. I remembered when it was rumored that Hammonds, your pa's old home, was to go under the hammer. What a pity, I said to Mr. Witherspoon, for it breaks my heart to see an old home going out of the family. 'Never fear, my love,' says he, 'for that young spark'll find the money even if he has to marry to get it.' "

There was an appalled silence which penetrated even Mrs. Witherspoon's thick hide, for she added hurriedly, "It was just his little joke for I can see by looking at you and your lovely wife, my lord, that if ever I did see a pair of lovebirds. . . ."

"Madam, pray keep your distasteful and vulgar observations to yourself," said Lord Hubert.

"That's right, my lord," remarked Mrs. Witherspoon complacently, "as I was saying to the dear Dook only yesterday, I says, 'Arthur,' I says, 'I likes a gentleman who can take a joke.' "

"Come Mrs. Witherspoon," said Lady Clarissa hurriedly, "you are not eating your food."

"We're newly married ourselves," said Major Godwin with a fond smile at his wife, Lucy, who pouted and stared at the table.

"Why must you tell everyone we're just married?" complained Lucy.

"Because it's true, my love," said Major Godwin in surprise.

"Oh, you're such a *dull* old stick, Freddie," said his wife with a brittle laugh.

There was another embarrassed silence and Mary racked her brains for something to say.

"Your little wife is very quiet," said Clarissa to Lord Hubert. "I do believe you beat her."

"Do you think this affair at Quatre Bras will come to anything?" Lord Hubert asked Major Freddie Godwin.

"Can't say till we join the chaps in the morning and see for ourselves," said Freddie.

Clarissa frowned and bit her lip. Hubert was not going to let her attack his little wife in any way. Why had he married that countrified nobody anyway? *She* could have given him money. And hadn't he been her lover for two delirious years before this strange marriage? Now Hubert was stuck with a wife he obviously did not want, and she had gone and got herself engaged to Perry in a fit of pique at the news of Hubert's wedding.

Well, she would punish. Somehow, she would have him back in her arms. She became aware that Mr. Witherspoon was addressing her.

"My lady," said that gentleman, "my good wife informs me that a young officer has just ridden up to your front door looking all of a lather." He paused and looked at Clarissa expectantly.

"*I,*" said Clarissa sweetly, "have servants to answer the door for me."

"But I wonder ..." began the unsnubbable Mr. Witherspoon. But at that moment a servant entered, and said that Captain Harry Black was anxious to have a word with Lord Challenge.

Lord Challenge left the room with the curious eyes of the Witherspoons boring into his back. Clarissa called the servant back. "Tell Captain Black to join us for a glass of wine."

The servant bowed and withdrew. A thin, nervous young Captain walked into the room carrying a portfolio which he clutched tightly under one arm, followed by Lord Hubert.

"Harry," smiled Clarissa, "how divine to see *you* again."

"Not another," said her fiancé, Lord Peregrine, with a heavy sneer, and Captain Black blushed. "I really must go," he said, but Clarissa stood up and wound her white arms around his neck. "We are just moving to the drawing room, dear Captain," she cooed. "Do put down that silly portfolio and come and join us."

"I am not supposed to let it out of my sight," said Captain Black. "I . . ."

"Oh, *silly,*" laughed Clarissa. "Which one of us here is going to steal it?"

"I didn't mean that, my lady. I meant . . ."

But Clarissa was already leading him out of the door after having taken the portfolio from under his arm and dropped it carelessly onto the table.

Mary looked sympathetically towards Lord Peregrine. She did not like him, but she could not help feeling sorry for him as he stood by the empty fireplace, scowling furiously at the hearth.

She looked round for her husband but Lucy Godwin was

talking to him in a very animated fashion. Lord Hubert was smiling down into her eyes in a way that he certainly never showed to poor Mary.

She gave a tiny sigh and turned as she heard a small echo of it behind her. Major Freddie Godwin was standing miserably behind her, fingering his sideburns and watching his wife.

"Do I look like that?" thought Mary suddenly. "Hurt and lost and oh! so transparent?"

"Come, Captain Godwin," she said with a boldness that amazed her, "you shall escort me to the drawing room. Tell me, do you think we shall still be going on to the ball?"

"Oh, I think so," said the Major, reluctantly tearing his eyes away from his wife and offering Mary his arm. "We've orders to march in the morning, but Wellington's to be at the ball so we may as well be there too."

"Does Hubert march too?" asked Mary faintly.

"Dash it, didn't he tell you? He's bound to, you know. His regiment's out there already."

He led her into the drawing room and sat next to her on a small sofa.

Ignoring Mary's obvious distress, the Major took her gloved hands in his and looked earnestly into her eyes.

"I say, Lady Challenge, do you think you could keep an eye on little Lucy for me while I'm away? She's just a child, you know. So beautiful and, well," here the poor Major tugged desperately at his sideburns, "if something happens to me I'd like to think that she's in capable hands."

For all her distress, Mary could not help reflecting bitterly that she, Mary, was seventeen and the beautiful Lucy a mature twenty. But beauty, she thought sadly, is always considered vulnerable.

"What are our chances of victory?" she asked in a low voice.

"Oh, we'll win," said the large Major cheerfully. "Napoleon's nothing compared to our Duke. Why, look how Wellington routed them in the Peninsula!" But his eyes held a worried look.

"But *why*," said Mary intensely, "*why* must we all go to this ball? It is eleven o'clock in the evening and if you must march in the morning, surely you at least want to spend some time alone with your wife?"

"Well, I would and that's a fact," he said miserably. "But Lucy was so thrilled to get the Duchess of Richmond's invitation, that she would go even if Napoleon himself, and all his troops, were to be there.

"Fact is," he said with a sudden burst of confidence, "I feel Lucy's had rather a hard time of it. We were neighbors, you know, and she had never really met any other fellows when she married me. I've got the family place in London and the minute we were married I decided to give her a Season. She got a great deal of attention for she is so very beautiful, you know, and she sometimes feels that perhaps she could have done better than have married a stick-in-the-mud like me."

"She surely did not say so!" exclaimed Mary, shocked.

"No," lied the gallant Major, "but I love her and I notice things."

Mary was overcome by a rush of affection for the miserable Major. After all, who knew better than herself what it was like to be married to someone one adored, and to receive no love in return?

"I shall take care of her," she said in a quiet voice, squeezing the Major's large hands sympathetically in her own, and smiling up into his eyes.

She then looked across the room and caught the faintly surprised look on her husband's face and the hard, china blue stare of Lucy.

At that moment, the Captain took his leave and Clarissa announced gaily that they should leave for the ball.

Once more into the warm night they went, with the Witherspoons clinging like limpets.

"Surely *they* are not invited to the Richmonds?" said Lord Hubert as they stood on the street outside waiting for their carriages. "Where did you find such pushing mushrooms, Clarissa?"

But Clarissa only laughed and would not reply.

They made their way towards the Duchess of Richmond's house as the drums began to beat and the trumpets sounded, calling the soldiers to arms.

The ballroom was on the ground floor of the Richmond's rented house in the Rue de la Blanchisserie. All the curtains were drawn back, and golden light flooded out onto the cobbles of the street.

All the beauties were there, and all the list of chivalry—ambassadors, generals and aristocrats, and dashing young officers.

Mary felt suddenly weary and wished she could go home to lie down and sleep. She clung to her husband's arm as they entered the ballroom and, wide-eyed, looked round at the magnificence of the tent-like hangings in the royal colors of crimson, gold and black, the rose-trellised wallpaper and the glittering chandeliers.

She made her curtsy to the Duke and Duchess of Richmond, and turned to say something to her husband. But he was staring towards the doorway where a tall figure, glittering with orders, had just entered. The newcomer had a handsome tanned face, close-cropped black hair and a hooked nose. He laughed at something the Duke of Richmond was saying and his laugh echoed round the ballroom in great jerks of sound, like a hyena with the whooping cough. There was no mistaking that laugh or those vivid blue eyes. The Duke of Wellington had arrived.

A seventeen-year-old beauty, Lady Georgiana Lennox, left off dancing and rushed up to the Duke asking whether the rumors of war were true.

Wellington replied gravely, "Yes, they are true. We are off tomorrow."

"Oh, let us go home," Mary urged her husband.

"In such a hurry to see me die?" he asked cruelly. He then shook off her arm with some impatience, leaving her to find her own way to a sofa in an embrasure.

The ballroom vibrated with whispers and hurried leave-takings as the officers whose regiments were farthest away slipped quietly from the ballroom. The Duke of Brunswick felt a premonition of death and dropped the little Prince de Ligne off his lap. Wellington sat on a sofa next to Lady Hamilton-Dalrymple, chatting with her and looking very much at his ease, although he kept turning round to whisper orders to various officers who came up to him, one of whom was Lord Hubert.

Clarissa caught hold of Hubert's arm as he was making his way back across the ballroom. "Hubert," she breathed huskily. "When am I to see you alone?"

"Perhaps tonight," he replied seriously. "For tonight may be my last."

"Then spend it with *me*," she urged, and then reluctantly released his arm as Lord Peregrine came scowling up to them.

Major Godwin detached Lucy from her court of admirers. "I've got to go now, Lucy. At least I've got one hour before I join my regiment. Come home with me."

"No," pouted Lucy. "Why are you so dramatic? Everyone knows that the dear Duke will defeat Boney. You simply don't want me to have any fun. You may have the next dance with me before you go but that is all."

"Oh, Lucy," groaned the Major sadly, but couples were already making up sets for the quadrille.

Hubert strolled towards where his wife was sitting. She looked timid, sad and colorless and he suddenly felt impatient with her. Clarissa had issued an invitation, and he had a good mind to accept it. Mary need never know.

But if he died, he would like to think he had left an heir to inherit Hammonds.

"We leave after this dance, Mary," he said, looking down at her and holding out his hand. "Come!"

"Wasn't this a clever idea of mine, my love," Mr. Witherspoon was saying gleefully to his wife. "These grand folk who would look down their noses at us at home are all too anxious to be civil when there's a war in the offing."

Mrs. Maria Witherspoon nodded her turbaned head vigorously. Mr. Witherspoon's fortune hailed from a series of Yorkshire mills. The Witherspoons were therefore "in trade," and had found that their vast wealth would not open one society door to them in London. It was then that Mr. Josiah Witherspoon had hit on the idea of going to Brussels.

By being very free with his money and giving various sumptuous banquets in restaurants, he had soon found himself on hobnobbing terms with a variety of titled names who would have cut him dead in Bond Street.

The Witherspoons were an unprepossessing couple, both being on the plump side and a similarity of disposition having marked each face with a permanent ingratiating leer. They had secured invitations to the Duchess of Richmond's ball by simply buying two cards of invitation from a pair of impecunious aristocrats.

But Mrs. Witherspoon's sharp ears had caught a nasty comment earlier that evening. "My dear," one lady had said to the other, "aren't the Witherspoons too simply terrible for words? But after all, one need not recognize them in London."

She saw Lord Hubert and his wife standing up for the quadrille and noticed that they needed one other couple and accordingly urged her husband into the dance.

The eight members of Lord Hubert's quadrille waited for the opening chords of the music.

"I shall never forget this evening or these dreadful people," thought Mary, looking round at the other members of the quadrille. "Apart from Hubert, I never want to see any of them again."

There were the Witherspoons, simpering awfully and calculating how much social use each member of the quadrille could possibly be to them. There was Lucy, her large eyes roving in every direction but that of her husband. Clarissa was staring at Mary with a hard, calculating look and Lord Peregrine was looking as restless and angry as ever.

The band struck up. The couples bowed and curtsied. They crossed and recrossed, weaving out the patterns of the dance, sometimes dancing with their own partner, sometimes with someone else's.

And the members of Lord Hubert's quadrille did not know that they could at that moment have been acting out a pattern of their lives to come.

In another room of the Richmond's rented mansion, the Duke of Wellington and the Duke of Richmond were poring over a map.

"Napoleon has *humbugged* me, by God!" said Wellington angrily. "He has gained twenty-four hours' march on me."

"What do you intend doing?"

Wellington stared down at the map. "I have ordered the army to concentrate at Quatre Bras, but we shall not stop him there, and if so," the Duke passed his thumb-nail over the map, "I must fight him *here*."

The Duke of Richmond stared down at the little black name on the map indicated by Wellington's thumbnail.

Waterloo.

Chapter Two

"WHY THIS SUDDEN desire to have me in your bed, my lord?" said Mary wearily.

No reply as her husband unwound his cravat from his neck and shrugged his broad shoulders out of his evening jacket. Hubert had drunk quite a lot of wine that evening. He was tired and he was also excited and elated at the thought of the battle to come.

Mary stood by the window, looking across the shadowed room at his back. She longed to feel his arms around her and at the same time she was alarmed at his air of detachment about the whole thing. He stripped off his shirt and flung it onto a chair where it lay against the dark red plush of the upholstery, gleaming whitely against the darkness of the room.

He turned abruptly and looked at her. He lifted the branch of candles from the mantelpiece and held it high, sending long shadows running and dancing up the walls. Her eyes looked enormous in her white face and she seemed little more than a schoolgirl. He suddenly felt that the correct thing to do would be to deposit a chaste kiss on her forehead and then tuck her into bed. But she was his wife after all and she could really not, in all fairness, expect to remain a virgin for the rest of her life.

He replaced the candelabra on the mantelpiece and walked slowly towards her.

Mary waited, trembling, hanging onto her pride. How dare he flirt with Clarissa one minute and expect her to fall into his arms the next? How dare he shun her for all those long and lonely nights after their marriage? Had he pulled her into his arms as ruthlessly as she expected, then she would have remained still and unresponsive. But instead, he folded his arms gently round her and rocked her against the warmth of his naked chest. "Come, Mary," he said softly. "There is no need to be afraid."

He tilted her chin and bent his head and kissed her very gently on the mouth, feeling her soft lips cling and tremble against his own. The great love she had for him could no longer be hidden. She gave a little broken sound, half sigh, half sob, and wound her arms round his neck as he lifted her up and carried her to the bed.

Clear and loud below the window came the imperative call of a bugle, and in the nearby squares the drums began to beat to arms. In the back of his brain, he had a nagging feeling of guilt. He should have waited. It was her first night after all and it should not be a hurried affair like this. He should be able to lie at her side late in the morning instead of hurrying off to the battle. But the trembling passion of her immature body against his own suddenly excited him more than anything he could remember before.

He at last fell completely and soundlessly asleep, lying across her body while Mary, cradling him in her arms, dazed with love and happiness, lay awake for a few minutes longer than her lord.

After an hour, a louder bugle call sounded outside and Hubert woke immediately and sat up. Mary awoke as well and stared up at him, eyes almost blind with love. He looked down at her with a strange, abstracted stare. He felt acutely responsible for her for the first time since their marriage and this new feeling of responsibility irked him immensely. And in the same misguided way of parents who are cruel to be kind, he said harshly, "Dammit, I have overslept!"

Without another look at her, he stalked off to his dressing room, shouting for his valet.

Mary lay, stunned. She felt as if he had slapped her across the face. She could feel the tears pricking at the back of her eyes but she would not let them form. After a few minutes, she got up and wrapped a blanket around herself and crossed to the wash stand in the corner to splash cold water over her face.

She put on a fussy and elaborate pink morning dress, hoping to look her best, but the masses of frills and furbelows only succeeded in making her look younger than ever.

Lord Hubert came into the room, dressed in his scarlet

and gold regimentals, looking magnificent, handsome and remote. She stared at him, her eyes wide with hurt, begging for reassurance.

But he avoided her gaze, saying abruptly, "Should anything happen to me, will you look after Hammonds? It's been in my family for centuries and I would like our son to inherit it . . . if we have a son."

She nodded dumbly, twisting one of the silly frills of her dress nervously in her fingers.

He crossed the room with easy, athletic strides and called down into the street below for assurance that his horse had been brought round.

"Very well then, Mary," he said, turning back and dropping a cool kiss on her cheek. "I must be away. Pray for me."

"Of course," said Mary quietly.

He crossed to the door.

"Mary . . ."

"Yes, Hubert?"

"Oh, nothing. Goodbye." And with that he was gone.

She crossed to the window and leaned out. A rosy dawn was rising over the jumbled gables of Brussels. The air was warm and still and heavy. A flock of pigeons rose and wheeled up to the brightening sky.

A Scotch regiment swung down the street to the skirl of the pipes, then came a regiment of Hussars in their magnificent uniforms.

Then came her husband.

He was sitting on his dappled horse talking to Major Godwin who rode beside him. He seemed to be trying to cheer the Major up. Major Godwin was still in evening dress and dancing pumps, his wife having kept him at the ball until the very last minute.

Hubert suddenly looked up and saw Mary at the window. He raised his arm in a brief salute and rode on.

The regimental band was playing, "The Girl I Left Behind Me," a jaunty rousing tune. Mary leaned farther from the window, craning her neck for a last look at her husband, as the remainder of the regiment swung out along the Charleroi road in the rosy glow of the sunrise to join the rest already on the battlefield. She stayed there as all the regiments that had been left in Brussels marched out. She stayed there until the drums and the bugles and the pipes and the marching, marching feet had all filed by and the last fixed bayonet glinted in the sun.

And then she went back into the room to pray.

But Mary was not destined to be allowed to pray in peace. Scarcely had the last military sound disappeared from the streets of Brussels to be replaced by the rumbling of the farm carts arriving for the market than Mrs. Witherspoon was announced.

Mary had not been out in the world enough to recognize a pushing mushroom, or to know what to do about it. Mrs. Witherspoon announced she had come to sit with "the poor love" and comfort her. Mary did not like Mrs. Witherspoon but she had no one else in Brussels to share her fears with, and so suffered that vulgar lady to stay all morning and then to join her for lunch.

Not that Mrs. Witherspoon seemed very prepared to listen. She had so much to say herself! "Faith, Lady Mary," she gushed. "I feel I have known you this twelvemonth instead of us meeting only the other day. Such a handsome man your husband is and such a rip with the ladies! Ah, now, there's your pretty eyes filling with tears. I do let my tongue rattle on so. Why, the dear Duke—Wellington, you know—was saying only t'other day, 'I should have you at the front of the fighting, ma'am. That tongue of yours would put the Frenchies to flight.' "

Despite her misery, Mary had to suppress a smile. It did indeed, for once, sound like something the Duke of Wellington might say.

Mrs. Witherspoon continued to eat great quantities of food, seated comfortably in Mary's little dining room, her elbows on the table and a chicken wing in her hand. Her large bosom spilled over the square neckline of a purple silk gown. A purple turban ornamented with an ostrich plume covered her sparse hair, and a stream of non-stop name-dropping issued from her pouting, rosebud mouth as her three chins wiggled vigorously in accompaniment.

Then all of a sudden, Mrs. Witherspoon began to talk about Lord Hubert and Mary learned a great deal about her husband that she did not know before.

Like herself, Lord Hubert had been born when his parents were middle-aged and his mother had not survived the birth. The family fortunes had been dwindling for generations and

Hammonds, where Hubert had been brought up, had fallen almost into decay.

His father had died while Hubert was at Oxford; and Hubert had taken what little money there was and had bought himself a captaincy in a regiment which was ordered to Portugal the day he joined it.

He had followed Wellington through Portugal and up the long corridors of Spain to France. At the age of thirty, he had found himself a full colonel with a resounding list of battles behind him: Badajoz, Salamanca and Vittorio to name a few. He had seen more death and bloodshed than he had ever dreamed of. Sometimes in his dreams, he could still hear the screech of the wheels of the bullock carts as they hauled his regiment's provisions across the endless barren sierras. There was the prize money, of course, but every bit of it seemed to be swallowed up in repairs to Hammonds. Wellington forbade looting, and Lord Hubert agreed with this law. But it was not always easy to impose it when the men seemed hell-bent on looting whole towns and sometimes, seeing brother officers made rich by stolen jewels, wished his conscience would allow him to do the same. At last, in desperation, he began to look about him for a rich wife. Mrs. Witherspoon paused for breath and Mary stared at her, her young face almost hard.

"Tell me, Mrs. Witherspoon," she said in arctic tones, "where did you come by such intimate information about my husband? How could you possible know of his dreams?"

Mrs. Witherspoon bit her lip. She loved gossip and realized she had allowed herself to become carried away. The gossip had mostly come from Lady Clarissa. Even Mrs. Witherspoon, by dint of listening in to everyone else's conversation, had quickly learned that Clarissa had been Lord Hubert's mistress and had wondered along with society why Lord Hubert had not married Clarissa, who was reputed to be mistress of a sizeable fortune.

But the bit about hearing the bullock carts in his dreams she had gleaned from overhearing him talk at a party to one of his brother officers, Peter Bennet. That would do.

"Why, my dear, Lord Hubert told Captain Peter Bennet and that young fellow told me. I don't like to listen to gossip, and that's a fact, but that there Peter was forever talking to me like I was his mother."

Mary blinked. Peter Bennet was an extremely elegant and fastidious young man. She could not for a minute imagine him confiding in anyone, let alone Mrs. Witherspoon. But she did, however, dismally feel as if the whole of Brussels knew of her husband's innermost thoughts and plans while she, his wife, had only been treated to a few common pleasantries.

The day was hot and hazy and Mary reflected that she had never seen anyone perspire with such unembarrassed abandon as Mrs. Witherspoon. Little rivulets ran down from her forehead, across her chins and joined somewhere at the base of the last chin forming a river which plunged down into the chasm formed by her cleavage. Mary was all at once too tired to school her expression. Open distaste was mirrored in her eyes. Mrs. Witherspoon caught the look as she raised her head from a dish of tansy pudding and her brain began to churn. She would lose this little lady if she did not find some way to make Lady Mary obliged to her.

All at once the hot stillness of the day was broken by a muffled boom.

"What's that!" cried Mary, starting to her feet. "Thunder?"

Again it sounded and suddenly the street below became alive with the sound of running feet and shouting voices.

Mary leaned out of the window. "Qui se passe?" she yelled down to the fleeting figures. One Brussels shopkeeper heard her cry and twisted up his head. "Le feu," he screamed. "Le feu, madame! La bataille commence!"

As the sounds of the cannonade boomed even clearer, Mary ran down the stairs and out into the street completely forgetting about Mrs. Witherspoon, and joined the hustling frightened crowd as they streamed towards the Namur Gate to look out across the fields in the direction of Quatre Bras.

All afternoon she stood there, listening in dread to that dull *boom boom boom* which sounded across the heavy air like a death knell. Rumors flew about her. Napoleon had driven a wedge between the British and their allies the Prussians, and he was taking his time to massacre them both. At last, at sunset, the noise of the cannonade died away. Trembling from worry and fatigue, Mary returned to her lodgings.

But she was still not to have her home to herself. Lucy Godwin was waiting for her, her pretty face drawn and pale.

Mary felt a rush of pity for her. "Do not look *so*, Mrs.

153

Godwin," she urged. "Our men will come home victorious, never fear."

"I'm not worried about Freddie," said Lucy, hitching a callous shoulder. "He's used to battles. The thing is—how are we going to escape? Every horse and carriage has been taken and the few seats that are left are going for fabulous sums."

Mary stared at her amazed. "But surely you would not contemplate leaving before your husband gets back? How can you dream of leaving, not knowing what has happened to him?"

"I think you're very cold and unfeeling," pouted Lucy. "You *promised* Freddie you'd look after me, yes you *did*, for he told me so. And looking after me doesn't mean leaving me here to be raped by a lot of Frenchies."

"But what can I do? We have no carriage. I have my own horse and you are welcome to that."

"I couldn't ride all the way out of here on my own," protested Lucy. "It must be a carriage or nothing. Mr. Witherspoon, 'tis said, bought a great deal of horses and at least two carriages apart from his own, and he is selling seats in them at fabulous prices which I cannot afford. *You* are very rich . . ."

"My husband has control of any money we have," said Mary stiffly. "I do not inherit any wealth until my parents die."

"But the Witherspoons are friends of yours . . ."

"I did not set eyes on them until last night."

"Oh, you're *horrid*," said Lucy, beginning to sob. "And so I shall tell Freddie."

"I shall, however, go and see Mr. Witherspoon," went on Mary quietly, "and see what I can do."

Lucy's tears dried like magic.

The two women had to walk on foot since neither had a carriage and all vehicles of any description had been bought in order to escape the doomed city. The British did not quite realize that the people of Brussels were mostly pro-French and delighted in spreading rumors of Napoleon's successes. The roads from the city were jammed with the carriages of society who had believed up to the very last minute of the ball that Wellington would succeed as he had always done, but no longer had any faith in that great leader.

The Witherspoons had a suite of rooms in the Hotel du Parc. They were delighted to see the ladies, especially Lady

Mary. Mrs. Witherspoon and her husband had been plotting all day for some way in which to be of service to young Lady Mary so that they should have subsequent claims on her society in London. As soon as Mary asked for a carriage seat on Lucy's behalf, they brightened considerably. Mr. Witherspoon drooped an eyelid at his wife, which was his signal to tell her to leave things to him. He led Mary into an adjoining room and studied her thoughtfully although the ingratiating leer never left his face. The girl looked exhausted—and vulnerable.

"I shall put it to you plain, my lady," began Mr. Witherspoon at last. "I have a seat left in a carriage which is to leave Brussels in an hour's time. Now I will gladly let Mrs. Godwin have it and at no cost whatsoever."

"You are very kind," exclaimed Mary, her face lighting up.

"Why, she's quite a little beauty!" thought Mr. Witherspoon. Nonetheless, he pressed on. "I would like to say I am doing this solely to oblige *you*, Lady Mary, being as how my wife has taken a fancy to you."

"Too kind," murmured Mary.

"Now my good wife is very sensitive, very sensitive indeed. Her sensibilities are easily wounded. I would, for example, not like to think that should she wish to call on you in London she would be met with a rebuff."

Mary was young and immature and unused to the ways of the world. Nonetheless, she knew what was being asked of her and why it was being asked. But she had promised Major Godwin to take care of Lucy.

"I would not dream of rebuffing your wife," she said gently.

"And I would hope that you would introduce my good Maria to some of the delights of the *ton*? She has no acquaintance in London, you see," added Mr. Witherspoon, speaking the truth for once.

Mary felt suddenly that should she ever gain safety and feel her husband's arms around her again, she would gladly entertain every pushing Cit in the country.

"Of course. I should be delighted."

"I hope you don't forget," said Mr. Witherspoon, his face momentarily losing its habitual leer.

"I am not used to having my word doubted."

Mr. Witherspoon studied her face for a few seconds and then slowly nodded. "Best tell Mrs. Lucy to get packed."

Lucy was ecstatic. She hugged Mary. She even kissed the Witherspoons. She begged Mary to return with her to her lodgings to help her pack.

The sky outside was very black. From overhead came the sinister rumble of thunder. Mary thought dismally of the mud of a water-clogged battlefield and Lucy stared upwards, thinking of all those beautiful roads to freedom which might be washed away.

At last Lucy was packed and seated in the carriage. She looked radiant, flashing smiles at her fellow passengers and chattering nineteen to the dozen.

Mary heaved a sigh of relief and made her way back to her temporary home.

"God protect Hubert," muttered Mary desperately, "and all those poor boys."

She staggered up the stairs to her bedroom, still wearing the silly, ruffled morning gown and collapsed on the bed, too tired to undress and mercifully too tired to worry any more.

The next day, Mary found her servants inclined to be surly, particularly her lady's maid, a resident of Brussels, who was convinced that the French would beat the British and wondered why her mistress had not flown. The other servants were also locals and appeared to be dedicated Bonapartistes.

Mary regretted not having hired a lady's maid in England. She had always dressed herself, but on her arrival in Brussels she found that her husband had hired a local staff, and that included a pert lady's maid, Marie Juneaux. Mary kept to her rooms that day, resting and praying, no longer wishing to venture into the streets for news of the battle since, from what she heard through the open windows, the whole of Brussels was convinced that Napoleon had won.

The night of the seventeenth of June was miserable. Rain poured down in a steady deluge and Mary was more afraid for her husband than for herself.

She was roused from her prayers by the unwelcome visit of Lady Clarissa.

Lady Clarissa was not a coward and had not fled Brussels. On the contrary, the nearness of the battle and the scent of danger seemed to exhilarate her. Her cats' eyes flashed fire like emeralds and, in defiance of the atmosphere of fear and defeat, she was bedecked with jewels and wearing her best silk gown.

"I do not know how the men will survive this night," said Mary miserably. Although she both despised and was jealous of her beautiful guest, she found she could not keep her fears to herself.

"Pooh!" laughed Clarissa. "It will take more than a little rain to vanquish our brave Hubert."

Mary stiffened at the use of her husband's Christian name, a fact which Clarissa gleefully noticed.

"Your fiancé," asked Mary stiffly. "Is he on the battlefield?"

"Perry? Good God, no. He is too concerned for the safety of his skin. Also he is a Whig, you know, and thinks it might not be too bad if Boney won."

"For shame!" cried Mary, forgetting her natural timidity in a burst of outrage.

"Claws in, my dear," cooed Clarissa. "I said these were Perry's views, not mine. I do confess I have a soft spot in my heart for a soldier. Dear Hubert, so strong, so brave."

"You knew my husband before our marriage, I believe," said Mary, desperately wishing this woman would go away, and at the same time, desperately wishing to hear the worst.

"Oh, yes, *very well*," smiled Clarissa languorously. "One never thought Hubert would get married, you know. But ah me! The things men do for money."

Mary rose to her feet and stood looking down at Clarissa, her large eyes sparkling with anger. "You are offensive," she said coldly. "I have worries enough without your malice. Please leave."

"Oh, 'tis a jealous little wife," said Clarissa rising languidly to her feet and patting Mary on the cheek. "But it is the truth after all."

"My husband loves me—and only me," lied Mary, her anger giving her voice a ring of conviction. "I am annoyed and irritated by your impertinence, that is all."

Clarissa surveyed her for a few seconds, her green eyes narrowed into slits. Why, when the little thing was animated, she was quite beautiful. "I shall lose the game," thought Clarissa, "and I make an enemy of her. Hubert will take her part simply because she *is* his wife. He always was a bit of a stuffed shirt after all."

She accordingly threw her arms round Mary and cried, "Ah, you must forgive me. I was in love with Hubert once, Lady Mary, and I am still a little jealous. I have a wicked tongue and see how these rumors and dangers have upset me and make me say stupid things. Please forgive me."

She stared appealingly at Mary, opening her eyes to their widest.

Mary was lonely and afraid. She was not yet aware that Clarissa was a superb actress. "Please," urged Clarissa softly. "I am engaged to Perry after all, and I am not the kind of woman to become affianced to a man I do not love."

Mary gave a little sigh. "I forgive you," she said quietly. "There are too many enemies out there. I do not wish to have any at home."

"Splendid!" cried Clarissa. "Come now. I see a backgammon board over there. Why do we not have a game to pass the waiting hours and I shall tell you all the scandal of London."

During the next few hours, Mary had to admit that Clarissa was extremely entertaining company. When Clarissa put her mind to it, she could charm both women and men. And Mary was still too young to realize that beautiful and charming people can often be quite nasty and cruel. She found herself laughing at Clarissa's stories. Clarissa did not mention Hubert again and Mary became convinced that Clarissa could not have been her husband's mistress. In her innocence, she believed that Clarissa's desire to please her and keep her company was ample proof of that.

Unaware that his wife and his former mistress were cosily engaged in a game of backgammon, Lord Hubert lay in the muddy battlefield and wrestled with his guilty conscience. He was old campaigner enough to have smeared his blankets with clay to waterproof them but, nonetheless, the unceasing pounding of the rain got on his nerves.

Tomorrow might be his last day. They had held the French at Quatre Bras, but God alone knew how long he and his men could stand up to this ceaseless pounding. So many had already fallen. The Duke of Brunswick was dead as was most of Wellington's staff. Wellington himself had remained miraculously untouched, riding here and there in the very thick of the battle; his calm, deep voice urging the men on.

Hubert wished he had left a happy wife behind him. He had not meant to be so cruel to her, and now he wondered if he would now have a chance to return from the battle and make amends. If only the damnable rain would cease, then he would be able to pen a letter. He wondered what she thought of him behind that madonna-like mask of a face. Her eyes had registered a lost, hurt bewilderment as she looked down at him from the window as he rode away. But then, he thought cynically, any nicely-bred girl would look exactly the same after the sort of night she had endured. Perhaps she might not care if he never returned. That thought annoyed him. He did not love her but she was his wife after all and he did not want to think of her enjoying all the license of a young widow in the saloons of London.

The sky turned pale gray and the rain ceased as abruptly as it had begun. He sat up stiffly. A flaming red sun climbed up over the fields of rye, turning them as bloody a color as they were going to be before this hellish day was ended.

He looked across the fields to the small ridge above Waterloo and recognized the trim figure of the Duke of Wellington astride his horse Copenhagen. He was wearing his blue frock coat and a low cocked hat that bore the black cockade of England with the colors of Spain, Portugal and the Netherlands.

Hubert felt a lifting of his heart. The Duke had pulled them through so very many times when all the odds seemed against them. Surely he would do the same again today!

"I shall write to Mary this evening," thought Hubert, rising stiffly to his feet. "This evening will be time enough."

The Brussels morning dawned. Knots of people stood around their doorways, dreading the arrival of the French. Rumors flew from mouth to mouth. The Prussians had been defeated, the English had been defeated, the English had won. And then the carts began to arrive.

They rolled into Brussels in a seemingly endless stream, carrying the dying and the wounded. Mary, who had been up all night, ran downstairs rushing from one wagonload to the other, searching for her husband, searching for anyone who might be able to give her news.

At last, she saw the white, drawn and bloodied face of Peter Bennet. "Carry him into my house," she cried to some soldiers, "and anyone else you think I can help."

She rushed back and roused her surly servants to action, crying for medicine and kettles of hot water, promising a footman a small fortune if only he could find a doctor.

"My husband?" she asked Peter Bennet. "I know you are most dreadfully ill, but my husband . . . ?"

"I don't know," said Peter faintly. "Oh God, my head."

He put a thin shaking hand up to the bloodstained and dirty bandage and moaned.

At that moment, the footman arrived triumphantly with the doctor in tow. Peter was pronounced not to be critical, although he had a high fever. The doctor turned his attention to the four other wounded men who lay in makeshift beds in Mary's sitting room. Mary frantically fought down her fears for her husband and listened carefully to the doctor's instructions. When he had gone, she busied herself attending to the wounded as the long hot day dragged on. And far away across the fields outside the city, the cannons of Waterloo began to sound, pounding and pounding through the heavy air. All day long the noise of cannons rolled, all day long Mary worked and prayed until she was dropping with exhaustion.

She had a brief visit from Mrs. Witherspoon, who soon lost interest when she found that Mary was not housing a title.

Mrs. Witherspoon was very sour. She had nursed a young man diligently all day, had given him her bed, and had paid the doctor, all in the belief that her patient was none other than the Duke of Hamden, only to find, when her patient had recovered enough to whisper his thanks, that she had wasted her time nursing a mere Mr. Hamden who was nothing more than a foot soldier. The glorious regimental jacket of the Hussars which had been draped round his shoulders had been put there by the sympathetic hands of his commanding officer.

By nightfall, the bells in all the steeples began to ring and the news was out. Napoleon was defeated. Waterloo had been held by the British and allies. Mary's servants promptly dropped their Bonapartiste sympathies and became tremendously pro-British, offering all kinds of help to the wounded, leaving Mary to fall into an exhausted sleep at last.

Lord Hubert Challenge rode wearily into Brussels on the following morning behind the ragged remains of his regimental band who were playing "Rule Britannia" in double quick time. The Duke of Wellington had forbade the playing of the song for fear it might offend the allied armies, but Hubert hadn't the heart to check them. He was bone weary, exhausted. He felt they had suffered a crushing defeat rather than a victory. So many, oh so many, dead.

Beside him rode Major Godwin in the tattered remains of his evening dress. But the sun shone bravely and the fickle people of Brussels were all out to cheer the victors and suddenly Hubert realized he was alive. By some miracle he had emerged from that dreadful carnage, unscathed.

He stared wonderingly down at his bloodstained uniform and marvelled that it was not his own blood. "Hey, be of cheer, man," he called across to Major Godwin. "Don't want Lucy to see you with a long face!"

Major Godwin brightened and his eyes began to search the crowds. "She's probably billeted with your wife," he said hopefully. "I asked Lady Mary to look after her."

Hubert felt an almost drunken sense of exhilaration, and his head reeled like the bells tumbling and clanging above in the city steeples. He reined in at his house and dismounted. As he turned round after tethering his horse, his first thought was to look up at the window to see if Mary was there. But suddenly a pair of white arms were wound round his neck and he looked, instead, down into the beautiful face of Clarissa. "See the conquering hero comes," she murmured.

He threw back his head and laughed, laughed because he was alive and there were still pretty women in the world. He bent his head and kissed her.

Upstairs, Mary let the curtain fall and turned and stared blindly across the darkened room, darkened so that the bright sunlight would not hurt the eyes of the wounded.

Her love for Hubert, that first, fragile, tender and delicate adolescent love, withered and died. Mary was a very human girl. She thirsted for revenge. She crossed to the looking glass and stared at her reflection, at the pale face with the wide eyes

161

and the demure wings of brown hair, then down at her fussy, frilly, outmoded gown. Her trousseau had been chosen by her mother.

As she heard her husband's heavy tread on the stairs, she muttered to herself, "I shall become the most dashing young matron in London. Two can play at that game and a married woman does not have the same restrictions as a young girl. Damn him to hell!"

Peter Bennet sat quietly in a chair in the corner, studying the expressions on her face. He had been looking out from another window and had seen Hubert's arrival. He felt bitterly sorry for Mary, but good breeding stopped him from interfering in a marriage which was none of his business.

"Mary!"

Lord Hubert stood in the doorway, his arms outstretched.

"I am glad you are safe, my lord," said Mary in a cold, formal voice. "But be so good as to lower your voice. We have wounded here."

Hubert looked around, aware of the other men in the room for the first time. Major Godwin walked in after him.

"Lucy?" asked the Major, staring at Mary, his eyes wide with hope.

Mary bit her lip, and Hubert saw her gray eyes were filled with pity for the large major. Then she walked forward and said softly, "Lucy has left for England, Major Godwin. I insisted that she go. You did place her in my care, after all."

The Major's face fell, but he tried to be fair. "Thank you, my lady, I am sure that was the best thing to do. But it sort of casts a fellow down, you know, to dream of nothing on the road home but of seeing his wife again, and to find . . ."

"There were very frightening rumors," interrupted Mary gently. "At one point it seemed almost certain that we had been defeated. Practically everyone was trying to flee. It was best that she should go."

"Yes, but *you* waited," pointed out the Major miserably.

"Then you must blame me," said Mary with a cheerfulness she did not feel. "I am afraid I all but *forced* your wife into the carriage. Now, sit down here by me and tell me about the battle and I shall send one of my servants to your lodgings to fetch you fresh linen."

Hubert watched her as she listened intently to the Major as

162

if he were the only man in the room. He found himself becoming very angry indeed. She should have been bustling about in a wifely manner, fetching *him* fresh clothes and seeing to his needs.

At last he could not bear it any longer and interrupted them with, "If you will excuse my wife, Major Godwin, I would like some words with her in private."

"Of course," mumbled the Major guiltily. "Forgot."

Hubert led Mary into the bedroom and slammed the door. "Well, madam," he grated. "Would you care to explain the coldness of my welcome?"

"What else could it be but cold?" said Mary lightly. "There is no love in our marriage as you have often pointed out."

"Your duty as a wife . . ."

"My duty, sirrah," said Mary tartly, "has been amply fulfilled. You have saved your family home through the marriage settlements. You have my money and that, my lord, is all you are going to get. I shall not interfere with your pleasures."

"How dare you! You lay in my arms not so many nights ago."

Mary winced. "You do not love me," she said flatly.

Hubert shook his head wearily. He felt he should apologize but it was not in the nature of his class to apologize for anything at all—particularly to one's wife.

"I find this shrewish discussion fatiguing," he said, beginning to strip off his clothes. "We must be in Paris in twelve days."

"You," said Mary evenly, "can go to Paris or go to hell for all I care. I shall be in London."

He whipped round and struck her across the face. She looked at him coldly and then turned on her heel and slammed the door.

He started after her to beg forgiveness. But what was the use. She was a woman, after all. And women never understood anything anyway. He was sorry he had struck her. The room suddenly seemed to swirl in front of him. God, he was tired! Mary must understand he was suffering from nerves and battle fatigue. He would make things all right with her. Just as soon as he had an hour's sleep. That was all he needed.

* * *

The clocks of Brussels were chiming eight o'clock in the evening when he finally awoke.

Mary sat on the cabin roof of a public boat and watched with dull eyes as the placid fields and quaint villages slid past. Across the fields, the spires of Ghent rose in the evening air. Behind lay Brussels, with its smells of blood and gangrene. She was going home.

She was going to change. First she would go to her parents' home and demand money—money to pay for the best dressmakers and hairdressers in the kingdom. "If a Clarissa is what he admires," she thought savagely, "a Clarissa is what he will get."

A little nagging voice in her brain tried to tell her she was being too hard on him, that she had not given him a chance, that he had been battle-weary and at the end of his tether, and that was why he had struck her. But the louder voice in her brain crying for revenge, crying over the ruin of wasted love, soon silenced the other.

Down below in the cabin she could hear the clink of glasses and the loud, jolly voices of her compatriots, celebrating their release from Brussels.

"He has won his battle," she thought grimly. "Now I must win mine. No man shall hurt me again. No man shall touch me again."

Chapter Three

THE TYRES, MARY'S parents, lived a prim well-ordered life in a prim well-ordered mansion. A trim line of pollarded elms marched all the way up to the well-scrubbed steps. The lawns were smooth and shaved like billiard tables, and the neat, well-ordered patchwork fields seemed to frown under the unruly shadows of the large fleecy clouds romping in an indecorous way across a pale blue summer sky.

Mrs. Tyre was as prim and upright as her home. She had gone into mourning some twenty years ago for a second cousin and had affected deep mourning ever since, enjoying the interest it caused, but always failing to discuss the reason for her mourning weeds, merely sighing mysteriously, into a black edged handkerchief, "Poor Albert." (Albert having been the name of the second cousin.) Her figure was spare and straight, with never an ounce of womanly flesh to relieve her stern silhouette. She had a neat, prim mouth and well guarded eyes which surveyed the world from behind a barrier of thin, white eyelashes. She wore black mittens, winter and summer, and her pale, lavender-scented skin was cold to the touch.

She kissed the air some two inches from her daughter's cheek and remarked in her high, drawling voice, "Do not, pray, fatigue me with boring battle stories, Mary. It's Waterloo this and Waterloo that, and one will be glad when one can return to the more important business of the everyday world. Now, why are you come home and where is your husband?"

Mary walked with her mother through the familiar dark square entrance hall which smelled of beeswax and woodsmoke. Mrs. Tyre kept fires burning in all rooms of the house despite the warmth of the sunny day outside.

"My husband is stationed in Paris with his regiment," said Mary, removing her bonnet. "I am come to ask for money."

"Money!" A startled look flashed across the arctic wastes of Mrs. Tyre's pale eyes. "We were exceeding generous with the marriage settlements."

"I know," said Mary, turning to face her mother at the door of the Rose Saloon. "But I am a lady of title now, mother, and it is essential that I dress according to my rank."

"Come in," said her mother holding open the door. "We cannot discuss such matters *devant les domestiques*."

The Rose Saloon remained the same. Perhaps it had been rosy sometime in the early eighteenth century when the house was built, but now it had plain white walls with the familiar prim landscapes of country roads running straight as rulers into the middle distance; or long lines of poplars running straight into the middle distance; or an avenue of funeral urns marching away into the middle distance. A straight, tall grandfather clock stood as rigidly as any soldier in the corner, its heavy tick-tock seeming to issue orders to the seconds—"Left-right! Left-right!"

Mrs. Tyre sat down on the very edge of an upright chair and placed her mittened hands along its arms, placed her feet neatly together and surveyed her daughter.

"Well, Mary, you may tell me now. What is all this fustian about dressing to suit your station in life. Did I not furnish you with a monstrous elegant trousseau?"

A thirst for revenge had made Mary dishonest. She knew she had only to appeal to her mother's snobbery and so she decided to lie.

"I had better explain," said Mary calmly. "I was at the Duchess of Richmond's ball in Brussels . . ."

"Indeed," said Mrs. Tyre with a pale smile of satisfaction. "The Duchess of Richmond. Very good."

"And," went on Mary, "I overheard the Duchess saying to her husband that the new Lady Challenge would do very well but 'twas a pity her clothes were so provincial."

"Indeed!" exclaimed Mrs. Tyre in quite a different tone of voice.

She sat for a long moment in complete silence while Mary patiently waited for her mother's snobbery to do its inevitable work.

"Very well," said Mrs. Tyre. "I appreciate your good sense, Mary. I am glad to see you have finally come to appreciate your position. Your clothes looked very well to me but . . . alas, I must admit I am not *au fait* with the current modes. How much?"

"Two thousand pounds," said Mary grimly, "just to start my wardrobe."

Mary had deliberately asked for much more than she needed. She knew instinctively that her mother would be impressed by the outrageous figure.

Mrs. Tyre's white lashes flickered rapidly, but she was too proud to say she was astonished at the amount. She felt, instead, a dawning admiration for her daughter.

"I shall speak to your father, Mary," she replied. "Now, why do you not go to your room and change for dinner. We still keep country hours you know."

Mary rose and went upstairs to her old familiar bedroom on the second floor. She sat down in the old ladder-backed chair by the open window, and felt her courage desert her.

She had written to her husband's servants at their town house, informing them of her imminent arrival. She had now all but got the money she required to cut a dash in polite society. But, how could she cut a dash when she suddenly felt very young, inexperienced and unsophisticated?

Mary conjured up a vision of her husband as a cold, autocratic boor. The more she concentrated on this image the more it solidified in her mind, until at the end of some half hour's meditation, she thoroughly hated her husband and was once again hell-bent on revenge.

Her lady's maid, Marie Juneaux, who had sulkily followed her mistress to this foreign land, answered Mary's summons and laid out a fussy, frilly dinner dress of pale pink sarcanet on the bed and proceeded to groom her mistress.

Mary entered the cool, square dining room with its square mahogany table and prim regiment of hard, upright chairs an hour later to greet her father.

Her father was fat where his wife was thin, but he contracted his bulk under a formidable pair of Cumberland corsets and, in general, contrived to look as prim as his wife. His shaven head was covered by a plain brown wig and he wore an old-fashioned chintz coat, a striped waistcoat and knee breeches.

He had a soft white face which seemed to be pinned in

place by two short narrow lines for the eyes, one short narrow vertical line for the nose and one long, thin horizontal line for the mouth. Mary had never really known her father, and often wondered if she ever would.

He did not ask her how she was after her journey, or waste any time at all on social chit-chat, but went straight to the point. "Your mother says you need two thousand pounds to rig yourself out in style," he remarked in that high drawling voice which was so like his wife's. "And so you shall have it. Never let it be said that a Tyre was not of the first stare."

"Thank you, father," murmured Mary. "I shall indeed do the family name credit, when I am suitable at-Tyred."

"Quite so. Now, come kiss me child, before we enjoy our dinner."

Mary dutifully bent over him as he screwed up his face until all the lines quite disappeared into the flesh. He looked for all the world like a singularly tough baby suffering its mother's embrace.

He then bent his head and said Grace, and the Tyre family began to eat in their usual silence. For as long as Mary could remember, there had been no conversation at mealtimes.

A soft twilight settled down on the garden outside, and, one by one, the birds went to sleep. Mary remembered the clamor and noise of Brussels and the booming of the guns sounding from the battlefield. For the first time she enjoyed the peace and dull quiet of her home.

But she excused herself directly after dinner and went back to her bedroom only to lie awake for a long time into the night, nourishing her anger against her husband, so that she might draw courage from it. She could not hope to conquer the fashionable world, but at least if she tried very, very hard she could make enough of a ripple in it and bring a look of surprise to her husband's arrogant face.

With a draft on her parents' bank securely in her reticule, Mary set out for London a week later. She had never stayed in London in her life before, she and her husband having spent the first days of their marriage with the Tyres, and then at a succession of posting houses in England and the Low Countries on the road to Brussels.

The noise and dirt and bustle of the great city alarmed her

and she shrank back against the squabs of the Tyre traveling carriage and wondered how on earth she was going to fare alone in this large city.

By the time the carriage rolled to a halt in front of the mansion in St. James's Square, she was feeling dirty and tired and defeated.

Her groom ran lightly up the steps to ring the bell, only finding, after repeated pulling on something like an organ stop, that it did not work. He applied himself to the knocker and at last the door swung open and the strangest butler Mary had ever seen stood on the threshold. He had a large squashed-looking face and little twinkling eyes like boot buttons. His livery consisted of a much darned, red military coat, worn over a yellowing white waistcoat and a yellow-white neckerchief.

His hair stood up like a scrubbing brush and was imperfectly powdered, making him look a bit like a porcupine that had strolled through a bucket of whitewash.

Behind him, a swarthy footman, who looked like a reformed assassin, was diligently swabbing the hall floor.

The butler made Mary a jerky little bow. Then he straightened up and saluted smartly. "Name of Biggs, my lady," he announced, staring straight ahead. "Butler to my lord. Servants present and correct, my lady. 'TENSHUN!"

A strange assortment of servants filed into the hall and lined up for their new mistress's inspection. Instead of livery, all wore remnants of military uniforms. The cook was a large, bearded highlander with a white apron tied over his kilt. Mary was introduced to them all. When the introductions were over, she sent her maid upstairs to superintend her unpacking and asked Biggs to follow her into a saloon on the first floor.

"Biggs," said Mary wonderingly, "are there no female servants employed in this household?"

"No, my lady," barked Biggs, springing to attention. "All of us is soldiers what was invalided home after the Peninsula so Captain Challenge—he was a captain then, my lady—he says he can't pay us much but he can house us and feed us and give us these here jobs."

Biggs suddenly ran his thick hands through his hair making it stand more on end than ever, producing a small cloud of flour dust. "See here, my lady," he said anxiously, looking full at Mary for the first time. "We're a rough and ready lot, ma'am, and we've not been in the way of being servants except to His Majesty, King George, so to speak, and God bless him, but we has kept the house as clean as a pin."

Mary looked about her. The saloon was very large. The floor was scrubbed and bare. A few dingy, dark paintings ornamented the faded wallpaper, and a few ancient chairs stood about the room, looking as if they had dropped in a century ago for a visit and had not yet summoned up the social courage to leave. The room was dominated by a vast black marble fireplace depicting the rape of some unfortunate Greek maidens who screamed soundlessly into the long room.

"How can I become fashionable with such unfashionable servants as these?" thought Mary. But, sheltered as her life had been, she had heard many stories of soldiers starving in the gutters of London when their country no longer needed them. So instead, she cleared her throat nervously and said, "Yes, I can see the house is very clean, Biggs, but sorely in need of carpets and curtains and furniture. Also, you must order livery *immediately* for yourself and the other servants. This day, I shall make good your wages. You will be paid as fits your station in this household."

"Thank you, my lady," said Biggs, and to Mary's embarrassment she thought she heard the sound of tears at the back of the butler's voice. "We never thought for a minute you would let us stay, ma'am. I took a ball in the chest at Salamanca and it's still in there somewhere."

He stiffly saluted. "Just you give orders and we will follow them out, ma'am—my lady. Stand by you to the death, we will. Lay down our lives for you!"

Mary felt a lump in her own throat but she answered quietly. "I shall indeed need your help, Biggs. I am determined to surprise your master by becoming the fashion. I shall need to set up my stables since he is still in Paris. I must also find a good dressmaker, which is really why I would have liked to see some female member of the staff. My own maid is still new to London."

Biggs's face lit up with genuine joy at being able to help. "James, the first footman, my lady, him what got it in the leg at Vittoria, is a-courting a housemaid at the Duchess of Badmont's. I'll send him there drecktly and he will find your ladyship all necessary directions. As to your stables, ma'am, you can't do better than to ask John, the groom who looked after the best horses in the cavalry and he got his in the arm, my lady, at Badajoz. I knows Gilberts is the best warehouse for furnishings, my lady, and I shall have a gent from that there establishment call any time you wish. We are sparse on provisions in the kitchens, my lady, so if you were desirous of a tasty dinner, it would be . . ."

"Send all bills to my mother and father," said Mary firmly, "and order all that is necessary for the kitchens." She sent up a private prayer that her parents' snobbery would honor the bills. "I am sure you will prove a good general, Biggs."

Biggs saluted. "Sergeant, my lady. Sergeant Biggs it is."

Mary dismissed him with a nod of her head and Biggs clattered joyfully off down the stairs, his heavy boots doing a sort of clog hornpipe.

Mary rested her chin on her hand and prayed for courage. Perhaps she was lucky in these strange servants. A fashionable butler would not have been nearly so sympathetic.

"I shall become fashionable," she vowed, "even if I kill myself in the process."

And during the next few weeks, she indeed thought at times she might die from exhaustion. The house was jam-packed from morning to night with a succession of dress-makers, milliners, haberdashers, decorators, carpenters and grocers.

Many cards were deposited on the hall table, but Mary did not yet feel ready to venture into society. The court hairdresser himself cropped her long hair into a short cap of saucy curls, and although Marie Juneaux, the lady's maid, assured her mistress it was all the crack, Mary felt very strange, getting a shock every time she caught her reflection in the looking glass.

At last the day arrived when she felt ready to receive visitors. She informed Biggs—resplendent in a new claret and silver livery—that she was "at home."

The house was not as large as many of the other London town houses, but it had a certain quiet charm. The ground floor boasted two public rooms, a study and a library, the first floor, four connecting saloons, each now decorated in a different color, the third floor held the bedrooms, including a new suite for his lordship and one for her ladyship, as well as the guest bedrooms, and the top floor, a chain of attics.

The saloon where Mary had first interviewed Biggs was now called the Green Saloon, its walls now panelled in green watered silk. The black marble fireplace was still there but did not seem so grim, now that the rest of the room was softened by rugs and vases of flowers and *objets d'art*. Brussels-lace curtains floated beside the open windows, for the weather remained sunny and warm.

Mary now sat in the Green Saloon. Her cropped hair had given her face an elfin look, and her gray eyes looked larger than ever. She was wearing a deceptively simple white muslin dress, tied under the bosom with long gold ribbons. The delicate white of her gown gave Mary a charming look of vulnerable virginity. She longed for a friend or companion to support her in her debut. In fact, she longed for any company but that of her husband.

All at once, she heard Biggs's heavy tread of the stairs. He had changed his thick-soled boots for a pair of equally thick-soled shoes and was so obviously proud of his new feathers that Mary had not had the heart to tell him that a good servant should be seen and never heard.

He swung open the double doors and announced, "Mr. and Mrs. Witherspoon and the Honorable Cyril Trimmer," and with a click of his heels, and a stiff salute, he clattered off, leaving Mary to rise and greet her guests with a sinking heart.

"La! Don't we look grand!" cried Mrs. Witherspoon, seizing Mary in a hot embrace. "We called and called and you wasn't at home but Mr. Witherspoon says to me, he says, 'Lady Challenge won't forget a promise not after the way we took care of Mrs. Godwin,' so here we are."

The Witherspoons were exactly as Mary remembered them in Brussels. Mrs. Witherspoon's bosom and turban were the same. Both she and her husband carried the same ingratiating leer. Their companion, the Honorable Cyril Trimmer, came forward to be introduced.

To Mary's inexperienced eyes, he looked a very grand young man indeed. His cravat was like a foot high snow drift, and his coat of Bath superfine had the highest, most buckram-wadded shoulders she had ever seen and was nipped in at the waist and very full about the skirt.

His waistcoat was embroidered with a whole covey of scarlet and gold pheasants and his very thin, very long legs were encased in lavender pantaloons ornamented down the sides with a multitude of vertical black silk stripes. His pale blue eyes held a calm contented look of absolute stupidity, and his sparse light brown hair was pomaded and curled and waved into an elaborate style. He had an eyeglass wedged in one eye so tightly that Mary could not help wondering if he ever managed to get it out. Mr. Trimmer had compressed his mouth into a tiny fashionable "O," from which emerged a thin, ultra-refined fluting voice. He looked as if his governess had made him practice saying his prunes and prisms for years.

Mary was very impressed.

He made her a very low bow, pointing his left foot with all the elegance of a ballet master. "Charmed, Lady Challenge. Utterly charmed," he said.

He sat down beside Mary on one of the new backless sofas, arranging his coat skirts very carefully. "And now, Lady Challenge," he began, "you must tell me how you go on. Look here, interested in fine women, don't you see. Ecod!"

Having made this speech, he relapsed into silence.

Biggs and two of the footmen entered, bearing trays of cakes and wine. Mrs. Witherspoon stared at the servants avidly as they thrust the trays in front of her with military precision. Then having seen that Mrs. Witherspoon and the other guests were served, they wheeled about, formed a line and filed out before Biggs, who stood grimly at the door as if taking a march past.

"Shoulders back! Heads up, men!" rapped Biggs, swinging into line behind the last of them.

"Well, I never did!" crowed Mrs. Witherspoon in amazement. "What odd servants!"

"They are all ex-soldiers," said Mary gently.

"Oooh! You must be careful, my dear," cried Mrs. Witherspoon. "These men come from the gutter. Very useful when there's a war on but after all . . ."

"After all, I do not know what I would have done without them," said Mary firmly. "I have never known such a loyal hard-working bunch of men before."

Mary listened in surprise to the sound of her own voice. She had never taken a social stand on anything before. But she had just done it and, although Mrs. Witherspoon's habitual leer seemed a trifle fixed, the heavens hadn't fallen in. Suddenly Mary found that her new gown did not feel in the least strange, and she caught a glimpse of herself in a looking glass on the opposite wall and saw to her surprise that she actually looked quite fashionable. She realized that she had not answered Mr. Trimmer's question.

"I have not been anywhere," she confessed. "I have been putting things in order here and I had to arrange a new wardrobe since my old one was sadly unfashionable."

"I think you are very fashionable," said Mr. Trimmer. "I am accounted an expert in such matters, Lady Challenge. Permit me to be your escort and guide in society."

Mary blinked and then recovered her composure. She had been about to point out that she was married but surely, this very fashionable young man was just the sort of person she needed to show her husband that she could attract a spendid member of the *beau monde*.

She smiled and thanked him, and then caught a little triumphant look that flashed between Mr. and Mrs. Witherspoon and wondered why.

She did not know that the acute social climbing Witherspoons had quickly divined Mr. Trimmer's problem. He wished a young lady to squire around to save himself from the unfashionable stigma of effeminacy. Unfortunately, he had very little fortune, although he was related to a duke, and fashionable young ladies were apt to dislike his posturing. The Witherspoons had promised to find him just the young lady to suit his needs and of course, should his noble relative, the duke, ever consider inviting them to a little soiree or something of that nature, they would be grateful to accept an invitation. They decided to strike while the iron was hot.

"We are making up a little party tonight," said Mr. Witherspoon. "A little evening at the opera and supper afterwards. Mrs. Godwin is our guest. Her husband is still in foreign parts."

"Yes, indeed," burst in his wife. "Poor little Mrs. Godwin. She does hang around us so. Of course, we did say to her not to feel under any obligation to us, although we did arrange for her to leave Brussels but, I declare, she loves us for ourselves alone."

"Ecod! I say, who wouldn't?" put in Mr. Trimmer gallantly.

Mary thought quickly. She did not want to go with the Witherspoons nor did she want to see Lucy again. But she did so long for a little gaiety. The monster she had created out of her husband lurked always in the back of her mind. Why should she pine alone, while he frolicked with the *mademoiselles* in Paris and did not even find time to write?

She accordingly said she would be delighted. Mr. Trimmer indicated to the less fashionable Witherspoons that ten minutes had passed since they had arrived and that to stay longer would, of course, be monstrous vulgar. He took his leave with many elaborate bows and great wavings of a scented handkerchief.

After they had all left, Mary ran lightly to her bedchamber to begin preparations for her social debut. She finally decided on a pale green lingerie gown cut fashionably low on the bosom, with an over-tunic of tobacco brown velvet trimmed with gold bugle beads. The hairdresser was summoned to brush her short curls into the style known as *à la Titus*. She debated whether to carry a lace muff, and decided against it, substituting a handsome painted fan with mother of pearl sticks. The hairdresser finished his art by placing a little coronet of gold silk roses on top of her shining curls. With great daring, she applied a little rouge to each of her pale cheeks.

When she descended the stairs that evening to where the Witherspoons and Mr. Trimmer were waiting, her heart misgave her. Her ensemble, which had seemed so elegant in the privacy of her bedchamber, now seemed shabby in front of the magnificence of her escort.

Mr. Trimmer was wearing a blue silk evening coat which was padded on the chest as well as the shoulders, and his waist appeared smaller than Mary's own. His face was highly painted, and his hair gleamed with Rowlandson's maccassar oil. His silk waistcoat was embroidered with brilliants, his knee breeches were skin tight and his white silk stockings had large clocks on the sides, and his legs appeared to have grown muscular calves, which indeed they had, his valet having arranged a false, wooden calf in each stocking.

His gaze, however, was more vacant than ever, and Mary finally realized that Mr. Trimmer was a trifle disguised, having resorted to the brandy bottle before leaving his apartments and therefore would not have noticed had she descended the stairs in sackcloth.

"Tol rol, Lady Challenge," said that young gentleman, waggling his fingers at her by way of greeting. "Tol rol."

Mrs. Witherspoon again crushed Mary to her bosom while her husband leered fondly on. "And if she isn't my own sweet love," cooed Mrs. Witherspoon. "I declare you are like a sister to me, so I shall call you Mary and you shall call me Marie. Little Mrs. Godwin is going to join us in our box. Now hant you got any jewels, dear?"

"I did not consider jewelry necessary," said Mary, feeling that Mrs. Witherspoon's personal remarks were the outside of enough. "I am sure you have enough for both of us."

This indeed was true, Mrs. Witherspoon's massive bosom being laid out with gems like a jeweler's tray.

Mary felt suddenly depressed. Mr. Trimmer was surely very fine but the vulgar, pushing Witherspoons were a decided disadvantage.

Mr. Trimmer however seemed much struck with Mary, volunteering that he thought her "a deuced fine girl."

And Mary, who was unused to receiving praise, blossomed under his flowery compliments and soon began to look forward to the evening after all. When she sailed out of the house on Mr. Trimmer's arm, her only regret was that her horrible husband could not see her at that very moment.

The short carriage ride through the cobbled streets was exciting, flambeaux blazing outside the mansions, carriage lights winking like fireflies, carriage wheels rumbling like thunder as polite society came awake for the evening.

The Haymarket Theater was ablaze with candles from top to bottom, and myriads of jewels flashed on bosoms and cravats behind the red curtains of the boxes.

Lucy Godwin was already waiting for them, escorted by a very aloof young man who volunteered the information that he was Giles Bartley. Bartley stared at the magnificent Mr. Trimmer through his quizzing glass, remarked loudly and rudely, "By God!" He paid them no further attention, flirting desperately with Lucy instead.

Lucy at last turned her attention to Mary. "Isn't it fun with our husbands away?" she whispered. "This is our last evening of freedom, though."

"What?" cried Mary.

"Shhh!" admonished several voices from the neighboring boxes for the opera had begun.

Mary sat in an agony of worry as Catalini's shrill voice soared from the stage to drown out the chorus and the orchestra. Was he back already? Was that what Lucy had meant? She tried to concentrate her attention on the stage, but the colors swam and blurred before her worried eyes.

Lord Hubert Challenge strode into the hall of his town house and blinked in surprise. The tiled floor gleamed like a looking glass, the walls were painted Nile green, flowers glowed from vases on occasional tables, and a new turkey-red carpet climbed the staircase to the upper floors.

He then focused his gaze on the splendor of his butler, Biggs, who stood preening himself in his new livery.

"Am I in the right house?" asked Lord Hubert wonderingly.

"Indeed that you are," beamed Biggs. "Missus—I mean, my lady—has put everything in order, including me."

Biggs turned slowly so that his master could admire the effect.

"Very fine," commented Lord Hubert dryly. "Where is my lady?"

"Gone to the opera," said Biggs, running his stubby fingers through his powdered hair and sending a cloud of flour-dandruff onto the claret-colored shoulders of his livery.

"Not alone, I trust."

Biggs shuffled in his heavy shoes. "Well, no, my lord. There was a kind of tailor's dummy called Mr. Trimmer . . ."

"Good God!"

"Zackly. And a couple of mushrooms by the name of Witherspoon."

"I think I had better change and join my wife, if I can tear her away from that man-milliner," said Lord Hubert grimly.

He mounted the stairs two at a time and was bathed and barbered by his valet while he stared around at the splendor of his new apartment. His favorite hunting pictures had been cleaned and rehung on tasteful pastel walls. His ancient four-poster bed had been hung with new curtains, and when he sat gingerly down on the edge of it, he discovered it boasted a new feather mattress.

He was pleased with the transformation, but at the same time he felt Mary might at least have waited for his return. He had not thought of her much when he was in Paris. She was a woman, after all, and women were subject to all sorts of fits and tantrums. He had only behaved like a husband, and she had reacted like a typical wife. He had nothing to reproach himself with.

At last, resplendent in dark blue evening coat, exquisite cravat and knee breeches, he set out for the opera to find his wife.

As he was entering the theater, he met a doleful-looking Major Godwin who told him that he too, was in search of his wife.

"We're a bit late," said Hubert cheerfully. "We'll take my box and then catch them when the performance is over."

When they were ensconced in his box, he pulled aside the red curtains and, raising his quizzing glass, stared across the brightly lit theater. He could not see his wife at all.

"There's Lucy!" suddenly whispered the Major. Lord Hubert followed his pointing finger and gave a start of surprise. For seated next to Lucy was a vastly attractive young lady who could not possibly be the pale, colorless girl he had married. But it must be! There were the Witherspoons and there, by all heaven, was that court card, Trimmer.

At the same time, Mary looked across the theater and saw him. Her eyes immediately darted away and he realized in some bewilderment that Mary did not want him to know she had recognized him. Then she turned and laughed over her shoulder to Mr. Trimmer—and there was no doubt about it. Mary was flirting! And she wanted him to know it!

He leaned lazily back in his chair, beginning to feel amused. What a naive girl she was, despite her new appearance! Did she honestly think he could be made jealous by a fool like Trimmer? Obviously she did.

Then he noticed Lady Clarissa, with a party in a box near his own. He decided to go and flirt with Clarissa and see how his little wife liked that. He still felt terribly amused by the whole situation. The fact that his flirting with Clarissa would hurt his wife never entered his head. Mary was a woman, after all, and women naturally did not suffer from the same deep and intense feelings as men.

Major Godwin was already rising to join his wife. "Don't know what Lucy thinks she's doing with that feller but I'm going to throw him out that box right now."

"You would fare better if you threw your wife out," retorted Lord Hubert lazily, but Major Godwin had already gone.

Lord Hubert made his way to Clarissa's box where he received a very warm welcome indeed. Viscount Perry was not in evidence, and Clarissa quickly vouchsafed the information that her fiancé was abroad "on business."

Across the theater, Mary tried not to stare. She felt shocked and miserable. She had built up a picture in her mind of her husband as a beetle-browed, sweaty, boorish soldier. She had forgotten he was so handsome, with those black wings of hair falling over his high-nosed, tanned face. She had forgotten he could look so elegant. Suddenly, Mr. Trimmer appeared silly, fussy, stupid and overdressed. When she had flirted with him, she had caught the amused and cynical look her husband had thrown in her direction and had blushed to the soles of her feet. She had hoped to make him jealous by becoming a fashionable young lady. How on earth could he find her fashionable, accompanied as she was by this fop, by two of London's most vulgar Cits and that silly, fickle beauty Lucy Godwin, who seemed determined to torture her patient husband.

Mary sat miserably deaf to the music, learning one of her first hard lessons—that you cannot choose your friends for any reason other than friendship. Choose them for reflected glory, choose them to help you cut a dash, and in the long run you are left looking very silly—and friendless.

She saw Hubert's handsome head bent over Clarissa's beautiful one, and all her misery fled in a burst of rage and her courage came back. How dare he! How dare he, on his first night home, flirt with that . . . that *doxy*. How could she be so naive as to have ever believed there was one ounce of good in the beautiful Clarissa? Mary clenched her fan so violently that the sticks snapped.

There was further humiliation in store for her. Her handsome husband was, admittedly, waiting for her in the press in the theater foyer after the show.

Admittedly, he was alone.

But he treated her as if she were some tiresome little cousin up from the country. He bent his head and kissed her hand lightly, wished her the pleasure of her company of friends in a light mocking voice which bordered on insult, and said he was going to Watier's for a rubber of piquet and would, no doubt, see her later.

There was worse to come. After her husband had melted off into the crowd, Mary heard a loud, carrying female voice declaring with awful clarity, "Did you see the new Lady Challenge? Pretty little thing, ain't she, but no *ton*. And such company! Even Brummell couldn't bring her into fashion now."

That voice resounded in her ears even as she sat at her dressing table later that evening, after dismissing her maid. She had taken off her cambric wrapper and was sitting gloomily in a near transparent Indian muslin nightgown. She might have felt less miserable had she known that the famous Beau Brummell, that arbiter of fashion and leader of the *beau monde*, had also heard the spiteful remark and had not liked it one bit.

There was a faint scratching at the door and she swung round. Her husband strolled into the room.

"God, I'm tired, Mary," he yawned, beginning to tear off his cravat.

Mary turned back to the looking glass.

"Get out," she said in an even tone.

The hand tugging at the cravat stopped. Hubert turned and looked at his wife. She certainly had become an amazingly pretty girl, he noticed, with her saucy brown curls peeping out from under a lacy nightcap, and tantalizing glimpses of her white body showing through the thin stuff of her nightgown.

"I know what it is," he said with an indulgent laugh. "You haven't forgiven me for that scene in Brussels. Well, I apologize. I kneel before you. I kiss your feet." He suited the action to the words.

Mary jerked her feet under her chair and glared at him like an infuriated kitten. "I don't like you, Hubert," she explained in a maddening voice of weary patience. "Do get up and stop making a cake of yourself."

Hubert rose, hanging onto his fast mounting temper. He

tried to kiss her cheek, but she ducked her head and his kiss landed on the top of her cap.

"Look, Mary," said Hubert, standing back apace. "I know you were trying to make me jealous this evening. But you must do far better than that idiot Trimmer."

"I was NOT trying to make you jealous. 'Tis only your overweening conceit that makes you think so, sir."

"By God," he said. "I've a good mind to teach you a lesson."

"Don't you dare touch me," cried Mary, leaping to her feet and backing to the other side of the room. She suddenly became aware that she was dressed only in the transparent nightgown, and a furious blush seemed to cover her whole body. "You have my money," she shouted, goaded beyond reason by rage and embarrassment. "Must you rape me as well?"

"I wouldn't need to," he said, becoming as cold as he had been hot a minute before. "But I do not waste my talents on gauche, little schoolgirls who think they are cutting a dash by being escorted by the silliest fribble in London."

"Just you wait!" howled Mary, jumping up and down with rage.

"I am too bored to school you tonight," he said, walking over and casually flicking her under the chin. "You need a lesson in how to behave like a wife."

"You would beat me?"

"I would kiss you."

Before she had time to retreat, he clipped her in his arms and forced his mouth down on hers. She struggled furiously to no avail, and then decided to stand cold and unresponsive in his arms. He relaxed the pressure of his lips and began instead to move them gently back and forth against her own until he felt her lips begin to tremble against his. She felt her bones melting and her senses reeling.

"Oh, Hubert," she sighed against his mouth.

He abruptly released her and gave her a hearty slap across the buttocks. "Good night, my sweet," he remarked cheerfully, and striding out of the room, slammed the door behind him.

Chapter Four

𝒯HE USUAL UNPREDICTABILITY of the English weather struck fashionable London. A greasy drizzle fell steadily, trickling down the windows of Mary's bedroom in sad little tears. The weather had turned chilly as well, and Mary's sheets already felt damp to her touch.

She felt tired and low and despondent. She had lain awake into the small hours, waiting in dread in case her husband should visit her bedroom; or rather part of her mind dreaded the visit and another small mischievous part hoped that he would.

When her maid, Marie Juneaux, arrived with the morning's post and the morning's chocolate, Mary settled back against her pillows to survey the sheaf of letters which were, as usual, mostly bills. Then a gilt-edged card caught her eye. Someone—Biggs probably—had written laboriously in pencil, "delivered by hand."

She picked it up and squinted at the convoluted script, and then lit her bed candle and leaning over, scanned the lines and then read them again, as if she could not believe her eyes. The Duchess of Pellicombe requested the pleasure of Lady Mary Challenge at a ball that very evening!

Mary had not been very long in town—but long enough to know that the Duchess was one of London's highest sticklers. An invitation to her home was tantamount to a royal command. It was almost insulting that the card should have arrived at the last minute. But then, perhaps the formidable Duchess had only just learned of her existence.

She was not to know, until long afterwards, that she owed the invitation to the wiles of Beau Brummell. That fashionable leader had been determined to prove that he *could* make Lady Challenge the fashion, and had accordingly used his considerable influence on the Duchess.

A footman entered with a coal scuttle and proceeded to light a fire in the grate. The cheerful light from the flames soon danced around the walls and Mary began to feel very excited indeed. She had a new ball gown which had, so far, never been out of its wrappings. She lay back against the pillows and dreamed of entering the ballroom on her husband's arm, basking in the glory of his admiring stare.

Her husband!

She sat bolt upright in bed. He must go with her. She could not go without an escort.

She rang the bell and when her maid arrived, began to dress feverishly. She ran lightly down the stairs to the dining room to find her husband had already finished his breakfast and was preparing to leave. She rushed into speech.

"My lord,"—she waved the gilt-edged card excitedly—"I have here an invitation to the Duchess of Pellicombe's. Do say you will go with me."

Hubert stared down at the card and then flicked it with his finger. "I see my name is not on the invitation," he remarked lazily. "In any case, I have other plans for this evening. You did say, did you not, that you would not interfere with my . . . er . . . pleasures?"

"But I must have an escort," wailed Mary staring at him with wide, shocked eyes. "I do not know of any woman who could act as chaperone. I do not know any man who . . ." She broke off and bit her lip.

"Exactly," said Lord Hubert. "Your friend Trimmer. I am sure he will do very nicely."

"But I don't want to go with him. I want to go with you. How can you be so stupid!" cried Mary, stamping her foot in exasperation.

"You must learn that you cannot insult me one minute and ask favors of me the next," said Hubert in an indifferent voice. "The fact remains that I am not going with you."

He gave her a slight bow and strode from the room, leaving Mary to burst into stormy tears.

Mary bitterly wondered what was happening to her.

She was behaving like a spoilt child. She had been disappointed before, many times, and each of those times she had borne her disappointment with stoic calm.

"What is happening to me?" she wailed out loud, clutching a sodden piece of cambric handkerchief.

"I'm sure I don't know, my lady," came the voice of Biggs from the sideboard. Mary turned round. Through a mist of tears, she saw the broad back of her butler, his head bent over a dish of grilled kidneys which he was examining with intense concentration.

"Oh, I didn't know you were in the room, Biggs," said Mary, trying to recover.

Had Biggs been a properly trained butler of many years standing, he would have bowed and left the room. But he was not. He was an old soldier with an ugly, pudgy face and a graceless, stocky body—and a heart as big as St. James's Square. So instead, he edged nearer to the table and said in a hushed voice, "If there is anything I can do to help, my lady . . . anything at all."

Mary ran distracted fingers through her mop of curls. "I can't tell you, Biggs. It's something you can't help me with. I can't possibly tell you." Mary's voice choked.

"There, there, my lady," said Biggs. "You tell old Biggsy and you'll feel better."

And Mary did. Mary who had never discussed anything with a servant in her life since her mama had taught her that to do so would be vulgar in the extreme and, furthermore, would cause a revolution among the "lower orders."

Biggs listened carefully, his great head on one side and then an unholy twinkle lit up his small eyes.

"Well, now, my lady," he said slowly. "I might just have the answer to your problem but you'll probably not like it."

"Oh, I will! I will!" cried Mary, grasping hold of the butler's hand.

"See now," said Biggs awkwardly, "it's like this. When I was in the army, we had a lot of them there theatricals and me and some of the lads used to dress up and act in the plays, seeing as how the Duke, God bless 'im, liked a bit of theatre around the camp.

"Now in one of them plays, I took the part of a Spanish lady of quality. I was the Marquise Elvira Dobones deLorca y Viedda y Crummers. One of the officers wrote the play. Very naughty it was an' all. I still have the costume belowstairs. Very grand costume it is, too, for it belonged originally to one of them great Spanish ladies. So, if I were to put it on and keep me trap shut, and sit with the chaperones, you could go to your ball. 'Course, we mustn't tell his lordship for though he's the finest man in the English army, he can be a bit of a tartar."

"It would never do," said Mary dismally, while her eyes began to fill with tears again. "It . . ."

"What the hell is going on here?"

Lord Hubert stood glaring from the doorway. Mary became aware she was still clutching the butler's hand and blushed fiery red.

"My lady had something in her eye and I was endeavoring for to take it out," said Biggs woodenly.

"Really?" commented his lordship cynically. Then his shrewd eyes noticed his wife's tear-stained face. He walked towards the table and stood over her.

"I gather you have been crying like Cinderella, because you cannot go to the ball. Very well then, my child. If it means so much to you, I shall take you."

But a few minutes ago Mary would have thrown herself into his arms had he volunteered to escort her. But now, Biggs's sympathy had made her resent what she now considered to be a piece of autocratic condescension.

"I don't want to go now," she remarked, wondering in amazement if her voice sounded as childish and sulky to her lord as it did to herself. Evidently it did.

"Sulk, then," said Lord Hubert carelessly. And the next second he was gone.

"Now you've been and gone and done it," said Biggs with gloomy relish. "It would have been silly of me to go with you my lady. I don't know what came over me."

"Oh, please Biggs . . . do try," cried Lady Mary, while somewhere in the back of her brain, the old self-controlled, madonna-like Mary looked on in amazement at the vacillating child she had become.

Lord Hubert Challenge had dreamt of this sort of evening for a long time. Now he was beginning to wonder why he wasn't enjoying it one bit.

He was ensconced in his club with a few of his favorite military friends. The play was deep, the wine was good, and a huge log fire crackled in the club fireplace, dispersing the unseasonable chill of the evening. For the drizzle had changed to a downpour, slashing against the windows, driven by a wild gale. He was both comfortable and fashionably dressed in a double-breasted tail coat with a deep M-shaped collar, short-waisted waistcoat and close fitting knee-breeches. He had run into the Duke of Pellicombe earlier in the day and the Duke had been almost alarmingly effusive in his apologies. He would deem it a tremendous honor if Challenge would but grace his wife's little ball. Hubert had said firmly that he had a previous commitment but had, nonetheless, accepted the card which the Duke had pressed upon him.

He shifted slightly in his chair and he could feel the stiff edges of the card in his pocket pressing against his hip. Well, he had offered to escort her, hadn't he? And she had refused, hadn't she? And furthermore, she was a silly chit and he didn't care a rap for her . . . did he? But she was his wife and dammit, he had to admit he had not liked to see her cry.

He abruptly stood up and walked to the window and stared out into the street where a lamplighter battled with the gale, nipping up and down the posts like a monkey, filling the lamps from his oil can. The cowls on the chimney tops spun round and round, sending streams of black smoke down into the rain-drenched street below.

All at once he remembered the rain-soaked fields of Waterloo. He turned and looked at his group of friends round the card table. How few of them had survived! All at once the screams of the wind were the screams of the wounded and dying. Damn it all! He was blue-devilled. He would go to the ball after all.

When he arrived at his house to deliver the news to his wife, it was to discover with some anger that she had left. Asked who was escorting her, his footman became shifty-looking and muttered that it was by some Spanish lady.

"Probably some mushroom friend that the Witherspoons picked up in Brussels," he thought haughtily.

He changed quickly into his ball dress, allowed his thick black hair to be teased into the artistic disorder of a style called *coup de vent*, tucked his *chapeau bras* under his arm and set out.

* * *

Some streets away, Lucy Godwin strode up and down the room waiting for her husband to get ready. "I declare I do not know what is taking you this age," she stormed. "I had as well gone with young Haverstock. He dances so exquisitely. Do you remember . . . ?"

"Young Haverstock died with a ball in his heart," said Major Godwin as he struggled with the intricacies of his cravat.

Lucy bit her lip in vexation. "Now you have upset me by talking of death."

"I am sorry, my dear," replied the Major quietly. "It seems as if death is my trade. I shall never forget that battle, or the useless waste. So very many dead."

"Ooooh!" cried Lucy, bursting into ready tears. "Are we to have no fun? You make me feel guilty. You prose so."

The Major turned slowly. Large tears were rolling down Lucy's heart-shaped face.

"There now," he said in a softer voice. "You are spoiling your looks, my sweetheart. Come, I am an old bear to depress you so. I shall be the happiest man at the ball tonight if only you will smile on me."

Lucy gave him a petulant, watery smile. And with that he had to be content, although his heart was very sore. He was still troubled by feverish nightmares of death and disaster. But he was a mean and selfish brute to expect this fairy-like creature to share his grim agonies. Wasn't he . . . ?

Mary Challenge found that she was able to forget her husband for at least two whole minutes at a time. She was the *succès fou* of the evening. She had entered the ballroom very nervously escorted by Biggs, expecting any minute that someone would cry, "Imposter!" But it had all gone as smoothly as a dream. Biggs, a splendid Marchese in purple velvet, lavishly trimmed with crystals from the dining room chandelier, and with his brushlike hair covered by an enormous turban, had sailed off sedately to sit with the chaperones. Mary was quickly taken in charge by none other than the famous Mr. Brummell himself. She was at first overawed, but he seemed to find everything she said so excruciatingly funny that she began to relax after her first surprise, and when he at last asked her how she was enjoying her first season, she found the courage to reply calmly, "Absolutely terrifying, Mr. Brummell," which sent the famous Beau off into whoops.

Her success was assured. Everyone was anxious to find what it was about Lady Mary which had kept London's leader of fashion so amused.

Without his patronage, most might have found her a pretty enough girl with her large clear eyes and saucy fair curls tied up in a gold filet to match her gold-spangled gown. But because of the Beau's obvious interest, she was at once declared to be "quite beautiful" and her dance card was quickly filled.

Mary was determined to enjoy her success, and the only thing she found lacking was that her infuriating husband was not present to see it. Even the arrival of Lady Clarissa, who was dressed in silver gauze, damped so that it molded her body, could not dim Mary's enjoyment.

She was, however, slightly disturbed to notice that minx Lucy Godwin flirting with all and sundry, while her large husband propped up one of the pillars and watched. It really was too bad of the girl, thought Mary, smiling sympathetically across at him.

The next dance was a waltz and as Mary had not yet received permission to dance it, she decided to stroll over and join her friend, the "Marquise." But before she could reach Biggs, she was accosted by Major Godwin.

"I say, Lady Challenge," he began. "I must speak to you. Just a little of your time."

Mary nodded and took his arm and they walked to the adjoining saloon where refreshments were being served. The Major found them a table in a corner, away from the other guests. He sat down heavily and looked at Mary like a large, sad dog who has just received a whipping from its master.

"I don't know how to begin," he blurted out at last.

"It's Lucy, isn't it?" asked Mary gently. "She is very young, you know."

"But dash it all, we're *married*," groaned the Major. "I try to tell her not to flirt with the other fellows and she glares at me and calls me an old stick-in-the-mud. I tell you Lady Challenge, it's no go. You're a fine girl but you cannot understand what it means to love someone desperately and not be loved in return."

Mary's beautiful eyes filled with tears as she felt a sympathetic knot of pain in her stomach. "Oh, yes I know," she said sadly.

The Major fingered his sideburns and looked at her awkwardly. "I say, I didn't know. You mean . . . ?"

Mary nodded. The burden of her unrequited love for her husband was suddenly too much for her to bear alone. For in that second she realized bitterly that she loved him with all her heart.

"Perhaps," she volunteered slowly, "your situation is not as bad as mine. You see, Hubert married me for my money. He never pretended anything else. But Lucy must have loved you."

"She did at first," said the Major, covering Mary's hand with his own large one. "Those were marvellous days. Then we came to London. After that she had no time for me. She . . . she said I had stolen her youth."

Mary pressed his hand in return and forbore from remarking that Lucy Godwin had obviously read too many novels.

"La! How comfortable you look together. 'Tis said you are the latest fashion, Mary. So you are become like the rest of us. Setting up a flirt!"

Lady Clarissa stood looking down at their joined hands, her cat's eyes alight with lazy malice. Mary snatched her hand from the Major's, but not before her startled eyes had caught sight of the tall figure of her husband blocking the doorway.

"I doubt if I shall ever become so fashionable," said Mary quietly. "Major Godwin is a friend. You must not mistake friendship and loyalty for anything else, Lady Clarissa. Love is a different matter."

"In what way," drawled her husband, strolling up to their table. He had only just caught Mary's last remarks.

Clarissa swung round so that the drying gauze of her dress floated out from her body, showing tantalizing glimpses of the white flesh beneath. "Hubert darling," she exclaimed, clinging to his arm. "Your little wife was just expounding upon the virtues of love. She and Major Godwin make quite a fuss about it."

"Indeed!" said Hubert casually. "You must tell me all about it, Mary. We shall dance, I think."

Mary rose to her feet, all poise gone. The sophisticated Clarissa and her tall, handsome husband seemed to belong together. Their eyes, as they surveyed her, held the same look of mocking mischief.

"I have no dances l-left," stammered Mary. "Only the waltzes and I have not yet received permission to dance those."

"Then I shall find permission," he said smoothly. "Ah, I believe your next partner approaches." He bowed and walked off with Clarissa on his arm, bowing and nodding to various acquaintances. He had not noticed her success! The evening fell in glittering ruins at her feet.

Her partner was young Lord Fitzwilliam, a dashing exquisite who usually only favored beauties of the first stare with his attentions. He danced smoothly and expertly, chatting amiably when the movement of the dance brought them together. He gradually grew a little piqued. The Season's newly risen star seemed unaware of his condescension, replying only in monosyllables to all his wittiest sallies. When the dance came to an end, and he was allowed that very English privilege of walking about the floor with her until the beginning of the next dance, he asked her flatly, "I fear you are not enjoying the evening or my company either, Lady Challenge."

Her gray eyes flew up to his face in startled wonder and dismay. "I am so sorry," said Mary contritely. "I am tired and my feet hurt. I would normally be extremely flattered that you should single me out for such distinguished notice, my lord, but I fear I would rather be home in bed."

Lord Fitzwilliam laughed appreciatively, long and loudly, drawing interested stares from all corners. "By Jove," he gasped at last. "Brummell was right. You are an original. I declare, honesty shall be the latest fashion."

And Mary, who knew she had said nothing witty, extraordinary, or funny was left to stare after him in a bewildered way as she was led off by her next partner. Lord Fitzwilliam hastened to tell a highly embellished story of Mary's honesty.

His group of exquisites were delighted. Honesty became the new thing. People began to complain of their corns, their disordered livers and their tight corsets. One young fashionable aspirant became so carried away by this new vogue that he told the bewildered Duchess of Pellicombe that her ball was "curst flat" and got ordered home by the duke.

After the next dance, Mary glanced at her card and saw with relief that it was to be another waltz. She could rest and find out how the stalwart Biggs was faring with the dowagers. She was relieved to see that, since her husband's arrival, Biggs had opened an enormous ostrich fan in front of his face and kept it there.

"My dance I think," came a well known voice. Her husband stood looking down at her. Beside him was the slightly flustered Duchess of Pellicombe who was still wondering what had gone wrong with her ball that people should keep complaining so. "The Duchess has given us permission to waltz," added Hubert gently. "By the way, I trust you did not come unescorted."

"Indeed no," said the Duchess before Mary could reply. "A most exceptionable lady. Very *grande dame*. The Marquise Elvira Dobones deLorca y Viedda y Crummers, no less."

"The *what*?" Hubert's eyes raked the line of chaperones. "You must present me, Mary. Where did you find this lady?"

"I m-met her in Brussels after you had g-gone," lied Mary wildly. "B-but I want to waltz, Hubert. I shall introduce you afterwards."

As they moved about the room, Mary tried to stand on tiptoe so that she could signal over Hubert's shoulder to warn Biggs. But Biggs had disappeared.

Then Mary suddenly saw Biggs. He was dancing with the elderly Colonel Fairfax and, as the ill-assorted couple drifted past, Mary heard Biggs say in a high falsetto voice, "Oh, ain't you the one, Colonel. You must be a fair old rip!"

Mary closed her eyes and Hubert looked down at her curiously. "Feeling faint?" he asked.

"Y-yes," gasped Mary. "Take me home, Hubert."

"So I shall. Directly after you have introduced me to your Marquise."

"She's . . . she's gone," squeaked Mary.

The dance came to a stop.

"I say, Challenge," roared Colonel Fairfax. "Want you to meet this splendid lady. Fine woman, damme. The Marquise de something or other Crummers. Sorry, ma'am. Never could get my tongue round those names."

"Call me Elvira," simpered Biggs awfully.

Hubert made a low bow. "You bear a startling resemblance

to an old friend of mine, Marchese," he said, staring into those boot-button eyes.

Biggs rapped his lordship painfully across the knuckles with the sticks of his large fan. "I declare you're flirting with me, my lord," he leered.

Hubert's face went rigid with distaste. "Your imagination does you credit, madam," he said. "Come Mary."

But Mary had to be surrendered to her next partner and went off with many an anguished look towards Biggs. But Biggs's familiarity with Hubert had done its work. Lord Challenge had privately damned the Marquise as a pushing vulgarian—worse than Mrs. Witherspoon—and did not look at her again.

He propped his broad shoulders against a paneled wall and waited for the dance to end. Then he would take Mary home. She did indeed look white and strained.

He felt a gentle tug at his sleeve and found himself looking down into the lovely face of Clarissa. "I must talk with you, Hubert," she said urgently.

"Is it very important?" said Hubert, his eyes never leaving his wife's slim figure.

"Very," she whispered. "*Please* Hubert. Where we can be private."

"Oh very well," he said reluctantly.

He led her out of the ballroom and across the hall and pushed open the door to the library.

"Now Clarissa . . ." he began impatiently, but she was in his arms, her own wrapped tightly round his neck and her thinly clad body pressed hard against the length of his own, awakening reluctant memories of old desires.

"What is all this?" he asked huskily.

"I want you," she said in a low voice, her mouth inches from his own.

Hubert forgot about Mary, he forgot that Clarissa was engaged to another man. It seemed to him that since that terrible battle he had been living each minute of the day as it came along, glad only to be alive with all that hell and carnage behind him.

He bent his head and explored her mouth, his mind beginning to register with reluctant surprise that nothing was happening to his senses.

* * *

"Oh, please Major Godwin. Do find Hubert for me," said Mary her voice breaking on a sob.

The ball had turned into a glittering nightmare for her. Her disjointed, murmured comments were treated as the height of wit. Mr. Brummell had made her the fashion, and London society would not allow her to be anything else.

"I shall fetch the Marquise," said the Major.

Mary looked wildly towards the refreshment room. Biggs stood with Colonel Fairfax at his side. He was surrounded by a court of elderly admirers. He bent his great turbaned head and began recounting something in a low voice. His audience listened intently and then burst out into roars of salacious laughter. Mary shuddered. She remembered that her maid Marie Juneaux had told her indignantly that the butler, when he was in his cups, had the bad habit of regaling the servants' hall with a stream of warm anecdotes. And Biggs's pudgy gloved hand was tightly holding onto a large bumper of champagne.

"No, leave her," said Mary. "Just take me to Hubert."

"He left with Lady Clarissa. That is he left the room," said Major Godwin pulling feverishly at his sideburns.

"Oh," said Mary in a small voice.

"Look here," said the Major awkwardly. "Hubert's the soul of honor. We'll look about. Bound to be somewhere around."

They entered the hall in time to witness the arrival of Viscount Peregrine St. James, Clarissa's fiancé.

Lord Peregrine looked as unappealing as ever, despite the magnificence of his evening dress. His great hooked nose seemed almost to reach his blue chin.

"Where's Clarissa?" he demanded.

"We're just looking for her," said Major Godwin so ingenuously that Mary felt a sudden stab of sympathy for Lucy. "She's with Lord Hubert."

"Is she, by God," said Lord Peregrine unpleasantly.

"I think perhaps I shall not trouble Hubert . . ." began Mary weakly, but Lord Peregrine had turned his great head and summoned one of the footmen. "In the library, eh?" he said after a low-voiced consultation with the servant. "Follow me!"

They trailed awkwardly behind him as he threw open the library door.

Clarissa had been disappointed and furious at Hubert's coldness. She heard the steps outside, and thinking that with any luck it might be Mary, she threw herself again into Hubert's surprised arms and pressed her mouth hotly against his own.

The library door swung open.

"You harlot!" said Lord Peregrine thickly. "I'll horsewhip you."

"Can I depend on that?" asked Clarissa, her green eyes alive with amusement. "Perry darling. How marvellous to see you."

She ran forward lightly and tried to embrace him but he pushed her aside.

"I demand an explanation, Challenge!" his voice grated.

"I haven't got one," said Hubert lazily, although he looked past Lord Peregrine to where Mary stood, clutching Major Godwin's arm. "Do you demand satisfaction?"

Lord Peregrine flushed. He knew Lord Challenge to be one of the most notable shots in England and a fine swordsman. "Don't talk fustian," he blustered. "I shall ask Clarissa."

"Do that," said Hubert with insolent contempt. "And now if you will all forgive me, I will take my wife home."

"No," said Mary in a sudden burst of rage. "Major Godwin shall take me home."

The Major looked awkwardly at Hubert, but at that moment Lucy's tinkling laugh sounded from the ballroom. "Oh, my dear sir, *what* husband?" she said.

"Yes, I'll take you home," said Major Godwin.

"It's *my* wife, Freddie," said Lord Hubert lazily.

"I shall not interfere between man and wife," said the large Major stiffly.

There was a commotion behind them as the Marquise sailed into the hall with her entourage. "Oh, there you is, my pet," called Biggs cheerfully.

"Oh, Bi . . . I mean, Marquise. Take me home."

"Home it is," said the Marquise, the boot-button eyes darting from Hubert's mocking face, to the Major's stern one, to Mary's pleading eyes burning in her white face.

The Marquise gathered Mary in one plump arm. "Come along precious," she said in a gruff voice. "Men, my love, are all a lot of rots!" And with that the Marquise bore her charge off into the night.

"Well, I'll be demned," said Colonel Fairfax.

"Probably," said Hubert, staring with hard eyes in the direction his wife had gone.

The Duchess of Pellicombe came sailing up. "I trust you gallant gentlemen are enjoying my little *affaire*?" she called gaily. "What think you, Lord Challenge?"

"I'm getting out of here," said Hubert still staring at the door. "This is a madhouse—a veritable madhouse!"

"Oh!" wailed the poor Duchess. "Whatever have I done?"

But Lord Hubert had gone.

He walked through the pouring rain to cool his fast-rising temper. By the time he reached St. James's Square, his reason had taken over and he was feeling heartily sorry for Mary. She must consider him the worst sort of rake. She must be crying her eyes out. Poor thing. And she had looked so pretty and, dammit, he was proud of her. There might be more to this marriage business than he had imagined. He would take her in his arms. He would tell her about Clarissa. He would convince her that it was all over. Finished and dead. Feeling very noble he let himself in with his own door key and hastened up the steps to her room.

Empty.

It was four in the morning. Where could she be?

He ran down the stairs to the hallway again and was about to ring the bell, when he heard the sound of laughter from the servants quarters. He pushed open the green baize door and walked lightly down the shallow steps, his dancing pumps making no sound upon the stairs.

He pushed open the kitchen door.

His wife and Biggs were seated on either side of the kitchen table with two empty champagne bottles between them, laughing uproariously. Biggs's face had a scrubbed look and his hair was unpowdered, and his livery looked as if it had been thrown onto his stocky body from a long way off.

Both saw Hubert at the same time. Biggs leapt to his feet and stood swaying slightly. Mary giggled and hiccupped, and the tighter and sterner her husband's face became the more she giggled.

"You, madam, are drunk," said Hubert furiously. "What is the meaning of this?"

"Why not ask Clarissa?" giggled Mary.

"Biggs, you are dismissed," said Lord Hubert, his eyes glittering with rage.

"Very good, my lord," said Biggs woodenly.

"Shan't!" said Mary, leaping to her feet, staggering wildly and ending up falling against the butler. "I *made* Biggsy drink with me. Made him, d'ye hear? I ordered him. Stuffed shirt. Stuffed stupid lecherous *owl*."

"My apologies Biggs," said Hubert coldly, not noticing in his rage that his butler could hardly stand. "I understand you were obeying orders. I shall take her ladyship upstairs. Come, Mary."

"Shan't. Stay with Biggsy. Only friend I've got. Biggsy."

Hubert picked her up and threw her over his shoulder and marched off up the stairs, not releasing her until he reached her bedroom where he deposited her unceremoniously on her bed and stood looking down at her.

"Pig," said his wife pleasantly. "Lecherous piggy-wiggy-wig."

"I shall talk to you in the morning, madam," said Hubert. "Get your clothes off. I do not want your maid to find you in this state."

"What *will* the servants say," exclaimed Mary with an awful titter. "Pig," she added flatly. "Owl. Greater stuffed owl."

He deftly removed her clothes until she was naked. She lay back against the lace pillows with her hands locked behind her head, and stared blandly up at him with drunken unconcern while the candlelight flickered over her body.

It was a slim body with skin like satin, and small high breasts. He felt his pulses begin to quicken. He knelt beside the bed and put a hand over her breast. She studied the hand, with its large sapphire ring, with clinical interest and then yawned. "It should be through your nose," she said clearly. "That's where pigs wear them."

His hand moved gently and slowly over her breast and he bent his mouth to hers, kissing her long and deeply and feeling waves of almost suffocating passion rise to his brain.

But the passion was all his own. When he at last removed his mouth, it was to find his wife had fallen asleep. He lifted her gently up, and covered her with the blankets and then went slowly downstairs to the kitchen.

Biggs's hair looked wilder than ever, for he had guessed

there was a confrontation to come and had gone and put his head under the pump.

"Well Biggs," said Hubert. "How much did my lady drink?"

"Two bottles," said Biggs in a low voice. "Said she needed a laugh." His little eyes peered shrewdly at his master. "Didn't stop 'er my lord for she was a-crying when she came in."

"Very good, Biggs," said Hubert curtly. "I understand in this case. But my lady is not to be found in such a situation again. Do I make myself clear?"

"Yes, my lord. Very good, my lord."

Hubert stalked off up the stairs and Biggs sank wearily down and rested his head on the table. What a night!

Chapter Five

MARY CREPT SLOWLY downstairs in the morning. She felt strung up and nervous. The storm had blown itself out and yellow watery sunlight blazed in at the windows, hurting her eyes and making her head ache. Her mouth was dry as dust and she longed for a cup of tea, since the thought of her usual morning drink of chocolate made her feel acutely ill.

Memories of the end of the evening came to her in bright flashes of color interspersed with long vistas of cloudy gray. She remembered arriving home tearful and distressed. She remembered begging Biggs to stay with her for a little and Biggs, who was cheerfully drunk, suggesting they should repair to the kitchens after he had changed, in case Lord Hubert should find them. After the first bottle of champagne, she remembered talking long and earnestly to Biggs about love and life. After the second, Biggs's stories had seemed excruciatingly funny, and after that she could not remember a thing.

Tea! Fragrant Bohea in a thin cup drunk in a cool, silent room would put her to rights. She pushed open the door of the breakfast room.

Her husband was seated at the end of the table reading his newspaper. Biggs was not on duty. She ordered tea in a faint voice and he lowered his newspaper and looked at her. Mary had never realized how much noise a freshly ironed morning paper could make, and put her hand to her brow.

"That is a very becoming dress, my love," commented her husband. "Gray with touches of pink. It matches your eyes."

"Very funny," said Mary sourly. "Must you crackle and rustle so, Hubert?"

"I am not crackling and rustling," he said mildly. "You are suffering from the effects of too much champagne."

"Fustian," said Mary, raising her cup and drinking thirstily.

"Pray return to your paper, sir. I am not in the mood for conversation."

Last night she had been dying by inches because of love and jealousy. Now she simply wished he would go away. His strong aura of sexuality seemed to fill the room to suffocation. Nonetheless, some imp prompted her to add: "Or perhaps you have some pressing social business . . . like entertaining Clarissa."

"I am glad you reminded me," he said putting down his paper. "I am driving with Clarissa this afternoon."

"You sit there as cool as . . . as cool as . . . as . . . as *anything* and tell me that you're going to drive out with that trollop!"

"Now listen to me, Mary," said Hubert. "I had a certain involvement with Clarissa before our marriage. It is finished, over and done. I wish to make it quite clear to Lady Clarissa that there must be no repetition of last night. I am doing it for your sake."

"Not for our sake?" said Mary, clutching the edge of the table.

"For our sake, then."

"I don't believe you."

"If I returned your brand of trust, my dear, I would assume that you were hell-bent on setting up Freddie Godwin as a flirt."

"Nonsense!"

"Exactly," he said with infuriating calm. "I suggest you go and lie down and . . ."

"Mr. and Mrs. Witherspoon," uttered Biggs in lugubrious tones from the doorway.

"We are not at home," snapped Hubert.

"Oh, yes, Biggs, I shall see them," said Mary blushing under her husband's surprised stare. She opened her mouth to tell him of her promise to the Witherspoons in Brussels and then closed it again. He would surely consider her a fool.

So under his curious stare, she left to join the leering Witherspoons in the Green Saloon. They had Mr. Trimmer in tow and Mary suffered a most unpleasant ten minutes. The Witherspoons and Mr. Trimmer had learned of her social success and were anxious to stake their claim to her society. She firmly turned down their pressing invitation to go for a drive and subsequently endured Mr. Witherspoon's particular brand of emotional blackmail.

When the Witherspoons and Mr. Trimmer had taken their leave, she returned to the breakfast room to find that Hubert had gone. She felt strangely flat and sick. Why should she trust him?

She trailed wearily up to her bedroom and fell into a hot, sweating, nightmare-racked sleep from which she arose some two hours later feeling worn out and depressed.

Although all the shutters were closed, the house seemed stifling and hot, and angry bluebottles buzzed over the gallipots with a monotonous drone. She dressed with more care than usual in a light, sprigged muslin gown with deep flounces at the hem and little puffed sleeves.

On descending the stairs again, she learned with some surprise that Viscount Peregrine St. James was waiting to see her.

He was standing in the Green Saloon with his back to the empty fireplace. His hair was powdered and tied at the nape of his neck by a black silk ribbon. This outmoded fashion seemed to add to his brutish air. He surveyed Mary with hot angry eyes.

"If I had a little wife like you waiting for me I would not waste my time philandering with old loves," he said.

Mary put a nervous hand to the little necklace of seed pearls round her neck.

"I do not understand you, my lord."

"Your husband and Clarissa. She told me they were going for a little drive in the Park for old times' sake. Old times' sake be damned. I know where they are. They are lying in each others arms right at this minute in an inn bedroom. An inn off the Chiswick Road called The Green Man."

Mary began to tremble. "It can't be true," she exclaimed.

"I shall take you with me and we shall confront them," he said heavily. "My carriage is outside."

"No!" said Mary wildly. "I don't believe you."

"You must," he said with an almost pitying note in his voice. "It is the only way. Unless you see for yourself, you will go on hoping . . . go on believing . . . like me."

"I am loyal to my husband," said Mary stiffly.

"But he is not loyal to you." Viscount Peregrine's flat, reasonable voice convinced Mary more than blustering or rage would have done. Her heart seemed to die within her and she felt faint. Then the faintness was replaced by a burning feeling of rage and desire for revenge. At least all lies would be at an end.

"I will go with you," she said flatly. "Wait until I fetch my bonnet."

Lucy Godwin slipped quietly away from the saloon doors and ran lightly down into the hall where she nearly collided with Biggs.

"Didn't you see my lady?" asked Biggs looking surprised.

"She is driving out with Lord Peregrine," said Lucy hurriedly. "I shall not trouble her this afternoon."

"You should have let me announce you, ma'am," said Biggs looking at her curiously.

Lucy's beautiful eyes slid away from his gaze. "Yes, so I should," she laughed. "Do not trouble to tell her I called. I shall let myself out."

Lucy unfurled her parasol and settled back in her barouche, a malicious little smile of pleasure playing about her mouth. It served prim and proper Lady Mary right. She *deserved* an unfaithful husband! How dare she hold hands with Freddie! She, Lucy, would drive in the Park and enjoy the cool shade from the trees. Then she bit her lip. She had promised Freddie to go with him to see his mother. But there would be so many dashing gallants in the Park. Freddie must wait, as he had waited before. He would sulk, of course, but she could always charm him out of it. The barouche rolled forwards and turned the corner just as Mary and Lord Peregrine appeared on the doorstep.

Mary began to feel hot and anxious. She wished she had not come. Lord Peregrine was driving at a furious pace. He had chatted amiably enough to her, explaining that he had only just returned from France the evening before, as he skillfully negotiated the Kensington traffic. But once through Kensington turnpike, he had sprung his horses and had set a hell-for-leather pace down the Chiswick Road while Mary clung to the side of the carriage.

Flat, empty, hot fields flashed by on either side and then the carriage veered over as Lord Peregrine swung it off the road and down a network of country lanes.

"Please slacken your pace, sir," cried Mary, hanging onto her pretty straw bonnet. "You will overturn us!"

"Nearly there!" he shouted over the rushing wind.

To Mary's relief, the carriage slackened its nightmare pace, slowed and finally rolled to a halt outside a tavern.

"This is a common alehouse," exclaimed Mary in surprise. "You must be mistaken."

"Unfortunately, I am not," said Lord Peregrine bitingly. "Clarissa likes this milieu. She says it adds edge to the excitement."

Mary winced. She could almost hear Clarissa saying it in her laughing, mocking voice. She wished she had not come.

Everything was very quiet and still except for the dry wind rustling through the hedgerows and the creaking and rattling of the inn sign. The inn was low and thatched. There was no sign of any other carriage, but Mary assumed that the guilty lovers had hidden it round at the back, out of sight.

"Come!" said Lord Peregrine, jumping down and holding out his hand. Mary hesitated. In her burning jealousy and rage, Hubert, with Clarissa in his arms in some romantic inn, had seemed a reality when she left London. Now confronted with this silent hedge tavern miles from anywhere, she began to think the whole thing impossible.

"I was silly to come," she began but Lord Peregrine held up his hand. "Hush!" he said. "I can hear that laugh of Clarissa's."

Jealousy is a marvelous thing. Mary listened intently and could swear that she, too, had heard Clarissa's high mocking laugh.

Grasping her parasol firmly in her hand, she marched into the inn, followed closely by Lord Peregrine.

The tap was deserted except for a thick, heavy-set landlord who looked remarkably like Lord Peregrine.

"We are looking for a certain lord and lady . . ." began Lord Peregrine. Mary stared at the landlord hopefully. Now that she was actually inside the building, the whole business began to seem unreal. But to her dismay, the landlord jerked his thumb towards the back quarters of the inn. "In there," he said laconically.

Mary pushed open a low door and found herself in a short

narrow corridor. Lord Peregrine was so close behind her that she could feel his hot breath on the back of her neck.

With her heart thudding against her ribs, she walked forward and pushed open the door of the room.

Empty!

Nothing but a low iron bedstead covered with a greasy quilt. She swung around.

Lord Peregrine had his back to her. He was locking the door.

"Why?" said Mary through white lips. "You tricked me. Why?"

"Revenge," he snarled. "I shall have from you what that husband of yours has been taking from my fiancée so freely."

Mary began to scream. He studied her thoughtfully and then slapped her across the mouth.

"No one will hear you, I've paid the landlord enough," he said. "But I can't stand the row." He began to tug at his cravat. "You can take your clothes off or let me rip them off for you. When I'm finished with you, you'll have learned every trick I've picked up in about five hundred brothels between here and Rome."

He moved toward her and she backed away, looking wildly around for a means of escape, but the only window was barred. Lord Peregrine put out a large, beefy hand and hooked it into the bodice of her gown. He pulled her into his arms and rammed his hot mouth down over her own.

With a demented strength she wrenched her mouth away and screamed "Hubert!" her voice like a clarion call.

Peregrine pinned her savagely down with his great bulk. Her hat was crushed over one eye and he wrenched it off and threw it into the corner.

"Now," he said between clenched teeth. "Now."

But it was like trying to rape an eel, he thought savagely, as Mary twisted and writhed. He held her down by the neck with one hand and drew back his fist to knock some sense into her when the lock of the door shattered in pieces as a pistol shot ripped the country silence.

Lord Hubert Challenge stood on the threshold, a smoking pistol in his hand and black murder in his eyes.

Lord Peregrine's beefy face which had been flushed a moment before, turned ashen.

"Out!" said Lord Hubert, jerking his head at Mary. "Out and wait for me."

On trembling legs, which were barely able to support her, Mary tottered past him. She clutched at his sleeve. "He will kill you, Hubert," she whispered.

"Get out!" said Hubert savagely, "and don't talk fustian."

Mary tottered through the taproom. There was no sign of the landlord. Out into the dazzling sunlight she swayed and collapsed onto the grass verge of the lane, covering her ears with her hands. Lord Peregrine was so strong, so brutish, he was probably massacring Hubert right now. She must run for help.

But still she sat there, wincing at each muffled thump and cry from the inn. Then there was a great cry and a long silence.

She heard a sound and looked up.

Lord Peregrine stood swaying in the doorway of the inn. Blood was streaming down his face and one arm hung limply at an awkward angle at his side.

"Hubert!" she cried desperately. "What have you done with Hubert?"

But he said not a word. He pulled himself 'round the low building, hanging onto the wattle with one hand until he reached his carriage. He crawled into it on his hands and knees and painfully took up the reins.

Mary leapt up to her feet and ran into the inn, visions of her husband's dead body flashing before her eyes.

Hubert walked into the taproom. His blue swallowtail coat moulded his form without a crease, his cravat was spotless. He looked down into her anguished face with a smile in his eyes.

"Dear heart," he said gently. "What a mull we have made of our marriage."

Mary fled into his arms, sobbing and crying. "How did you find me? Why is Perry so bloody and you untouched? Oh, Hubert, I am so sorry. I should never have believed him!"

"Hush," he said, holding her tightly and putting his lips to her curls. "Lucy Godwin fortunately could not wait to tell me the news. Somehow she overheard Perry telling you lies. She seemed so disappointed to find me respectably driving in the Park, instead of philandering in Chiswick. Perry is all bully and bluster, but an arrant coward in a fight. Now have I answered all your questions?"

"Yes ... no ..." gabbled Mary quite overset. "Do you love me?"

His brown eyes held the old mocking glint.

"Come home with me and I'll show you," he teased.

Mary buried her aching head against his broad chest and sighed. Could he not have said, "Yes?"

"I must rest my cattle," he said holding her a little away from him. "Let us see if this hedge tavern has a hair of the dog. You look as if you could do with one."

"The landlord?"

"I ... er ... persuaded him to leave," said his lordship, smoothing down the ruffles at his wrists. "Ah, what have we here? French brandy no less. Probably smuggled." He found two glasses and stared at them thoughtfully and then, producing a large handkerchief, wiped them carefully.

With equal deliberation, he poured two large measures, holding one out to Mary and saying in a peculiarly colorless voice, "Now drink that down like a good girl. I shall ask you questions afterwards."

Mary looked anxiously at him. "But Perry tricked me, Hubert. You know that. What questions?"

"Drink," he commanded, holding the glass to her lips.

She drank the strong measure in one gulp, shuddered and blinked, and then smiled at him weakly.

He dusted a chair with his handkerchief and drew it forward for her. Sitting down opposite, he leaned back, his thumbs in his waistcoat, affording Mary an excellent view of his broken knuckles.

"You are hurt," she exclaimed.

"It's nothing," he shrugged. "Tell me, why were you holding hands with Major Godwin last night?"

Mary flushed and looked down. She thought of the large Major and the pain in his eyes.

"It is not my secret," she said at last, looking down into her empty glass. "I cannot tell you."

"I don't like you having secrets with another man."

Her eyes flew up. "You have secrets with Clarissa."

"No longer," he said. "I explained all that, if you will remember."

"Clarissa—she heard Lucy's story too?"

He nodded.

"Then she will no longer be engaged to Lord Peregrine."

"Oh, I think she will," remarked Lord Hubert in a bored voice. "It titillated her no end. That sort of woman finds brutish indiscretions exciting."

"And that is the sort of woman you have consorted with in the past? That explains . . ." Mary bit her lip. She had been going to explain that that explains his brand of violent love making on that night in Brussels, but lost her courage.

But he seemed to read her thoughts for he said gently, "I have not yet made love to you, Mary. I do not count that episode as love."

Mary looked at him in embarrassed anguish. How could he sit there so coolly discussing such things which were surely reserved for the privacy of the marital bedchamber? One did not discuss such things with the hot sun blazing outside.

"Poor Mary," he murmured. "So much to learn."

He stood over her and raised her to her feet. She looked up into his eyes and then closed her own as his mouth came relentlessly down on hers.

The world swayed and spun. The floor seemed to disappear from beneath her feet and a heavy, drugged sweetness took possession of her body as his mouth moved against her own, parting her lips and exploring her mouth.

Still keeping his mouth against her own, he swept her up in his arms and carried her down the corridor toward the bedroom.

She pulled her mouth free. "What are you doing?" she cried.

"Taking you to bed," he smiled.

"To . . . It's the middle of the afternoon, sir!" cried Mary appalled. "That bed, no doubt, is full of livestock and you want to . . . oooh!"

He dropped her abruptly to her feet. "Not yet a woman," he remarked coldly, his eyes like pieces of agate.

"Me, not yet a woman," said Mary shrilly, hurt unreasonably. "I may not be one of the strumpets you are used to bedding but I am a lady, sir, and I will not soil my dress on that filthy bed."

"Oh, really," he said savagely. "Did you mean to keep it on? How quaint. Very well, madam. We shall return home and draw the shades and extinguish the candles and you may keep all your clothes on and, if it pleases you, I will go to bed in my boots and breeches, but have you I will."

Mary was shocked. That anyone should dare to be so crude in the presence of a lady!

She folded her lips into a thin line and marched back down the corridor and through the inn. Then she saw with dismay that his horse, Vittoria, was tethered to a tree outside and there was no sign of a carriage.

"I could not bring the carriage to your rescue," he said behind her. "It would have taken too much time. With one horse I was able to cut across the fields. You must ride with me . . . on the horse I mean, my love, in case I have offended your delicate sensibilities with my boorish masculinity."

She said nothing but allowed him to throw her up into the saddle. He mounted behind her and gathered the reins in one hand, holding her lightly with the other. She sat bolt upright, feeling faint at the sensations caused by that light touch.

The air was hot and humid and still, heavy with the scent of the hedgeroses, and the long shining grass still wet from last night's storm.

She wondered bitterly whether her husband could sense the churning emotions in her body, but he said not a word until Chiswick Mall was reached and he rode into the yard of a posting inn under the curious stares of the ostlers. "We will bespeak a carriage here," he said curtly. He swung her lightly to the ground and then turned and strode off into the inn, not once looking behind him to see if she were following.

Suddenly she remembered that quadrille on the night of the Duchess of Richmond's ball. Was she never to be free of Perry and Clarissa and the problems of Lucy and Freddie, not to mention the pushing Witherspoons?

"I am going to the opera tonight. So there!" screamed Lucy Godwin at her large husband. "And if you need feminine company, I suggest you go and hold hands again with Mary Challenge!"

"I thought we might spend an evening together like the old days," said Freddie Godwin miserably.

Lucy stared angrily at him. He made her feel so guilty. If only he would shake her or beat her or do anything other than sit there like a great lummox.

But goaded on by the pain shown in his eyes, she went from bad to worse. "Don't talk to me of the old days," she sneered. "What a pair of little country bumpkins we were then."

"Don't call me little, Lucy."

"Little, little, *little*. Awful *little* man!"

The Major took a step toward her and raised his hand.

"That's right!" screamed Lucy. "Beat me like the brute you are."

He dropped his arm and then said in a measured voice. "Very well, Lucy. Have your fun. But show one serious *tendre* for any man and I will shoot him first and strangle you afterwards."

"Mr. and Mrs. Witherspoon," announced a servant.

Lucy stared at her husband uncertainly. Then, "Pooh!" she said, shrugging a muslin shoulder, and went off impatiently to see the Witherspoons. Really, they were the outside of enough. She must tell the servants not to admit them.

The Witherspoons had their customary leer pinned on their large faces, but for once it did not reach up to their eyes. They had received snub after snub since their return from Brussels. Money they had in plenty. But what they desired was social acceptance and they were prepared to get it any way they could.

After the tea tray had been brought in and social chit-chat exchanged, Mr. Witherspoon fixed Lucy with a steely gaze and said, "I fear Lady Challenge has forgotten the great service we did her in getting you out of Brussels. Begging and crying and pleading you were. 'What about your husband?' asks one lady. 'Oh, I don't care,' you says. 'Freddie can take care of himself.' Tut-tut. Society don't like that kind of behavior, Mrs. Godwin."

Lucy sat very still. Society had indeed begun to circulate stories of those who had fled from Brussels, leaving their men to die on the battlefield. If the Witherspoons circulated such a story, she would be socially damned, and some of her best and brightest flirts were among the military.

"But you have not told anyone since we are friends," she said at last with a lightness she did not feel.

"Not yet." The two words fell, carefully measured, into the hot, still room.

"I am grateful to you for all you have done. Do you want money?" asked Lucy hopefully.

Mr. Witherspoon shook his head while his wife munched cake after cake, her eyes never leaving Lucy's face.

"It is not your gratitude we want," said Mr. Witherspoon. "We want Lady Challenge's gratitude. She is all the crack now, and it would be deemed a mark of distinction if we could be seen abroad with her. You must remind her of her social obligation."

"Oh, very well," said Lucy pettishly.

"See that you do," said Mr. Witherspoon. "Just see that you do."

"You are looking particularly dowdy tonight, my love," remarked Lord Hubert Challenge to his wife as they faced each other down the length of the dining table.

Mary looked down guiltily at her dress. It was of gray silk in an old-fashioned mode, with a high-neck and long tight sleeves. She had suddenly been terrified of the night to come and had chosen the most repelling gown she could find.

"Do you wish me to change my clothes?" she asked.

"No," remarked Lord Hubert lazily. "Just take them off. What's the matter Biggs? Got a cold?"

"No, my lord. Must have burnt me hand on this 'ere chafing dish."

"Then we are quite well able to serve ourselves. You may go to the kitchens and have it attended to and ... er ... Biggs."

"Yes, my lord."

"Don't come back, there's a good fellow."

"Monstrous!" cried Mary after Biggs had gone. "To make such remarks, and in front of a servant too!"

"You drive me to it, Mary," he said, his eyes mocking her. "Miss Prunes and Prisms. You are so easily shocked."

Mary gulped at her wine and picking up the decanter, poured herself another glass.

Lord Hubert's black brows rose in surprise. "Does your mother drink? Or your father?"

"Of course," snapped Mary.

"I mean to excess."

"No."

"Splendid. I was beginning to fear you had inherited one of the Fatal Tendencies. Come and kiss me."

Mary put down her glass. She was too frightened. Love should be a gentle and delicate minuet, not this constant assault upon the senses. She must have courage. She had been abducted, nearly raped. She had had insufficient sleep.

"Hubert," she said desperately. "You must excuse me."

"You have a headache, of course."

"Oh, yes," cried Mary, delighted to find him so reasonable.

"Then you may retire," he rejoined equably.

She looked at him doubtfully. He had changed into evening dress although they were dining at home and looked very splendid and remote.

"And where are you going, my lord?"

"Ah," he teased. "That is my secret. Come and kiss me, Mary!"

She walked slowly towards him. He lay back in his chair, his eyes glinting up at her from under their heavy lashes. She looked down at him and then stooped to plant a brief kiss on his cheek. He turned his head abruptly so that the kiss fell full on his mouth, and his lips seemed to cling and burn although he did not raise his hands to touch her. She stayed there for a long time, imprisoned by his kiss, feeling her head reel.

Finally he held her away from him with gentle hands.

"Go to bed, Mary," he said quietly.

She hung her head and walked slowly away, feeling bitterly disappointed. Now that he was obviously not going to spend the night with her, she wanted his body pressed against her own more than anything in the world.

Juneaux chattered away as she unpinned her mistress's hair and prepared her for bed, but Mary only replied in monosyllables, her mind busy with the problem of her husband.

When Juneaux had gone, Mary climbed into bed and stared sightlessly at the canopy. The room was uncomfortably warm and sticky and smelled of sugar and vinegar from the gallipots. She threw back the blankets and restlessly stretched her legs. The flame of the candle beside the bed burned clear and straight without a flicker.

"It is not my fault," she whispered to the uncaring shadows. "It is too soon. I have known no courtship. I am frightened. But I need not be frightened for he will not come this night."

210

Two restless hours later she heard his steps in the corridor outside and stiffened against the pillows. But he walked past the door of her room without a pause and seconds later she heard the door of his bedroom close.

She bit her lip, suddenly troubled. She could not expect a man of his caliber to remain celibate. He would soon find consolation elsewhere. She had a vivid picture of Clarissa, lying back in his arms, and she groaned aloud. Was she, Mary, less of a woman than Clarissa? No! But a very inexperienced one, whispered a frightened voice in her brain.

Another hour passed while she tossed and turned fretfully. At last, she slowly climbed down from the bed. She would just look in at his bedroom. There was no harm in that. If he was awake, they could talk and perhaps she could explain her fears.

She gently pushed open the door to his bedroom and went in.

The bed curtains were drawn back and he was sprawled back against the pillows, fast asleep. The blankets were thrown onto the floor, where they lay in a tangled knot. He was stark naked, the faint yellow light from the oil lamp outside the window gleaming on the muscles of his back, which was turned to her.

She took a hurried step backwards and then stopped. He was asleep after all. He did not look so terrifying naked, nor so shocking as she had thought. His face probably looked softer and younger in repose, she thought.

She tiptoed forwards holding her bed candle high and bent over him. The long lashes lay on his cheek softening the harsh lean lines of his face. His long, mobile, sensuous mouth was curved in a half smile and the white-muscled column of his throat rose above the dark hair of his chest. As she bent over him, a drop of hot wax from the candle fell on his shoulder and his eyes flew open.

She retreated hurriedly. "I had a nightmare," she whispered. He reached out a strong white hand and pulled her roughly into bed, and then rolled over on top of her.

"Let me up," she breathed. "A nightmare, yes, that's what it was."

He did not seem to hear her. His eyelids half closed, he simply began to kiss her, slowly and lingeringly until she

211

groaned against his mouth. His lips moved downwards across her body, burning through the thin material of her nightgown, caressing and teasing, while his long strong fingers roved and probed. He made love to her slowly, sensuously and lingeringly, with a single-minded absorption, until she was digging her nails into his back and crying out for she knew not what.

When he at last moved inside her, the bed began to creak alarmingly like a ship in a high storm, and she had a sudden, panicky feeling, "What on earth will the servants think?" before her senses took over and she was never to know that even her delirious cry of fulfillment went unnoticed by everyone except Biggs, who opened the window and shied his army boots at a perfectly innocent cat who had not said a word.

When she awoke, dawn was pearling the sky and the watch was crying five o'clock. He was sprawled across her body and awoke the minute she moved and smiled down at her, his eyes very wide and tender. "What are you thinking of, my sweet?" he whispered.

"I am worried about the servants," said Mary anxiously. "I should be so embarrassed to be found here when your man comes in with your chocolate in the morning."

Did he look disappointed or was it a trick of the light?

"Then I shall escort you to your own room, my prude," he said, climbing out of bed and shrugging into his dressing gown.

"You *do* understand," pleaded Mary, feeling she had said entirely the wrong thing. She should have told him she loved him, which she did, but at that moment she could not bring herself to say so.

He opened the door of her bedroom and ushered her in.

"Goodnight, my sweet," he said, looking down at her. "You kept your clothes on after all . . . or nearly on."

She looked down at her crumpled nightdress and blushed. He put out a long finger and tilted her face up to his.

It seemed that seconds later she was in his arms, he was in her bed, and her nightgown lay crumpled in a ball in the corner of the room where it had been thrown by an impatient hand.

"Bleeding cats," said Biggs, throwing up the sash and poking his rifle through the bars.

Juneaux nearly dropped her mistress's tray of chocolate

when she blithely marched into the room in the morning, stopping short in amazement at the sight of the tangled figures on the bed.

Pursing her lips in disapproval, she turned about and marched out. The English were so indecorous!

"Hubert, it is noon," wailed Mary some time later. "Oh, my goodness, Juneaux must have seen us."

"Fascinating," said her lord lazily. "You blush all over. Noon is it? Then let us celebrate the dawning of the afternoon."

"Oh, Hubert. No, we can't possibly . . ."

"Darling!"

"Oh, Hubert!"

Two hours later, Mary awoke feeling dizzy and light-headed. "Hubert. I am so hungry."

"A healthy sign. So am I. I shall eat your left ear."

"Please don't, darling. This is impossible. You know quite well I did not mean that sort of hunger. My lord, I pray you listen to me. Only think of the servants. Only think of the . . . Oh, Hubert . . ."

They did not eat till dinner time. Served by an indulgent and cheerful Biggs, they made but poor work of their evening meal, drinking more than they should and staring into each other's eyes in sleepy fascination.

"We shall give a party," said Mary, slightly tipsily. "An Impromptu Party. We shall invite everyone. A great, big, beautiful party."

"A party you shall have," said Hubert sleepily. "See that you are not overworked, Biggs!"

"No, my lord. It'll be like a campaign," said Biggs cheerfully. "I'll leave my lord and my lady to their wine."

He went out and quietly closed the door.

Hubert flashed a wicked smile down the table at his wife. "Come and kiss me, Mary."

And she did. Long into the night while the candles burned down and the untouched food congealed on the table, and the tactful servants stayed belowstairs and Biggs laid wagers on his lordship's stamina.

Chapter Six

LUCY GODWIN PACED nervously up and down Mary's drawing room, the sarcanet flounces of her gown swishing over the
carpet.

"I declare, Mary," said Lucy coming to a halt. "It is too
vexing of you. Too monstrous thoughtless. Why did you not
send the Witherspoons a card to your rout?"

"It is an informal, impromptu party, Lucy," said Mary
gently. "They really only like grand affairs. I am obliged to
them for their kind offices in Brussels but, in all faith, I cannot
like them."

"Like them?" sneered Lucy awfully. "When did one ever
have to like people to invite them? I tell you this, if you do not
invite them, they will tell the world and his wife that I abandoned poor Freddie on the battlefield."

"You imagine things. Surely they would not say so."

"Oh, yes they would," cried Lucy pettishly. "I shall be
socially ruined and it's all your fault. You p-promised Freddie
you'd take care of me."

"Only in his absence."

Lucy burst into noisy tears. "I think you're horrid," she
sobbed.

"Very well then," said Mary on a sigh. She was so happy
she could not bear to see anyone else unhappy. "I shall send
them a card. But will they not be insulted? The party is this
very evening after all."

"Oh, no," said Lucy cynically, her tears drying like magic,
"so long as they are invited."

She slid a curious look at Mary's radiant face, out of the
corner of her eyes. "I declare I am surprised you should
condone the presence of Lady Clarissa and her fiancé, Lord
Peregrine."

"You must be mistaken," said Mary coldly. "I sent no invitation."

"Really," said Lucy with a little titter. "I would ask dear Lord Hubert about it. Good-bye, dear."

She kissed the air somewhere in the region of Mary's cheek and floated out.

Mary went in search of her husband. He was sitting in his study brooding over a glass of madeira and nursing a blinding headache. That morning, while Mary lay asleep, recuperating after another energetic night, he found himself strangely restless. He had gone out riding and had come across an old friend he had thought dead on the battlefield of Waterloo. They had gone off to celebrate too much, and too wildly. He had returned to find his house in an uproar. Decorators were draping the saloons in swathes of silk. Footmen were staggering around with potted plants. Strange housemaids hired for the occasion were flirting shrilly with his military servants and nowhere could he find peace except in his study. He slammed the shutters closed and decided to have a glass of wine, and then an hour's sleep, before preparing for the rigors of the evening.

He winced as his wife crashed through the door, two bright spots of color burning on her cheek.

"Did you or did you not invite Clarissa and Perry?" she stormed.

"Yes," he said, "and don't shout!"

"Is this some mad joke?" asked Mary, staring at him with hauteur. "I would have thought that Lord Peregrine would have taken himself out of the country."

"He had no need," said Hubert curtly, suddenly disliking his wife excrutiatingly. "He knew I did not want your name dragged into any scandal. I have no further quarrel with either of them. He called on me and explained in a very gentlemanly fashion that he had been driven insane with jealousy."

"You should have horsewhipped him," shouted Mary.

Hubert clutched his fevered forehead and groaned. "Leave me alone, Mary. My hea . . ."

"No I will not leave you alone. You will send a footman round to Lady Clarissa immediately cancelling the invitation. Do you hear me?"

"I hear you, madam. The whole of St. James's can hear you, dammit."

"I order you . . ."

She broke off as he sprang wrathfully to his feet. "You *order* me. Who in hell do you think you are? Get out of here before I slap you to your senses."

"You're a monster," screamed Mary, jumping up and down. "And . . . and . . . your nose is too big."

There was a shocked silence.

He stalked to the mirror over the mantle and twisted his head from side to side.

"It is a splendid nose," he pronounced at last.

"It's big! It's enormous! I hate it," Mary screamed even louder, quite beside herself.

"It is a fine example of an aristocratic nose," he said, glaring at her. "I do not have a common feature in my face—unlike yours."

"What is wrong with my face?"

"You've got a great long trap of a mouth. Vulgar, common, faugh!"

"Eh hiv nit," piped Mary pursing her lips into as small a shape as she could manage.

"And talking of being common," pursued Hubert. "Why not ask your so dear friends the Witherspoons."

"I will do that directly." Mary burst into noisy tears and fled from the room, crashing the door so violently so that it rocked on its hinges.

She rushed to her writing desk and scrawled a fulsome invitation to the Witherspoons and sent it off by hand. She then scrambled up the stairs to her bedroom where she lay on the bed and cried her eyes out. She thought she heard her husband's footsteps outside the door, so she cried even louder but all she heard in reply was the slamming of his bedroom door.

Why did I ever get married? thought Hubert as he buried his face in his pillows. Suffocating, demanding women! This rout would be a disaster. She was overworking the servants. Biggs was in a shaky condition with that ball in his chest. He would die. And it would be Mary's fault. And so he would tell her. And with that comforting thought, he fell asleep.

When he awoke, it was already dark. The sound of music

filtered up the stairs and he sat up in alarm and, lighting the candle, peered at his watch. Ten o'clock! Why had no one wakened him?

Then he remembered the insane quarrel of the afternoon. He wondered if they had both been mad. He rang for his valet.

"Tell me Mr. Jones," he said silkily. "Why was I not aroused? Am I not to greet my own guests?"

"Her ladyship gave strict instructions that you were not to be disturbed on account of you having the headache," said his valet nervously, scurrying to lay out his evening clothes.

"She did, did she?" snapped Hubert, all his irrational hatred returning. "No, lay out my dress uniform. I shall not look like a crow this evening."

A bare half hour later, he joined his wife at the top of the first floor stairs leading to the chain of saloons and took his place beside her. The first of the guests were only just beginning to arrive, but he felt his fury mounting.

Mary, who had tried to make amends to him by respecting his headache, took one look at his icy face and her heart sank.

"What is the matter?" she whispered.

"Matter?" he hissed. "You did not intend me to come to this rout, madam. A shabby trick!"

"But I gave the servants orders to leave you asleep," whispered Mary savagely. "I think you are drunk or mad or both."

"By God! You shall suffer for this insolence," he whispered viciously, just as the Duchess of Pellicombe ascended the stairs.

"Dear Lady Mary and Lord Hubert," she cried. "Such a delightful idea. Isn't it delightful?"

"No, it's not," snapped Hubert. "I wish the curst flat evening were over."

"Oh dear," wailed the Duchess, hastening off on her husband's arm. "What on earth happened to the motto, 'Manners maketh the man'?"

"Control yourself," hissed Mary to Hubert as the Duchess moved away.

He opened his mouth to make a reply, and then he saw Lady Clarissa coming towards him up the stairs on the arm of Lord Peregrine. Clarissa had surpassed herself. Her burnished hair gleamed like fire, and her green eyes sparkled like the magnificent collar of emeralds round her neck. In fact, at first glance, it looked as if Lady Clarissa were wearing the emeralds and nothing else. Her dress of the finest silk was in a creamy skin color and dampened to mold her body. Lord Peregrine had painted his face to disguise his bruises.

To Mary's surprise, he greeted both of them jovially, despite the fact that Hubert was smiling intimately into Clarissa's eyes. Clarissa laughed lightly and murmured to Lord Peregrine. "You must not take our dear Hubert so seriously, Perry. Once a rake—always a rake. It is only naive little girls who believe in reformed rakes."

Mary heard the murmur and her heart sank like a stone. She felt pallid and mousey compared to the glittering Clarissa. Her own dress of silver net, which had seemed daringly low in the privacy of the bedroom, now seemed the height of governess propriety.

Hubert had not yet learned one of the most difficult lessons of marriage—that you cannot give love and affection just when you feel like it. He had spent a long and energetic love-making with Mary and for the moment he did not desire her. He therefore felt trapped, and the hurt in her large gray eyes intensified the feeling. He longed to flirt with all the girls in the room and then see the dawn come up through the bow window at White's in St. James's.

Mary felt bewildered and lost. Her husband had suddenly turned into a hard, elegant and indifferent stranger. He looked heartbreakingly handsome in his uniform, and she noticed how other women looked at him and felt a lump of suffocating hurt in her throat.

This rout had really been to show the world that Lord Hubert and his wife were in love—a love such as fickle society had never known before. Still she hoped that when they danced together, he might warm to her. There was to be dancing and cards.

But no sooner had they joined the other guests than her husband abandoned her for the card room. She numbly conversed with various strange faces, and when the dancing began she found with some trepidation that Major Godwin was her first waltz partner. He plunged into his woes immediately and she could not help putting a sad little hand up to sympathetically caress his cheek.

She immediately realized what she had done and quickly

218

took her hand away, but not before she had caught the malice in Clarissa's green eyes and the speculative look on Lord Peregrine's face.

The Witherspoons seemed to be everywhere, pushing and gossiping. At first, they were snubbed as usual but as Mary watched them, she noticed that they were finally gathering an audience and then many startled looks were being cast in Lucy's direction. The Witherspoons were cheerfully burning Lucy's reputation on the social pyre.

Lucy gradually became aware of the hard stares. She looked desperately around for Freddie but he had taken Mary into the refreshment room and seemed absorbed in conversation.

Lucy had arrived late, hoping to make an entrance. Now it seemed she was destined to prop up the wall, while her husband broadcast his infatuation for a married woman.

Her eyes filled with ready tears of self-pity.

"Like Niobe, all tears," said a gentle voice at her elbow. Lucy looked up into the calm, austere face of Captain Peter Bennet. He made her a low bow. "We met in Brussels," he said. "Peter Bennet at your service."

"Oh, of course I remember you," said Lucy. Her heart-shaped face was animated and her tears dried without leaving any unsightly blotches. "Like a summer flower after rain," said Peter almost wonderingly.

"How pretty," laughed Lucy, her vanity restored. "How is it we have not seen you in town?"

"I have been ill," he said briefly. How could he tell this beautiful little creature of the horrid dreams and nervous exhaustion which had plagued his days and nights after the battle? He was normally a cynical and sophisticated man about town. But he had served in the Peninsular Wars from beginning to end, and then had survived the hell of Waterloo. Normally he would have found Lucy vapid and silly and his code of honor would not have allowed him to flirt with a married woman. But in his present state of mind, he would probably have fallen in love with the first pretty girl he saw at the rout. With the luck of the bewitched Titania, the first person he saw had to be Lucy Godwin and, like the fairy queen, he did not even notice the asses ears.

He gazed into her eyes and Lucy exclaimed, "You should not look so, Mr. Bennet! People will talk."

"Let them," he laughed, drawing her into his arms at the sound of the opening strains of the waltz. "Do you care?"

Lucy's eyes flicked from the gossiping Witherspoons to her husband in the refreshment room with Mary. "No," she said breathlessly, feeling the hard grasp of his arm at her waist. "No, not a bit."

Mary emerged from the refreshment room on Major Godwin's arm, just as her husband came out of the card room at the opposite side of the saloon where the dancing was being held.

Their eyes locked and held and one would have said their glances swore at each other. Clarissa floated past him and he caught her arm and said something in her ear. She threw back her head and laughed, her green eyes sliding towards Mary, holding a world of mockery. Hubert had not said anything about Mary at all, he had merely paid Clarissa a light compliment. But Clarissa meant Mary to be hurt and hurt she was. Hubert was being eaten alive with jealousy. He did not recognize the emotion that was tearing him apart. He only knew that everything was dreadfully wrong and that somehow it was all Mary's fault.

From then on the evening did become a nightmare for Mary. Her eyes kept blurring with tears as she danced and laughed and sparkled as best she could, while the tall figure of her husband in his scarlet regimentals seemed to haunt her as he flirted outrageously with not only Clarissa, but half the ladies in the ballroom.

At the third waltz, she found herself in Major Godwin's arms. "She won't look at me," he mumbled. "Peter Bennet of all people. Fine soldier and a good captain. I must speak to him!"

"So far he has done nothing wrong," said Mary gently.

"I wish I were dead," he said gloomily, treading on her toes. "Ah, you wince in pain. You know how I am feeling!"

"I am wincing because you are treading on my slippers," Mary pointed out reasonably. The Major gave her a hurt look. What a child he is, thought Mary.

When the dance came to an end, she began to walk about with him until her next partner should claim her.

Suddenly there was a loud commotion at the top of the stairs. The ballroom fell silent and all eyes turned upwards.

Guests crowded to the doors of the refreshment and card rooms to see what was amiss.

Biggs, who had been stationed at the top of the red carpeted stairs to announce the guests, came staggering forward. His face was deathly pale. His hand was pressed to his chest. He staggered painfully halfway down the steps and clutched onto the bannisters. Several of the guests rushed forward, but Biggs suddenly made a superhuman effort and hauled himself to his feet and stared down at the shocked faces of the guests.

His eyes dimly sought out Lord Hubert. "I'm a-going, Cap'n," he said. "Remember Vittoria! Remember Salamanca! Those were the days, Cap'n. I don't regret nothing."

He staggered on the bottom three steps and turned his white face to the painted ceiling. "Come on boys!" he yelled suddenly. "Come along you lazy bleeders or Frenchie'll get you." His dim boot-button eyes stared down from some dream escarpment across the baking sierras of Spain.

"God save King George," he cried in a great voice and fell in a crumpled heap on the ballroom floor.

"Dead!" screamed the Duchess of Pellicombe and fainted.

Lord Hubert pushed past the crowd of guests and knelt down on one knee by the side of his old comrade at arms. His hard, bright eyes lighted on his wife who was standing only a few inches from him. She was sobbing uncontrollably. Major Godwin was cradling her in his arms and murmuring soothing things into her curls.

Hubert's distress manifested itself in an all-consuming burst of fury.

"You silly bitch!" he yelled at Mary. "This is your doing and may God forgive you. You've worked the man to death!"

There was an indrawn hiss of almost shocked enjoyment. The death of a butler, although beautifully staged, was as nothing compared to the delicious sight of the handsome Lord Hubert, "Beau" Challenge, publically humiliating his wife.

Peter Bennet gently untangled himself from Lucy Godwin's arms and knelt on the other side of the butler. He thumbed open the butler's eye and then put his head to Biggs's massive chest.

"He's dead all right," said Peter cheerfully. "Dead drunk!"

Chapter Seven

𝒯HE CHALLENGE ROUT was discussed for days afterwards—but not in the way that Mary had hoped. The party, which was to demonstrate her husband's love for her to all the Polite World, had ended in showing them that he heartily detested her.

Lord Hubert did not know how to apologize. It was a wife's place to forgive her husband, after all. But no sooner had he tried to take her in his arms after the last guest had left and tell her soothingly that Biggs should be pensioned off, than she had beat at his chest with her fists and called him a monster of ingratitude.

Biggs was the one who had apologized most heartily to both master and mistress, who both readily forgave him but would not forgive each other, Mary feeling she had nothing to forgive and Hubert not wishing to believe that he had.

He took himself off to his beloved Hammonds and Mary did not see him for three whole weeks. When he returned, he promptly set about escorting Clarissa, while Lord Peregrine smouldered in the background. Mary felt her heart would break, but Major Godwin at least was always there to take her about and comfort her.

The Witherspoons avidly watched the members of the quadrille. Their gossip about Lucy had been a great success and they were anxious to supply more. They were to be frequently seen either in Mary's company or in Lucy's, and gradually their malicious gossip that Mary was having an affair with Major Godwin and that Lucy was having an affair with Peter Bennet began to be believed.

Peter Bennet was the first to hear the gossip. He had escorted Lucy to a turtle breakfast and when he had left her to find refreshments for them, he had overheard two dowagers carefully picking Lucy's character to pieces. His infatuation had fled leaving him feeling foolish and appalled at his behavior.

He was no longer available to help Lucy into her carriage or to stand holding her shawl and fan at the opera. He at last also heard the gossip about Lucy's flight from Brussels, and he could hardly bear to look at her. Lucy, deprived of her last flirt, turned her hurt attention on her husband to find that he had apparently deserted her for Lady Mary Challenge.

Lord Hubert seemed much as he had been in his bachelor days. His clothes were the envy of the clubs, his graceful, muscular figure graced every ballroom in London. It was just as well, people said, that his little wife had found a flirt for herself.

When they met in their home, they treated each other with the polite formality of strangers, while Biggs looked on with anxious, worried eyes. He felt he had been the cause of the break-up in the marriage but, for the life of him, he could not think what to do about it.

He confided as much to the Highland cook who consoled him not at all by pointing out that it was none of his business, whereupon the much-incensed Biggs had called him a haggis-faced petticoat-wearing dumpling, and nearly got a pot of turtle soup over his head.

Then one late summer morning, the eight members of the Brussels quadrille found themselves face to face again—in a room in Horseguards. Each eagerly asked the other why they had been summoned, and finding that no one knew why, their various hatreds reasserted themselves and they glowered at each other in a laden silence.

The door opened at last and the well-known, portly figure of General Brian Deveney rolled in with a pale and silent Captain Harry Black.

The General sat down at the head of a long oaken table and motioned the members of the quadrille to take their places around it.

The General ruffled a sheet of paper and cleared his throat. "You will all recognize Captain Harry Black," he began. "He called at the residence of Clarissa, Lady Thorbury in Brussels. Explain, Captain Black."

Captain Black wetted his lips and looked nervously around

at the party. "I called at Lady Thorbury's," he said in a low voice. "I was to inform Colonel Challenge that we had orders to march. I had a portfolio with me. In it were papers and maps showing the strength of our allied troops, and the placing of the various regiments, particularly near Quatre Bras.

"Lady Thorbury begged me to join them for an after-dinner drink. When I returned to staff headquarters, I left the portfolio in the care of the Adjutant. During the battle of Quatre Bras, it was discovered that the portfolio contained nothing but blank sheets of papers. For a while it was assumed that a traitor had stolen them from staff headquarters."

"But," interrupted the General, "after a rigorous investigation, headed by none other than His Grace, the Duke of Wellington, it was discovered the papers were removed from the portfolio at your house, Lady Thorbury."

"Madness!" said Clarissa, her eyes flashing. "Just because I asked Captain Black to stay for a drink does not make me a traitor."

"I agree," said Lucy Godwin surprisingly. "I am sure it was not Lady Clarissa. But there are some people who would do anything for power and money. Blackmailers!" She stared straight at the Witherspoons.

"Ho, indeed," snarled Mr. Witherspoon. "And what about young wives who run away and leave their husbands to die on the battlefield?"

"Freddie didn't die, but that piece of malicious gossip just did," raged Lucy.

"I think of a spy as one of the *quiet* ones," said Clarissa lazily, looking pointedly at Mary.

The General held up his hands for silence.

"These pointless accusations are not getting us anywhere," he said. "I want each of you during the next week to write down everything you remember about that evening from the moment Captain Black arrived. I shall not detain you any longer—with the exception of you, Colonel Challenge—a word with you in private, I beg."

The party filed from the room and then hesitated on the steps outside. The Witherspoons went home to rehearse this latest gem of gossip. Lucy looked at Major Godwin in a furious way and insisted on going home alone. Major Godwin escorted Mary. Clarissa looked curiously at Peregrine. "Here's a coil," she murmured. "Who do you think did it, Perry?"

"The General himself," said Peregrine with a great bark of laughter. Clarissa giggled. "Of course, you must be right. But now we have to remember all sorts of dreary things. You shall help me write them, won't you darling?"

"After," he said.

"After what?"

"After this."

"Perry! In the street. I declare you are becoming as wild as Hubert."

"Don't mention his name to me. What's your game, Clarissa? You say you are playing him along to revenge me, but it seems to me as if you're enjoying yourself a bit too much."

"Pooh!" said Clarissa. "I am a good actress. Come, if you tease me you shall not have your Before."

Lord Hubert Challenge left Horseguards an hour later in a thoughtful mood. He had no clue as to the identity of the traitor. He only knew it was not himself. It could not be Mary. Freddie would never betray his country. But Lucy Godwin was greedy and silly. The Witherspoons would do anything for social power whether in this country or in France. Clarissa might do it to discover a new thrill. But Lord Peregrine was too cowardly, too much the John Bull in an unappetizingly brutish way.

On his return home, he paced through the spacious, fragrant rooms of his house, looking for his wife but she had not yet returned. He sat down and tried to think clearly. He had to admit he was driving her into the arms of Freddie Godwin and he did not quite know why. He looked back on their quarrel and wondered if he had run mad. He had always been so sure of himself, so ruthless in attaining his aims. He had married to keep Hammonds in the family. He had married for money. He had not dreamed for a minute that the shy, countrified girl he had wed would turn into a woman with a tempestuous range of moods. He suddenly knew that he wanted her in his arms again, so badly it made him feel quite ill.

He wondered again what she thought of him. Her new

225

vivacity had dimmed and her face had resumed some of its old madonna-mask, the eyes wary and guarded.

He had imagined a wife as being someone grateful, admiring and compliant who would be ready to accept his love and affection at precisely the time he felt like giving them, and at all other times would sit somewhere unobtrusively with her sewing, until he was ready to notice her again—not racket around the town with a married army officer.

He realized that if he wanted her he would have to go about courting her, and the idea made him angry. One should not have to court one's own wife.

Nonetheless, as the day wore on and she did not return, he changed into his evening clothes, dressing with elaborate care and sent orders to the kitchen to prepare an especially good dinner.

MacGregor, the Highland cook, drove Biggs into a fury by pointing out smugly that his best French dishes would be just the thing to restore tranquility to the household. But Biggs was a devoted servant, so he swallowed his spleen and lined his army of servants up for inspection and gave them their orders. They were to be quiet and unobtrusive. James, the first footman, was to order flowers for the dining room and for my lady's bedroom. Then Biggs hit on a brainwave. A band of musicians should be hired to play soft romantic music in the hall—there was some Viennese lot who were fashionable at the moment.

His heart quailed however when he took a tray of decanters in to the Green Saloon early in the evening. Her ladyship had not returned, and his lordship was looking about as romantic as a thunderstorm.

As he was gloomily descending to the hall, the street door opened and Mary came in. She looked white and tired, as indeed she was. She was tired of listening to Major Godwin's troubles and had snapped at him that all Lucy needed was a good shaking. She loathed the very sight of Clarissa and was sure that Hubert was in love with her. That time of passion, which had meant all the world to her, had been, she was sure, merely a *divertissement* for her sophisticated husband. She had been on the town for long enough to realize that a great proportion of society treated their sex lives in the same way they treated gourmet cooking, something to be savored and enjoyed while someone else did the dirty dishes. One had affairs with anyone other than one's spouse, and never let messy emotions like love spoil the fun.

She looked up and saw the anxious face of Biggs.

"I shall not be dining this evening," she said quietly. "I am very tired."

"Oh, you can't do that, my lady," said Biggs anxiously. "His lordship has commanded such excellent dishes and Mac-Gregor would break his heart, my lady, if they were to go to waste."

"My lord is dining at home!" exclaimed Mary in surprise.

"Yes, my lady," said Biggs, "and he has already changed for dinner and awaits you in the Green Saloon."

Mary gave a sigh. "Very well, Biggs. Tell my lord I shall join him shortly."

Biggs made her such a low bow that his bristling head nearly touched his shoes and then rushed off to tell Mac-Gregor of his splendid diplomacy in getting my lady to take dinner.

Hubert was seated by a small fire in the saloon and looked up briefly as his wife entered the room. She was wearing a lingerie gown of pale green muslin trimmed with little gold oak leaves. Her hair which had grown longer was piled on top of her head in an artless cluster of curls. A chain of gold oak leaves had been threaded through her curls. She looked remarkably pretty and very young.

She dropped a curtsy to her husband, who was once again staring at the fire, and sat down in a high backed chair opposite him.

Had she arrived some two hours earlier, he would have swept her into his arms. But he had grown angry at being kept waiting, forgetting that he had not dined at home for some time. As if remembering his obligations to an unwanted guest, he rose to his feet and poured her a small glass of wine, placed it on a table beside her, and resumed his brooding over the fire, the flames playing on the stern plains of his face and sparking fire from the diamond pin in his stock and the diamond rings on his long fingers.

"Was it not a strange meeting at Horseguards?" asked Mary timidly at last.

"Very," he said coldly. "I am sure you have already mulled over the matter with Major Freddie Godwin."

"As you no doubt have with Clarissa."

"We will leave Clarissa's name out of this, if you please."

"Of course," sneered Mary nastily.

"I merely do not wish to bicker this evening."

"Dinner is served," announced Biggs.

Lord Hubert offered his arm to his wife. Mary put the tips of her fingers on his sleeve as if she were afraid of contracting some contagious disease. Biggs's boot-button eyes darted from one angry face to the other and with a little sigh he made a smart rightabout turn and led the way downstairs.

As soon as his master and mistress were seated at the table, Biggs realized it was going to be a bad evening. Both my lord and my lady were usually in the habit of noticing and appreciating any special effort on the part of the servants. But the splendor of the dining table, with its beautifully polished silver and crystal, its elaborate flower decorations, its tempting dishes, went unnoticed by the glacial pair.

Remove after remove was carried back to the kitchens untouched, as the couple sipped their wine and brooded on each other's iniquities.

How long this state of affairs would have lasted is hard to say. But the cook, MacGregor, finally could not stand the insults to his art any longer. He erupted into the dining room, an angry barbaric figure in his military kilt, his red beard glistening with rage.

"It iss mair that the flesh and bluid can stand," he roared, advancing on Lord Hubert. "Sassenachs wass always the same. Ice water in your veins. My verra soul went into those dishes, my lady, my lord. Do you care? Och, it takes the heart out of a body."

With that he tore off his chef's cap and flung it on the floor and then collapsed into a chair, hugging his large body and rocking backwards and forwards, wailing, "Ochone, ochone!" in a high keening voice.

Mary sat in shocked silence. Biggs was wringing his hands. Lord Hubert raised his quizzing glass and studied his cook in startled amazement.

"If you will stop that demned Gaelic wailing, MacGregor,"

he said icily, "and try to explain slowly and carefully in English the reason for this disgraceful behavior."

"It iss yourselves," moaned the cook, too distressed to guard his tongue or remember his place. "We are sad to see my lord and my lady at odds so we work and slave to bring ye together again. I am inspired. Neffer haff I cooked as I haff cooked this night. Och, what's the use!"

He resumed his keening, while his master slowly lowered his quizzing glass.

Out in the hallway, the small six-piece orchestra hired for the occasion burst into the opening chords of 'Oh, Nights of Passion.'

"Stop that damned caterwauling, MacGregor," snapped Lord Hubert, "and bring all the dishes back and you, Biggs, bring all the servants here! Bustle about man!"

MacGregor stopped his wailing and fled from the room. Biggs marched after him, while the orchestra played on.

"Oh, Hubert," said Mary, the tears standing out in her large eyes. "I feel we are behaving very badly."

One by one the servants marched in the room and stood against the wall. MacGregor and the kitchen staff followed, bearing the rejected dishes.

Lord Hubert stood up while they all hung their heads and waited for the outburst. "Now," he said, "I and my lady are indeed touched by your efforts to please us. We have indeed been remiss in not noticing your attentions." He smiled down the long length of the table at Mary, and her heart gave a painful lurch. "You must not be so depressed by our marital rows, must they, my love?"

Mary smiled back at him weakly.

"So, my lady wife," said Hubert, stretching out his hand, "if you will come and sit by me, I think we shall celebrate our loyal servants' devotion. All of you, pull your chairs to the table, and we shall sample the MacGregor's art!"

The Duchess of Pellicombe's carriage swung over the cobbles of St. James's Square in front of the Challenge mansion. The dining room curtains were drawn back, affording the Duchess an excellent view of Lord and Lady Challenge entertaining their servants to dinner.

"Good gracious!" she cried, her eyes almost popping out

of her head. "Do but look. The Challenges dining with their servants!"

The Duke leaned across her and stared from the carriage window at the brightly lit tableau.

"Challenge must have turned radical," he grunted, settling back in his seat. "That sort of thing breeds anarchy. I shall speak to that young man very sternly."

Mary watched her husband's animated face as he refought old battles with his servants. The wine was flowing freely, his face was flushed and alive. He had never looked so handsome. He had never before looked so much a stranger.

"Right you are, Captain—I mean my lord," cried Biggs, excited by the tales of battle. The butler turned his twinkling gaze on Mary. "Saved my life, many's the time, 'is lordship did. 'Member when Frenchie was levelling a pistol at me and I was saying me prayers. His lordship creeps up behind Frenchie and slices 'is 'ead clean off. How we laughed! That poor Frenchie's 'ead was a-rollin' on the ground with sech a look of surprise on 'is face as you never did see, my lady."

Mary repressed a shudder and gave a weak laugh. Then she felt the pressure of her husband's hand on her knee under the table.

How could she possibly go to bed this night with this bloodthirsty stranger? She moved her knee away from his hand and he snapped his head round and stared down at her, as if finding some subaltern guilty of dereliction of duty.

Then a faint, wicked gleam began to burn at the back of his eyes. "Come, my love," he said, throwing down his napkin. "It is time we retired."

Mary blushed painfully, and all the servants got to their feet and stood waiting.

"Three cheers for the Captain!" shouted Biggs. There was nothing else to do but to take her husband's arm and leave the room as the resounding *huzzas* split the quiet air of St. James's.

Her bedroom looked dark and mysterious and sinister to Mary's frightened eyes. It was lit by only one small candle placed beside the bed and the dark, saturnine face of her husband seemed to glow above the darkness of his body.

"No, I *can't*," said Mary helplessly. "Not tonight, Hubert. I am not feeling at all the thing. Hubert! Why are you taking off your clothes. You are not attending to me. Leave me *alone*. I am perfectly capable of undressing myself! Oh, my gown! You monster! You have ripped my gown! Oh, *no*! Oh, Hubert. Oh, *darling* . . ."

The watch announced to the interested that it was two o'clock and a fine night.

In the upstairs bedchamber of the Challenge mansion, Lord Hubert initiated his bride further into the mysteries of the marriage bed. At one point, Mary surfaced from a sea of passion to protest faintly, "The position is awkward and monstrous undignified, my lord." But her husband, his face strangely drawn and tense in the light of the guttering candle, merely looked down at her and said, "I love you, Mary," and she closed her eyes, grasped tightly onto the muscles of his shoulders, and forgot everything else.

The watchman announced the three o'clock in a hoarse stentorian voice, as if peeved at his lack of audience.

Mary turned sleepily in bed and looked at her husband. He was wide awake, staring up at the bed canopy.

"Clarissa," he said. "Clarissa, by all that's holy."

He hurtled from the bed and began to put on his clothes with the same rapidity with which he had taken them off.

Mary struggled out of the mists of sleep and fatigue and sat up in bed clutching the crumpled sheets to her naked breasts.

Her husband was emanating a quivering air of excitement, like a war horse scenting battle.

"If you go to Clarissa at this hour," said Mary in a low, even voice, "our marriage is finished."

Lord Hubert swung around, staring at her as if not quite hearing or seeing her. "Fustian," he said vaguely. "I shall return shortly."

Mary sank back against the pillows, as wave after wave of misery and shock engulfed her. After such a night of love, he had left her to go to Clarissa. He was a degenerate, an unfeeling monster. And she loved him.

She turned her face into the pillows and cried until a pale dawn began to streak the sky.

Chapter Eight

𝒜 THIN DRIZZLE was falling as a hired hack drew up outside Major Freddie Godwin's house. The Godwins lived in that network of small streets at the back of Park Lane. The houses were the same as those of the grand squares and of Park Lane itself, except that they were much smaller and had the appearance of being squeezed together to make room for as many desirable gentlemen's residences possible. Even the tiny shops considered it the height of vulgarity to display all their wares in their windows, so that you had to guess that it was, say, the grocers by one basket of plovers eggs in the window, or the bakers by two varnished wooden loaves.

Into this stagnant pool of gentility stepped Lady Mary Challenge at six o'clock in the morning.

She paid off the hack after the driver had deposited her trunks on the pavement, and brushed the straw from the skirt of her carriage dress before mounting the worn steps of the Godwins' residence. Assuming—quite rightly—that the bell probably did not work, she rapped loudly with the tarnished brass knocker and waited.

There was a long silence and then the slow, shuffling sound of footsteps.

A sleepy, cross butler opened the door a crack and stared disapprovingly at the heavily veiled figure of Lady Mary.

His eye swiveled round the crack, looking for an attendant maid and, finding none, began to close the door again.

Mary put her small half boot in the crack and, made courageous by misery, said in a loud voice, "I am come to see your master. Rouse him immediately or it will be the worse for you."

The butler opened the door two inches. He wanted to send

this unescorted young miss to the rightabout but something in her voice gave him pause.

"Master's asleep," he said sulkily. " 'Tis dawn and respectable people are abed."

"Fetch Major Godwin immediately," said Mary grimly.

Reluctantly the butler opened the door wide and led Mary into a small dingy saloon on the ground floor.

After some time, Mary heard him mount the stairs and then the shrill sounds of an altercation. She could not make out the words but she could recognize Lucy's voice. Then she heard a heavy tread of the stairs and Major Godwin walked in, looking as if he had hurriedly scrambled into his clothes—as indeed he had.

"Oh, *Freddie*," said Mary brokenly. "Take me home."

"Indeed, yes," said Freddie equably, as if being roused from his bed at dawn by young matrons was an everyday occurrence. "Delighted to be of service. I shall have my carriage brought round directly and you shall be home in St. James's Square in a few minutes."

"Not *there*," wailed Mary. "I mean *home*. My parents' home."

"Is anything wrong with Hubert?" asked Freddie.

"Everything's wrong with Hubert," said Mary bursting into tears. "He-he d-doesn't l-love me. He's gone to Clarissa. At three o'clock this morning. He l-left our b-bed and w-went to Clarissa."

"Here. Steady on. There must be some reasonable explanation."

"What?" demanded Mary through a mist of tears.

Major Godwin thought long and hard, twisting his sideburns in his large fingers. But it was too unusual and painful an exercise for him, so he at last said dismally, "Don't know."

And Mary, who had somehow hoped that he would come up with some dazzling explanation, threw herself into his arms and cried in earnest.

"There, there," said Freddie helplessly, putting back her veil and trying to dry her eyes with his pocket handkerchief. But she only cried harder than ever, so he merely hugged her close, trying to comfort her as he would a hurt child.

"Philanderer!" cried Lucy from the doorway. "What, pray, is the meaning of this?"

"I'm going off with Mary," said Major Godwin, made stupid by embarrassment.

"*What?*" screamed Lucy. "Explain yourself, sir, this instant."

"Oh, I say," began the Major awkwardly, about to make his usual humble apology. But in that moment, he saw the full blaze of jealousy in his wife's eyes and recognized it for what it was. He was overcome by a mad desire to hurt Lucy as badly as she had hurt him, so he turned his attention to Mary and stroked her back with a large, comforting hand. He then looked coldly at his furious wife over Mary's head.

"We're going off together," he said, savoring every word.

Lucy glared at him, and then her natural vanity reasserted itself and she laughed, "Stop teasing, Freddie. You would never leave me in a hundred years and you know it. I don't believe a word of it. And just to show you, I am going back to bed and I am going to leave you to your silly schoolboyish games."

She gave a malicious little titter and flounced out of the room.

"I'll escort you," said Freddie heavily. "Come, Mary. Dry your eyes. It will do us good to leave London for a bit. The servant shall bring you some tea while I fetch my trunk."

A bare half hour later, Lucy Godwin leapt from bed at the sound of her husband's carriage being brought round to the front of the house. With unbelieving eyes, she watched the servants strapping her husband's trunk up at the back, along with Lady Mary Challenge's luggage. She threw up the window and leaned out.

"*Freddie!*" she screamed. But the broad back of her husband disappeared into the darkness of the carriage and a footman slammed the door behind him. The coachman on the box cracked his whip, and the carriage swayed off down the narrow street.

Lucy's beautiful mouth folded into a thin line. Lord Hubert Challenge should hear of this.

Mrs. Witherspoon was awakened by a commotion below her bedroom window. Ever curious, she opened the window and leaned out, her great bosoms spilling over the sill.

A small trunk had rolled from the back of a traveling carriage and had broken open. Fine silks and satins were spilling out into the greasy mud of the street. Mrs. Witherspoon settled her elbows on the sill and prepared herself to thoroughly enjoy every bit of someone else's misfortune.

The carriage door opened and a heavily veiled young lady descended followed by a large young man. Mrs. Witherspoon recognized the young man as Major Godwin. Then the young lady, who was instructing a groom on the refastening of her damaged trunk, threw back her veil. Mrs. Witherspoon drew in her breath in a hiss of excitement. Mary Challenge! That high and mighty, hoity-toity Mary Challenge with none other than Freddie Godwin! Beau Brummell himself would listen to such a marvelous piece of gossip. And as for Lord Hubert who looked at the Witherspoons as if they had crawled out from under a rock—how he would smart.

She watched avidly until the couple reentered the carriage and moved off.

She was about to leave the window when she saw another familiar figure. She leaned out again. Viscount Lord Peregrine St. James was standing outside his house a little way down the street, staring after the departing carriage. Then he swung about and rushed indoors. Mrs. Witherspoon waited. Two minutes later, his horse was brought round and Lord Peregrine swung himself up into the saddle and galloped off in the direction the carriage had taken.

Lord Hubert Challenge should hear of this—for a price.

"I've told you and *told* you," said Lady Clarissa. "Now I wish you would go away."

How could I ever have loved this monster? thought Clarissa angrily. Lord Hubert had dragged her from her bed in the small hours of the morning and had questioned her over and over again about that wretched dinner party in Brussels. He was sure he remembered Perry sliding some papers behind the clock. "What of it?" Clarissa had yawned. She always stuffed letters and things behind the clock in the dining room. Perry probably thought they were love letters and had taken them out to look at them. Hubert must know by now how jealous Perry was.

"I am well aware of Perry's jealousy," said Hubert grimly. "But I am not leaving until you think a little harder. Did Perry

235

ever say or do anything that might lead you to believe that he would turn traitor?"

"Oh, anything to be rid of you," groaned Clarissa. "Very well. He rather admired Napoleon, but Perry is a Whig so that is nothing strange. I would not become affianced to a man who would betray his country."

"Why do you want to marry Lord Peregrine?" asked Hubert, stopping his pacing of her bedroom and coming to stand over her.

"Because you married that silly widgeon," snapped Clarissa, too tired to speak less than the truth.

"But you still mean to go through with it?"

"Oh, yes, yes, yes. He amuses me. He's a brute. I like brutes. But I no longer like you, Hubert. You are merely boorish and unpleasant and my head aches so. Go and ask Perry. That would surely have been a more intelligent thing to do than bursting into my bedroom and supplying my servants with gossip."

"I thought to find him here," said Hubert.

"And having not found him, why did you not leave immediately?"

"Because I want to confront him with some evidence. Now think again, Clarissa. We all left the dining room when Captain Black arrived. . . ."

Clarissa sighed loudly. The drizzle had thickened into a heavy rain which pattered mournfully against the windows.

"Well . . ." Clarissa was beginning, when there came a timid scratching at the door and a maid entered, her head down and eyes averted. One never knew, after all, what one would find in the Lady Clarissa's bedroom.

"An it please my lady," she whispered. "Mrs. Witherspoon is below demanding an audience. Mrs. Witherspoon says as how she has urgent news of Lord St. James."

"Tell the old baggage to take her gossip out into the kennel where it belongs . . ." began Clarissa wrathfully, but Lord Hubert was already at the door.

"I shall see her," he said to the maid, ignoring Clarissa's horrified cry of, "How dare you give that tattle tongue more food for gossip, Hubert!"

He ran lightly down the stairs and entered Clarissa's drawing room.

Mrs. Witherspoon dropped him a magnificent curtsy, the feathers on her turban quivering with anticipation.

"It is a shocking miserable day, is it not?" she said leering up at him as she rose from her curtsy.

"You did not come calling at this hour of the morning to exchange pleasantries on the weather. Out with it," said Hubert grimly.

Mrs. Witherspoon smiled at him coyly, not in the least put out by his angry manner. "I could not find you at home," she said, "and as it was a matter of some urgency, I thought Lady Clarissa might know your whereabouts."

"Now you found me," snapped Hubert. "But since your news is about Lord Peregrine, what concern is it of mine?"

"Ah, that would be telling," smirked Mrs. Witherspoon. "I would like it understood that if I do your lordship a favor I expect one in return."

"How much?"

"La, it ain't *money*," giggled Mrs. Witherspoon. "Me and my husband only ask for a little social kindness in return, if your lordship takes my meaning."

Hubert stared at her in baffled rage. Then he said in measured tones. "It is believed that Lord Peregrine may be a traitor to his country ma'am. You will give me any information you have, or by this night every fashionable drawing room in London will be calling you his collaborator."

Mrs. Witherspoon shrank back in her chair away from the blazing anger in his eyes. "Well, I don't want to be the one to pass along bad news," she said sulkily. "But your wife left at around six and a half hours of the morning with Major Godwin."

Hubert looked down at her with an expression she could not fathom.

"And," he suddenly said quietly, looming over her, "you also mentioned Lord Peregrine—or had you forgotten."

Mrs. Witherspoon looked up into his eyes and what she now saw there terrified the wits out of her. She shakily stood up, edging sideways away from him and began to babble. "Lord Perry started riding after them. That's all, my lord. Please let me go. It's late I am for my dressmaker. That's all I know."

"Go then," said Hubert, looking at her with disgust. "But

keep that silly tattle-tale mouth of your closed, madam, or it will be the worse for you. I cannot call you out, more's the pity, but there is always your husband."

Mrs. Witherspoon gave a horrified squawk and, gathering up her voluminous skirts, fled the room.

Hubert barked out an order to one of Clarissa's footmen to fetch his racing curricle.

Returning to the drawing room Hubert sat down heavily and buried his head in his hands as wave after wave of hot, burning jealousy swept over him. He wanted to find Mary and take her in his arms and tell her he loved her; he wanted to choke the life out of her. Gradually his hot brain began to clear and he had a sudden and vivid memory of leaving Mary in the small hours of the morning to see Clarissa. He had expected her to know what he was thinking. She had obviously thought he had fled from her arms to Clarissa's and God only knew he had given her enough reason to think so. She was probably returning to her parents and had persuaded Freddie to take her. Freddie was not the man to elope with anyone else's wife. He roused himself and went to wait for his curricle.

Lucy Godwin went in search of Lord Challenge at St. James's, only to be told by a footman that he could be found at Lady Thorbury's.

As Lord Challenge was pulling on his York tan driving gloves and pacing up and down impatiently on the doorstep, he felt an imperative tug on his arm. Lucy Godwin looked up at him, her eyes bright with tears.

"Freddie has eloped with Mary," wailed Lucy.

"Fustian," snapped Lord Hubert. "He is merely escorting her to her parents."

"But he *told* me so," sobbed Lucy whose self pity had made Freddie's brief words appear to have been a full scale rejection. "He threw back his head and laughed at me and said he'd always loved Mary, and that he was leaving with her."

"Out of my way," said Hubert coldly. "I am going to follow them in any case."

"Take me with you!" screamed Lucy, hanging onto his arm.

"I am driving my curricle," said Hubert impatiently. "You are not dressed for an open carriage in this weather."

"I will not melt," said Lucy with surprising vigor. "I insist on going."

"Don't complain then," he rejoined curtly.

He sprang up into the curricle and a footman helped Lucy mount by way of the wheel. She wrapped herself in rugs and tried to ignore the driving rain which was making a sorry wreck of her new bonnet. After fifteen minutes of swaying and jolting, she whispered a complaint that she felt sick.

Lord Hubert Challenge paid her not the slightest heed whatsoever.

A watery sunlight was beginning to bathe the English fields as Mary and Major Freddie Godwin jolted along side by side, each silently immured in their own thoughts. Freddie was cursing himself for his weakness, but he could not help regretting not telling Lucy the true state of affairs. The poor little love had been so terribly jealous.

He had admired Mary as being a sensible woman, but now he began to feel that this situation was somehow all her fault and longed to return to Lucy to be bullied and humiliated once more. For her part, Mary was beginning to feel foolish. Perhaps she should have stayed until Hubert came home and asked him the meaning of his strange behavior. As the miles rolled under the carriage wheels, and London faded in the distance, she could only remember Hubert's voice as he said he loved her.

Freddie rapped on the roof of the carriage with his cane. "Pull up at the next posting house, John," he called to the coachman. He leaned back against the squabs. "We will both feel better when we have had something to eat," he explained gently.

Mary answered him with a miserable little nod. The sun was beginning to beat on the carriage roof making it uncomfortably warm inside. A hot tear ran down her cheek and splashed on the skirt of her gown. Love was not what she had imagined it would be.

She had dreamt of a tranquil, affectionate relationship. Not this burning, unsettling emotion that made you believe the worst of the one you loved. She suddenly could not bear it any longer. She did not care if Freddie was angry with her. She simply had to go back.

She turned to speak to her companion when the carriage lurched to a sudden halt, nearly throwing them on the floor.

"What the devil . . ." began Freddie, jerking down the carriage window and thrusting his head out.

Then in front of Mary's horrified eyes a pistol butt came down on the top of his head, and he slowly toppled forwards through the window. Then the carriage door was jerked open and Lord Peregrine St. James stood there with a more unpleasant expression than usual on his heavy face.

He pulled Mary out onto the grass beside the road and, as she kicked and screamed, called on some unseen assistant for help. Rough hands wrenched off her bonnet and turned her face down on the grass, while her wrists and ankles were firmly tied. Then she was twisted over and a wad of gun cotton was stuffed in her mouth and she was gagged with a handkerchief.

Mary rolled over and stared wildly upwards. Lord Peregrine had three uncouth helpers; coarse, brutal looking men. The coachman and the groom were lying trussed up beside the road, and Freddie was lying on the grass where he had fallen, blood streaming from an ugly gash on his head.

All was suddenly very quiet. The only sounds were of the birds chirping in the hedgerows and the faint barking of a dog several fields away. The black clouds of the morning had rolled away, leaving the day hot and sunny, smelling of the grasses and flowers of the countryside, the pastoral scene somehow intensifying the nightmare.

Lord Peregrine stooped down and picked Mary up into his arms. She averted her eyes from his leering face.

Still he did not speak. He carried her to another travelling carriage which had been swung across the road and threw her in on the floor among the straw. One of his helpers took the reins and the other two jumped up on the back strap.

Lord Peregrine prodded Mary lazily with his boot as she rolled backwards and forwards helplessly on the floor as the carriage sprang forward and lurched and swayed as it headed down the road towards its destination.

Mary closed her eyes tightly to blot out Lord Peregrine's face and tried to think. What would Hubert think if he did not find her at home? Perhaps he would not care. All her jealousy for Clarissa came pouring back and her anger gave her courage.

One thing was sure. Hubert would never find her. She would need to lie very still and watch and wait for a chance of escape. But secretly she felt this was the end. She looked up at Lord Peregrine and read her death warrant in his eyes.

The carriage rolled on and on. Once it slowed in the narrow streets of a market town and the shaggy head of a yokel peered in at the carriage window, his eyes popping out of his head at the sight of a gagged and bound young lady lying on the carriage floor. Mary stared up at him, her eyes dilated, pleading for help. Then Lord Peregrine shouted, "We'll never get to Dover at this pace!" and the carriage rolled on. No cry of alarm was raised. Mary had never felt more frightened or more alone.

At long last, they stopped to change horses. With a slow smile, Lord Peregrine threw a blanket over Mary and all hopes she had of rescue faded to one little dot of light. He has abducted you before, a little voice of hope nagged in her brain, and Hubert rescued you then. But that small gleam of hope was almost agonizing. Better to prepare her mind for death.

The blanket was removed and the headlong flight continued. Night fell and a pale sliver of moon lurched and swayed along beside the carriage. Lord Peregrine fell asleep, leaving Mary to stare up at the moving sky. Where was he taking her? And if he wanted to kill her, why take her so far?

At last, as a red dawn barred the sky, Mary fell asleep and did not awake when the carriage stopped to change the horses again.

She awoke to the sound of the carriage wheels rumbling over cobbles and then she thought she could smell the sea. Suddenly, from overhead came the high, thin scream of a seagull.

The carriage door was opened by one of the ruffians who jerked his thumb at Mary. "Best put her in a sack me lord so's we can take 'er on board without fuss."

Lord Peregrine nodded. "Fair enough, Jim. Slide it over her legs. Stay *still*, damn you." For Mary had begun to feebly kick out with her bound feet.

Then she lay still and let them bundle her up in the sack. When she was carried from the carriage, she planned to wriggle up onto and kick to attract attention. She felt herself being heaved up onto Jim's back. She waited until he had stumbled a few steps with her and then she began to kick and wriggle in earnest. "Seize 'er feet, man," Jim whispered to one of the ruffians.

"What have you got there?" called a jolly voice and Mary tried to wriggle harder, although her feet were now being held tight.

"As prime a porker as you ever did see," yelled Jim cheerfully.

"I like 'em with a bit of life in 'em," answered the jolly voice.

"Move once more and I'll knock you unconscious, you plaguey woman," muttered Jim, and Mary ceased her struggles.

Soon from the creaking of wood and the hiss of the wind, Mary judged she was being carried aboard a vessel. She was bumped and banged ruthlessly down a short flight of stairs. There was a grunting and wheezing as Jim dumped his load and searched for a key. Then she was picked up and, a short minute later, dumped onto the floor. The stifling sack was jerked from her head and then her body. Then the gag was taken from her mouth by an ungentle hand, and the ropes that bound her wrists and ankles were cut. She groaned aloud as the circulation began to return to her hands and feet, aimed a feeble punch at Jim, and fainted dead away.

"That'll keep 'er quiet till 'is lordship's ready for 'er," muttered Jim. He went out and carefully locked the cabin door behind him.

Chapter Nine

LUCY GODWIN HAD almost forgotten her misery over her husband's unfaithfulness. She had never felt so battered, beaten or bruised in her life.

Lord Hubert was driving neck or nothing through the now sunny countryside. She had screamed in protest several times as her ferocious driver had skimmed past a farm vehicle on the road with barely an inch to spare. The members of the Four-In-Hand Club would have cheered. Lucy begged in vain for Lord Hubert to stop the nightmarish pace.

The colors of the summer fields streamed past her terrified eyes. Then the horses surged over the crown of the road and Lucy screamed in earnest as she spied a carriage blocking the roadway, and the still figures of three men lying in the ditch. At one moment it seemed as if they surely must crash head-long into the stationary carriage. But the next, Lord Hubert had skimmed past it, grazing his nearside wheel.

He slowed his horses to a trot and then reined them in. His frightened groom ran to their heads and, without even looking at Lucy, Lord Hubert jumped lightly down and strode back along the muddy road which was steaming in the hot sun.

He walked round the carriage and looked down at the body of Major Freddie Godwin. "Help us!" cried a voice, and he turned and saw the coachman and groom struggling with their bonds. He quickly untied them and returned to Freddie, kneeling down beside him and examining the gash on his head.

"It wor that Lord Peregrine," gasped the coachman. "He hits master on the head with the blunt of his pistol, while his servants hold me and Johnnie up at pistol point."

A faint scream from behind him brought Lord Hubert's head round with a snap. "No, he is not dead—yet," he told the trembling Lucy. "I hear the sound of a stream nearby. You fellows, soak handkerchiefs and place them on Major Godwin's head and then convey him gently to the nearest inn and send for a physician."

Freddie groaned and opened his eyes. "Mary," he said weakly.

"What of her?" said Hubert in a low, tense voice. "What has he done with her?"

"Taken her off," said Freddie weakly. "I don't know where. They—they tied her up. I came out of my swoon for long enough to hear one of them say they had a long ways to go."

"I must go after them," said Hubert quietly. "Lucy is here and your servants will attend to you. Has no carriage passed here since?"

"I don't know," sighed Freddie. "I've been dead to the world. Mary was going home to her parents, Hubert. Wasn't going away with me, old fellow. Wanted an escort. I . . . I wanted to make Lucy jealous. Do you hear that, Lucy?" But Lucy had gone to fetch water.

Hubert pressed his hand in reply, and strode back towards his carriage. He could only hope and pray that he could keep a track of Lord Peregrine.

At first it was easy since Lord Peregrine had been traveling at a hectic enough pace to draw attention, but then at a large crossroads the trail went cold, and there was nothing he could do but scour the surrounding towns and villages.

He was weary, and hungry and mad with worry and concern when he finally stopped in the market town of Little Beddington. There had been a fair that day and knots of people were still standing around the town square. At first they seemed alarmed by his vehement questions, until one farmer vouchsafed that one of his men had a "powerful funny story" about looking in the window of some lord's carriage and seeing a young lady tied up on the floor; but no one had paid much attention seeing as how the fellow was "touched in his upperworks." The yokel who had seen Mary was at last found and slowly and painfully told his story.

"Where were they bound for?" cried Hubert. "Think! For God's sake *think*."

The yokel became sulky and hung his head and said he

didn't know, until his ox-like gaze fastened on the piece of gold that Lord Hubert was holding under his nose.

"Duvver!" he cried, all of a sudden anxious to please.

"Dover?" asked Hubert. "Are you sure?"

The yokel smiled, lolling his great head from side to side. "Duvver, it wor."

"Don't'ee believe our Clem," said the farmer soothingly.

"I'll have to," said Hubert grimly. "Pray God he is right!"

Peter Bennet was a very disturbed and worried young man. He sat in a corner, unobserved, at the Duchess of Pellicombe's breakfast, and listened to the ebb and flow of gossip around him.

The presence of the Witherspoons had been a shock. They had arrived with Mr. Cyril Trimmer, that young man being more pomaded and padded and corsetted and wasp-waisted than any other person in the room. Peter had mildly asked the Duchess the reason for the Witherspoons' invitation; to which that good lady had replied somewhat incoherently that England was heading for a revolution, and one could no longer be so high in the instep. Even the Challenges were entertaining their servants to dinner!

But it soon became all too evident that the Witherspoons' social value was in their fund of gossip and they were soon surrounded by a crowd of listeners three deep. Mrs. Witherspoon had happily forgotten Lord Hubert's threats as soon as she was safely back at her husband's side. Mr. Witherspoon had promptly sent a note to the Duke of Pellicombe hinting at all kinds of social outrages—hence the coveted invitation.

Peter listened to the gossip with growing alarm. Mary Challenge had fled with Major Godwin. Lord Hubert had been found at Clarissa's house. Lord Peregrine was a Bonapartiste spy. Only the famous Beau Brummell appeared indifferent to this fascinating news. It had amused him to bring little Lady Mary into fashion. But he had not thought of her for some time, and was supremely uninterested in the others.

A newcomer arrived with the information that Lord Hubert's servants had said that Lady Mary had gone to stay with her parents and that his lordship and Mrs. Godwin had gone to join them.

Peter still had a bad conscience over his flirtation with Lucy

Godwin. All of London society knew that the Godwins were becoming increasingly estranged, and Peter blamed himself for the breach in their marriage.

Whether Lord Peregrine were a traitor or not troubled him not in the slightest, but he felt that the least he could do was to try to get the Major and his wife together again.

He suddenly decided to ride down to Mary's parents and see what he could do. Peter was surprisingly unworldly at times for such a sophisticated man-about-town.

He accordingly returned to his lodgings to change and rode out from London in the pale, primrose light of late afternoon.

He had travelled several miles through the countryside when he came to a small town with an attractive-looking posting house. He was debating whether or not to stop for a glass of ale before continuing on his way, when, to his surprise, he heard his name being called. He looked up and there was the pretty face of Lucy Godwin looking down at him from a casement window.

He sat very still, his mind seduced by the romantic picture they made—the pretty girl leaning out of the window among the rambling roses under the golden thatch of the inn, the swimming lazy golden light of evening, the stillness of the countryside and the young cavalier, seated on his horse, looking up. Then he shook his head to banish such mawkish thoughts and sprang down lightly from his horse and entered the inn. Lucy met him at the foot of the stairs, her beautiful eyes brimful with excitement. She poured out the tale of their adventures leaving Peter with only one point to grasp hold of in all the outpourings. Major Godwin had been hurt.

"Take me to your husband immediately," he said more abruptly than he had intended.

Lucy smiled and shrugged. "Oh, if you please, but Freddie's all right now. The doctor says he has a thick skull." And with that she went off into a trill of laughter.

Nonetheless she ushered Peter into a low bedchamber where the Major sat in a chair beside the window.

Until Peter's arrival, the Major had been cursing himself for his stupidity. Lucy had at first crooned over him and nursed him tenderly. It had been wonderful. "Am I not better than that drab, Mary Challenge?" she had kept asking jealously. At last the tenderhearted Major had held her in his arms and had told her that Mary had been upset over something, and that he had merely been escorting her home and that he loved only Lucy. Lucy's affection had ceased from that moment, and she had spent more time in her room than in his.

He looked up as Peter Bennet entered the room. He looked from Peter's handsome face to Lucy's flushed and excited one, and his face hardened.

"Peter came looking for me," giggled Lucy who had managed to elicit the information that Peter had been on his way to the Tyres to see them.

"That is not the case at all," said Peter heavily. "Pray leave me with your husband, Mrs. Godwin."

Lucy started to protest and then backed away from the expression in Peter Bennet's eyes. He closed the door behind her and turned to the Major. He hardly knew how to begin.

Major Godwin continued to stare at him and at last, with a sigh, Peter drew up a chair and sat down.

"You may have been aware that at one time I nursed a certain *tendre* for your wife," began Peter awkwardly.

"Yes," said the Major in a flat voice.

"I came in search of you to offer you my sincerest apologies for my behavior," said Peter quietly. "I was, I believe, still shocked from the Battle of Waterloo and Mrs. Godwin seemed like an angel to me. If I have done anything to cause you distress, I am bitterly sorry for my conduct. Is there any way in which I can remedy the situation?"

He sat with his head bowed, his face taut with embarrassment and distress.

The Major's large heart was touched. "No, Captain Bennet," he said quietly. "The damage was done before you appeared. I have hung around like a fool watching Lucy flirt with one gallant after another. When she met you, I feared her heart was engaged . . . but she has no heart. I appreciate what it cost you to come here. But there is nothing anyone can do for me."

Peter's sensitive soul writhed under the other man's distress. He abruptly changed the subject. "What is this villainy of Lord Peregrine? What is all this about a meeting at Horseguards?"

"The Witherspoons I suppose," asked the Major heavily and Peter nodded.

"Then I may as well tell you." He told Peter about the

missing papers. "But that does not make Peregrine the villain," he pointed out at last. "He is mad with jealousy over Lady Clarissa's obvious interest in Lord Hubert."

"So you think that may be why he abducted Lady Mary?"

"It could be. Good God . . . someone must inform the authorities. Are you returning to town?"

Peter nodded. "I shall go straight to Horseguards, never fear. But surely, Lord Hubert would send one of his servants?"

The Major shook his large head. "That one would not stop or think until he found Peregrine. I informed the local magistrate of the abduction but not of the matter of treachery."

Peter rose and tried to find some words of comfort before he left. He could not bring himself to present his compliments to Lucy. He made the Major a stiff bow and turned towards the door.

"I say—Major Godwin," he said with his hand on the latch.

"Yes?"

"I would beat her, you know—beat her soundly." And with that he was gone.

A few minutes later, Lucy bounced into the room and made a *moue* of disappointment. "Oh, has Peter gone?"

She ran to the window. "*Cooee,* Peter!" She turned a laughing face to her husband before turning back to the window again. "Such a handsome young man! Peter! I shall see you when I return to London and you shall tell me all the *on-dits.*"

Lucy was leaning far out of the window, looking as if she might topple out at any minute.

Her husband surveyed her with a red mist of anger beginning to blur his eyes. He rose from his chair and walked over to where she stood with her back to him. He jerked her back with a rough hand and sitting down on the bed, he pulled her across his knee and proceeded to administer a good hiding, deaf to her screams.

Every inn servant listened to the screams with great satisfaction. They hoped the trollopy Major's wife was getting her just desserts. For Lucy had flirted with almost every customer in the inn.

His rage did not last long. He buried his head in his hands as she slumped to the floor at his knees. It was all so incredibly hopeless.

Then to his amazement, he felt a pair of soft arms winding

round his neck and a soft voice saying, "Oh, Freddie, I do love you so."

Major Godwin slowly took his hand away from his face and stared down into his wife's shining eyes. Of all things, he thought. His brutal handling of Lucy had won him the response he had dreamed of. It was a strange sort of love but if it made his wife look at him like that . . . well . . . He pulled her roughly into his arms and began to make love to her with a well-simulated savagery.

Peter Bennet rode slowly through the tranquil blue light of the evening. He thought of the Godwin's marriage with fastidious distaste. He thought of old battles, and once again his ears reeled with the thud of the cannonade and the bark of shot. The tranquil evening fled before his frightened eyes as the noise of battle became more deafening and he saw ghostly, mutilated bodies lying beside the road. He stumbled from his horse and sat beside the road, covering his head with his arms, trying to ward off the nightmare terrors of war. It was his worst attack yet.

And then he heard the bells of evensong.

Faintly, they sounded through the roar of battle and then gradually they came to his ears, sweet and clear.

He raised his head.

He only saw now the quiet fields and, some distance away, the gray walls of an Anglican monastery. The pale scents of the summer evening came to his nostrils. Up in the violet sky, the first star of evening shone bravely down.

With a calm, single-minded purpose, he remounted and road steadily across the fields towards the monastery, towards home.

And that is how Society lost one of its most elegant ornaments, and how the gentlemen of Horseguards heard nothing of Lord Peregrine's villainy that day.

Chapter Ten

THE WIND SIGHED and moaned in the shrouds of *The Avenger* as the trim sloop swung at anchor in Dover harbor.

Mary had pounded on the door of the cabin, and screamed until her lungs were hoarse, but the only sounds that came to her ears were the occasional high-pitched cry of a gull and the whining of the wind. Night had fallen. The small cabin was furnished with a table and two chairs and a low berth in one corner. A brass lamp swung dizzily from the low ceiling. Then, above the wind, she heard the sound of voices on the quay.

"It's a powerful deal of yelling she's doing," said a rough voice. And then quite distinctly came the smooth reply of Lord Peregrine. "I've told you all, my sister is mad and to pay no heed. It's a sad business, but mayhap she will fare better in a sunnier clime. Come, my friends. If I had not volunteered to remove her from these shores, our relatives would have had her in Bedlam."

Then came the sound of steps on the gangplank, then above Mary's head, and finally descending the ladder to the cabin. As he opened the door, Mary made one desperate bid for freedom, flinging herself on Lord Peregrine and clawing at his face with her nails. He gave her a violent shove and she fell back against the berth.

He lit the lamp, and then came and stood over her, dabbing at the scratches on his face with a handkerchief. "Now Lady Mary Challenge," he sneered. "I suppose you wonder why I have brought you here."

"Revenge," gasped Mary. "You would be revenged on Hubert because he gave you the thrashing you deserve."

"Correct," he smiled, "but I must also leave the country. It would only be a matter of time before those fools at Horseguards found out that it was I who stole the papers from Captain Black."

"You are a traitor," said Mary flatly.

"I am a loyal supporter of Napoleon. He will escape again, mark my words, and then I will come to power. England will be under French rule and I shall be regent."

"You're mad," said Mary in a voice that broke on a sob. "Why are you taking me with you?"

"I'm not," he said, moving closer to her while the lamp above them swung in a dizzying arc. "Your first guess was correct. I want revenge on that oaf, Hubert. I shall have you first, then I shall kill you and leave your remains in a sack on the quay for dear Lord Hubert Challenge to find. I cannot set sail because of this accursed storm, but it cannot last forever."

"What of Clarissa?" begged Mary desperately.

"That one will console herself with someone else soon enough—probably with your husband."

"He would not have her," cried Mary, steadying herself as the boat made a wild, bucking lurch. "He married me!"

"And regretted it ever since," sneered Lord Peregrine. "Clarissa was too unfaithful a type of woman for him. He wanted to gain his money by marrying a respectable little mouse."

"Then he will not care if I am dead," pointed out Mary, grimly trying to keep him talking.

"You forget, you are his possession like his horse or his dog. I shall have revenge enough."

Both stared at each other in silence, Lord Peregrine in greedy cruelty, Mary wide-eyed, almost numb with fatigue and shock.

Above and below them pounded the tumult of the storm. The boat plunged and reared, riding and tossing and straining at anchor like a nervous thoroughbred. The gale shrieked and hissed and moaned in the shrouds. A flicker of apprehension appeared in Lord Peregrine's eyes. Perhaps he had been foolish to allow his crew to spend such a night ashore.

Something broke loose on the deck above and set up a wild, rhythmic thudding.

There was another great heave and lurch and both staggered trying to gain their balance. Then with a great crack, *The Avenger* struck against the side of another boat. Lord Peregrine started in alarm and Mary began to hope again that there might be some way of escape. But Lord Peregrine's greed for revenge was too strong. He moved closer to Mary and put a large, beefy hand on her neck. "Plead for mercy, Mary," he laughed. "Plead for mercy and I might let you live!"

Mary stared up into his gross brutal face and all the fight left her. "Hubert," she said with a weary sigh and closed her eyes. She heard his excited labored breathing and waited for the feel of that awful, brutal mouth against her own.

There came a loud report and the sound of splintering wood. The cabin door flew open and Lord Peregrine abruptly released Mary and stared in alarm.

Lord Hubert Challenge loomed on the threshold. He held a smoking pistol in one hand and a drawn sword in the other. The door with its lock shattered from his shot swung wildly on its hinges as the boat plunged and heaved in the storm.

"Leave the cabin, Mary," shouted Hubert. "Get behind me!"

Lord Peregrine stood swaying, his face black with rage, his hands fumbling to fasten his breeches. His eyes never left Hubert's face as Mary, holding her hands to her face, scurried behind her husband and stood at the foot of the companionway.

"Your sword, Lord St. James," said Hubert in a voice like ice.

A gleam lit up Lord Peregrine's eyes. He would normally be no match for Hubert's swordsmanship, but in this reeling, plunging cabin he might have a chance.

Mary sat on the bottom step of the companionway as the rain lashed down on her and buried her head in her hands and prayed.

The two men began to thrust and lunge and parry, ducking their heads to avoid the swinging oil lamp which threw grotesque shadows on the cabin walls. Lord Peregrine fought with a mad courage born of desperation and once he slipped under Hubert's guard and his sword point pinked him on the shoulder. The sight of Hubert's blood drove Peregrine to further efforts. He thrust his sword point up through the glass of the lamp and plunged the cabin into darkness. He could just make out the doorway of the cabin as a sort of lighter blackness.

He heard a noise over to the left of him and made a dash

for the doorway, throwing his great bulk directly ahead to freedom.

He ran full headlong into the point of Lord Hubert's sword.

Lord Hubert pulled his sword clear and backed out of the cabin, fumbling behind him to find Mary and then pulling her to him in a strong grasp.

Lord Peregrine's heavy, dying body reeled blindly around the darkness of the cabin like some great moth looking for the light. At last there was the sound of a heavy fall, and then silence.

"Come, Mary," said Hubert urgently. "The boat has been holed. The water's coming in already."

They struggled up the companionway and up onto the deck, gasping as sheets of icy rain struck their faces. They ran along the plunging, reeling deck to the gangplank only to find it had been wrenched from its moorings and lay shattered like matchwood below them on the quay.

The air was full of rain and screaming wind and the smash and rattle of ships being battered at anchor. Great masts danced and dipped and bowed before the storm like some demented forest.

Hubert cupped his hands to his mouth. "John!" he yelled to his groom, who was standing guard on the quay. There came a faint answering shout above the storm.

"John, catch my lady. She's coming over." The white face of the groom suddenly appeared directly below them on the quay.

"Mary," said Hubert urgently. "I'm going to throw you over. John will catch you. Do you understand?"

"Yes," said Mary, dazed, and battered and buffeted. Would this ordeal never end?

He picked her up lightly in his arms. "Ready below?" he called, and, at John's answering call, he tossed her over.

Mary was expertly caught by John and placed on her feet. She stared upwards, seeing the black bulk of her husband leaping down towards her from the ship.

"She's a-going, my lord," said the groom, jerking his thumb in the direction of *The Avenger*. "She's been holed."

"Let her sink," said Hubert indifferently.

He huddled Mary close to him and began to run. "I have to

find us rooms and shelter," he shouted above the storm. "It won't be very long now."

It was well that Lord Hubert was known at that famous hostelry, The Blue Anchor, or the landlord would certainly not have unbarred his doors on such a night.

Mary was hustled into a warm bedchamber, sleepily clutching hold of her husband as he removed her sodden clothes. He shook her gently.

"Did I arrive in time, Mary?" And Mary could only dumbly nod, weak tears of relief beginning to pour down her face.

"I must go and report this to the authorities," he said quietly. "Sleep, Mary. You need no longer be afraid. Peregrine is dead."

But Mary had already fallen asleep in his arms. He picked her gently up and carried her to the bed, stroking her hair back from her white face.

"Thank God she is alive," he murmured. "I will never raise my voice to her again."

Chapter Eleven

"**I** SAID WE are going to the Duchess of Pellicombe's ball and let that be an end of it," shouted Lord Hubert Challenge at his wife, Mary. "Those damned, gossiping, tattling Witherspoons must be put a stop to. They have been having a tremendous time while we have been gone, planting and sowing all kinds of disgraceful rumors. You have had a full fortnight to recover from your ordeal, madam, which is more than is granted to any soldier."

"I am not in your regiment," snapped Mary, her eyes bright with tears. Men were so boorish, so stupid. How could she ever have believed she loved him. He was as insensitive as an . . . as an . . . as an *ox*. It was too good a piece of imagery to waste.

"You are as insensitive as an ox," said Lady Mary.

"You shall answer for that piece of impertinence later," said her husband grimly, winding his military sash round the waist of his red and gold dress uniform.

Mary turned and stared out of the window. She had hardly been able to believe her ears when Biggs had brought her a curt note from her husband, telling her to prepare herself for the Duchess's ball. She had reluctantly arrayed herself in a pretty silver-spangled gown and had sent for the hairdresser to tease her lengthening curls into one of the fashionable Grecian styles. But she could not resist walking along the corridor to her husband's rooms to protest at his accepting the invitation.

She had lain in the Dover inn for a week after her ordeal, feeling nervous and weak and shaken. On the seventh night Hubert had tried to share her bed and she had shrunk away from him with a cry of alarm as Lord Peregrine's brutal features seemed to be suddenly imposed over those of her husband.

He had brought her back to London where she had kept to her rooms, eating her meals from a tray. All her old timidity had returned and she shrank from seeing anyone, even Hubert.

But now her unfeeling husband was dragging her out into the world again.

She maintained a chilly silence all the way to the ball.

The Duchess of Pellicombe greeted them rather nervously. Really! One no longer knew what to expect from the Challenges. Or from anyone, for that matter. Clarissa had arrived with not a thread of mourning on her. The affair of Lord St. James had been hushed up but one *knew*. So many whispers and the Witherspoons appeared to be an endless source of fascinating gossip.

Lady Clarissa was the first guest to welcome the Challenges. She looked magnificent. She had lost weight and used more water than ever to damp her gown, hiding hardly an inch of her superb figure from the interested gaze.

She did not mention Lord Peregrine. It was as if the monster had never existed, thought Mary, hanging rather sulkily onto Hubert's arm. Clarissa rattled and chattered very amusingly and at a great rate, her beautiful face animated.

Hubert was at first all chilly condescension. But at last his eyes began to light up in a smile of appreciation at one of Clarissa's naughtier stories and Mary, unaware that her husband now cordially detested Clarissa but wished to punish his wife, heard him asking Clarissa for the next dance.

As they moved away together, Mary saw one of her former dancing partners approaching and hid behind a pillar. The ballroom was very hot, illuminated as it was with the light of hundreds of wax candles. The windows at the end of the room opened onto a terrace from which steps led down to a pleasant garden.

Mary made her way there and leaned over the balustrade and looked down. The Witherspoons were holding court beside a lily pond. Mrs. Witherspoon's feathered headdress nodded back and forth. There were excited *oohs* and *ahs* from their listeners. Suddenly the music behind Mary ceased, and Mrs. Witherspoon's voice rang out loud and clear, "I hear Lord Hubert's dancing with Lady Clarissa. That pair have no shame. His poor little wife . . ."

Not stopping to think, consumed by hurt and a burning

rage, Mary ran down the stairs to the garden and straight up behind Mrs. Witherspoon who stood facing the pool. Raising one little slippered foot, Mary kicked out with all her might and Mrs. Witherspoon sailed into the lily pond, face down in the water. Mr. Witherspoon turned round and his large ingratiating face with its permanent leer was too much for Mary. Still panting with rage and exertion, she kicked him in his well-stuffed stomach, and he toppled backwards to join his wife.

Lord Hubert, who had stood amazed on the terrace with Clarissa, watching the antics of his wife, ran down into the garden and swept Mary into his arms and gave her a kiss that left her breathless.

"Oh, my joy," he laughed. "I could not have done better myself. Mary, Mary, when you are cold with me, you make me behave so badly. What will you do with me?"

Mary clutched hold of him. "Take me home, Hubert."

He looked down at her blushing face and kissed her very tenderly. "Home it is," he said, leading her gently from the garden.

The Witherspoons sat in the lily pond and saw their social ruin in the disdainful faces looking down at them. Fickle society admired Mary's spirit, and now stood united against the upstart Witherspoons and their malicious gossip.

"Laugh!" said Mr. Witherspoon, poking his wife under the water. "Laugh as hard as you can."

Mrs. Witherspoon stared at her husband as if he had gone mad, but she dutifully began to laugh as hard as she could, joined by Mr. Witherspoon who bellowed with mirth as hard as he could.

The guests, who had been turning away, turned back and stared at them in amazement. Even mock laughter is infectious, and soon one joined in and then another until the Witherspoons were surrounded by a circle of guests howling with mirth.

One intoxicated young man became so carried away that he hurled himself into the water with a tremendous splash. Soon all sorts of people were leaping into the pool and tipsily congratulating the Witherspoons on their party spirit.

Mr. Witherspoon exchanged a covert wink with his wife. They were still in society—for the time being anyway.

The Duchess of Pellicombe stared into her garden as if

she couldn't believe her eyes. What a rowdy disgrace! What had happened to all the ladies and gentlemen? She closed her eyes firmly and turned around and then, opening them again, marched into the ballroom. If she did not watch the disgraceful goings-on, perhaps they would simply go away.

But the Duke had already seen the pool party. "You know," he confided to his wife, "there are some curst rum touches around society these days."

And the much-plagued Duchess of Pellicombe burst into tears.

Lord Hubert's carriage wound its way through the country lanes at a leisurely pace. Mary sat beside her husband with her hands tucked into her muff, for the sunny day was unusually cold for early autumn, and tried to fight down an attack of nerves. She was finally going to see Hammonds, and felt as nervous as if she were going to meet a rival. The wooded countryside grew more open and rolling and a stiff breeze sent a small hail of beech nuts rattling into the carriage roof. A field of grass stretched out to her left, rolling and turning in the glittering yellow light of the setting sun.

A pheasant, startled by the rumbling of the carriage wheels, rocketed up clumsily and disappeared over the hedge. A flock of starlings whirled and chattered against the lemon yellow sky.

Her husband was asleep, his body moving easily on the seat to the lurching and swaying of the carriage. Mary pressed her hand against her stomach. She was sure she was pregnant. Would her son—for she was sure to have a son—be worthy of this country estate she was at last going to see? Would she?

The carriage slowed and turned and swung through an ancient pair of moss-covered gates. Hammonds!

Her husband awoke and smiled at her sleepily. "Nearly there," he yawned. "Biggs has been there all day, marshalling his troops so we should have a comfortable night."

Mary smiled at him weakly, feeling increasingly nervous. Soon the carriage left the brown and gold fields of stubble behind and began to roll through wooded parkland where deer flitted silently through the trees, as fabulous and romantic in the flood of late golden light as unicorns. Everything seemed to be a rich blaze of green and gold as if a Gobelin tapestry had come to life.

"Hammonds!" said Hubert with a deep note of satisfaction in his voice.

The carriage had left the woods and was bowling through open parkland.

Hammonds nestled in the foot of a small fold in the landscape—or rather it crouched.

It was one of the nastiest houses Mary had ever seen. If a house could be said to grumble, then it certainly did. Heavy ivy hung over the windows, giving the ludicrous effect of heavy lowered brows. It was a jumble of roofs and fantastically twisted chimneys. It had been built in Tudor times out of a singularly repellent yellow brick. Some ancestor had tacked on a wing in a florid Gothic style, which sprang away from the main building at an awkward angle.

It will be charming inside, thought Mary, fighting down a feeling of disappointment.

Biggs stood on the worn steps, his large face looking strained and creased. But summoning up his best manner, he clicked his heels smartly together and said, "Welcome my lord, m'lady."

He turned about and led the way into a low dark hall where a great fire sent acrid puffs of smoke up to the already blackened beams. The whole place smelled of damp and dry rot and, despite the fire, had an all-pervading chill.

"Begging your lordship's parding," said Biggs, clearing his throat. "But was your lordship intending to make a long stay of it?"

Hubert smiled warmly round the decay of his family home.

"For the rest of our lives," he said.

"Blimey."

"I beg your pardon, Biggs."

"I said I was going to show you to your room, my lord."

"I can find my own way, Biggs," said Hubert, throwing his butler a suspicious look. "Come, Mary."

Mary obediently took his arm and allowed him to lead her up the stairs, which creaked and groaned in protest.

He led her down a low corridor on the second floor and down a small flight of steps to a low door at the end. He flung it open. "Our bedroom, my love," he said.

A small fire crackled on the hearth, hissing and spitting and sending vicious little puffs of smoke into the freezing air. One of the servants had left the small windows wide open, no doubt in an effort to dispel the smoke. A vast great four poster bed dominated the room. Its dingy, threadbare hangings moved in the breeze from the open windows. A smoke-blackened tapestry covered most of one wall. It depicted a deer being disembowelled in splendid clarity. There were no carpets on the floor. An enormous wardrobe which looked as if it could house a whole army of ghosts loomed from the gathering shadows.

"What do you think of your home, Mary," said Hubert, standing with his back to her and looking out of the window.

"It's *awful*," said Mary in a choked voice. "And you married me to save this ... this ... crumbling, smelly heap of decay."

Hubert swung around. "You must be mad," he said slowly. "Of course, it is hard for you to appreciate a *real* family home when one takes into account that prissy, prim, soulless box of a place you were brought up in."

"My home," grated Mary, "is well-run and isn't in any danger of falling down with dry rot and decay. This place stinks, my lord. It stinks of bad cess and all sorts of nasty, nasty things."

"Your mind is a cesspool," said her husband in a cold, level voice. "You see life accordingly. I have never been so insulted in all my life ..."

"Oh, Hubert," sighed Mary, "I am not insulting you. I am insulting this run-down hovel."

"Then don't live in it, madam," he said, his eyes hard and glittering in his flushed face. "I am going out riding and when I return, I expect you to have removed your presence from my home."

He stalked from the room and Mary ran furiously after him. "You can't expect me to travel all the way back to London when I have just arrived," she shouted to his retreating back.

"Go to London—go to hell for all I care," said Lord Hubert, descending the staircase. "Just get your unwanted presence out of my home!"

"Oh, Gawd," said Biggs, retreating hurriedly to the kitchen. "They're at it again."

He fortified himself with a bumper of brandy in the pantry and then made his way up the stairs, scratched on the door of his mistress's bedroom and walked in. Mary was sitting, dry-eyed in a chair by the window. She turned hard eyes on the butler.

"Ah, Biggs. I shall shortly be leaving for London. Please have the travelling carriage brought round and send Juneaux to me."

Biggs rubbed his hands distractedly through his powdered hair. "My lady," he began awkwardly. "It's not my place to say so but it's a bit sudden like and them 'orses—horses—is tired."

"My lord commands it, Biggs," said Mary with a dreary smile. "I offended his delicate sensibilities by pointing out that his ancestral home is a slum."

"And so it is," said Biggs eagerly. "I am talking out of hand, my lady, but think what that place in St. James's looked like before you changed it. There's a lovely little saloon on the ground floor, not half bad, and the fire draws sweet. If you was to let me lead you there, my lady, and have a cup of tea, you might see things different."

"Oh, very well," sighed Mary, anxious to postpone the long journey back to London.

The saloon was hardly lovely, but it was warm and cheerful and someone had placed a large copper bowl of beech leaves and chrysanthemums, a flower Mary had not seen before. The walls were covered in faded panels of yellow silk and the furniture was comfortable, if shabby.

Biggs set the tea table beside her and then went over to an old settle in the corner. He lifted up the lid and came back bearing a roll of gold brocade.

"See here, my lady. This here would look ever so fine as curtains. There's so much we could do."

He rolled out the cloth and held it up to his bosom, staring at her anxiously. The fold of rich gold cloth fell around his feet and Mary giggled, despite her misery. "You look very well, Biggs," she laughed. "Just like the Marquise Elvira."

Biggs's small eyes twinkled and then he cocked his head on one side. "Master's home," he said. Mary stiffened, her face going hard.

"Compringmise," whispered Biggs urgently. "That's what my Ma who had book-learning used to say. It don't hurt to tell a bit of a lie. Tell 'is nibs you like the dump."

261

Mary hesitated, torn between taking Biggs's advice and giving him a stern set-down for his over-familiarity.

The door opened and her husband walked in, drawing off his gloves. Mary rushed into his arms crying, "I am so sorry, Hubert. I was tired, that is all. I think it is my condition . . ."

"You mean . . ." Hubert's face changed from stern anger to radiant pleasure like lightning. "Biggs you may leave us— although what you are doing parading round in cloth of gold looking like . . . Hey, I think I know who you look like. You look exactly like that Marqu? . . ."

"Kiss me, Hubert," said Mary.

Biggs tactfully retreated, closing the door behind him and trailing the swathes of gold cloth to the kitchen.

"My lord and my lady are reconciled," he said dreamily to the cook, MacGregor.

MacGregor sniffed and rattled the pots and pans violently.

"It'll not last a day," he said gloomily.

But it did!

And for much, much longer than that. . . .

Want to know a secret?
It's sexy, informative, fun, and FREE!!!

❧ PILLOW TALK ❧

Join Pillow Talk and get advance information and sneak peeks at the best in romance coming from Ballantine. All you have to do is fill out the information below!

♥ My top five favorite authors are: _____

_____

_____

_____

_____

♥ Number of books I buy per month: ❑ 0-2 ❑ 3-5 ❑ 6 or more

♥ Preference: ❑ Regency Romance ❑ Historical Romance
     ❑ Contemporary Romance ❑ Other

♥ I read books by new authors: ❑ frequently ❑ sometimes ❑ rarely

Please print clearly:
Name _____

Address_____

City/State/Zip_____

Don't forget to visit us at
www.randomhouse.com/BB/loveletters

regency

**PLEASE SEND TO: PILLOW TALK
BALLANTINE BOOKS, CN/9-2
201 EAST 50TH STREET
NEW YORK, NY 10022
OR FAX TO PILLOW TALK, 212/940-7539**

*Coming next month, a sensual contemporary
love story you won't want to miss!*

BLUE CLOUDS

by Patricia Rice

Phillipa "Pippa" Cochran has a reputation of
being a regular Pollyanna who smiles her way
through life's tribulations. But when her mother
dies, her nursing career fails, and her fiancé
becomes abusive, Pippa loses her smile. She flees
across the country to live in California and is hired
sight unseen to care for the disabled young son of
Seth Wyatt, a wealthy, handsome, and difficult
recluse.

Unprepared for the altogether-too-attractive hur-
ricane that is Pippa, the troubled Seth and his
lonely son begin to blossom under her care. Then
a series of "accidents" threatens Seth's life as well
as the fragile love that has begun to grow between
Seth and Pippa. Determined to protect the man
she loves, Pippa is drawn into a dangerous game
of cat and mouse that could cost her this precious
new love.

Coming next month . . .

THE PIRATE PRINCE

by Gaelen Foley

Taken captive by a fearsome and infuriating pirate captain come to plunder her island home of Ascension, the beautiful Allegra Monteverdi struggles to deny her growing passion for her intriguing captor. Lazar di Fiore is a rogue with no honor and has nothing in common with the man of her dreams—the honorable and courageous crown prince of Ascension, who is presumed murdered with the rest of the royal family by treacherous enemies of the throne.

But Allegra has badly misjudged Lazar, a man with a tragic past and demons that give him no peace. He harbors a secret that could win him Allegra's love and restore freedom and prosperity to Ascension, if his sworn enemies do not destroy him first. And the greatest battle of all must be fought within Lazar's own heart as Allegra tries to prove that, prince or pirate, he is truly the man that she has always dreamed of.

Published by Fawcett Books.
Available wherever books are sold.

Patricia Veryan,
the reigning queen of Regency romance,
returns with

THE RIDDLE OF
ALABASTER ROYAL

Captain Jack Vespa, a soldier fresh from battling
Napoleon, is searching for a quiet, peaceful place
to recover from his wounds. To recuperate, he
heads for Alabaster Royal, his country mansion
rumored to be the local "haunted house." What
he does not know is that residing at his new
home is the bewitching Miss Consuela Jones.
Determined to solve a murder, this spirited young
woman believes the old manse is visited by ghosts.
But it is she who will come to haunt Captain
Vespa and bring him to his knees under the spell
of a love too fierce to be denied.

Published by Fawcett Books.
Coming next month to your local bookstore.